To the creators of a next generation of wonderment! May their imaginations continue to create new worlds and seek out new civilizations.

D1241060

Publisher and Designer: Hal Schuster   *Editor: David Lessnick*

CONTENTS

TREK: THE NEXT GENERATION

THE LONG JOURNEY

It was only supposed to last six years, and even then that figure was spoken of as a hope. Few TV series last more than two years these days. Only hits last for five or more. When the six year figure was bandied about, THE NEXT GENERATION was only two years old. Even the actors themselves admitted that after six years their contracts would need to be renegotiated and it was doubted that Paramount would want to pay the increases necessary to get the cast to all renew. It looked like six years would be it. But it wasn't.

While the terms of the new contracts have not been made public, they clearly involve the NEXT GENERATION motion pictures, the first of which goes into production in the spring of 1994 for a Christmas 1994 release. So after seven years, STAR TREK—THE NEXT GENERATION is making the leap the original STAR TREK wasn't able to accomplish until nearly a decade after it went off the air. But all of that groundwork in the '70s when fans called for STAR TREK's return has ultimately led to everything which has followed in the '80s and '90s. All of the STAR TREK conventions which began in 1973, and the letters to Paramount asking that they bring back STAR TREK in some form, led to that first motion picture in 1979. That of course led to subsequent motion pictures, which in 1987 led to Gene Roddenberry's television sequel to the original series. In 1991 this led to Berman and Piller's sequel to Roddenberry's sequel, and apparently the sequels will continue.

While the original STAR TREK bottomed out after 79 episodes, NEXT GENERATION, produced at a time when ratings are figured differently, has been crowned with success by appealing to basically the same type of audience. More than 150 episodes have been made for STAR TREK—THE NEXT GENERATION, and by the time it completes its run that number will top 175. Only hits produce 175 episodes and NEXT GENERATION has clearly entered the undeniable stratosphere of hit status.

—JAMES VAN HISE

ACTOR SPOTLIGHT

DATA SPEAKS OUT!

By Diana Collins

It was November 24, 1991 and promptly at 6:00 PM Brent Spiner cheerfully strolled on stage at the Sheraton Renaissance Tech World to a standing ovation. He was wearing white tennies, buff tone pants, a black long sleeved shirt, and his usual round wire-rimmed glasses. The one actual trace of Data was his darker hair color.

Brent Spiner opened his one hour presentation by thanking the audience for coming to see him. He explained that people at conventions usually ask if he gets a chance to see the local sights, but he confessed that this weekend's schedule, as with most, had been a very hectic one. Brent stated that the hotels, airports, and city streets between them are all that he gets to see. He reflected on the fact that it's becoming harder and harder to distinguish the difference between Indianapolis, Boston, D.C., Valley Forge, Dallas, etc.

Spiner remarked that the last time he'd been in Washington, D.C. was when the NEXT GENERATION cast members had been invited by then Vice-President Quayle for a NASA ceremony. That was the fateful day that while attendees were sitting in Dan Quayle's living room, he got an important phone call. The White House had called to say that President Bush had been rushed to the hospital suddenly for a heart condition. A senator sitting next to Brent looked at him and said, "Oh, oh."

Brent opened the question and answer session by jokingly stating that the audience could ask him anything at all—except about STAR TREK and his personal life. "But I'll be glad to discuss politics, news, historical events. . . anything." To which the crowd roared, and they also started asking questions, such as whether Brent was going to renew his contract when it expired. As recently as 1991 it was still believed that THE NEXT GENERATION would fold after six seasons.

"Our contracts are for six years," he explained. "I'm not a real long range planner. Paramount may elect to have a third generation cast replace us. Also we may be offered STAR TREK—THE NEXT GENERATION movies in the future after the series ends in the sixth year. I don't know exactly what will happen, but keep writing those cards and letters to let Paramount know you want us to make STAR TREK—THE NEXT GENERATION movies."

But how did Brent Spiner, struggling actor, become Data, one of the most popular characters on television?

"From being in several Broadway plays in New York I came to Los Angeles to do 'Little Shop of Horrors.' It was a tremendous play," he recalled. "After that I did mostly villain of the week guest appearances in HILL STREET BLUES, CHEERS, NIGHT COURT and other TV shows. I feel very fortunate to be doing something with this long a run and feel very proud of it.

Unlike so many other actors who do shows that aren't meaningful, STAR TREK is a show about the positive aspect of humanity which contains a morality play and an entertaining plot that holds to Gene Roddenberry's vision and values."

And as to how Brent actually landed that now popular role, he explained, "The producers interviewed many actors for the part. It came down to two of us. Fortunately Tom Cruise didn't want to commit himself for that long," which amused the audience. "Actually Eric Menyuk, who played the Traveler in two Wesley episodes, was the other candidate for the part of Data. Very fortunately for me, I got the part."

FOREVER DATA

Fans also wanted to know whether he was going to record another album.

"That's a good question. Actually when I recorded 'Old Yellow Eyes Is Back' I felt like George Plimpton. It was a gruesome schedule to do all of the recording during the hiatus. Fortunately I had the assistance of the Sunspots [Patrick Stewart, Michael Dorn and Jonathan Frakes] in making the work more fun. But it was so time consuming that I probably won't begin to cut another one before the end of the series, if I can convince a record company that I should have that opportunity. I had thought of the idea of doing duets with other famous people. But I'm not sure they'd be as interested in the idea as I am."

It was natural to ask Spiner what it is like being on a series which would live forever as an icon.

"I feel good about that," he stated. "It's odd even thinking about the idea of being immortalized in that way. But it's really a good feeling to know that the acting work that I've done, unlike other actors who work on other shows for six years, has been artful, has a positive purpose and is meaningful to a wide audience. Not many actors who do a TV series can feel the same way."

He's come a long way from the young boy who was teased for having his birthday on February 2nd—Groundhog Day. "My brother used to carry a picture in his wallet of a ground hog, point at the picture and tell people: That's my brother!"

DATA AND SPOCK

And then there's the matter of what it's like playing the character of Data himself, or is it itself?

"Every acting role has its set of problems to work out. I'm fortunate to be playing an android. Since nobody knows what it's like to be an android or what one is supposed to act like, I can play it any way I like. No one can be too critical about my style." And the contact lenses? "They're yellow on the iris part with a clear center which is a prescription contact. So fortunately I don't see everything in yellow."

Because he plays an android, he was asked whether the other actors try to make him laugh during scenes?

"Each episode is shot from five different angles. We have five to seven rehearsals before the final filming. I usually laugh during that time. The first time we say our lines, it's funny. By the second or third time it's no longer funny. By the tenth time it becomes funny again."

In "Reunification," Spock met the cast of the NEXT GENERATION for the first time, which couldn't help but make people wonder what it was like working with Leonard Nimoy?

"It was good to work with Leonard Nimoy," he explained. "He's very professional. It was like working with a visiting dignitary. At first we were all pretty nervous and on our best behavior. After awhile we realized that Leonard was a fun person on the set, too. So we went back to our usual antics after a few days and he seemed to enjoy our bad lounge act routines."

BEHIND THE SCENES

The episode "Loud As A Whisper," which featured an actual hearing impaired actor in a major supporting role, still arouses many questions and comments, such as whether Brent had to learn sign language for the show.

"Howie Seago, who is a deaf actor who played the Henry Kissinger in space, taught me everything I needed to know. It was a wonderful experience working with him and I hope he comes back on the show so we can find out about the outcome of his mission and what happened to his character."

What about Data? Will he have another relationship on the show?

"It's always a present to be able to develop another facet of Data's character. I don't know of any plans for that this season and haven't shot any episodes like that so far. But let's say a little prayer."

Wil Wheaton left the series in 1991 and Brent had some interesting comments about him. "Sea Breeze is his nickname because he's so cool. The cast calls me Hot Air. I was really sorry to see him leave the show. I sat next to him a lot on the set and I miss the interaction."

THE ASIMOV CONNECTION

Brent was asked about an supposed incident involving Marina Sirtis being mad at him about her pet.

"Marina had a dog named Skylugie. She said I told her I'd put him in the microwave. No, for the record, that's not true. I said I'd put him in the trash compactor."

Since Data seems to have been inspired by parameters for robots established by Isaac Asimov, Brent was asked whether the writers continue to draw inspiration from Asimov?

"I think Gene Roddenberry was very hip to that and Data's character is generally taken from that idea. But Gene didn't make Data exactly like Asimov's robots with Three Laws or anything that was precisely copied. Data has his own free will."

Does this mean that Data can kill? This was suggested in the episode "The Most Toys." "[That] episode is the closest Data has come to that. My own feeling is that I don't think so. My reasoning is that he can't lie. When Data told Riker that something must have happened during the transporter sequence, he was implying he didn't kill Faijo. However, had he not been beamed up at that point in the episode, who knows?"

FAVORITE TREKS

As Data, Spiner wears makeup to alter his facial color and texture, as well as the contact lenses, which makes it not as easy to recognize him in public as one might think.

"Sometimes people will see me in a restaurant and I can always tell because they get this puzzled look on their faces, so I try to help them out by. . . [He twitches his head with the jerky movements of an android]. Then they recognize me as the RCA dog."

There have been many novels written with additional adventures of the NEXT GENERATION characters, but Spiner has not had the time to read any of them. "I'm lucky to read one book per year. The filming schedule makes my day so long [12-16 hours on the set] that my main hobby is sleeping. I'm getting real good at it, too."

Asked what his favorite episodes of the old STAR TREK and THE NEXT GENERATION are, someone shouted out "The Naked Now" before he could even reply. Brent responded, "So you liked that one too, huh? I really enjoyed my interactions with Tasha. Completely arrogantly I like the episodes that I had major roles in, such as 'Measure of a Man' which had something to say about the state of

Brent at St. Sophia's Cathedral for Marina's wedding.

Brent at '92 VSDA in Las Vegas (Video Software Dealers Assoc.).

Photo © 1994 Albert L. Ortega

humanity. Also I liked 'Offspring' a lot due to the directing of Jonathan Frakes and working with the actress who did an outstanding job playing my daughter, Lal."

As to his favorite one of the original STAR TREK's, he zeroed in on one of the motion pictures. "I'd have to say the movie WRATH OF KHAN because Ricardo Montalban was brilliant in it. Critics and I especially liked the scene where Kirk is yelling, 'Kaaaaaaahhhhhhhhhhhnnnnnnnnnn!' " The audience cheered at Brent's William Shatner/Captain Kirk impression.

THE DIFFICULTIES OF BEING DATA

But what is it really like playing Data and what's the most difficult part of playing the role?

"I'd have to say that learning the lines is the hardest part. When you're a young actor in a school play, your family and friends always ask, 'How do you learn all those lines?' Well, in my role it's not just that I have to learn so many of them, but most of them are words I've never said before in my life! Mike Okuda and Rick Sternbach invent all of these wonderful futuristic technical-scientific things and make up words that don't exist to fit their ideas. Getting those words from my head to my mouth is the difficult part. I have a personal rule that I don't go to bed at night until I can get the next day's script words from my head to my mouth. So I spend many sleepless nights working on it 'till I can get it out of my mouth."

And what does he think about the way that the insides of Data's body have been exposed in certain episodes?

"At this time I think they have opened up every part of my body that's possible! Michael Westmore and his son, who are the makeup and electronic prosthetic geniuses, have done a fabulous job of making all of it appear so realistic."

One of the difficulties of playing Data involves the extensive makeup he must wear, which smears easily.

"I had to train myself over the years of production not to touch myself. Can you imagine just five years ago I didn't know how to do that? Actually it is very difficult not to smudge makeup all over everything. Particularly the face of the Comm Station that my fingers are frequently typing on will get pretty disgusting. Now and then the director or camera man will notice it looks awful, stop the camera and have someone clean off the Plexiglas."

THE MAN BEHIND PICARD

Regarding what personalities Brent likes to imitate, he zeroed in on a certain British cast member. "The person I most often like to imitate says this: Pontiac. Patrick Stewart says he does that commercial in his American accent."

The actor stated that he and Stewart might be doing Shakespeare together sometime in the future.

"Patrick Stewart and I have talked about doing 'The Merchant of Venice,' where I'll play Shylock one night and he'll play that character the next night."

And what is it like working with Patrick Stewart?

"Patrick is one of the best actors I know. In the beginning of STAR TREK—THE NEXT GENERATION's filming, he took everything very seriously. One day the director of an early episode complained to the producers that he didn't think he could stand to finish filming because we were too loud, boisterous and wild. Patrick was stricken by the comment and we were all hanging our heads in shame. Then the next day, as we're walking onto the rolling green hills in the Tasha holodeck goodbye scene, Patrick breaks into song: 'The hills are alive, with the sound of music!' Then we were sure that we'd loosened him up."

PERFORMING ART

On the subject of whether he actually plays any of the musical instruments Data is supposed to be able to master, he stated, "I play only a very bad guitar. Once I auditioned for a film about Horton Foot. During the audition the director requested that I play the guitar and sing. So I think I decided to play the Randy Newman song 'Marie.' He was listening and asked what the song was. After that I think Randy Newman got the part instead of me."

Regarding another type of performance art, he discussed the episode in which Dr. Crusher taught Data to dance.

"I do know some things about dance. I took tap dancing when I was 16 years old. The dancing for the episode took a week to rehearse. Gates did all of the choreography work to create the dance routine. Gates has tremendous experience in dance. For instance, she was the lead choreographer in a couple of Muppet Movies and has done several things along those lines."

But what was actually his most physically difficult episode to perform in? "Brothers" is the episode he cited as the one which he felt was almost technically impossible to do.

"There were many tiny sequences that had to be positioned right. I used a video feedback and split screen to do all three parts. Even then, it took many takes to get each sequence in sync. For example, when I was playing Dr. Soong's part, I would take a pencil and wave it in front of Data to make him follow its movement. Then as I switched roles to play Data, I had to remember exactly where my eyes should be focused to follow a pencil that wasn't there. The timing was too difficult to use a stand-in to copy Dr. Soong's motions.

All I could do was relate to the sequence of dialogue words to where each pencil movement should be. The most difficult thing to accomplish was when Dr. Soong held Data's face in his hands and patted it. That was something a stand-in had to do since it would be impossible for me to hold my face with my own hands. It took a long time to get it technically correct on film, but very satisfying to have accomplished."

THE DAY GENE DIED

Asked whether he had aspirations for Data to become more human by the end of the sixth season, the actor stated, "I'd be very interested in seeing Data's character grow. Let's say we are able to do a feature film and part of the plot shows the character becoming human. The film could explore what Data gains and what he loses and how it has affected him."

Regarding whether Brent would get to play Sherlock Holmes again, he revealed some interesting information about the problems involved with that.

"It was a dream come true to do the part of Sherlock Holmes. But Sir Arthur Conan Doyle's estate complained because we did that first episode without asking permission and paying a royalty fee. They gave the studio the okay for this one time, but wanted lots of money to ever do it again. Considering the STAR TREK—THE NEXT GENERATION budget has other needs, I doubt they would consider paying a royalty for a second episode."

An interesting question I'd never heard asked was what episode was being filmed when Gene Roddenberry died and how the cast reacted to the news?

"The episode was 'Hero Worship' — a story about a child who decides to imitate Data, which was directed by Patrick Stewart, by the way. As to how the cast reacted, they were, of course, understandably upset. The tone of the rest of the filming that day was very subdued. But they quote this line, 'Gene would have wanted the production to go on.' "

WORKING WITH WHOOPI

Does Brent plan to do any writing, directing or producing on STAR TREK—THE NEXT GENERATION?

"I haven't had the time to prepare to direct. I had thought of directing for awhile in the beginning. But after I saw how much extra time that Jonathan and Patrick had to spend learning the intricacies of directing, I changed my mind."

Regarding what it's like to work with Whoppi Goldberg, Brent enthusiastically replied, "Whoopi is sensational! It's a thrill to be working with her. She brought her well deserved Oscar on the set the next day after receiving it. She let everyone hold it, too! She's the most available person I've ever met. Whoopi knows everybody and everybody seems to know her.

We hang out together sometimes because we like the 30's, 40's and 50's music and movies. We recently went to the American Cinema Awards together. It's a benefit for the Old Actor's Home. We were sitting at a table with Dean Stockwell, Rutger Hauer and all kinds of famous stars. I got to meet the Bowery Boys, Clayton Moore and many other retired actors as well.

"When it was time for us to go home, Whoopi had Shelley Winters in tow, and asked if I could drive her home as well. I'm thinking, she's asking me if I want to drive Shelley Winters home? No problem! Shelley told us a story on the way home about how she's been living in the same house since 1952. When I let her out, I offered to walk her to the door. She said, 'Don't be silly, I'm fine.' To make sure she was all right, Whoopi and I wanted to wait there in the car until she went in.

She went up to the door, stopped, looked around, and walked back a few paces and seemed confused. I called out to her and asked if there was something we could do to help. Once she realized we were still there, Shelley walked back to my car and said that wasn't her house. So we had to drive around to find her house. Can you imagine she'd been living there since 1952 and couldn't find her house?"

COMEDY TREK

While Data has a cat named Spot, on the show, in real life Brent Spiner doesn't have any pets due to the long hours he has to work. "I have to get up at 5:30 am to be at the studio for makeup. If I had a pet I'd have to get up that much earlier and feed a dog or something."

Early in the series Joe Piscopo appeared in a holodeck sequence, and while Brent enjoyed working with him, he wasn't their original choice for that role.

"It was my idea to work with Jerry Lewis. Unfortunately Jerry was busy that week. We went through a lot of names of comedians before we were able to get one to perform on the show." These days that probably would not be as big a problem. As to whether Brent ever thought about doing stand-up comedy himself, he replied, "No, it's very dangerous work. When you're standing on stage doing comedy, it's not a character in wardrobe and makeup. It means they hate you if they don't clap, not your character."

A strangely worded question involved went: If Data lives forever, what did Brent like best about the character?

"I feel silly talking about him being immortal," Brent stated, and then added. "He's a character with no potential for cruelty. He's an outsider and yet he's incredibly capable, despite being an outsider. I think those qualities are his best ones."

A point often wondered about by fans is how much control or input the actors have regarding what their characters do on the show.

"We try to finesse it in the playing of the roles," Brent explained. "But we don't have much control over the actual lines."

FUTURE TREKS

Even two years ago (before the announcement of DEEP SPACE NINE), fans were wondering about the next stage of STAR TREK, either new NEXT GENERA-

TION movies or a new TV series. Brent made these observations about such possibilities, some of which are quite prescient.

"If I were Paramount, I'd be thinking about creating a next NEXT GENERATION as their new project, and be doing STAR TREK—THE NEXT GENERATION films, too. Just as they are doing with the STAR TREK—the original generation and talking about STAR TREK—THE NEXT GENERATION films today. Although my character, Data, is supposed to have a very long life span, I the actor do not have that luxury. Eventually I would have to be replaced or written out of the plot."

So what are Brent's plans after the series wraps?

"I don't make long term plans," he explained. "I don't even know any short term plans right now, aside from attending the conventions I'm signed up to appear at in the future. I'm hoping that Paramount will be interested in making STAR TREK—THE NEXT GENERATION feature movies. That is unless you folks and the studio aren't interested." But the audience assured him they were very interested!

Does it bother him that he'll be remembered by audiences as Data for the rest of his life?

"I don't mind at all. If Art Carnie doesn't mind being remembered as Norton on THE HONEYMOONERS, I certainly don't mind being Data."

Someone asked a rather silly question when you think about it—they wanted to know whether it was difficult for Spiner to say lines without contractions in them.

"It's not difficult," he explained patiently. "I memorize whatever is given to me. Since it has no contractions in it, I just don't say them."

DATA'S LAUGH

On the subject of laughter, Brent was asked whether he could perform for the audience the same laugh as Data did when Q gave him the brief ability to laugh in the "Hide and Q" episode.

"Sorry, I can't do that laugh on queue after so long a period. When I saw that the script called for Data's first laugh, I was very nervous about getting it just right. Originally that scene was supposed to be filmed at the end of the day on

Friday. Thankfully production delays caused them to not be unable to get to that scene until after the weekend. So I practiced and practiced all weekend until I felt it was right.

"Monday morning when I did the laugh for the camera, I got it right the first time! When the director said 'Cut!,' Patrick Stewart dared me to be able to do it again. As it turned out, I did it again three more times to capture it on film with different angles, and I was successful each time, fortunately."

SPINER'S STORY FINALE

"I had this idea for an episode, or as part of one," he explained. "The crew would go to the holodeck and play out an American Western." He stated that this would be different than the "Specter of the Gun" episode of the original STAR TREK. "I was telling my idea to LeVar Burton one day.

"Captain Picard would be wearing all black like Yul Brynner. Commander Riker would be dressed like Clint Eastwood or John Wayne. As Data, I would have to wear enormous chaps and a ten gallon hat. LeVar asked, 'But what would I be?' I replied, 'Why, the Lone Ranger, of course!' "

Finally the talk came to a close. He apologized for having looked at his watch a few times already, but explained that he had to get to the airport. Brent confessed ominously that if he didn't make this plane, the producers would never let him out of town again. He thanked the audience for being so kind during his speech and for coming to see him.

Upon receiving a standing ovation, thunderous clapping, high spirited cheering, and Arsenio Hall style hoots, Brent Spiner blushed as he slipped off stage.

Patrick, Marina and Gates at the Roddenberry building dedication.

SEASON ONE

SEASON ONE

In the beginning there was Gene Roddenberry, who decided to repeat himself in the mid-Eighties and succeeded. Despite countless nay sayers, STAR TREK—THE NEXT GENERATION reached the television screen full-blown, and became the highest-rated syndicated television series in history. Fine-tuning the character balance thrown slightly out of skew in the original classic STAR TREK, Roddenberry devised a larger cast and a wider range of dramatic possibilities. This time around, the Enterprise even had a Klingon on board.

Women were better represented, too: the doctor was Beverly Crusher. Complementing this role was that of the ship's Counselor, the empathic Betazoid, Deanna Troi. The blind engineer Geordi LaForge, who could see with his electronic VISOR, added even more diversity. And in a move inspired by James Kirk's seeming lack of caution, Roddenberry implemented a First Officer, William Riker, whose job it was to beam down while the Captain stayed on board. The Captain himself was a far cry from Kirk: an older Frenchman with no hair and an inexplicable British accent, Jean-Luc Picard would prove to be one of the cagiest men ever to preside over a ship called Enterprise. The first year would be a pretty rough shakedown cruise, but it was still a hell of a good start.

EPISODES ONE AND TWO: "ENCOUNTER AT FARPOINT "

Written by D.C. Fontana and Gene Roddenberry
Directed by Corey Allen
Guest Cast: John deLancie, Michael Bell, DeForest Kelley, Colm Meaney, Cary Hiroyuki, Timothy Dang, David Erskine, Evelyn Guerrero, Chuck Hicks

Captain Jean-Luc Picard has just been posted to the new Enterprise NCC 1701-D. On his way to pick up his first officer at Farpoint Station, he encounters a powerful being calling himself Q, who claims that humanity must stop its progress immediately. Q proves his knowledge of human history and its brutalities, but Picard points out that everything Q has described is centuries out of date. Humans are far different now, and Picard doesn't fear the facts.

This gives Q an idea. As soon as Q leaves, Picard orders the Enterprise to maximum warp. He and other bridge crew members descend to the battle bridge so that a saucer separation can take place, which sends the part of the ship with families off in another direction.

Q catches up with them and faced with the destruction of his ship, Picard surrenders. Picard, Yar, Troi and Data are taken to a trial chamber from the pre-holocaust period. They fence with words and Q impetuously freezes Troi and Yar, but finally unfreezes them when Data plays back Q's assurance that the prisoners would not be harmed. Q decides to submit the Enterprise crew to a test, which will take place at Farpoint Station.

Meanwhile, on Farpoint, Will Riker meets with Administrator Zorn. When Riker casually mentions that he wishes he had an apple, he suddenly finds a bowl full on the counter. When Riker leaves the office, Zorn seems to be speaking to empty air, threatening to punish someone for doing that.

Elsewhere in the Farpoint station, Riker encounters Dr. Crusher and her son Wesley, and meets Geordi; they've all been posted to the Enterprise.

When the stardrive section of the Enterprise reaches Farpoint, Riker is beamed aboard to meet Picard, who briefs him on Q. Riker's first duty is to oversee the rejoining of the two halves of the ship. Picard meets with Crusher, concerned that she might not have wanted to be posted there. But Beverly insists that she bears no grudge over the fact that her husband died while under Picard's command.

Later, Q reappears on the bridge and states that they have only 24 hours to solve the mystery of Farpoint. Then Q vanishes, but Picard states that he won't be rushed into making a rash decision.

Down on Farpoint in Zorn's office, Picard, Riker and Troi meet with him. Troi detects great pain and terrible despair. Zorn is offended by this, particularly when Picard doesn't believe Zorn's claim that he has no idea what Troi is talking about.

An unknown spacecraft appears and attacks the planet. The blast hits the city but not Farpoint Station. Q reappears, mocks Picard and coaxes him to blast the intruder. Zorn pleads for help but insists he doesn't know what's happening. Suddenly he vanishes before their eyes, taken aboard the other ship.

Picard orders Farpoint evacuated and sends an energy beam down to the planet. Jean-Luc manages to figure out that Farpoint is a huge alien being which had been wounded and had landed on the planet. The Bandi captured and enslaved it. Now its mate has found it. Energized by the Enterprise, it frees itself, leaves with the other creature, which in turn frees Zorn.

Q is disappointed that the humans didn't use brute force against what they didn't understand. He never expected them to pass his test. Picard orders Q off his ship and points out that Q is the only one who has been proven guilty of savagery in this encounter.

EPISODE THREE: "THE NAKED NOW"

Teleplay by J. Michael Bingham
Story by John D.F. Black and J. Michael Bingham
Directed by Paul Lynch
Guest Cast: Benjamin W.S. Lum, Michael Rider, David Renan, Skip Stellrecht, Kenny Koch

The Enterprise arrives too late to save a science ship in distress. Everyone is dead, and the final message from the ship was very strange. Riker reports to Picard, confirming that all 80 crewmen aboard the ship are dead, some having been blown out into space. Something about this situation jogs Riker's memory. Data begins searching the ship's records for such a reference.

Geordi, who seems ill after returning from the death ship, slips out of Sickbay. He encounters Yar, but Geordi doesn't realize that he's infected by something. But he does recognize that something is wrong and begs Yar to help him. She takes him back to Sickbay.

Data tracks the story to the Constitution class Enterprise commanded by James T. Kirk. The record even includes the cure created by McCoy 87 years before.

The illness spreads through the crew. Picard hears his own voice over the P.A. system handing control of the Enterprise over to Wesley in

Engineering. Wesley uses his new beam to create an impenetrable force field while he sits in engineering with the assistant Chief Engineer, who is pulling control chips from the computer control panel.

The original antidote discovered by McCoy is ineffective against this strain of the toxin. The control chips are scattered all over, and must be put back in order. Wes remarks that Data could do this quickly, a challenge which intrigues Data. He has only 14 minutes to accomplish it. A piece of a star is hurtling in their direction and unless the Enterprise can regain motion control, the ship will be smashed. Crusher finds a cure. The Enterprise still needs to move from the path of star matter, though.

Reversing the tractor beam, the Enterprise pushes away from the Tsiolovsky, which briefly blocks the star stuff. This gives the Enterprise time to allow Data to finish. The ship blasts out of orbit.

EPISODE FOUR: "CODE OF HONOR"

Teleplay by Kathryn Powers and Michael Baron
Directed by Russ Mayberry
Guest Cast: Jessie Lawrence Ferguson, Karole Selmon, James Louis Watkins, Michael Rider

The Enterprise goes to Ligon II to pick up a rare vaccine needed on Styris IV. A Ligonian legation beams aboard to greet Picard. He is accompanied by Riker, Troi and Tasha. The assistant to the leader, Hagon, bears a small box as a gift— then Lutan, the leader, appears.

When Hagon tries to present the box of vaccine to Picard, Tasha intercepts him. Hagon tries to brush her aside but is flipped on his back. Lutan is amused that a woman could do such a thing. He offers to open relations with the Federation so long as the customs of his people are respected.

When Riker explains that it is common for women to hold positions of authority on a starship, Lutan remarks that among his people the duty of women is only to own the land; men protect and rule it.

Lutan asks for a demonstration of Tasha Yar's skills. She agrees, and defeats an adversary created for her on the holodeck. Lutan reaches out to congratulate her while touching a jewel in his collar. The two vanish in a transporter beam. Picard puts the ship on full alert and sends a message demanding the release of Yar, but there is no response.

Another day passes without word from Lutan. Crusher reports that something must be done. The vaccine cannot be replicated in the lab and must be obtained from Ligon II. After an analysis of Ligonian society, Data reports that they live by a strict code of honor, and by Lutan's standards what he did is considered heroic.

Lutan contacts Picard and states that if he beams down to the surface of Ligon II, that Tasha will be returned. Picard complies and Lutan presents himself along with his primary wife Yareena , his "First One." Lutan promises that Yar will be returned at a banquet planned for that evening, and demonstrates his goodwill by proving that Tasha has not been harmed. At the banquet, Lutan announces that he doesn't want to return Yar after all. He wants Yar to become his wife. Yareena, Lutan's present wife (and primary wife, called "The First One") challenges Yar to a fight to the death.

Because they need to get the vaccine from them, Yar goes along with all this nonsense and accepts the challenge. If Yareena is killed, Lutan inherits all her land. Yareena is determined to fight Yar as she cannot believe that Tasha would not be attracted to a man like Lutan.

Once the battle starts they seem evenly matched, but the more Tasha becomes accustomed to the style of combat, the better she gets, and she defeats Yareena by scratching the woman's shoulder with her poisoned weapon. At the moment Yareena falls, they beam out of sight. Lutan is upset, because Yar is supposed to become his First One now. Picard says that he won't stop her, should she choose to claim the honor

Lutan releases the vaccine and it is beamed aboard the Enterprise. When Lutan and Hagon beam back down to the surface with Picard, Lutan is amazed to find that Yareena alive. She did die, but then Dr. Crusher revived her. Since their mating agreement ended with death, Yareena is free of Lutan, and turns her attentions to Hagon. Without Yareena's lands, Lutan is now powerless, and Hagon, who asks Yareena to be his First One, inherits Lutan's title.

The Ligonians return to their planet after negotiations are completed, and the Enterprise leaves orbit, carrying plenty of vaccine to fight the plague on Styris IV. Tasha chooses to remain on the Enterprise, having turned down Lutan's offer to be his "First One."

EPISODE FIVE: "THE LAST OUTPOST"
Teleplay by Herbert Wright
Story by Richard Krzemian
Directed by Richard Colla

Guest Cast: Darryl Henriques, Mike Gomez, Armin Shimerman, Jake Dengal, Tracey Walter

A pursuit of a Ferengi ship leads the Enterprise to a distant planet. The planet was once part of the T'Kan Empire which was destroyed by a supernova centuries ago. Shields and weapons systems fail. It seems that the Ferengi have some new, unknown but powerful weapon which puts them at a deadly advantage over the Enterprise.

Data reports that some force is reading all of the information in the ship's memory banks. Picard contacts the Ferengi again and offers to open negotiations for surrender. The response of the Ferengi indicates that they think that Picard wants them to surrender. The Ferengi have not disabled the Enterprise. Something on the planet below has affected both ships.

The Ferengi reluctantly agree to coopcrate, and to meet at predesignated coordinates on the planet below. But the Ferengi betray their trust and capture the Away Team. On the Enterprise, power continues to fail as the temperature drops. On the surface, Worf wakes and attacks the Ferengi. A free for all ensues until Yar arrives and points a phaser at the Ferengi. The Ferengi and the humans stand off but when they try to attack each other with their weapons, their energy beams are drawn into nearby crystalline structures.

Geordi realizes that the entire planet is a power accumulator. The guardian of the planet, Portal, appears. Portal was in suspended animation for hundreds of centuries until the two ships awakened him. He still believes that the T'Kan Empire exists. The Ferengi try to convince him that the humans are there to loot. Portal tells Riker that he will put him to a test: "He will triumph who knows when to fight and when not to fight."

Riker demonstrates his wisdom and Portal realizes who the civilized ones are. Portal returns the power to the Enterprise just in time to save the crew. He had seen the ships bent on combat, and his first impulse had been to destroy both. But when he saw them cooperating, he decided to wait. He offers to destroy the Ferengi, but Riker declines. Portal chooses to go back to sleep until needed again, and the two parties return to their ships.

EPISODE SIX: "WHERE NO ONE HAS GONE BEFORE"

Written by Diane Duane and Michael Reaves
Directed by Rob Bowman

Guest Cast: Biff Yeager, Charles Dayton, Victoria Dillard, Stanley Kamel, Eric Menyuk, Herta Ware

A Federation propulsion expert and his assistant are arriving to test new warp drive theories. Riker questions the value of this. The formula sent on ahead by Mr. Koszinski show no effect when run in computer simulations.

Koszinski is accompanied by his assistant, a humanoid from Tau Alpha-C. Troi scans the two men. Koszinski is exactly as he seems, arrogant and self-important, but she can't read his assistant. It seems as if he weren't even there.

Riker makes it clear that tests will not begin until approved by himself and the chief engineer. Eventually, Koszinski is allowed to proceed. The alien lays in the formula at a high speed, and allows Wesley to observe him. He seems strangely open to reinterpreting Koszinski's theories. During the test, something goes wrong. Wesley observes the alien momentarily phase.

Picard stops the ship; they are in a new star system 2,000,700 light years from their previous position. It will take 300 years to return to Federation space at top speed. Koszinski admits that he made mistakes, but he's certain he can get them back. He takes full credit for what has happened, but Wesley notices that the alien is tired.

Wesley asks if the formula was based on the concept that space and time and thought are not as different as generally believed. The alien is startled and asks him never to repeat this. Wesley tries to tell Riker that he doesn't think Koszinski was really responsible, but Riker pays no attention. When the procedure is repeated the Enterprise winds up further away than before, but Riker witnesses the alien phase in and out.

In this region, space and thought are linked, and people can materialize things from within their minds. Yar imagines herself back at the colony where she grew up, while Picard encounters his long dead mother. Realizing what is happening, Picard warns the crew to be careful what they think. The alien collapses and is taken to Sick Bay, but Picard insists that Crusher give him a stimulant, as he is the only one who can return them all.

The being is a Traveler, but is vague about where he comes from. He can act as a lens to focus thought and turn it into power. That is how the ship traveled millions of light years in moments.

The procedure is tried again. The Traveler has Koszinski help him enter the formula. They succeed, but in the process, the Traveler fades out completely.

Gates at the Coronet Theatre for her performance of "A Muse of Fire."

Photo © 1994 Albert L. Ortega

Patrick at the '93 Emmy Awards where he was a presenter.

Photo © 1994 Albert L. Ortega

TREK: THE NEXT GENERATION

Later, Captain Picard invites Wesley to the bridge, this time justifying the boy's presence in the command center by making him an acting ensign. Then Picard states that he has decided to sponsor Wesley's application to Starfleet Academy.

EPISODE SEVEN: "LONELY AMONG US"

Script by D.C. Fontana
Story by Michael Halperin
Directed by Cliff Bole
Guest Cast: Colm Meaney, Kavi Raz, John Durbin

As the story begins, the Enterprise brushes against an energy cloud. A bit of energy moves into the Enterprise. It flows into Worf, who is shocked unconscious. He is taken to sickbay, and the energy moves to Crusher. She goes to the bridge and makes an excuse to use one of the science stations, and the energy moves into the ship's systems. Controls malfunction, but they are easily repaired. Picard demands an answer be found as soon as possible.

Warp capabilities suddenly fade, along with subspace communications, but then it is restored. Mr. Singh, the Assistant Chief Engineer, receives the same shock and dies. Dr. Crusher realizes that she's suffering from a memory lapse just as Worf is, and asks Troi to hypnotize them in order to get to the truth. Under hypnosis, each reveals that they were under the control of another entity. The force emerges from the ship's systems and enters Picard, who immediately orders the Enterprise to double back to the mysterious cloud.

Crusher and Riker determine that something is wrong with Picard and confront him. Picard deftly turns the situation around. He admits to Crusher that he is an alien entity which has joined with Picard, and that he plans to take Picard with him into the cloud. Using strange powers, the Captain temporarily disables the bridge crew and transport chief. As the ship reaches the cloud, he beams himself into it as pure energy.

Troi detects the presence of Picard in the cloud as energy disconnected from the entity. They could not stay united in the cloud as the entity had thought. Picard's energy enters the ship. Since Picard was the last person to beam out, and since he did not reform outside, his pattern is still recorded in the transporter. Reforming on the transport pad, he doesn't remember what happened to him when he was just energy although he does have some memory of when the entity was controlling him.

EPISODE EIGHT: "JUSTICE"

Teleplay by Worley Thorne
Story by Ralph Willis and Worley Thorne
Directed by James L. Conway
Guest Cast: Josh Clark, David Q. Combs, Richard Lavin, Judith Jones, Eric Matthew, Brad Zerbst, David Michael Graves

The Enterprise discovers a new Class M planet where the people are not just friendly but downright over-affectionate. Initial surveys deem this world safe and Picard decides to grant the crew shore leave following a more detailed survey by an Away Team.

The Edo greet the team with embraces. Aboard the Enterprise, Data detects something off the bow. He broadcasts a beam asking the object to identify itself, and it appears. It looks like a huge space station but it straddles more than one dimension, allowing the entities in it to be in many different places at once.

A small globe shoots out of the craft, confronts Picard and asks the reason for his visit. Picard explains; the device says, "Do not interfere with my children below." The device confronts Data and attaches itself to him in order to learn what he knows. Down on the planet, Worf and Yar are conversing with two of the Edo and ask about laws

and crime. The Edo casually admit that no one breaks any law because no one wants to risk execution.

Yar is astonished and contacts Riker; they summon the rest of the landing team members, but they can't locate Wesley. He is playing ball with Edo teenagers and blunders into a small greenhouse. The Mediators appear and try to execute the death sentence. Riker and the others arrive in time to stop them. This creates great consternation among the Edo. No one is above the law, not even outsiders.

Picard beams down. The Edo explain their system to Picard while the Captain explains that his culture no longer practices capital punishment. It becomes clear to the Edo that Picard regards them as a primitive culture and they become defensive.

Picard then tries to calm things by stating his own Prime Directive contains a non-interference clause. Thus Wesley should be sacrificed to uphold this rule. The Edo state that the punishment of the boy can only be delayed until sundown.

Picard wants to know more about the entities in orbit nearby and beams up to the Enterprise with one of the Edo women. He takes her to the observation chamber and she reverently tells him that what they are seeing is "God." Suddenly the alien craft starts moving towards the Enterprise, demanding that their "child" be returned to the planet below. Picard acts quickly and has the woman beamed down.

Data states that the entities know all that he knows about the Federation, which would include the Prime Directive.

When Crusher asks Picard what he's going to do, he states that no matter what the cost, he will not allow Wesley to be executed. They beam down to confront the Edo again. Wes is brought out and Picard informs the Edo that he cannot allow the boy to be punished for a crime he wasn't even aware he was committing. Following a rousing speech, the entities agree to forego punishment and Wesley returns with Picard to the Enterprise.

EPISODE NINE: "THE BATTLE"

Teleplay by Herbert Wright
Story by Larry Forester
Directed by Rob Bowman
Guest Cast: Frank Corsentino, Doug Warhit, Robert Towers

The Enterprise meets with a Ferengi ship at their request. The Ferengi ship does not reply to the Enterprise's communications for three days. Then Bock, commander of the Ferengi ship, states that he wants to meet with Picard alone. Picard invites the Ferengi to meet him aboard his ship.

Picard has been suffering from severe headaches. Since this is an uncommon ailment in the 24th Century, Crusher is concerned, but can find no physical reason for the affliction.

As the Ferengi prepare to beam over, Wesley announces that he has detected the approach of a Constellation class ship on the scanners. The Ferengi beam aboard; Bock announces that this ship is a gift to Picard. Bock's comrades are shocked at this un-Ferengi display of foolish, unprofitable generosity.

Picard is just as shocked. This Federation ship is the Stargazer, his old ship. He and the crew had to abandon it nine years earlier after they were attacked by an unidentified ship (since revealed to be Ferengi) and only barely destroyed their attacker before having to flee in several shuttlecraft. Picard had believed the Stargazer lost in space. The Ferengi claim that they found it adrift on the far side of the galaxy.

They discuss Picard's fateful engagement with the Ferengi. It introduced a new method of warfare involving the use of warp drive over a short distance so that a ship would appear to be in two places at once, thereby confusing the enemy. Bock seems particularly sensitive about the Battle of Maxia, a name the Ferengi have applied to this encounter.

Picard's headache worsens. Bock asks if Picard's conscience is bothering him.

Yar, Geordi and Worf beam aboard the Stargazer and find it in remarkably good condition. Picard soon follows and is amazed. When he abandoned the ship, it was on fire. Picard goes to his old stateroom on the ship and packs some things which had been left behind nine years before. While Bock gloats over how he intends to destroy Picard with his secret device, Picard lies in his bunk and dreams of the Battle of Maxia.

Geordi finds Picard's personal log on the Stargazer. It indicates a different chronology to the Battle of Maxia than the official report submitted by Picard. Data proves that the log is a clever forgery. Someone is trying to discredit Picard. This is confirmed when Wesley Crusher reveals that he has detected low intensity transmissions from the Ferengi ship which match strange wave patterns in Picard's brain scan. Before the Captain can be contacted, it's discovered that he has beamed aboard the Stargazer and activated the shields.

Bock confronts Picard, revealing that his son was in command of the Ferengi ship that Picard destroyed. Bock has spent the wealth of a lifetime to acquire the forbidden device he is using against Picard. Bock beams back to his ship and leaves a brainwashed Picard thinking that he is back at the Battle of Maxia, and that he is under attack by a strange spacecraft— the Enterprise.

The Ferengi ship informs the Enterprise that Bock has been relieved of command because of his unprofitable quest for vengeance. Riker shows the Ferengi a device found in Picard's cabin; the Ferengi identify it as a forbidden mind control device.

Picard uses the warp drive maneuver against the Enterprise but is caught by the ship's tractor beam. Riker manages to get a message through, and tells Picard what is happening. Picard manages to destroy the mind control sphere and is freed from its influence.

EPISODE TEN: "HIDE AND Q"

Teleplay by C.J. Holland and Gene Roddenberry
Story by C.J. Holland
Directed by Cliff Bole
Guest Cast: John deLancie, Elaine Nalee, William A. Wallace

A barrier halts the progress of the Enterprise; a strange alien life form appears on the bridge— and plays a deadly game with the crew of the Enterprise. Yes, it's Q again. Q insists that he wants to involve the crew in some deadly games and vanishes, taking Riker, Worf, Data, LaForge and Yar to a barren planet surface.

Back on the Enterprise, Picard finds himself stranded on the bridge unable to contact any other part of the ship. On the planet below, Q appears dressed in the uniform of an American Revolutionary War commander and invites Riker to drink with him. Riker accepts but Worf refuses, turning the drink upside down.

When they ask what the rules of this game will be, Q states that it will be completely unfair. When Yar objects she is sent to the "penalty box." Q states that the next person to break a rule will also be sent to the penalty box, causing Yar's instant demise.

The penalty box that Yar is sent to is the bridge of the Enterprise, which is still trapped behind the barrier. Q appears to Picard and reveals that the one he's really interested in is Riker. Q plans to offer Number One something that he cannot refuse. Picard says that he will lose. Q agrees that if he does he'll leave humans alone forever after.

Q appears to Riker and states that he has given Number One the power of Q to use as he will. Riker sends the other crewmen back safely to the Enterprise. They find that the Enterprise is not only back on course, but was never behind any barrier. Q had just suspended time.

Down on the planet, Q and Riker converse, as Riker wants to know what Q wants from humans. Q explains that he's fascinated by the human race's ability for growth and wants Riker to become one of the Q so that they can learn more about this facet of humankind. Riker turns Q down.

Suddenly the entire bridge crew is back on the planet, along with Picard and Wesley. Alien warriors attack; Worf and Wesley are killed, but Riker uses his new power to return them all to the Enterprise, along with restoring Worf and Wesley to perfect health. On the Enterprise, Picard tells Riker that the only way he can not give in to Q is by refusing to use his power. The more Riker uses his power, the more he will want to use it. Riker promises Picard that he won't use the power.

The Enterprise arrives at Quadra Sigma II and the Away Team beams down on a rescue mission. They find many dead, including the body of a child. Riker doesn't use his power to revive her because he has promised Picard that he would not. Riker is angry at having to keep his word.

Riker summons the bridge crew, including Wesley, to discuss his situation. Picard points out that Riker is already being corrupted by the power as he's started calling the Captain by his first name. Q comes to observe the proceedings.

Riker wants to use his power to give his friends what they've always wanted. He makes Wesley ten years older.

Data refuses to be made human. He doesn't want to get his wish that way. Geordi is given human eyes, but then has Riker return him to the way he was. Worf is given a mate, a savage Klingon woman who he fights with and subdues as part of the courtship rite. He suddenly realizes that he can't continue, as this part of Klingon reality is no longer part of his life. He has Riker remove her. Wesley too asks Riker to take back his gift.

Riker rejects the power at last. Q has therefore failed. The other entities of the Q Continuum summon Q back to explain his failure, and the troublesome being disappears screaming.

EPISODE ELEVEN: "HAVEN"

Teleplay by Tracy Torme
Story by Tracy Torme and Lian Okun
Directed by Richard Compton
Guest Cast: Danzita Kingsley, Carel Struycken, Anna Katrina, Raye Birk, Michael Rider, Majel Barrett, Rob Knepper, Nan Martin, Robert Ellenstein

The Enterprise arrives at the planet Haven for some R & R. But no sooner does the grand starship arrive than an object beams up which announces to Troi that the marriage party will be arriving soon. Troi is crestfallen at the news; she had been promised in marriage as child but believed it would never really happen. She knows that she and her husband will not be staying with the ship. Troi tells Riker that she knows that he cares about her.

The Miller wedding party, consisting of the mother, father and their adult son Wyatt, beam aboard. Wyatt is a handsome young doctor. Troi warns Picard that her mother Lwaxana is eccentric, as well as a full Betazoid with telepathic powers. The woman is loud and obnoxious, and even though she has a seven foot tall servant with her, she asks Picard to carry her bag.

Troi tells her mother that she has doubts about her wedding vows but will uphold them. Lwaxana states that she understands and had all but forgotten about the arranged marriage herself until the Millers tracked her down and confronted her with the old promise.

Haven detects an unidentified ship approaching. The ship is too far off to be identified.

Troi visits Wyatt to learn more about him and discovers that he's an artist. His art repeats the image of a beautiful woman whom he has seen often in his dreams. He believed the woman to be Troi until they met.

The Enterprise identifies the unknown vessel as a Terellian plague ship. The ship carries the last survivors of a contagion created in a biological war. Haven demands that the Enterprise prevent the ship from approaching.

Troi visits Riker in the holodeck. He's unhappy over the impending marriage as he and Troi were once involved, although the relationship drifted apart. Wyatt enters and Riker decides to leave. Wyatt asks Troi if she really wants to marry him. They kiss.

Haven pleads with Picard to destroy the Terellian ship. The Enterprise traps it in a tractor beam instead.

The Terellians contact the Enterprise. Troi recognizes one of its passengers, Arianna, as the woman in Wyatt's drawings. She asks for Wyatt; he is amazed by what he sees. The Terellians explain that there are only eight of them left alive. All they crave is a remote area of Haven where they can be left alone to die.

Wyatt prepares medical supplies to be beamed over to the Terellians. He says good-bye to his parents and Troi, but they don't realize what he's planning. He goes to the transporter room, knocks out the technician and beams over to the Terellian ship before the beam can be overridden. He joins Arianna, who had also dreamed about him but was never completely sure if he was real.

Wyatt tells his parents that he'll try to cure the Terellians, who have chosen to remain aboard their ship and continue on their journey through space, away from Haven, as they will remain outcasts until the day they die.

EPISODE TWELVE: "THE BIG GOODBYE"

Written by Tracy Torme
Directed by Joseph L. Scanlan
Guest Cast: Mike Genovese, Dick Miller, Carolyn Alport, Rhonda Aldrich, Eric Cord, Lawrence Tierney, Harvey Jason, William Boyett, David Selburg, Gary Armagnal

Picard has been working hard to memorize an important greeting in Harada, a difficult alien language. Troi suggests that he take a break on the holodeck. Picard agrees and calls up the 1941 Dixon Hill program, based on the exploits of a fictional detective.

Picard enters the holodeck, still wearing his normal uniform, and walks into the office of Dixon Hill. A woman is waiting in his office; she wants to hire Dixon Hill to keep her from being killed. She gives him a C-note as a retainer and tells him to wear a suit the next time.

Picard looks around "Hill's" office, calls out "Exit" and leaves, even though someone is knocking at the office door. He tells them to come back later. But after Picard leaves the holodeck, the program keeps running; the person enters the office only to look around in confusion.

At a meeting, Picard can't contain his excitement over the holodeck and how real it all seems. It was so real that Crusher leans over and wipes some lipstick off Picard's face.

Picard dresses in clothes fitting the time period and has Mr. Whelan, an expert on 20th Century culture, accompany him. Data has just scanned the computer and absorbed all the information on Dixon Hill, so he dresses up in 1940s garb and joins them. They enter the holodeck and emerge on a street outside Dixon Hill's office. Picard sees a newspaper with a picture of the woman who'd hired him. She's been murdered. When a police detective sees Picard, he takes him in for questioning.

The Harada send a probe and announce that they want to hear from Picard immediately. When Riker tries to speak to the aliens, they angrily terminate their communications. Crusher puts on a 1940s style dress and enters the holodeck to find Picard. She learns that he's being interrogated by the police. Geordi tries to contact Picard on the holodeck, but the communication link fails, and the holodeck doors won't open. When the probe swept the ship, it disrupted the holodeck.

Picard is released from custody by a cop who's a friend of Hill. When Picard enters the lobby of the police station, he's surprised to see Crusher, and impressed by how she looks in her costume.

When they return to Dixon Hill's office, a little man named Leach is waiting. None of them take him seriously because he's a hologram. But when Felix Leach loses his composure and shoots Mr. Whelan, the historian is seriously wounded by the gunshot. Picard disarms Leach, who flees. Picard calls for the exit but it fails to appear. Whelan may die if he isn't taken to sick bay.

Redblock enters with his bodyguards and Leach, demanding to know where "the item" is. Picard claims ignorance. The policeman arrives and is taken prisoner as well. Picard confesses that they're from another world and that he's not really Dixon Hill. Redblock plans to test how real he is by killing one of Picard's people. Picard appeals to Redblock's greed by telling the man that he has "the item" in his world. He convinces Redblock when the holodeck momentarily flickers, replacing San Francisco with a blizzard.

The exit opens in the holodeck. Picard lures Leach and Redblock through it. Once they leave the holodeck, they vanish. Picard and friends then overpower the thugs remaining in the holodeck, and take Whelan to sick bay.

Picard says farewell to his friend, who wonders if he'll exist after Picard leaves. Picard doesn't know. When Captain Picard leaves, the holodeck goes dark.

Picard, still dressed as Dixon Hill, then flawlessly delivers the Federation's greeting to the Harada.

EPISODE THIRTEEN: "DATALORE"

Teleplay by Robert Lewin and Gene Roddenberry
Story by Robert Lewin and Maurice Hurley
Directed by Rob Bowman
Guest Cast: Biff Yeager

The Enterprise achieves orbit around the planet in the Omicron Theta star system where Data was found. Data holds the complete recorded knowledge and experiences of the 411 members of the Earth colony that once existed there but who disappeared shortly before Data was found, in a non-functional state. No life exists there now. An Away Team down, and Data shows them where he was found.

Geordi's artificially enhanced sight detects a false wall of rock which conceals a cave, not apparent to the unaided normal human eye. He finds a way in and they discover a fully functional laboratory— the lab where Data was created. They also find something odd— children's drawings of a weird configuration in the sky.

Data's creator was Dr. Noonian Soong, Earth's foremost cybernetic scientist until he tried to make Asimov's dream of a positronic brain come true. When his attempts to accomplish this failed, he disappeared from Earth.

The Away Team locates Data's patterns and an epidermal mold, as well as parts for another Data. They return to the Enterprise with them and assemble the second android.

The android is activated and says that its name is Lore. It looks exactly like Data, but has a facial tic and an attitude that sets it apart from its 'brother', whom Lore claims is an imperfect version of himself. Soon, Lore manages to replace Data, disabling the real Data and triggering a facial tic like his own. Lore is also able to halt his own twitch, and replaces Data on the bridge.

Lore contacts a strange space creature which feeds on life and summons it toward the Enterprise. This crystalline entity is the same creature depicted in the children's drawings on the planet in the Omicron Theta system, and is the force which destroyed the colony. Wesley is suspicious of Data and senses the truth of his identity. They try to revive the unconscious android in Data's quarters, but without success.

The huge crystalline creature attacks the Enterprise but Lore warns it off. He offers to go over to it and goes to the Transporter room. Wesley protests but Riker belittles him. Wesley complains that people would listen to him if he were older. Worf follows Lore and is cornered and attacked in the turbolift. Lore demonstrates that his strength and fighting skill can defeat even a Klingon warrior.

After Wesley and Dr. Crusher manage to reactivate Data, they confront Lore in the transporter room. The rogue android grabs a phaser and threatens the boy, forcing Dr. Crusher to leave. As a parting gesture, he shoots the doctor in the arm.

Data attacks Lore and during their struggle, Data maneuvers Lore into the transporter and Wesley hits the controls, beaming Lore into space—but not reintegrating the android once its out there. Without Lore to communicate with it, the huge crystalline entity departs.

EPISODE FOURTEEN: "ANGEL ONE"

Teleplay by Patrick Berry
Directed by Michael Rhodes
Guest Cast: Karen Montgomery, Sam Hennings, Leonard John Crowfoot, Patricia McPherson,

The Enterprise encounters the freighter Odin, now a derelict ship which had been reported lost reportedly lost seven years before. Three escape pods had been jettisoned, leading the Enterprise to believe there may be survivors. The nearest planet is Angel One, so their search for possible survivors begins there.

While similar to mid-20th Century Earth in technology, Angel One is a matriarchal society in which men are the meek servitors of women. It has been 62 years since a Federation ship last visited that world. When the Enterprise requests permission to send down an Away Team, they receive a cool reception since men are the ones in command on the Enterprise.

Riker, Data, Troi and Yar beam down and ask for information regarding possible survivors. The ruler is evasive and says that she is not yet prepared to answer their questions. When she does answer them, she reveals that there are four survivors who are now radical fugitives from Angel One society.

On the Enterprise, Wesley and another boy contract a respiratory ailment.

The Enterprise plans to scan the surface of Angel One for survivors. The Elected One agrees to this so long as the Enterprise crew promise to take the rebels with them, since they are an unwanted disruptive force.

On the surface, Riker is given a garment to wear for his audience with the Elected One. Yar and Troi are at first annoyed by Riker's submission to the ruler's sartorial demands, but are amused when they see Riker dressed in the skimpy outfit.

Picard contracts the virus which afflicted Wesley, and orders Geordi to take the bridge.

The survivors are located. Data, Yar and Troi are beamed to their position. A man there, Ramsey, greets them as though he'd been expecting them.

On the Enterprise, 82 more cases of the virus are reported.

The survivors of Odin reveal that, while they have families now, they are prepared to leave the planet.

Riker and the Elected One get along well, as she makes no effort to conceal her feelings of physical attraction for Riker.

Elsewhere, Ramsey explains that he and the other survivors felt alienated in the matriarchal society. They change their minds and decide to stay, and Data points out that they cannot be forced to leave.

On the Enterprise, there are now 300 people ill with the virus.

Data, Yar and Troi return to the palace of the Elected One to report to Commander Riker. The Elected One becomes furious when the Away Team explains that the Enterprise isn't going to take the radicals away. She claims to have no choice but to sentence Ramsey and the others to death.

Aboard the Enterprise, Dr. Crusher comes up with a temporary remedy when she discovers how the virus is transmitted. It has a pleasing scent and when people inhale deeply to enjoy it, it goes deep into their lungs. The Enterprise is subjected to further pressure when it receives orders to aid an outpost which is being threatened by the Romulans.

On Angel One, Ramsey and the others are captured, and condemned to death unless they agree to leave the planet.

Riker tries to convince Ramsey to leave on the Enterprise, but he and his people refuse. Riker tries to force them, but Crusher won't let them be beamed up while the virus is still a threat.

Data is beamed up to pilot the ship since he is not affected by the virus. Data tells Riker that they have 48 minutes before they must leave orbit.

The execution of Ramsey and his people is scheduled. It is to be carried out by means of disintegration.

Riker points out that the execution could make Ramsey's people martyrs, and make them symbols of discontent, or even of evolution, instead of revolution. The Elected One rescinds the death order.

Crusher comes up with a cure for the viral infection.

The rest of the Away Team beams up and they are inoculated as the Enterprise heads for its next mission in the Neutral Zone.

EPISODE FIFTEEN: "11001001"

Written by Maurice Hurley and Robert Lewin
Directed by Paul Lynch
Guest Cast: Carolyn McCormack, Iva Lane, Kelli Ann McNally, Jack Sheldon, Abdul Salaam El Razzac, Ron Brown, Gene Dynarski, Katy Boyer, Alexandra Johnson

When the holodeck requires repairs (see "The Long Goodbye") the Enterprise stops off at Starbase 74 to undergo the required diagnostic work. The repair team includes a pair of Binars, who come from a world where a humanoid race has become closely linked with the computers which run their world.

When more Binars arrive to join the original team, they explain that since they must complete their repairs more quickly than they originally thought, they need more help. Although Wesley Crusher is concerned by this, Commander Riker says that there's nothing to be worried about. As more and more people exit the Enterprise, unoccupied areas of the ship are shut down to clear space in the computer banks.

Riker and Picard return to the Enterprise after work on the holodeck is completed. Riker uses the holodeck to create a nightclub in New Orleans on Bourbon Street, complete with sultry brunette. When Riker enters the program, he meets the girl named Minuet.

Riker plays a trombone in the bar and Minuet watches admiringly. When Riker starts thinking about leaving to return to work, Minuet dissuades him by wanting to dance. Riker is interested in her. When he asks how real she is, Minuet replies, "I'm as real as you need me to be."

Picard enters and sits down at the bar with Riker and Minuet. She speaks to him in French and he tells her how impressed he is with her adaptability.

Wesley contacts Data about a problem in Engineering with the magnetic containment field. Data detects that it is deteriorating. If this continues, the anti-matter will be released. Data orders that everyone abandon ship. He and Geordi program the Enterprise to leave so that when the anti-matter is released, the ship will be far enough away not to be a hazard to anyone. The ship is abandoned, but the alarms do not penetrate the holodeck. Riker and Picard remain on, unaware of the process, and whenever Picard tries to leave he is distracted by Minuet.

The Enterprise leaves Starbase 74 under computer control. Only then is it realized that the two ranking officers are still on their ship. Just as the Enterprise exits the Starbase, Data detects that the magnetic containment field has stabilized. The ship is out of danger. By this time, the ship has prepared to enter warp speed, and vanishes.

When Picard tries to exit the holodeck again, Minuet tries too hard to convince him to stay, which arouses his suspicions that things are not all that

they seem. He calls for the exit and finds his ship empty, undergoing a crisis alert.

When Picard learns from the computer that the ship has been evacuated, he realizes that the Enterprise has been hijacked by the Binars. The two officers decide that it would be better the Enterprise was destroyed than that it fall into the hands of hostile forces. They activate the auto-destruct sequence and have themselves beamed to the bridge. There they find the Binars unconscious.

Picard and Riker cancel the destruct sequence and find their ship going into orbit around the planet of the Binars.

The Enterprise computer is filled with information. They return to the holodeck, guessing correctly that Minuet had been created by the Binars to keep them aboard the Enterprise. She explains that a nova had knocked out the computer on their world and they need another computer to reactivate it. This is why they stole the Enterprise.

Returning to the bridge, Riker and Picard try to access the computer but cannot get in. Picard contacts Data at the Starbase. After assuring them that they are well, he asks Data what the access code might be. They finally figure out what it is and access the information which is moved to the computer on Binars, reactivating that world.

The Binars revive. When Picard questions them as to why they stole the Enterprise rather than asking for help, the Binars explain that there was a chance they might be turned down. They couldn't take that risk. They surrender themselves to be returned to Starbase 74 for a hearing.

Will Riker returns to the holodeck, but although the New Orleans setting remains, he can no longer summon Minuet. She had been a part of the Binar's programming. She had truly been a fascinating character to know, and he misses her.

EPISODE SIXTEEN: "TOO SHORT A SEASON"

Teleplay by Michael Michaelian and D.C. Fontana
Story by Michael Michaelian
Directed by Rob Bowman
Guest Cast: Clayton Rohner, Marsha Hunt, Michael Pataki

A planetary ruler, Karnas, contacts the Federation after a group of terrorists take an ambassador and his staff hostage. The terrorists want Admiral Mark Jameson as negotiator. Jameson is the one who negotiated during another hostage situation 45 years before. The Federation complies with the request.

Mark Jameson, now elderly and infirm, beams aboard the Enterprise along with his wife where the admiral is designated senior officer. Karnas contacts Picard and stresses that the terrorists will only negotiate with Jameson in person. Crusher wants to schedule Jameson for a routine physical, but this prospect seems to disturb him for some reason.

Alone with his wife in their quarters, Jameson steps from his wheelchair. He seems to be a little stronger, but suffers a sudden spasm. He claims that it's just natural body changes.

Crusher talks with Picard and wonders why Jameson gave her medical records which show his last physical was two months before. When Jameson demonstrates his ability leave his support chair and to walk, Crusher wonders how Jameson could have recovered from Iverson's Disease, which is incurable. When Jameson has a mysterious spasm, his wife calls sick bay. Unable to dodge a medical scan, Dr. Crusher's tests reveal an unknown substance in the Admiral's body.

Picard discovers that the Admiral has been using an illegal youth restorative drug. He had been taking the drug slowly, as intended, until the hostage situation developed— then he took the rest of the drug to accelerate the process. He's never told this to his wife, and she becomes furious with him when the truth is revealed.

Admiral Jameson contacts Karnas privately because he knows that Karnas is lying. There are no terrorists. Karnas is the one who has taken the hostages in order to lure Jameson back to that world and exact his revenge after 45 long years of waiting.

Picard wants to know what secret Jameson is hiding. The Admiral reveals that 45 years before, when he secured the release of hostages from Karnas, he did so by giving the man the weapons he wanted. Then, to balance this inequity, he gave the same weapons to Karnas' enemies.

In this way, Jameson thought he could stay within the boundaries of the Prime Directive. But the result of his actions was 40 years of warfare on the planet, which ended only five years earlier.

Jameson leads the Away Team because he believes he knows where Karnas is keeping the hostages. His youth has almost been completely restored and he is relishing his renewed vigor, although he is still having occasional spasms. Accelerating the drug's usage carries certain dangers with it. Picard refuses to remain on the ship and accompanies the Away Team himself.

Upon beaming down into the tunnels, Jameson finds them changed from what he knew of them 45 years before. He points to a new wall and tells the Away Team to cut an opening in it. As soon as they break through the wall they are attacked and a pitched battle is fought. When Jameson suffers another spasm, Picard has the Away Team beamed up.

Although gravely ill, Jameson offers to trade himself to Karnas for the hostages. When Picard and Crusher beam down with the young but dying Jameson, Karnas accuses them of trying to trick him. Karnas wants the real admiral or he'll start killing the hostages. But Jameson finally convinces Karnas of the truth and drops dead in front of him. Karnas agrees to releases the hostages. He's had his revenge, at last.

EPISODE SEVENTEEN: "WHEN THE BOUGH BREAKS"

Teleplay by Hannah Louise Shearer
Directed by Kim Manners
Guest Cast: Dierk Torsek, Michele Marsh, Dan Mason, Philip N. Waller, Connie Danese, Jessica and Vanessa Bova, Jerry Hardin, Brenda Strong, Jandi Swanson, Paul Lambert, Ivy Bethune

The Enterprise nears the legendary location of the planet Aldea, a mystery which Riker has long been interested in. Amazingly, they do detect a planet which is using a cloaking device, a device which is dropped as the Enterprise nears.

They are contacted by a woman who welcomes them to her world. She says the Aldeans want to discuss something with the Enterprise crew, and two Aldeans beam themselves to the bridge. They invite Picard and his people to a gathering. The Aldeans then beam Riker, Crusher and Troi down to the planet.

While they're planetside, powerful beams probe all decks of the Enterprise but seem to contact only the children.

The Aldeans explain to Picard that they have no children and want to trade technological secrets for some of the children on the Enterprise. Riker rejects the suggestion out of hand. The trio are beamed back to the Enterprise, and several children, including Wesley, disappear from the ship via the Aldean's beam.

When the Aldeans contact Picard to discuss the terms of an equitable trade, Jean-Luc is furious and demands the return of the children immediately. The Aldeans regret Captain Picard's position in the matter.

On the shielded planet below, the children from the Enterprise are friendly with the Aldeans and in turn are well

treated. But Wesley refuses to accept what has happened to him and he demands that they all be returned to their parents.

The Aldeans ignore the request, stating that they'll come to love their new lives. Wesley is shown a computer, called a "Custodian." By asking the Aldeans questions, he quickly figures out that they don't understand a great deal about their own technology.

On the Enterprise, Data detects weaknesses and fluctuations in the force shield around Aldea. He works on a way to break through.

Picard and Crusher are beamed down for negotiations, but are not allowed to see the children— except her son. She slips him a miniature medical monitor which he uses to scan one of the Aldeans and then surreptitiously returns it to his mother.

The negotiations do not proceed well as each side is firm and immovable in their demands. Captain Picard and Dr. Crusher are beamed back aboard the Enterprise. Then the great starship is hurled three days from Aldea in a matter of moments. Captain Picard is sternly told that if he refuses to cooperate, the Enterprise will be hurled decades away.

By the time the Enterprise returns to Aldea, Beverly Crusher has completed her analysis of the medical scan she had Wesley make and has determined that the Aldeans are dying as a race, but she can't yet determine the reason.

That night he learns where all of the children are from the Custodian. He goes to each of them, gathering them together to organize passive resistance in the form of a hunger strike. The Aldeans don't know what to make of this.

Dr. Crusher discovers that the Aldeans are dying from radiation poisoning caused by their depletion of their world's ozone layer.

The Aldeans want help in dealing with the children's resistance. When Crusher and Picard beam down, Data and Riker also beam down at the same moment, and beam through the defensive screen around the planet. Dr. Crusher reveals to the Aldeans what is afflicting them, but they think it is just a trick.

Riker and Data find a Custodian and get control of the computer so that the Aldeans can't silence Crusher and Picard by beaming them back to the Enterprise. Finally, the Aldeans accept that the power source of their defense screen must be shut down if they are to survive, otherwise even the children will suffer the same fate. With the power net terminated, it is possible that the Aldeans may once again be able to have children of their own, and so the Aldeans return the Enterprise children they had kidnapped.

EPISODE EIGHTEEN: "HOME SOIL"

Teleplay by Robert Sabaroff
Story by Karl Guers, Ralph Sanchez and Robert Sabaroff
Directed by Corey Allen
Guest Cast: Walter Gotell, Elizabeth Lidsey, Mario Roccuzzo, Carolyn Barry, Gerard Pendergast

The Enterprise makes a stopover at a terraforming base where something is being covered up. When Picard contacts the base leader, Director Mandel, Troi detects fear in the man. He tries to dissuade them from coming down but Picard is insistent and sends down an Away Team.

Mandel shows them the procedures they are working on. Mandel orders Arthur Malencon to work in a chamber with the laser drill, and Malencon reluctantly complies. Once he's in the sealed chamber, they hear screaming and force the door open. The man had been attacked by the laser drill. Yar immediately beams up to the Enterprise with him. The rest of the Terraforming crew beam up as well. Geordi and Data remain behind to investigate.

Data seals himself in the chamber and has the program reactivated. The laser attacks him, but Data is able to dodge it. When they unseal the door, they find that Data is fine, but he's destroyed the expensive laser drill.

Picard catches Mandel by surprise by asking him what he's trying to hide. Mandel claims he has nothing to hide, he's just worried about his timetable.

The injured hydraulics expert dies from his injuries.

Data and Geordi return to the planet and encounter strange flashes in a drill tunnel where the laser drill had been aimed. They wonder whether these flashes are a life form.

A sample is beamed aboard. They examine it and conclude that it is inorganic life which reacts to the presence of a probe, as well as to a human presence. The computer tests confirm that it is alive.

Mandel is questioned because the presence of the life form means that all terraforming must stop. Troi reveals that Mandel knew of the life form.

The life form reproduces, thus proving that it is alive. The life form then links with the computer to try a translation of its language into human terms, proving that it is also intelligent. It takes over the Med Lab, which is put under quarantine.

The thing continues to reproduce and tries to break the quarantine seal. It then attempts to communicate, referring to humans as "Ugly bags of mostly water." It wants to kill the terraformers, and declares war on the Enterprise.

They try to beam it back to the planet, but it resists the transporter beams and redirects the power. They figure out how it was threatened on the planet, and that it is photoelectric. By reducing the lights in the lab, they force the life form to end hostilities. The crystal is beamed back down to the planet. The life form tells the humans to return in 300 years.

The terraformers are evacuated and the planet is placed under quarantine.

EPISODE NINETEEN: "COMING OF AGE"

Written by Sandy Fries
Directed by Michael Vejar
Guest stars: Estee Chandler, Daniel Riordan, Brendan McKane, Wyatt Knight, Ward Costello, Robert Schekkan, Robert Ito, John Putch, Stephan Gregory, Tasia Valenza

The Enterprise is in orbit over the planet Relba where a group of Academy candidates, including Wesley, are to be tested.

Meanwhile, Admiral Quinn beams aboard and asks for a private meeting with Captain Picard. Commander Remmick is with Quinn and will investigate the Enterprise. They believe something may be wrong on the ship but are not prepared to say what they are looking for.

On Relba, Wesley meets Oliana Mirren, one of the other candidates. She's an attractive young woman who is nervous about the upcoming tests. He also meets the other candidates, Rondon and Mordak. Mordak is already widely known and respected. Wesley is surprised to learn that he isn't already in Starfleet.

On the Enterprise, Remmick is observing as well as annoying everyone. Riker asks Picard what Remmick is doing there, but Picard is not at liberty to say.

Wesley takes a hyperspace physics test. When he realizes that it is really a trick question, he passes it easily, to the mild annoyance of Oliana Mirren. She tells Wesley that if he wasn't so cute, he'd be obnoxious. Wes is concerned about the upcoming psych test which is based on exploring someone's deepest fear. He discusses this with Worf.

Remmick questions Riker about discrepancies in Picard's log, but Riker doesn't like the tone or direction of the questions. Remmick questions Geordi about the incident in "Where No One Has Gone Before" and asks Troi about Picard's mental state in "The Battle."

A crisis arises when Crewman Kurland steals a shuttle, stating that he's moving to a freighter. Picard orders the man back just before the shuttle malfunctions. Picard miraculously talks the shuttle in to safety by giving Kurland specific directions on how to save himself.

On Relba, Wesley is bullied and reacts aggressively, according to the alien's culture, as the alien's people detest politeness. It turns out to have been a test.

Remmick interviews Data and tries to tell him that Picard is not who he appears to be. Data rejects this premise as being totally without foundation. Remmick interviews other crew members, including Picard.

Picard confronts Admiral Quinn, demanding to know what's going on. Quinn says he'll be able to reveal the answer soon.

Wesley is taking another test when he helps Mordak, who finishes first. Chang announces that the psych tests will be in one hour.

Remmick presents his report to Quinn and Picard and reveals that he could find nothing wrong with the Enterprise. After giving his reports, he turns to leave, but pauses to mention that his tour of duty in the Inspector General's office will end in six months. He says that he would like to serve on the Enterprise then, if it is possible.

Quinn reveals to Picard that something is wrong in the Federation and that he wants to promote Picard to Commandant of Starfleet Academy because he needs someone there that he can trust. Picard decides to turn down Quinn's offer of promotion. Quinn wonders if he's just imagining a conspiracy after all.

While Wesley Crusher is waiting to take his psych test, there is a sudden explosion in the environmental lab. Two men are trapped. Wes helps one of the injured men but the other one is too frightened to move. Wesley manages to drag one man out just before the lab self-seals, trapping the other man inside. This turns out to have been Wesley's psych test. The Academy knew that Wesley feared fire and that he would be unable to make a decision to leave a man behind in a life-or-death situation. This is how Wesley's father died.

It turns out that Mordak is the candidate who wins selection to Starfleet Academy. Wesley feels that he has failed the Enterprise, but Picard assures him that is not the case. Picard admits that even he failed the entrance tests the first time around—but not the second time.

EPISODE TWENTY: "HEART OF GLORY"

Teleplay by Maurice Hurley
Story by Maurice Hurley and Herb Wright & D.C. Fontana
Directed by Rob Bowman
Guest Cast: Vaughn Armstrong, Robert Bauer, Brad Zerbst, Dennis Madalone, Charles H. Hyman

Life signs are detected aboard a disabled ship. The Away Team finds the compartment where the survivors were detected and forces the door open. Inside they find three Klingons, one of whom is badly hurt. They barely manage to escape before the ship explodes.

The Klingons claim they were passengers on the vessel when it was attacked by the Ferengi. The three Klingons are surprised to see Worf aboard the Enterprise and they question Worf as to why he is in the Federation. They also try to provoke him to determine whether he's just a tame Klingon. But Worf is no tame Klingon, and Koris and Kunivas are pleased that Worf can display anger.

The wounded Klingon is near death so Koris, Kunivas and Worf go to be with him in sick bay, finally emitting a loud, frightening chant when their comrade dies. While talking to Worf, they let slip that their companion's death was not in battle at the hands of an enemy. They question Worf about how he came to be in the Federation and Worf reveals that he was the sole survivor of a Romulan attack and was rescued by a human. The other Klingons state that they understand his solitude and confess that they are warriors without a war, fugitives who destroyed a Klingon cruiser sent to bring them back to the Klingon Empire.

When the Enterprise detects a Klingon ship approaching, the Klingon Captain contacts Picard and states that Koris and the others are fugitives and requests that they be turned over to him. When the security team, commanded by Yar, arrives to take the two Klingons into custody, Koris and Kunivas appeal to Worf for help.

Worf seems confused. When a child runs into them and one of Klingons picks her up, Yar thinks a hostage situation is underway, but Kunivas hands the child to Worf, explaining that Klingons do not stoop to taking hostages. They surrender willingly and are taken to a security cell.

Worf asks that he be allowed to speak to the captain of the Klingon ship and pleads for the hostages, asking that they at least be allowed to die as warriors on a hostile world, rather than be executed while bound and helpless. The Klingon Captain admits that they are all diminished when a Klingon dies in such a manner, but they pose a threat to the Klingon alliance with the Federation and so he must recapture them and return them to the Klingon homeworld where they will no longer pose a threat in confinement.

The two Klingons are locked in a cell on the Enterprise but manage to construct a weapon from parts cleverly secreted in their uniforms. The Klingons kill two guards while escaping but Kunivas is killed as well, leaving Koris alone.

Koris goes to Main Engineering and threatens to use his weapon to blast the dilithium crystal chamber. Worf and Picard go to engineering, and Worf talks to Koris, who pleads with him to join him as a warrior, reject the Federation, take over the battle bridge, steal the saucer section and launch a rampage through space.

Worf tells Koris that a man cannot be a warrior without duty and honor, and is finally forced to shoot and mortally wound Koris in order to save the Enterprise. Worf goes to Koris and performs the Klingon death ritual, howling a warning as the Klingon dies. Picard and the others are strangely moved by the sight.

The Klingon Captain receives Worf's message that Koris and Kunivas are dead, and he does not seem surprised by the news. He invites Worf to join him when his tour of duty with the Enterprise is over. Worf says that he would feel honored to do so. But after the Klingon ship departs, Worf reassures Captain Picard that he was just being polite. Worf has no desire to leave the Enterprise. Jean-Luc replies that the bridge of the Enterprise certainly wouldn't be the same without Worf there.

EPISODE TWENTY-ONE: "ARSENAL OF FREEDOM"

Teleplay by Richard Manning and Hans Beimler
Story by Maurice Hurley and Robert Lewin
Directed by Les Landau
Guest Cast: Vincent Schiavelli, Marco Rodriguez, Vyto Ruginis, Julia Nickson, George De La Pena

A small landing team, consisting of Riker, Yar and Data, beams down to a planet near the spot where the USS Drake vanished. They find an abandoned high-tech weapon but no signs of life. Data states that he believes they are being watched, but since there is no life on the planet, the question is: what is watching them?

Riker sees the captain of the Drake, who is an old friend of his, but realizes that this is a fraud. The man tries to get information from Riker on the weaponry of the Enterprise. When Riker states that the man is a phony, it disappears, replaced by a small flying robot which encases Riker in an energy field. They destroy the robot but the field remains.

Picard and Crusher beam down to see what has happened to Riker while Data works at removing the force field.

The ship reports energy readings in the area of the Away Team. The team is attacked by another small robot, and they split up to find cover. Picard and Crusher fall through a hole in the ground. The doctor is hurt when they hit the bottom.

Data removes the force field from Riker and tells him that they must find Picard and Crusher.

The Enterprise locates the Away Team with their sensors and is about to beam them up when the ship is attacked. Chief Engineer Logan wants the Enterprise to leave orbit.

They try to compute the pattern of attack of the object, which has a cloaking device, but are unsuccessful.

On Minos, Data and Yar are attacked by small robots again, defeating them only with great difficulty. They note that the robots appear every

Wil at the Chinese Theatre for the premiere of YOUNG GUNS II.

Photo ©
1994
Albert L.
Ortega

Denise at the screening of JACK THE BEAR.

Photo © 1994 Albert L. Ortega

twelve minutes and are more difficult to defeat each time, as though they are upgrading their tactics with data derived from their earlier attacks.

The Enterprise tries to outguess its invisible attacker but fails. Geordi orders the Enterprise out of orbit. They enter warp briefly and then stop. Geordi puts Logan in charge of the saucer and then does a separation. Geordi and Worf go to the battle bridge to control the main section of the ship, and return to Minos.

Picard looks around in the cavern and finds an operational unit with a view screen and tracking system, realizing for the first time that the Enterprise itself may be in danger. The projection appears again, programmed to answer questions about the demonstration of weaponry which is presently underway. The weapons being demonstrated work so well that they annihilated the population of the world which created them.

Data and the others find Picard, and the agile android is easily able to leap down eleven meters and save them.

The fourth version of the robot weaponry attacks while Data and Picard try to figure out how the control system works. Finally Picard tells the projection to end the demonstration because he likes what he's seen and wants to buy it. The projection is pleased. The robot

vanishes before it can home in on Riker and Yar.

When the Enterprise returns to Minos it encounters the invisible attacker again. Determined to outsmart the device this time, Geordi orders the Enterprise to enter the edge of the planet's atmosphere. The disturbance created by this action causes the invisible attacker to show up on their detection systems, and they're able to blast it out of existence.

The Away Team is beamed back aboard and they go to link back up with the saucer section once more.

EPISODE TWENTY-TWO: "SYMBIOSIS"

Teleplay by Robert Lewin, Richard Manning, and Hans Beimler
Story by Robert Lewin
Directed by Win Phelps
Guest Cast: Merritt Butrick, Judson Scott, Kimberly Farr, Richard Lineback

The Enterprise rescues some humanoids from their doomed ship. Four people materialize in the transporter. Two were lost with the freighter. Their first concern, though, is not their fellows, but rather their cargo.

The cargo is Felicium. The four begin to argue over its ownership since the material traded for it had been aboard the destroyed freighter. Yar removes them to an observation lounge, where they continue to quarrel.

Picard requests information about the two planets the people are from, but little is known about them.

Crusher reveals that two of the people appear to be plague carriers, but that while they show symptoms, there is no apparent cause for them.

Picard talks to the Brekians, the traders, about getting two doses of Felicium for the stricken Onarians. They agree to this.

The plague on Onara has afflicted that world's population for two centuries. The Brekians make the drug which controls the plague from a plant which cannot thrive on Onara.

When the Onarians get their doses of Felicium, she observes that they respond like drug addicts getting a fix, and perceives from this that everyone on Onara is addicted to Felicium.

Several thousand years before, Onara traded its advanced technology to the Brekians for the drug which controls the plague.

Dr. Crusher opposes allowing this exploitation of the Onarians and wants the truth revealed. Picard is against interfering because it would violate the Prime Directive's non-interference clause by disrupting the cultural symbiosis between the two planets.

Onara contacts the Enterprise, to say that their world is suffering and its people dying.

T'Jon and his people can discharge electricity from their bodies, and he threatens to kill Riker unless the Onarians are given the drug now, with terms to be worked out later. Picard refuses to be blackmailed, and T'Jon relents.

The Brakians agree to provide the Felicium and work out trade terms later. Picard realizes that the Brakians know exactly what they are doing to the Onarians. But the Brakians know that he won't tell the Onarians this since that, too, would be interference.

Using the Prime Directive as the basis of his decision, Picard chooses to withhold the control coils from the Onarians. Unable to repair their aging freighters, the Onarians will be forced to find an alternative to the Felicium. The Brakians are upset by this as well.

Defending the Prime Directive, Jean-Luc firmly states that even well-intentioned interference can be disastrous, which is why the Prime Directive is a strict non-interference clause in Starfleet regulations.

EPISODE TWENTY-THREE: "SKIN OF EVIL"

Teleplay by Joseph Stephano and Hannah Louise Shearer

Story by Joseph Stephano
Directed by Joseph L. Scanlan
Guest Cast: Walker Boone, Brad Zerbst, Raymond Forchion, Mart McChesney and Ron Gans as the voice of Armus

When an Away Team goes to rescue Troi from a shuttle crash, a strange black slick moves along the ground to block their path. This unknown life form generates a tar-like humanoid figure which talks to them. It is named Armus, and it will not let them pass. It doesn't think that their rescue mission is a good enough reason to move out of their way.

Yar tries to pass anyway and it lashes out at her, knocking her to the ground, lifeless. The others attack it with phasers, but to no effect.

The Away Team beams up, but it is too late to save Yar. There is a black mark on her cheek where the creature touched her.

Armus flows over the shuttle and communicates with Troi. She sensed Yar's death and knows Armus killed her thinking the death would be amusing. Armus is disappointed because Yar did not suffer.

On the Enterprise, Worf becomes acting chief of security. The Away Team returns, with Geordi, but Worf remains at his post on the Enterprise.

Armus covers the shuttle again, and won't let Troi contact the ship. Troi realizes that Armus is surprised that the Away Team returned, because the creature had been abandoned on Vagra II.

On the Enterprise it is noted that the energy field covering the shuttle had momentarily decreased while Armus was covering it. If the energy field were to drop far enough, the occupants of the shuttle could be beamed out safely.

The creature allows Crusher to communicate with Troi to determine her condition, and that of the shuttle pilot, to prove that his hostages are secure. Troi is indeed all right, but the pilot is seriously injured.

Then Armus toys with the landing party, demonstrating his power over them.

Armus flows over the shuttle again like a blanket of tar. Troi communicates with it and learns that is stranded on Vagra II. Armus is the sum total of the evil of an alien race which learned how to bring their negative aspects to the surface and then discard them. Once created in this manner, Armus was abandoned by the purified beings.

Troi angers Armus by pitying him. Enraged, Armus kidnaps Riker, enveloping him in his body to torment him. Again, the energy field over the shuttle drops, providing a vital clue for the freeing of Troi.

Troi offers to trade herself to Armus for Riker, but the offer is refused.

Picard beams down. He wants to see those in the shuttle. Armus demands to be entertained and controls Data's body to point a phaser at the other Away Team members, each in turn, threatening to kill one of them. Finally, Armus relents and regurgitates Riker, but he won't let Picard see Troi.

Riker, Geordi, Data and Crusher are beamed back to the Enterprise.

Armus tells Picard that it wants to leave the planet and lets Picard into the shuttle, hoping he will help the being escape from Vagra II. Picard and Troi discuss how they might escape— by exploiting the creature's rage.

Outside, Picard talks with Armus about how it was abandoned, and taunts him about it.

On the Enterprise, they prepare for the parallel beam of Picard, Troi and the shuttle pilot. They succeed when Picard tells Armus that he won't take him anywhere. The creature's rage diverts its energies, and the humans are saved, leaving the evil entity alone. Picard has the shuttle destroyed so that Armus cannot use it to escape either.

Back on the Enterprise, in the holodeck, a funeral is held for Tasha Yar. As part of it a holo-tape is played which Tasha had made as a farewell message for her friends should anything ever happen to her.

EPISODE TWENTY-FOUR: "WE'LL ALWAYS HAVE PARIS"

Teleplay by Deborah Dean Davis and Hannah Louise Shearer
Directed by Robert Becker
Guest stars: Isabel Lorca, Rod Loomis, Dan Kern, Jean-Paul Vignon, Kelly Ashmore, Lance Spellerberg, Michelle Phillips

The Enterprise investigates a distress call from Paul Mannheim— and discovers that his long-lost lover Gabrielle has married Mannheim. Twenty-two years earlier, Picard missed a rendezvous with her in Paris, a fact he has always regretted.

Gabrielle explains that the rest of their research crew were killed in a base on the other side of the planet. She doesn't know what the goal of her husband's experiments were.

Crusher reveals that Dr. Mannheim is dying. He seems to be trapped part way into another dimension, and his body can't take the strain.

They experience another time loop.

Two of the crew beam down to the lab but a security device prevents them from materializing.

Paul Mannheim comes through but is agitated. He says that he's touched another dimension and that part of him is still there. Mannheim knows that the experiment must be stopped.

Dr. Mannheim reveals that they have to go down to his lab and penetrate the elaborate security mechanisms. He reveals as many of the security devices as he can remember, but in his condition his memory is not reliable. He gives them codes which will allow them to beam down safely.

Mrs. Mannheim visits Picard. They recall the time he stood her up in Paris, 22 years earlier. He'd been afraid that if he saw her again, he wouldn't be able to leave.

Troi talks to Crusher, who is troubled by Gabrielle Mannheim's effect on Picard.

Mannheim asks to see Picard. He's not sure that he remembered all the security codes. He also asks Picard to take care of his wife if he dies.

Picard wants Data to be the only one in the Away Team, because he can handle time distortions better than the others.

Data beams down and is attacked by lasers, but bypasses them. He enters the lab and finds the point of time distortion. Data calculates that the next time loop is in 90 seconds. He must add antimatter at the moment of distortion. The time loop occurs and suddenly there are three Datas, but they combine in time and patch the distortion.

Mannheim recovers and wants to return to his work. His wife agrees to accompany him.

Gabrielle Mannheim enters the holodeck where Picard has recreated the setting for their unkept appointment. He tells her that he wants to say goodbye properly. She leaves, and Picard returns to the bridge and to his duties as captain of the Enterprise.

EPISODE TWENTY-FIVE: "CONSPIRACY"

Teleplay by Tracy Torme
Story by Robert Sabaroff
Directed by Cliff Bole
Guest Cast: Michael Berryman, Ursaline Bryant, Henry Darrow, Robert Schenkkan, Jonathan Farwell

The Enterprise receives a Starfleet Emergency Communiqué— for the eyes of the Captain only. Picard receives the message from his old friend Walker Kiel. Kiel warns Picard that Starfleet is in danger, but he can't be more specific. Picard is told to meet Walker for a face-to-face entente on a remote planet.

The Captain has the Enterprise alter course and orders that no log be kept. The Enterprise arrives to find three Federation cruisers in orbit around the planet. Three life forms are detected on the surface, and Picard beams down alone to that position.

Picard arrives at the entrance of an abandoned mine and finds Walker Kiel there with two other well-known Starfleet officers, Captain Rixx and Captain Tryla Scott— three of Starfleet's finest. They interrogate Picard to assure themselves that he's not an impostor.

Finally the three reveal their concerns, citing strange orders from Starfleet as well as the mysterious deaths of key personnel. Picard finds the conspiracy theory hard to believe. Walker asks Picard to at least be alert and to stay in touch secretly.

Returning to the Enterprise, Picard confides in Troi the events that have just occurred, and has Data access Starfleet orders for the past six months to search for any unusual entries.

A disturbance is detected nearby in sector 63, and they divert to investigate. They find the debris of a ship, the Horatio— the ship of Walker Kiel. The sudden and mysterious death of Kiel has a profound effect on Picard. He no longer considers Kiel's theories unbelievable. The timing of the death is too critical. Walker Kiel was killed to silence him.

Data discovers something in his record scan. There have been odd reassignments which seem to form a pattern to gain control of certain regions. Picard reveals what he knows to the bridge crew. He has them alter course and head directly to Starfleet headquarters on Earth.

Upon arrival, Picard requests a personal meeting with Starfleet Command. They oblige, and invite Picard and Riker to be their dinner guests.

Starfleet Admiral Gregory Quinn beams over to the Enterprise, bringing a small black case with him. In it is a small creature which he keeps hidden. Picard quizzes the Admiral and is disturbed by what he learns. Picard warns Riker to keep his eye on Quinn. Picard then beams down and meets with the head of Starfleet.

On the Enterprise, Quinn attacks Riker and knocks him around as though he were toying with the man. Quinn refers to a recently discovered life form, superior to humanity. Riker summons security, but Quinn knocks out Geordi and attacks Worf.

Crusher arrives and uses a phaser on Quinn, knocking him out after three blasts. She has Quinn taken to sick bay where a scan reveals something in his body, attached to his neck.

At Starfleet, Picard secretly contacts the Enterprise and learns what has happened. Picard is summoned to dinner. He enters and is seated at a table, but when he removes the lid from his dish, he discovers it is filled with wriggling grub worms. The other three Starfleet officers at the table are undeterred by this, and munch away on the worms quite happily.

When Picard tries to flee, he reaches the door just as it opens for Commander Riker, who won't allow Picard leave. All indications are that he has been taken over by the creature that Admiral Quinn had brought on the Enterprise.

Riker explains that the creature Quinn brought aboard had been intended for Crusher, but it was necessary to use it on him instead. He sits down at the table but suddenly whips out a phaser and starts blasting away at the Starfleet Council. As the men fall, small creatures crawl from their mouths and flee.

Riker and Picard follow them and see them enter the body of Remmick. Riker and Picard both blast the man with their phasers and are satisfied to see Remmick's head explode. As the man's body disintegrates, a larger version of the creatures they'd just seen is revealed within Remmick's ruined torso. It is a queen which had been controlling the others. Picard and Riker fire their phasers again to make certain that it is blasted out of existence.

They discover that Remmick had been sending a homing beacon from Earth to a remote sector of the galaxy, obviously the home of the creatures. But does this mean that the battle is over, or that it has just begun? Will more creatures come in response to the signal? Only time will tell.

EPISODE TWENTY-SIX: "THE NEUTRAL ZONE"

Written by Maurice Hurley
From a story by Deborah McIntyre and Mona Clee
Directed by James L. Conway
Guest Cast: Marc Alaimo, Anthony James, Leon Rippy, Gracie Harrison

The Enterprise discovers a 20th Century Earth satellite containing three people in suspended animation. Picard orders a course through the Neutral Zone. Some outposts in the Zone have gone silent. Picard wonders why the Romulans would be active now when the Federation has heard nothing from them in 50 years.

Crusher thaws out the three people and learns that each had been frozen after death through the process known as cryonics, a 20th century fad which was abandoned in the early 21st century. Crusher has repaired the damage that killed them. She now has them sedated.

Picard reluctantly has them awakened. The woman wakes up, sees Worf and faints. According to the disc Data recovered, she is Clair Raymond. The other two people are Sonny Clemons, a good-old-boy type, and a formerly-rich industrialist named Ralph. Picard leaves them in the care of Crusher, and Riker explains to them where and when they are.

Troi talks to Picard about Romulans, and how they are fascinated by humans. She says they should meet. Romulans would wait for humans to make the first move.

Picard meets with his bridge crew six hours before their arrival at the Neutral Zone. Riker thinks the Romulans want to see how much the Federation has advanced technologically in 50 years. Data points out that Romulan intentions might not be hostile.

Ralph demands that they contact Geneva to check on his stock holdings and accumulated wealth. He's annoyed that no one seems interested in helping him make his phone calls from the ship. When Ralph summons Picard as though he were a steward on a cruise ship, Picard tells him that a lot has changed in 370 years.

Clair begins to cry, remembering her children, who are now long dead. Picard summons Troi to help her. Troi uses a computer terminal to trace Claire's family.

The Enterprise arrives at the Neutral Zone. Outpost Delta 0-5 has vanished from the face of the planet. The same is true of the next outpost they investigate.

Ralph wanders around the ship until he enters a turbolift and finds his way to the bridge. When he enters the bridge silently, he is at first not noticed.

The Enterprise detects the approach of something but Picard refuses to attack. When the Romulans appear near the Enterprise, Picard won't respond with hostility. Worf is annoyed because the Romulans killed his parents even though the Klingons and Romulans were allied at the time. He says that Romulans cannot be trusted.

Picard communicates with the Romulans. They explain that they are investigating attacks on their own outposts. Picard asks for cooperation to learn the truth, but the Romulans find this idea amusing. The Romulans explain that they had been busy with other things but will no longer remain hidden.

Somehow, this isn't very alarming. The Romulans posture a bit but don't seem to be much of a real threat. The 20th Century humans are sent to Earth, graciously bowing out of the NEXT GENERATION saga before more harm is done.

END OF SEASON ONE

Michelle at the Director's Guild for her screening of KALI-FORNIA.

Norman at the Director's Guild for a tribute to Jean Stapelton.

SEASON TWO

SEASON TWO

Cast changes abound as the second season begins. Gates McFadden was out, Diana Muldaur was in, and Whoopi Goldberg signed on as Guinan, the mysterious alien bartender of Ten Forward. The quality of the show improved somewhat this year despite the poor development of Muldaur's character.

Geordi LaForge moved into a more prominent role as he was promoted to Chief Engineer; the first season's equivalent character was rather vague and ill-defined by comparison. The best of the second season would outstrip the best of the first. Highlights included the holodeck classic "Elementary, Dear Data," the brilliant Klingon episode "A Matter of Honor," and the introduction of the implacable Borg in "Q Who."

EPISODE TWENTY-SEVEN: "THE CHILD"

Written by Jaron Summer, Jon Povil and Maurice Hurley
Directed by Rob Bowman
Guest Cast: Seymour Cassel, R.J. Williams, Dawn Arnemann, Zachary Benjamin, Dore Keller

Beverly Crusher goes on to head Starfleet Medical, and Dr. Catherine Pulaski comes aboard as her replacement. LaForge creates new containment modules that will allow the Enterprise to transport samples of a plasma virus to a science station. Meanwhile, an entity resembling a point of light enters the Enterprise and finds Troi sleeping.

Ten Forward is a rest area where the hostess is the mysterious, ancient alien named Guinan. Picard goes there to find Dr. Pulaski, who directs his attention to Troi. She is pregnant. The fetus is already six weeks old, a mere eleven hours after its unusual conception. Delivery will occur in another thirty-six hours. The only genetic material involved is Troi's.

Worf recommends immediate termination, while Data advises letting the life form grow. Troi states her intention to bear the child.

The delivery is completely painless for mother and child. Within 24 hours, the child, named Ian, is physically four years old. There is no physical sign to indicate that Troi's body ever carried or delivered a child. When Picard drops in to visit later that day, Ian is eight; he tells Picard that everything is okay.

Plague samples are beamed into the containment units; if any get out, everyone on the Enterprise will die within hours.

Picard asks Ian why he has come, but the child says he is not yet ready to explain. According to Troi, he has the knowledge within him, but is not developed enough to express it in words.

Something goes wrong with one of the containment units: the strain of plague inside will break through in two hours. This strain was mutated in a laboratory experiment, by exposure to Eichner radiation. Renewed exposure could provoke growth, and Data detects Eichner radiation on board the ship.

The tricorder leads them to Troi's quarters, where Ian has already told Troi that he must leave in order to discontinue the threat to the Enterprise. He dies, or so it seems. Troi is grief stricken, but the entity emerges and communicates with her. It assumed human form to learn about humans, and thanks Troi for helping him do so, and then the glowing entity leaves the Enterprise and continues its explorations of space.

EPISODE TWENTY-EIGHT: "WHERE SILENCE HAS LEASE"

Written by Jack B. Sowards
Directed by Winrich Kolbe
Guest Cast: Earl Boen, Charles Douglas

A black area in space appears on the view screen. A complete absence of matter and energy, it provokes Picard's curiosity. Probes simply vanish into it. Worf recommends Yellow Alert status. When asked why, he seems embarrassed, and admits that it reminded him of an ancient Klingon legend of a black space being which ate ships. When the Enterprise moves closer, the void envelops it.

This new area of "space" lacks dimension. When the ship retraces its course, it does not return to its original place, but remains in the void. A Romulan ship uncloaks and attacks. A single photon torpedo destroys it utterly. This was too easy. Sensors reveal no debris from the Romulan vessel.

Then a Federation ship is sighted, although the Yamato should be nowhere near the area. There are no life signs. When Riker and Worf beam aboard, they find themselves lost in a shifting maze. Readings show that the ship is some sort of replica. When Riker and Worf beam back, they almost don't make it. Openings appear in the void, but disappear as the ship changes course.

Captain Picard realizes that this is some sort of test. They decide to stop playing along. A face appears in the screen. It is an entity calling itself Nagilum. It kills a crew member, and decides to learn about all the possible means of death for humans, a process that shouldn't take more than a third of the crew.

Picard and Riker set the auto-destruct mechanism. As Picard faces the end in his quarters, he is visited by Troi and Data. They both tell Picard that he should abort the destruct sequence. He realizes that they are simulations created by Nagilum.

They vanish, and Picard receives word that his ship is now free of the void. Sensing that this might be another experiment, Picard does not abort the destruct sequence until the last possible second.

The entity calling itself Nagilum appears on the viewscreen in Picard's office and states that it learned much about humans from this experiment. Picard angrily dismisses the alien's observations and the being vanishes as the Enterprise re-enters normal space once more.

EPISODE TWENTY-NINE: "ELEMENTARY, DEAR DATA"

Written by Brian Alan Lane
Directed by Rob Bowman
Guest Cast: Daniel Davis, Alan Shearman, Biff Manard, Diz White, Anne Ramsay, Richard Merson

While Data gets carried away in his Sherlock Holmes holodeck simulation, LaForge has no fun at all, because Data already knows the solutions in all the Holmes stories. He understands the process of deductive reasoning, but he can't savor the mystery itself.

Pulaski contends that Data can't solve a mystery that he doesn't already know the answer to. He accepts the challenge, and programs the computer to create a new mystery. Pulaski and LaForge accompany him. He solves it in no time, but only because he recognizes diverse elements from several Holmes stories. LaForge programs a mystery to challenge Data, with an adversary capable of defeating Data. This is witnessed by the holodeck's Professor Moriarty.

Moriarty abducts Pulaski. The search for her is too easy, and Data realizes that their adversary—Moriarty—wants them to find him. Face to face with him, they find that he has learned a great deal, and wants to know more. When he hands Data a piece of paper with a drawing of the Enterprise on it,

the android detective rushes out of the holodeck, only to find that he cannot terminate the program.

He informs Picard of the problem. Moriarty has control of the holodeck. The holographic projections could be wiped out by a particle beam, but this would also kill Pulaski. Suddenly, the ship rocks: Moriarty has gained access to the ship's propulsion and guidance systems.

Picard enters the holodeck, hoping to defeat Moriarty by giving him everything he wants. He concedes defeat to the Professor, hoping that this will bring the program to its end. Unfortunately, Moriarty has developed real consciousness; LaForge goofed by asking for an adversary capable of defeating Data, when he meant to say "Holmes."

Moriarty has become more than just a fictional character. He explains that he is not evil, but just wants to live and think. Jean-Luc is impressed, but holodeck technology has not progressed sufficiently to allow holodeck creations to exist off the deck. Since the technology is related to transporter beams, it may be possible some day, and Picard assures Prof. Moriarty that he'll keep his program safely in storage until the day that the technology makes it possible to allow the hologram to exist in normal reality. Moriarty graciously accepts, and order is restored.

EPISODE THIRTY: "THE OUTRAGEOUS OKONA"

Teleplay by Burton Armus
Story by Les Menchen, Lance Dickson and Kieran Mulroney
Directed by Robert Becker
Guest Cast: William O. Campbell, Douglas Rowe, Albert Stratton, Joe Piscopo

When Thaduin Okona beams aboard with his damaged guidance system, he turns out to be a real joker. Data is confounded by Okona's jokes, and goes to the holodeck to learn about humor. Data selects a 20th Century standup comic, who tells Data jokes, which the android proceeds to memorize at high speed. When Data tries to share his jokes, he comes across as a bad impression of a bad comedian. He is still baffled by the human concept of humor.

The Enterprise finds itself confronted by a small craft, armed only with lasers, which is threatening to attack. The captain of the small vessel claims that Okona is a wanted criminal. When pressed, he admits that he's after Okona for getting his daughter Y'Nar pregnant.

Matters are complicated further when a ship from Straleb also arrives, intending to arrest Okona for the theft of the Jewel of Thesia, a national treasure. Straleb is represented by Kushell and his son.

Okona assures Picard that he is innocent of both charges. Okona agrees to surrender, but won't say who he's surrendering to until both parties have beamed aboard. He then agrees to marry Y'Nar, only to have Kushnell's son protest. The truth emerges: the two young people had been seeing each other secretly with Okona's help. Kushnell's son had made Y'Nar pregnant, and had taken the Jewel, which was his right as the heir, to give to Y'Nar as a betrothal gift.

Okona turns over the Jewel to the young woman, leaving the elder statesmen baffled. He leaves, and Picard gets the two factions off his ship before an argument about the upbringing of the baby can get out of hand.

Having been tutored extensively by the holodeck comedian, Joe Piscopo, Data asks Guinan to come and see to see him perform. A preprogrammed holodeck audience loves his act, but Data comes to realize that they laugh at everything he does, down to the smallest physical movement. This is not what he wanted.

Data wants to elicit genuine laughter, not the phony laughter of a laugh track. He ends the program, understanding now that humor is something which will take a great deal of work for him to perfect so that he can play before a real audience.

EPISODE THIRTY-ONE: "LOUD AS A WHISPER"

Written by Jacqueline Zambrano
Directed by Larry Shaw
Guest Cast: Howie Seago, Marnie Mosiman, Thomas Oglesby, Leo Damian

Famed negotiator Riva has no gene for hearing, so he uses three companions— the Chorus— to express his thoughts for him. Riva is benign but perhaps arrogant, never having failed to settle a conflict, and he is immediately taken with Troi.

But when Riva and the Chorus beam down with an Away Team to negotiate a peace treaty, one of the delegates tries to kill the mediator. Riker knocks Riva out of the way, but the Chorus is vaporized, leaving Riva without a voice.

Riva is guilt stricken, and cannot go on. Troi tries to convince him, but he is too despondent, so she determines to mediate the affair herself. She asks Riva what his secret is. He responds that it is very simple. He finds some common ground, however small, between the opposing factions, and works from there.

He realizes that he can do it after all, and resumes his mission. He will teach the warring parties his sign language. It may take months, but it will create a new common ground for peace.

EPISODE THIRTY-TWO: "UNNATURAL SELECTION"

Written by John Mason and Mike Gray
Directed by Paul Lynch
Guest Cast: Patricia Smith, J. Patrick McNamara, Scott Trost

When the Enterprise receives a distress call from the SS Langtry, they arrive too late. The Langtry's crew is dead of old age, but the Enterprise surely wasn't that late! Picard quarantines the ship and heads for its last known stop, the Darwin Science Station.

At the Darwin Station they find that the station personnel are already suffering from the accelerated aging process, which begins with arthritic inflammation. The head doctor of the station claims that their children there are not affected, having been placed in isolation.

Picard and Pulaski debate bringing one of the children on board the Enterprise. Picard relents, as long as there is a force field containment in place, and the child is in suspended animation. The twelve year old "child" is physically an adult, however, and Troi senses that he has a telepathic consciousness.

All tests indicate that he is not infected. Pulaski wants to remove the stasis field and awaken him. Picard resists until she suggests taking the child aboard a shuttlecraft, which will be a close system separate from the Enterprise. With Data as pilot, a shuttle is launched, and the child is beamed aboard and removed from stasis.

Once it has awakened, the unusual child communicates telepathically with the doctor. The result of this exchange is that Dr. Pulaski is immediately stricken with the aging disease and proceeds to the Darwin Station. The children are the cause, although they are perfectly healthy. They are genetically engineered and have active aggressive immune systems, which attack viruses before they reach their bodies. A harmless flu virus triggered their systems to create an antibody fatal to normal humans.

Picard, LaForge and O'Brien entertain the possibility that the transporter's trace records could be used to reconstitute Pulaski as she was before the infection. Pulaski has an aversion to transporter use, and has never used the Enterprise's system. O'Brien believes that it may be possible to alter the bio-filter to use a DNA sample to reconstitute Pulaski.

They locate some of the doctor's hair in a hairbrush, and use DNA from the intact follicles to program the transporter. Picard takes the responsibility of operating the transporter; the process works. The staff at Darwin Station will have to leave their "children" behind, but they are saved by the new transporter technique.

The Enterprise returns to the derelict Langtry, and the bridge crew stands at attention while the death ship is destroyed to insure that no infection which may be aboard the ship can be spread.

EPISODE THIRTY-THREE: "A MATTER OF HONOR"

Teleplay by Burton Armus
From a story by Wanda M. Haight, Gregory Amos and Burton Armus
Directed by Rob Bowman
Guest Cast: John Putch, Christopher Collins, Brian Thompson,

Riker volunteers to be the first human to serve with the Klingons. The First Officer's primary obligation, on a Klingon ship, is to kill his captain if the captain seems weak or indecisive. The Second Officer is likewise obligated to his immediate superior. Riker prepares for the mission by sampling Klingon food in Ten Forward, much to the disgust of the other humans.

Before Riker beams over to the Klingon ship Pagh, Worf gives him a transponder.

Riker swears loyalty to the captain and the ship but the Klingons he is now serving with question the capabilities of their new officer. After all, he is only a human. When his Second Officer challenges him, he beats him soundly, winning his respect. Captain K'Argan is amused.

A microbe— a subatomic bacteria that eats metal— is discovered on the hull of the Enterprise. One of the crewmen notes that he'd also detected it on the Klingon ship as well. The Enterprise determines that the microbe has eaten a 12 centimeter hole in the Pagh's hull, and follows the Pagh to warn it.

Two Klingon women express curiosity about Riker, prompting some ribald humor. When Riker returns to the bridge, the Captain has discovered the hole in the hull, and believes that the Enterprise is responsible. Riker stands his ground; having vowed loyalty, he will serve the Pagh even in an attack on the Enterprise.

When the Captain demands the Enterprise's security codes and other secrets, Riker refuses. The Captain says that he would have killed Riker on the spot as a traitor if he had revealed those secrets; now he may have the honor of dying in battle among Klingons.

The Enterprise finds a way to remove the microbes, and sends a message to the Klingons. K'Argan does not believe them, and prepares to attack. K'Argan prepares to fire, and also gives this honor to Riker. Riker says he will obey, but tells the captain that his reasons are wrong, and triggers the transponder. K'Argan demands the device, which Riker yields to him.

As K'Argan grabs the transponder, Worf activates it expecting to retrieve Commander Riker. Instead they discover that they've beamed over angry Klingon captain instead. Worf subdues K'Argan and puts him under guard. Riker hails the Enterprise, as acting Captain of the Pagh, and demands the surrender of the Federation ship. Picard surrenders, and the Klingons decloak. K'Argan returns to his ship.

Riker has cleverly maintained the honor of all involved. His only shortcoming, in Klingon eyes, was that he did not assassinate his superior officer. K'Argan strikes Riker a vicious blow, thus reestablishing K'Argan's authority. The status quo re-established, Riker returns to the Enterprise.

EPISODE THIRTY-FOUR: "THE MEASURE OF A MAN"

Written by Melinda M. Snodgrass
Directed by Robert Scheerer
Guest Cast: Amanda McBroom, Clyde Kusatsu, Brian Brophy

Commander Maddox comes aboard. He is a cyberneticist who plans to disassemble Data and download his mind in order to test the positronic brain he has built. His goal is to create more androids for Starfleet use. Data finds the idea interesting, but refuses the procedure on the grounds that Maddox's procedure might risk the loss of Data's personality. To avoid transfer, he resigns from Starfleet. Maddox seeks to define Data as the property of Starfleet. Picard demands a hearing.

Picard acts as defense; the prosecution goes to the next highest ranking officer, a reluctant Riker. As prosecutor, Riker contends that Data is a machine, made by a man, and thus subject to human ownership. Picard tries to determine the nature of sentience. Can Maddox prove that Picard is a sentient being?

The issues become cloudy, until Picard questions Maddox's desire to create a race of androids like Data. The issue of slavery arises, and Picard declares that a slave race is what Maddox has in mind. The final ruling:

Data is not property, and has the right to make his own decisions.

EPISODE THIRTY-FIVE: "THE SCHIZOID MAN"

Teleplay by Tracy Torme
Story by Richard Manning and Hans Beimler
Directed by Les Landau
Guest Cast: W. Morgan Sheppard, Suzie Plakson, Barbara Alyn Woods

Ira Graves is a cantankerous genius who insists that his health his fine, but a medical scan reveals that he is dying. Graves is impressed by Data, the creation of Graves' former student Soong, and the two spend a time together. Graves plans to transfer his knowledge to a computer so that it will not be lost. When he talks of his fear of death to Data, the android trustingly reveals his on/off switch.

When the Enterprise returns and prepares to beam everyone up, Data emerges from Graves' office and announces the scientist's death. Later, on the ship, Data seems changed. Giving a speech at Graves' funeral, the android heaps lavish praise on the dead man.

When Picard brings Corinne, Graves' assistant, on the bridge, Data actually acts jealous, an emotion which Troi can sense. But Data doesn't have emotions, or at least he's never been capable of experiencing them before. A psychological test reveals that Data's personality has been submerged beneath a second, stronger personality of Ira Graves. Later, Graves admits this to Corinne, but this frightens her, and he hurts her hand, not realizing the strength of the body he has commandeered.

Picard confronts Graves and demands that he give up Data's body. He refuses, and knocks out Picard. He then begins to realize the damage that he is doing, damage that he never intended. Later, LaForge finds Data on the floor of his quarters, unable to remember anything since Graves took over his body.

Graves has downloaded his vast scientific knowledge into the ship's computer, but his personality did not survive. At the end Graves did the right thing when he realized what he was becoming inside the superhuman android body of Data.

EPISODE THIRTY-SIX: "THE DAUPHIN"

Written by Scott Rubinstein and Leonard Mlodinow
Directed by Rob Bowman

Guest Cast: Paddi Edwards, Jamie Hubbard, Madchen Amick, Cindy Sorenson, Jennifer Barlow

The Dauphin is Salia, a young woman on her way to rule her home planet of Daled IV. She is accompanied by her guardian, Anya, who refuses to allow Salia to tour the ship; she sees everything as a potential threat to Salia. When she encounters a sick patient, she insists that Pulaski kill the crewman to prevent the spread of the disease.

When Pulaski refuses, Anya takes matters into her own hands, transforming into a monstrous creature. Worf fights her until Picard arrives; Anya resumes her unassuming human form, and Picard confines her to her quarters for the duration of the trip.

Wesley takes Salia to the holodeck. In Ten Forward, they talk about her future. Wesley insists it will be wonderful, but she's afraid that her responsibilities will be oppressive. Picard asks Wesley to stay away from Salia and he reluctantly agrees.

But Salia doesn't consider herself to be under any such restriction, and so she chooses to visits Wesley herself. Anya barges in, again in her monstrous form, but Salia faces her down by shifting her own shape. Anya backs down, and she and Salia leave the surprised ensign alone.

Wesley never realized that Salia wasn't really human and the revelation unnerves him. When the Enterprise reaches Daled IV, Wesley avoids saying good-bye to Salia, but finally changes his mind and goes to see her in the transporter room just before she departs. Salia reveals her true form to Wesley, who accepts the truth more graciously now.

EPISODE THIRTY-SEVEN: "CONTAGION"

Written by Steve Gerber and Beth Woods
Directed by Joseph L. Scanlan
Guest Cast: Thalmus Rasulala, Carolyn Seymour, Dana Sparks

The Enterprise arrives just in time to see the Yamato explode, killing the thousand persons on board. Picard studies the Yamato's logs and learns that its captain believed himself to have discovered the planet of Iconia, home of a race that could travel through space without use of vessels.

Picard decides to investigate further, although Iconia is located close to the Romulan side of the Neutral Zone. The planet Iconia bears the signs of a civilization bombed out 200 thousand years earlier.

A probe is launched from the planet. LaForge warns Picard to destroy it before it can scan the Enterprise: the Yamato's destruction was caused by an alien computer program from the earlier probe. The Enterprise's problems are less drastic because they downloaded the program along with the Yamato's logs, and it needs to work its way through the system.

Picard leads a team to the ancient command center below, where Data deciphers the computer by extrapolating the root language from the tongues of several worlds believed to have been colonized by the Iconians. A gateway is found there which opens onto a variety of locations, including the bridge of the Enterprise.

The Enterprise is confronted by a Romulan ship, which is also malfunctioning. Data tries to access the Iconian computer, but it is incompatible with his systems, and he malfunctions. Picard realizes that the Iconian technology must not fall into Romulan hands, and sends Worf and Data back to the Enterprise through the gateway, while he arranges to destroy the ancient gateway.

Back on the Enterprise, Data "dies," only to revive again, with no memory of his experience. This provides a solution to the problem: download and wipe all affected systems. LaForge does the same to the computer, and regains control of the ship.

Levar at the Director's Guild hosting a night of Indian art for Reading Rainbow.

John with wife at the Beverly Hilton for Lily Tartikoff's Fire & Ice Ball (UCLA's breast cancer benefit).

Photo © 1994 Albert L. Ortega

When Picard jumps through the gateway, he finds himself on the bridge of the Romulan ship, which is about to self-destruct like the Yamato. The Romulan captain is pleased that Picard will die with her ship, but the Enterprise scans and locates Jean-Luc, beaming him back home. Captain Picard has the Enterprise transmit the necessary information to the Romulans which enables them to save their vessel just as the Enterprise did, and then they turn and leave the Neutral Zone.

EPISODE THIRTY-EIGHT: "THE ROYALE"

Written by Keith Mills
Directed by Cliff Bole
Guest Cast: Sam Anderson, Jill Jacobson, Leo Garcia, Noble Willingham

When the Enterprise encounters a distant, unexplored world, the crew is amazed to discover 21st century NASA debris is found orbiting the planet. This world is much too far from Earth to have been reached by that era's technology. The mystery deepens when the Enterprise's sensors locate a small area of Earth-like atmosphere on the planet's surface, which is otherwise covered with violent ammonia-methane storms.

Riker leads an Away Team down to the anomalous area, where they dis-cover an ancient revolving door. Inside, they find a 20th century casino, complete with sarcastic hotel clerk, who welcomes them to the Hotel Royale. In fact, a "trio of foreign gents" were expected.

Riker witnesses a bit of drama: a young bellhop, involved with gangster Mickey D's girlfriend, seems headed for serious trouble. Tricorder readings reveal that all the people in the Royale are not alive; although real, they are neither men nor machines, with no trace of life signs.

Although no danger threatens them, the Away Team can't communicate with the ship, and the revolving doors will not let them out. A tricorder scan reveals DNA on the second floor. Riker and his team discover a room with a 283-year-old corpse, which turns out to be a NASA astronaut from the period between 20333 and 2079. (This is determined by the presence of 52 stars on the US flag on his uniform.)

Colonel S. Richey's effects are few: a second rate novel entitled Hotel Royale, and a diary with one entry. It seems that Richey's craft was damaged by an alien life form, killing all the crew but Richey. Out of guilt, the aliens created a slice of Earth culture for the astronaut— using the novel as their guide! After thirty-eight years, trapped in the novel, Richey almost welcomed death.

The Enterprises finally manages to contact the Away Team. Commander Riker what they have found and Captain Picard accesses the novel on the computer, enduring its tortuous prose to the end; the final scenes include Mickey D's murder of the bell boy, after which a trio of foreign gentlemen buy the hotel and leave it in the care of the assistant manager.

When Riker witnesses the murder, he realizes a means of escape. Data embarks on a winning streak at the craps table, and parlays a handful of chips into millions of dollars. This breaks the casino's bank, but Riker takes the deed to the hotel as payment, and the Away Team assumes the characters of the "trio of foreign gents." They then leave, having brought the silly scenario to an end.

EPISODE THIRTY-NINE: "TIME SQUARED"

Teleplay by Maurice Hurley
From a story by Kurt Michael Bensmiller
Directed by Joseph L. Scanlan

A shuttlecraft found adrift has one occupant— Picard. But Picard is also at his place on the bridge! The unconscious $Picard_2$ is taken to sick bay.

His brainwaves are out of synch. The shuttlecraft (apparently damaged in an anti-matter explosion) circuits seems to be reversed. Data uses a phase inverter to align it with the Enterprise's power, but finds that it works only when adjusted in the opposite direction than expected. Efforts to revive $Picard_2$ with stimulants have the opposite effect.

Shuttle logs reveal that the craft came from six hours in the future. Visual logs reveal that the Enterprise was destroyed, with Picard as the sole survivor, in a strange vortex in space. Picard is assailed with doubt, for he can't understand why he would abandon his ship, and wonders if he can avoid making a predetermined mistake.

As the event nears, $Picard_2$ becomes coherent, but communication is remains impossible. When the vortex appears, it draws the ship in and attacks both Picards with bolts of energy. Troi senses that it has some sort of awareness, and that it has identified Picard as the "brain" of the ship.

Picard realizes that his other self tried to save the ship by drawing the vortex's attention. $Picard_2$ revives and heads for the shuttle bay: Picard tries to get $Picard_2$ to tell him what his other choice was, but $Picard_2$ is unaware of anything but the crisis at hand. At last $Picard_2$ reveals that he had discarded going through the vortex as too risky.

Picard shoots Picard$_2$ with a phaser and orders the crew to take the ship through the vortex. Then the duplicate captain and shuttle vanish as it passes through, to emerge unscathed on the other side. Now the real Jean-Luc can get back to his command.

EPISODE FORTY: "THE ICARUS FACTOR"

Teleplay by David Assael and Robert L. McCullough
Story by David Assael
Directed by Robert Iscove
Guest Cast: Mitchell Ryan, Lance Spellerberg

The chance to command his own ship is soured for Riker when the offer is delivered by his father, who he hasn't seen in fifteen years. Tension escalates between the two Rikers, the younger one refusing to talk.

When Worf seems disturbed, or at least more disturbed than usual for a Klingon, Wesley enlists the aid of Data and Geordi in helping the Klingon. Worf, hoping to immerse himself in danger, asks Riker to take him along when he takes charge of the Ares.

It is the tenth anniversary of Worf's Age of Ascension, an important Klingon ritual. Using the holodeck, his comrades provide Worf with an appropriate anniversary celebration, which involves running a gauntlet of Klingon "pain-sticks." Worf endures the ordeal and thanks his friends for helping him "celebrate,' as it were, this important occasion. Klingons like pain. Pain is their friend. It makes them feel alive.

Will and his father manage to come to terms with their problems by working out their aggressions in the gym. Kyle gets the better of son Will, but only by cheating. When Will realizes that his father had always cheated in their competitions, it acts as a kind of breakthrough for him.

His father had always bested him by cheating, but before he had been too young to realize it. Kyle admits that he did it as a means of keeping his son motivated. An uneasy rapport is achieved as a result, although they are still hardly a loving father and son.

Riker decides to turn down the commission he's been offered so that he can remain on the Enterprise, the flagship of Starfleet. When he accepts a promotion, it will be because he wants it, not because someone else wants him to accept the promotion. Riker has been in control of his career for a long time and he intends to keep it that way.

EPISODE FORTY-ONE: "PEN PALS"

Teleplay by Melinda M. Snodgrass

From a story by Hannah Louise Shearer
Directed by Winrich Kolbe
Guest Cast: Nicholas Cascone, Nikki Cox, Ann H. Gillespie, Whitney Rydbeck

Data communicates with an alien child, but things get complicated when it becomes apparent that she's alone on a planet racked by seismic disturbances.

The Enterprise continues on course for the endangered system and it soon becomes evident that Data's young friend lives on of one of the threatened planets. Since this world has had no contact with space faring peoples, Picard is concerned about the Prime Directive,. His officers voice a variety of opinions.

For once, Pulaski sides with Data, although she expresses her argument with more emotion than the android. A plea from the child weakens Picard's resolve, however, and he gives Data permission to contact her. When transmission proves impossible, Data is allowed to beam down to the planet.

Meanwhile, Wesley perceives that he is having problems with his support team, because he's much younger than any of them. He wants a certain test done, but the expert on that subject thinks it will be a waste of time. Wesley consults with Riker, and finally simply tells the other officer that he wants the test done. Much to Wesley's surprise, the officer takes this order cheerfully and without question.

The test reveals that subterranean layers of dilithium crystals are forming lattice-like structures which transform the planet's heat into tectonic movement. The Engineering staff believes that the process can be halted by converting probes into resonators which, burrowed into the planet's surface, could break up the dilithium crystal lattices.

Data beams down and finds the young alien child alone in her home. She had hidden when the rest of her family fled. She wanted to stay with her transmitter and talk to Data. Data beams her up with him, much to his captain's dismay. The plan they use to stop the tectonic activity works, however, and Pulaski uses a process to wipe the child's memory of all knowledge of Data and what she saw on the Enterprise.

Thus the Prime Directive is preserved and the child will be able to resume her normal life. Data returns the sleeping child to her hideaway, but leaves a gift in the sleeping child's hand. While Data will never forget his young friend, she will also have a keepsake of Data with her, which perhaps one day she will recognize for what it means.

EPISODE FORTY-TWO: "Q WHO"

Written by Maurice Hurley
Directed by Rob Bowman
Guest Cast: John deLancie, Lycia Naff

Q, that rascally omnipotent alien troublemaker, gets around his promise to stay off the Enterprise by whisking Picard away in Shuttlecraft 6. Guinan senses Q, but by then he and Picard are beyond the Enterprise's sensor range. Riker seeks Picard without success.

After some time adrift, Picard agrees to listen to Q, who immediately returns Picard and the shuttle to the ship. In Ten Forward, Guinan recognizes Q, and he seems to feel threatened by her; they met 200 years earlier, and Guinan, according to Q, wore a different form at the time.

Q's desires are simple, however; he wants to join the crew of the Enterprise. He contends that the Federation cannot proceed in its exploration of the cosmos without encountering things beyond their comprehension; Q offers himself as their guide. Besides, he's been kicked out of the Continuum and has nowhere else to go. Picard does not trust him, and turns down Q's request.

Q sends the Enterprise 7000 light years off course. It would take them two years and seven months at Warp 9 to return to Federation Space. Guinan suggests that they head back immediately, for there is great danger, but Picard decides to explore.

The Enterprise locate a Class M planet with signs of civilization: ancient roads remain all over its surface. Where cities once were, however, there are only vast pits, as if all technology had been ripped off the planet. This is identical to the destruction of outposts along the Neutral Zone.

A huge, cubical ship appears. Guinan tells Picard that it is the Borg, who destroyed Guinan's homeworld and dispersed her people. A Borg, a humanoid extensively implanted with machinery, appears on the bridge and begins draining power. Worf kills it with a phaser blast. A second Borg appears, and raises a shield when it is fired on.

It seems to adapt almost immediately to anything. It takes some components from the dead Borg and returns to its ship. A tractor beam locks on to the Enterprise. It takes photon torpedoes to damage the Borg ship and free the Enterprise.

The Enterprise dispatches an Away Team over to the Borg ship. There they find a vast vessel in which the Borg act as components in a huge hive mind, plugging into outlets and becoming physically dormant. The Borg are born biologically but begin implantation at birth, with mechanical devices attached to them even in infancy. They are the perfect fusion of artificial intelligence and biological brains. In their regenerative mode, the Borg don't perceive the Away Team as a threat and just ignore their presence.

The Away Team returns to the Enterprise and they try to put as much distance between themselves and the Borg ship as they can. But the Borg ship begins to pursue them as it finishes its self-repairs. Photon torpedoes now have no effect, and the Borg are able to match any warp speed. The Borg fire weapons designed to drain shield power, and soon the Enterprise is defenseless.

As things begin to look grim for the Enterprise, Q returns. He needles Picard, who admits that Q was right: they do need his help. Ecstatic, Q abruptly returns the Enterprise to its original location and departs happily, having proven his point. But now Jean-Luc is left Picard feeling uneasy. Q made his point by exposing the Enterprise to the Borg, a threat greater than any previously encountered. And there can be no doubt that now the Borg will come after them in order to absorbed the Federation into the Borg collective. They may have two year's warning, but is that enough time to prepare for their colossal threat?

EPISODE FORTY-THREE: "SAMARITAN SNARE"
Written by Robert L. McCullough
Directed by Les Landau
Guest Cast: Christopher Collins, Leslie Morris, Daniel Bemzau, Lycia Naff, Tzi Ma

The Enterprise, under Riker's command, proceeds with a scientific mission, only to receive a distress call from a small vessel, which only has sublight capacity.

The Paklids seem simple people, with no knack for technology. LaForge beams over to fix their simple guidance system. Although Troi believes that LaForge is in danger, it doesn't seem to be true, but as soon as LaForge fixes one thing, another system goes down. The Paklids, impressed by LaForge's know-how, decide to keep him, grab his phaser, and stun him. They raise Romulan-type shields and ignore all the demands the Enterprise broadcasts for Geordi's return.

Aboard the shuttle, Picard explains that he needs his cardiac implant replaced. Loosening up somewhat, he tells Wesley Crusher the story of how his original heart was damaged. Wesley is astounded to learn of the young, undisciplined Picard, and the fight which ended with a spear through his torso. This is a side of Picard few people have seen.

Meanwhile, back on the Enterprise Data is trying to somehow pierce the Paklid's shields. Troi senses that the Paklids are a very tricky people, and that they programmed their computer to fake various problems. They want LaForge to make them more phasers. When communication is reestablished, the Paklids stun LaForge repeatedly, and demand all computer information from the Enterprise.

The Paklids have no technology of their own, but have borrowed and stolen from just about everybody in their impatience to get ahead. Riker plays along; he and the crew stage an elaborate "farewell" to LaForge, who they will miss as their resident "weapons expert." His death will be remembered, says Worf, but he will never achieve the 24th Level. "24," says Worf, "is the gateway to heroic salvation." The Paklids become convinced that LaForge is a weapons expert, but LaForge is baffled by the crew's behavior.

At Starbase 515, Picard's heart operation starts going bad. The finest cardiac expert on the base cannot save him, and they put out a call for another one who has the required skills .

When Enterprise sensors detect that the Paklid ship now has photon torpedo capacity, Riker orders Gomez to fire on the Paklids after a 24-second countdown. At this, LaForge delays the Paklids from responding by "adjusting" the torpedo array for maximum efficiency, while dismantling the system.

When the countdown ends, the Enterprise emits a red cloud of gas. LaForge feigns dismay, and tells the Paklids that the "crimson force field" has disarmed the torpedoes. Overwhelmed by the Enterprise's show of strength, the Paklids return LaForge. The "force field' was merely hydrogen discharged through the Broussard collectors.

The menace of the Paklids settled, the Enterprise speeds to Starbase 515 at maximum warp. Picard awakens from his operation to discover Dr. Pulaski at his bedside. She was the cardiac expert who saved him. Now Jean-Luc's well kept secret about his artificial heart is no longer a secret, but it turns out that no one is bothered by the news after all, nor do they think that he is less than capable because of it.

EPISODE FORTY-FOUR: "UP THE LONG LADDER"

Written by Melinda M. Snodgrass
Directed by Winrich Kolbe
Guest Cast: Barrie Ingham, Jon deVries, Rosalyn Landor

The Enterprise reaches the source of a distress signal, a class-M planet threatened by solar flares, and evacuates the entire population of several hundred. They beam up with their livestock, which creates some confusion in the transporter room, and are given a cargo bay as temporary quarters.

Their leader is O'Dell, a crazy, hard-drinking Irishman, but the real power is his headstrong, beautiful daughter. Riker is taken with her immediately, and sparks fly. The colonists have some difficulty coping with advanced technology; when Picard asks O'Dell about the computers and such, he is asked if he'd heard anything from "the other colony."

When sensors detect a class-M planet half a light year away, the Enterprise proceeds on the assumption that this is the home of the second colony. They find a planet of scientists, headed by Wilson Granger, who is "not exactly" a descendant of the Mariposa's Captain Walter Granger. When an Away Team, with Pulaski and Riker among its number, beams down, they discover several men identical to Granger, and a number of identical women as well.

In Granger's office, Pulaski scans him, and realizes that the planet is populated by clones. It seems that only five of the Mariposa's passengers reached the planet. Cloning was their only option. Sexual reproduction has faded out and become a repugnant concept.

The Mariposans are faced with the problem of replicative fading: their gene pool is weakening. When they cannot get tissue samples freely, they abduct Riker and Pulaski, and steal cells from their stomach linings. Back on the Enterprise, they realize what has happened, and a furious Riker beams down and destroys his clones.

The Mariposans need new breeding stock in order to enrich their DNA base. Centuries of inbreeding, as it were, has weakened them, making some recessive characteristic dominant more and more, and thereby weakening the population as more clones are made. Further cloning, even with new cells, will only prolong their problems another generation or two.

After some maneuvering, Picard manages to unite the two colonies: the Mariposans will have to learn to reproduce the old-fashioned way, and polyandry will have to be the norm for a century or so. While no one can be certain how this will work out, it is a solution the Mariposans accept, however much it will change their lifestyle.

EPISODE FORTY-FIVE: "MANHUNT"
Written by Terry Devereaux
Directed by Rob Bowman

Guest Cast: Majel Barrett, Robert Costanzo, Rod Arrants, Carel Struycken, Robert O'Reilly, Rhonda Aldrich, Mick Fleetwood

Lwaxana Troi returns. She has been appointed Ambassador to the Pacifica conference, and must be accorded full diplomatic treatment. She immediately invites Picard to a diplomatic dinner, but neglects to invite anyone else: she's out to snare the good captain with her romantic wiles.

Picard picks up on this fast and invites Data to join them for some after-dinner conversation. The android is all too willing to entertain them with anecdotes of various scientific matters, which Picard greatly prefers to being left alone with the overly aggressive Lwaxana.

Troi tells Pulaski that her mother is going through "The Phase," during which Betazoid women quadruple their sex drive, which also impairs their telepathic powers, at least with men. All her energies arc directed to winning a husband by any means.

Confronted by this news, Jean-Luc takes refuge in a Dixon Hill holodeck program for the duration of the trip to Pacifica. This is not as peaceful as he'd hoped, since various characters keep trying to kill "Hill." Unfortunately, the program must conform to the parameters of the published Dixon Hill novels. Finally, he asks holographic secretary Madeline to join him for drinks at Rex's Bar, where he has a meeting with Rex. Madeline hands him a gun, which she says he'll need.

Lwaxana tires of trying to locate Jean-Luc and so chooses another mate, without asking him first, of course. Thus the bridge crew is astonished when Lwaxana announces her impending marriage to Riker. Riker flees, joining Picard on the holodeck, along with Data. When Lwaxana finally tracks them down, she walks into the holodeck into a barroom setting where she is hit on by Rex the bartender, who is after her wealth. She is immediately taken by Rex, and intrigued that she cannot read his thoughts. The officers withdraw, leaving Lwaxana with her holographic beau.

When the Enterprise reaches Pacific, the delegates begin beaming down. Just before departing Lwaxana casually reveals that the Antedians are assassins who plan to blow up the entire conference with undetectable explosives hidden in their robes. The terrorists are quickly taken into custody and relieved of their explosives.

But just before she beams down, Lwaxana expresses mock indignation over the naughty thoughts Picard is having about her at that moment, an accusation which Jean-Luc is helpless to defend himself against because there are no other telepaths around to prove otherwise.

EPISODE FORTY-SIX: "THE EMISSARY"

Television story and teleplay by Richard Manning and Hans Beimler
From a story by Thomas H. Calder
Directed by Cliff Bole
Guest Cast: Suzie Plakson, Lance LeGault, Georgann Johnson

K'Ehleyr, a half Klingon, half human woman, has a mission which involves a Klingon ship with a crew that has been in cryonic suspension for seventy-five years. The Enterprise must try to reach them in time to delay their awakening, for they will believe that the Federation/Klingon war is still going on.

K'Ehleyr knows Worf; they have an unresolved relationship. When they meet in a holodeck battle simulation, Klingon passions are aroused and old business soon becomes new business. Worf feels obligated to take the vow of mating, but K'Ehleyr, who is scornful of Klingon traditions, declines.

The Enterprise arrives too late and the Klingon ship attacks. They may well be forced to destroy it until Worf comes up with the perfect plan. Worf poses as the captain of the Enterprise, with K'Ehleyr his second in command, and convinces the Klingon captain that the war is over— with the Klingons as the victors. The Klingon ship happily accepts this news and agrees to stand down. Now

all they have to do is get them to accept the truth just as graciously.

EPISODE FORTY-SEVEN: "PEAK PERFORMANCE"

Written by David Kemper
Directed by Robert Scheerer
Guest Cast: Roy Brocksmith, Armin Shimerman, David L. Lander

The forthcoming threat of the Borg has been taken quite seriously by Starfleet and so war games are scheduled, among other defensive strategies. As part of the mock conflict, Will Riker is assigned the command of the starcruiser Hathaway, an eighty-year-old relic which he has 48 hours to get into shape. Both ships, of course, will convert their weapons to harmless laser pulses, which their computers will interpret in terms of "real" damage.

On their way to rendezvous with the Hathaway, the Enterprise takes on a passenger, the master strategist Kohlrami. Kohlrami will act as observer during the wargames and grade the captains accordingly. His race has had such a reputation as brilliant strategists that no one has attacked their planet for over nine thousand years. Kohlrami is also a master of the game Strategema, and easily defeats both Riker and Data.

Along with LaForge, Wesley and Worf, Riker takes command of the

Hathaway. The Hathaway has no warp drive, until Wesley returns to the Enterprise briefly to check up on a science experiment, which he beams over to the Hathaway. This device will give them two seconds at warp two. When the games begin, Worf tricks the Enterprise sensors into seeing a Klingon warbird, which distracts Picard long enough for Riker to score a significant "hit."

When a Ferengi warship enters the area, they observe the Federation ships firing on each other. Picard sees the Ferengi ship but wrongly believes it to be another illusion, until it attacks with real weapons. The Ferengi are curious: why would one Federation ship fire on another? Nothing makes sense to them but acquisition, so they assume that the Hathaway hides something of great value, and demand that it be turned over.

Data proposes a daring plan: if the Enterprise fires photon torpedoes at the Hathaway, and the Hathaway uses its limited warp ability to outrun the explosion, then the Ferengi will have nothing to motivate them to attack the Enterprise. The plan works, and the Ferengi flee when Worf tricks their sensors into seeing another ship as the brief warp surge creates an illusion of there being two versions of the Hathaways.

Following the successful completion of the wargames, Data plays Strategema with Kohlrami, who finally gives up when the android creates a spectacular stalemate. The android's strategy was not to seek victory against Kohlrami, but to match him move for move and stymie him at ever juncture. Since Kohlrami's only goal was to win, this was a maddening strategy he could not hope to defeat. By quitting, the arrogant Kohlrami automatically makes Data the winner.

EPISODE FORTY-EIGHT: "SHADES OF GREY"

Teleplay by Maurice Hurley, Richard Manning and Hans Beimler
Story by Maurice Hurley
Directed by Rob Bowman

While surveying an uncharted planet, Riker is stung by an indigenous life form. When he tries to beam up, the transporter registers a micro- organism in his system that cannot be filtered out. Pulaski (in her last episode) authorizes a medical override.

In sick bay, it is determined that the microbe has bonded with his nervous system on the molecular level, and is taking over his spinal cord. The unconscious Riker is placed on direct brain stimulation, which retards the microbes fatal progress to his brain. The brain stimulation causes Riker to relive scenes from the first two seasons. The endorphins released by the emotions of these memories have an effect on the microbe, and Pulaski, with Deanna's help, tries to find the right emotional "frequency" to save him.

Riker experiences a wide array of memories, from pleasant to passionate ones, as well as violent episode from his recent past. A cascade of crises he re-experiences becomes so intense that it risks his life, only to finally drive the infection out of his body and save him. Easily the cheapest episode of the series, and the last time that THE NEXT GENERATION would end a season on a low note.

END OF SEASON TWO

Jonathan at the cast Q&A for Creation Con.

Photo ©
1994
Albert L.
Ortega

Marina at '92 VSDA (Video Software Dealers Assoc.) in Las Vegas.

Photo © 1994 Albert L. Ortega

SEASON THREE

SEASON THREE

THE NEXT GENERATION finally hit its stride in its third season. Gates McFadden returned as Dr. Crusher, restoring the show's chemistry after Roddenberry's momentary lapse of reason. Some real classics would emerge, including the alternative-history episode which brought back Tasha Yar, "Yesterday's Enterprise."

Worf continued to deepen in episodes like "The Enemy," in which he refuses to give the blood that could save a dying Romulan's life. "The Defector" would reveal more aspects of the Romulan character, while Klingon culture— and Worf's personal history— would dominate "Sins Of The Father." Federation ethics, most notably the Prime directive, would get a real workout in "Who Watches The Watchers."

The rather dubious matter of holodeck abuse would be examined, rather gingerly, in "Hollow Pursuits." And die-hard fans of classic STAR TREK would get a real treat in the dramatic storyline of "Sarek," the first step in a real continuity link between the generations.

EPISODE FORTY-NINE: "EVOLUTION"

Teleplay by Michael Piller
Story by Michael Piller and Michael Wagner
Directed by Winrich Kolbe
Guest Cast: Ken Jenkins

Dr. Paul Stubbs is on board to launch a special probe, "The Egg," which will gather data from an event which happens only once every 192 years—a buildup of stellar matter which produces a spectacular explosion. When the Enterprise goes briefly out of control, almost veering into the stream of stellar matter, everyone is mystified as no malfunction can be detected.

More things start going wrong. In sickbay, a food slot malfunctions, even though the computer insists that it is working perfectly.

When a Borg vessel is sighted, the Enterprise goes to Red Alert. As if to mock them the shields drop, leaving the Enterprise helpless as the Borg prepare to fire. But then the Borg abruptly disappear. The computer seems to be going haywire; there was no Borg ship.

Stubbs is angry. If he misses this chance, his work is all in vain. Picard is more concerned that his ship is stranded right where the explosion will take place, but Stubbs values his experiment more than the lives of the crew.

When it becomes apparent that the ship's computer core has been tampered with, Wesley realizes that it's his fault. Two nanites he had been working with have escaped, reproduced, and infiltrated the computer. The nanites seem to be evolving, too, and eat bits of the computer memory core. There are even indications that they might have a collective intelligence.

Stubbs tells Geordi that gamma radiation might clear the cores. Geordi responds that this would kill the Nanites, and Stubbs agrees, firing a blast of gamma radiation at the core, killing the Nanites in it.

The Nanites do have a collective intelligence and they retaliate by altering the atmosphere of the ship. Manual control restores normal air, but Stubbs has inadvertently proven that the Nanites have intelligence because they track him down that and exact revenge by zapping him with a bolt of energy. While Picard plans to use gamma radiation to disposes of the nanite menace once and for all, Data manages to communicate with the Nanites, and allows them to use him as a host.

Picard explains what has happened to them, and gives them the standard Starfleet "peace between entities" speech. The Nanites explain that they needed raw materials for replication, but meant no harm. Stubbs apologizes for his thoughtless action.

The Nanites have evolved beyond the need to use the Enterprise computer core and undo their damage by repairing the core. Picard arranges for a planet for the Nanites which they can transfer them to. Stubbs and the Enterprise crew are able to witness the stellar blast from a safe distance, and thereby appreciate its stellar majesty without being consumed by it.

EPISODE FIFTY: "THE ENSIGNS OF COMMAND"

Written by Melinda M. Snodgrass
Directed by Cliff Bole
Guest Cast: Eileen Seeley, Mark L. Taylor, Richard Allen

The mysterious Sheliak finally speak to the Federation. They have discovered humans on a planet ceded to them by treaty, and demand their removal so they can colonize. The Federation has no knowledge of humans on that world. It is blanketed by heavy hyperonic radiation, which is fatal to humans. It is possible that humans could adapt, however, and the Enterprise is sent to investigate. The Sheliak regard humans as inferior beings, and will exterminate them if their deadline is not met.

While the Enterprise Sensors do detect life forms, the radiation in the area is making the transporters and phasers useless. Data is unaffected by the hyperonic radiation blanketing the planet and uses a shuttle to get down to the surface. There he finds a thriving community of 15 thousand settlers.

It would take over four weeks to shuttle them all up to the Enterprise, and there are only three days until the deadline. Even worse, Data cannot convince Gosheven, the colony leader, that there is a threat. Gosheven is proud of the colony and its accomplishments, especially its water system, and will not consider leaving these monuments.

But a young woman, Ardrian McKenzie, who is fascinated by Data due to her interest in cybernetics, offers to help Data. Together the two discover that not everyone in the colony agrees with Gosheven. Even so, not many are interested in leaving everything behind that they've worked so hard to build.

Jean-Luc pours over the Sheliak treaty, hoping to find a loophole. Complicating this is the fact that it required 372 Federation legal experts to negotiate the treaty to begin with. In the meantime the Sheliak refuse any sort of compromise or extended timetable beyond their demanded pull-out date.

At a meeting called by Gosheven, Data uses various arguments for evacuating and a lot of discussion is brought about, but Gosheven rallies his people together and Data is stalemated. Still, there are dissenters, and they meet at McKenzie's house. Gosheven intrudes, and shoots Data with an energy weapon. The meeting breaks up.

Ardrian McKenzie helps Data revives, and it becomes clear that a debate will not solve the dilemma. If the people do not leave the Sheliak will destroy them, and this is what Data must impress upon the colony. He rigs his phaser, using parts of his neural processor, to work despite the radiation, and sends a message to Gosheven telling him that he plans to destroy the aqueduct.

When Data arrives at the aqueduct, he finds the area protected, but stuns the armed guards, and sends a maximum-power phaser burst up the waterway, demonstrating his power. If one android can do this, he tells them, think what the Sheliak can do. This finally convinces the colonists that evacuation is a good idea, and preparations begin.

Finally Picard finds his loophole. A clause in the treaty enables either side to call in a third-party arbitrator in any dispute. Jean-Luc chooses a race that won't emerge from hibernation for nearly six months. Confronted with this, the Sheliak agree to the three weeks Picard wants to and needs to evacuate the 15 thousand colonists.

EPISODE FIFTY-ONE: "THE SURVIVORS"

Written by Michael Wagner
Directed by Les Landau
Guest Cast: John Anderson, Anne Haney

When a Federation colony is attacked and sends out a distress call, the Enterprise arrives too late to assist them. All life on Delta Rana IV has been obliterated, with one exception. There is a small plot of greenery occupied by a pair of elderly Earth botanists, the Oxbridges, and there is no clue as to why they were spared. Sensors cannot detect any sign of the alien battle cruiser responsible for the devastation.

The Enterprise beams down an Away Team to visit the Oxbridges, who are as perplexed by their survival as Picard is. Even so they remain content to stay where they are. Data is intrigued by one of their artifacts, an ancient music box topped by a pair of mechanical dancers. On board the Enterprise, Deanna Troi finds her mind assailed by an endlessly repeating piece of music, the same one played by the Oxbridge's music box, and it is slowly driving her mad.

The Enterprise is suddenly attacked by the alien ship, which appears almost out of nowhere, as though it had been a cloaked vessel. While the vessel fires on the Enterprise, it does no damage. The battle cruiser flees, and the Enterprise pursues it, until Picard decides that he's being toyed with and returns to Delta Rana IV.

Back at the planet, Picard beams down to meet with the Oxbridges. But all Jean-Luc can discover is that Mr. Oxbridge holds a strong moral position against killing, and refused to join in the defense of the colony. He believes that perhaps this was why he and his wife were spared.

Jean-Luc is not convinced. Something is going on that he cannot see. No sooner does Picard beams up, than the Enterprise is attacked again by the same mystery ship, only to have its shields destroyed and its weapons systems rendered inoperable. The aliens do not pursue when the Enterprise flees, but remain in orbit around the planet.

When the Enterprise returns, testing a theory Picard has, the mystery attacker has vanished once again, just as he expected. Jean-Luc beams down, and tells the Oxbridges that he will never enter their house again, but that the Enterprise will stay in orbit around Delta Rana IV as long as they are alive. As soon as he beams up, the aliens reappear. When Picard refuses to respond to its attack, it veers off and destroys the Oxbridges instead.

Picard then orders Worf to fire upon the ship, which disintegrates when hit by a single photon torpedo. Sensors indicate no life on the planet, but Picard waits. After a few hours, the Oxbridge home reappears. Picard claims that he is acting on the assumption that there is only one survivor of the alien attack, which baffles Riker. The Oxbridges are beamed onto the bridge, where Picard confronts them with his deductions.

Jean-Luc postulates that not only was the colony destroyed, but Oxbridges wife as well, and that the woman with him is just an illusion he created, along with the house and everything around it. At this, Mrs. Oxbridge vanishes. The alien ship that fought the Enterprise was one, too, and when Picard set the conditions for his departure they were all too quickly fulfilled.

"Kevin Oxbridge" vanishes, and reappears in sick bay, where he removes the music from Deanna's mind. He had used it to block her from learning his true nature. He reveals that he is a being thousands of years old which fell in love while in human form and married Rishanna. She never knew his true nature.

When the colony was attacked by a warlike alien race, she joined the resistance and died. His grief and rage were so great that, in the space of a moment, he destroyed the attackers— not just those in the ship, but all fifty billion of them, everywhere in the universe.

A peaceful being, the terrible guilt he feels is overwhelming. Picard understands and the being returns to the planet, to the recreations of the real life he had known, which are now just momentos of his guilt.

EPISODE FIFTY-TWO: "WHO WATCHES THE WATCHERS"

Written by Richard Manning and Hans Beimler

Directed by Robert Weimer

Guest Cast: Kathryn Leigh Scott, Ray Wise, James Greene, Pamela Segall, John McLiam, James McIntire, Lois Hall

The arrival of an Enterprise Away Team coincides with a survey post's discovery by two Mentakans. Liko, a man still grieving his wife's death, peers into the outpost, only to be shocked by energy which causes him to fall from a great height. Doctor Crusher helps him, and beams him up to the Enterprise. This is witnessed by his daughter, Oji, who is hiding nearby.

Liko awakens briefly on the Enterprise, and, through a haze, sees Picard, who is obviously in charge. Crusher tries Pulaski's memory wiping technique, but it doesn't work, and when he awakens on Mentaka-III he believes that he has seen a god out of his people's ancient legends.

Troi and Riker are altered to resemble Mentakans, and, outfitted with implanted transmitters, beam down to locate the missing scientist Palmer. They are welcomed to the village, where Liko is telling his people of the miracle that brought him back to life, and of the god he calls "The Picard." In the village is Palmer, the missing scientist.

The Mentakans remain skeptical, particularly Nouria, the village leader. Other villagers soon arrive with the injured Palmer in tow. While the villagers debate this, Troi slips out, and returns claiming to have seen another stranger. When they go to investigate, Riker makes off with Palmer, only to be pursued by a bow-wielding Mentakan. He manages to beam up unobserved, but Troi is held by the Mentakans now.

Picard beams Nouria to the Enterprise to convince her that he is not a god. He doesn't want to do this but he has no choice. By letting the people being in the god Picard would violate the Prime Directive by causing the people to become diverted by superstition and thereby misdirect their evolvement towards civilization.

Nouria grasps the concept of that there are different levels of social and technological development, and that Picard is not supernatural, but still thinks that he has the power to bring back the dead until he takes her to sick bay and allows her to witness the death of one of the injured anthropologists.

Jean-Luc returns to the planet with Nouria, only to face the unstable Liko, who begs for the return of his dead wife. When Liko tries to prove Picard's powers by shooting him with an arrow; his daughter pushes him, and Picard is only wounded in the shoulder. He bleeds, which convinces Liko that he is mortal after all.

Finally The Mentakans prove their intelligence when they accept Picard's explanation of the Prime Directive. He oversees the dismantling of the observation post and the Away Team leaves, secure in the belief that these people, too, will one day evolve into a race which will reach for the stars.

EPISODE FIFTY-THREE: "THE BONDING"
Written by Ronald D. Moore
Directed by Winrich Kolbe

Guest Cast: Susan Powell, Gabriel Damon, Raymond D. Turner

Worf's Away Team explores ancient ruins on a planet depopulated by war millennia earlier, but an explosive device left over from that conflict explodes, killing the ship's archaeologist, Lt. Marla Astor. Her 12 year old son Jeremy, who lost his father a few years earlier, is on board the Enterprise, and Picard once again faces the unhappy task of breaking the news, as he once did to Wesley Crusher.

When Geordi beams down to the surface of the lifeless planet to investigate the incident, he finds more of the bombs. They have apparently been all dug up and disarmed. Because Worf was in command of the Away Team, he feels responsible for Astor's death, which was senseless, and at the hands of a long-dead enemy which Worf cannot take vengeance against. He considers performing the Klingon bonding ceremony with Jeremy, but Deanna advises him to wait, as the boy has not yet started to deal with his emotions.

While Jeremy Astor is watching video records of his family, his mother reappears in their quarters and tries to take him to the planet below. Worf discovers this but is told not to interfere. When Picard confronts Astor, she vanishes. When Deanna takes Jeremy back to his quarters, Astor is there again, and the rooms have been transformed into Jeremy's home on Earth, right down to his favorite cat. Jeremy is convinced that it is all real. The being posing as his mother does not understand the other humans' interference, since all she wants to do is make Jeremy happy.

Geordi has detected an energy field near the explosion site and Deanna has detected a presence there as well. This has apparently extended itself to the Enterprise. Geordi determines that he can cut off the energy's access to the Enterprise by adjusting the shield harmonics. It works, and the illusion vanishes, but the energy field leaves the planet and re-enters the vessel. The illusion is restored, while the energy goes through the ship's systems, learning all about them.

Jean-Luc attempts to reason with the image which calls itself Marla Astor. He learns that she was created by a race of energy beings who vowed to stop all wars after another race, made of matter, destroyed itself. Picard insists that it is not in the boy's best interest to be given a comforting illusion. Jeremy must be allowed to mature, despite the pain that often accompanies that process.

Wesley is reluctantly brought into the debate by Jean-Luc, who wants him to tell Jeremy about his own feelings when his father died, a subject Wes has been unwilling to discuss with anyone other than his mother, until now. Wes explains that at first be blamed Captain Picard, but soon came to realize that he was wrong to do this. Finally Jeremy expresses his anger at Worf, who reveals his own parents' deaths, and offers to help the boy.

Witnessing how these beings called human deal with the pain of their emotions, the aliens withdraw back down to the planet. Later, Worf and Jeremy enter the holodeck and perform the Bonding ceremony, which honors their dead mothers and makes them brothers.

EPISODE FIFTY-FOUR: "BOOBY TRAP"

Written by Ron Roman, Michael Pillar, Richard Danus and Michael Wagner
Directed by Gabrielle Beaumont
Guest Cast: Susan Gibney, Albert Hall, Julie Warner

The Enterprise finds the perfectly preserved remains of a thousand-year-old Promelian battle cruiser in an asteroid field that was the site of an ancient space battle. Picard, Data and Worf beam over to the old battle cruiser and discover the bodies of the crew. A computer memory coil provides them with the Promelian captain's last message, in which he praises his crew and takes all responsibility for his ship's fate.

They complete their exploration of the ship, but when the Enterprise tries to leave the area, they can't. The Enterprise experiences a power drain while simultaneously being bombarded by lethal radiation. This will destroy the shields in several hours. It appears that the Enterprise has fallen into the same booby trap which destroyed the Promelian vessel.

Using holodeck simulations, Geordi studies the problem with the help of a simulation of Dr. Leah Brahms, the designer of the Enterprise's propulsion systems. Data recovers more coils from the dead ship and repairs them. They reveal that the trap involves energy assimilators hidden in the asteroids: these draw off power and transform it into radiation. Any power use fuels it, even that of the shields.

Geordi and "Leah Brahms" work up computer simulations that will enable the Enterprise computer to run the ship, making split-second alterations that might save them, but none of the simulations succeed. In a moment of inspiration, Geordi turns the whole idea around: why not cut the power completely? Picard accepts the idea as their best chance, and takes the con himself.

A single impulse burst first sets the Enterprise into motion. Then all power except for minimal life support systems are shut off. Picard uses the thrusters to direct the drifting Enterprise through the asteroid field. When their momentum seems about to give out, he uses the gravity of a large asteroid to swing the Enterprise around and out of harm's way.

Upon clearing the boundary of the asteroid field the Enterprise destroys the Promelian battle cruiser so that no one else will ever be lured into this deadly booby trap.

EPISODE FIFTY-FIVE: "THE ENEMY"

Written by David Kemper and Michael Piller
Directed by David Carson
Guest Cast: John Snyder, Andreas Katsulas, Steve Rankin

Geordi is stranded on a world ravaged by electromagnetic storms. Separated from his Away Team, he falls into a deep cavern. The team beams up with an injured Romulan, but cannot locate Geordi with their sensors.

The Enterprise drops a neutrino beam probe, which emits a beam visible to Geordi's VISOR. All he needs to do is locate it and alter its frequency. He sees it, but is taken suddenly captive by a Romulan. When they are threatened by a rock slide, he helps the Romulan to a sheltering cave, but the Centurion still regards the human as his prisoner.

Aboard the Enterprise, the Romulan they rescued from the surface needs a blood transfusion. But the only one on board whose blood will serve is also the one who hates the Romulans most: Worf. Data intercepts a Romulan response to the distress call, which reveals that a Romulan ship is six hours away from the Neutral Zone border. Picard warns them not to enter Federation space. They insist that the Enterprise meet them at the border in five hours and turn over the injured Romulan, but Picard will not abandon Geordi.

Geordi manages to convince his Romulan captor that they have to help each other if they're going to have a chance of getting out of the fix they're in. But then the neural interface with his VISOR fails, which effectively leaves Geordi blind. Now he can't see the beacon.

The Romulan on the Enterprise states that he would rather die than accept Klingon blood. This is just as well because Worf refuses to budge from his refusal to give any of his blood to the Romulan. Since Geordi's VISOR is still functional, his new-found ally suggests rigging it to his tricorder. Acting as Geordi's eyes and hands, the Centurion completes the connection,

creating a crude neutrino detector. Now they're able to detect the beacon and reach the rescue point.

Meanwhile the Romulan ship passes the border of the neutral zone and heads toward a confrontation with the Enterprise. Without a blood transfusion, the Romulan aboard the Enterprise dies. Worf has no regrets. The Romulan ship arrives, ready for battle. The beacon changes, but Geordi can't be beamed up with the shields raised, so Picard makes a gesture of peace and lowers them. Conflict is averted, and the Centurion is returned to the Romulans.

EPISODE FIFTY-SIX: "THE PRICE"

Written by Hannah Louise Shearer
Directed Robert Scheerer
Guest Cast: Matt McCoy, Elizabeth Hoffman, Castulo Guerra, Scott Thomson, Dan Shor, Kevin Peter Hall

When a wormhole appears in the Barzan system, the exploitation rights are opened for negotiation. The wormhole opens on a sector which can only be reached in a hundred years at Warp 9, but through the wormhole, the trip will only take a few seconds. At the negotiations, the Federation is represented by its top negotiator, Mendoza. The Caldonians are also present for the talks, hosted by Picard on board the Enterprise. A Ferengi delegation appears, demanding to be let in on the proceedings. The Premiere of Barzan invites the greedy Ferengi to participate in the negotiations.

The alien Chrysalians are employing a human negotiator named Ral, and as soon as they meet he is attracted to Deanna Troi. She is also attracted to him, and their romance develops quickly. Meanwhile, the Ferengi delegate administers a chemical to Mendoza by shaking hands, incapacitating him with an extreme allergic reaction. Riker takes Mendoza's place at Picard's insistence, for the captain is certain that his First Officer's poker skills will serve him well at the bargaining table.

Geordi and Data prepare to travel through the wormhole in a shuttle when it next appears due to the fact that all of the information known about it is based on the findings of a single probe. But the treacherous Ferengi see treachery everywhere and think that the Federation is up to something.

They insist on accompanying the Enterprise shuttle with a Ferengi travel pod. Geordi and Data pass through the wormhole with the Ferengi close behind. They discover that their location is 200 light years off from the expected sector.

It turns out that the far end of the wormhole is actually unstable, and is not at all as reliable as the original probe led everyone to believe. When Geordi notifies the Ferengi and warns them that they have to get back through the wormhole or risk being stranded, the Ferengi think that it's some kind of trick.

Geordi can see the wormhole a few moments before it becomes visible, through his visors ability to see subatomic energy patterns. He and Data enter it early, but the stubborn Ferengi crew will not follow. When the wormhole becomes visible to them, it only holds its position only for a second before vanishing. The Ferengi are stranded thousands of light years from home.

The Ferengi ship suddenly fires on the Enterprise, drawing Riker away from the negotiating table as he goes to the bridge to deal with the crisis. The Ferengi complain that the Federation has rigged the negotiations, cutting the Ferengi out of the action. They fire on the wormhole, a pointless maneuver, and the Enterprise easily destroys their missile. Ral and the Premiere come on the bridge and Ral announces that he has closed the deal.

Troi determines that the Ferengi are lying and that this was all a ploy to disrupt negotiations. Ral comes on the

Gates at the L.A. Airport Hilton for a Creation Con.

Photo © 1994 Albert L. Ortega

Brent at the screening for ROOKIE OF THE YEAR.

Photo © 1994 Albert L. Ortega

bridge and takes charge, getting the Ferengi to back down by cutting them in on the wormhole deal. Deanna figures out what's going on and reveals Ral's secret: he and the Ferengi staged the entire conflict to get Riker out of the way.

Just then Data and Geordi return, revealing that the wormhole has no practical value after all. But Ral's employers are still stuck with holding up their end of the bargain—paying for the rights to a wormhole they can't use. Deanna also rejects Ral due to his unscrupulous negotiation tactics. Riker offers his congratulations to Ral for his hollow victory.

EPISODE FIFTY-SEVEN: "THE VENGEANCE FAC-TOR"

Written by Sam Rolfe
Directed by Timothy Bond
Guest Cast: Lisa Wilcox, Joey Aresco, Nancy Parsons, Stephen Lee, Mark Lawrence

A world once torn by clan warfare, Acamar has achieved unity after many generations. One faction, which split off years earlier, is a group of thieves and scavengers known as the Gatherers. When traces of Acamar blood is found at a raided science station, Picard goes to the Sovereign of that world and con-vinces her to talk to the Gatherers in an effort to reintegrate them into the society of their homeworld. The Sovereign, Marouk, is accompanied by her cook and food taster, the beautiful Yuta, who catches Riker's eye.

Riker leads an Away Team to a Gatherer outpost they discover and convince the ranking Gatherer, B'rull, to talk to the Sovereign. Marouk and Yuta beam down. While Marouk and B'Rull talk, Yuta confronts an old Gatherer of the Lornak clan, who is astounded to recognize her. When she touches him lightly, he dies.

She is the last of her clan, she says, but she will outlive his clan nevertheless. When the body is discovered, it is believed that he died of natural causes, but Crusher beams the body up for examination. B'Rull, meanwhile, has agreed to lead the Sovereign to the Gatherer leader, Chorgan.

An examination of Lornak by Dr. Crusher reveals that the man had a perfectly healthy heart. His cardiac arrest was actually caused by a micro-virus, apparently tailored to his genetic pattern, which blocked the impulses of his autonomic nervous system. In a word, he was murdered. The virus could be carried without harm to the carrier, only to be deadly for anyone with the right DNA.

The Gatherers fire on the Enterprise, but Picard knocks out their shields and beams over for talks with Marouk, who, as always, takes Yuta along. Dr. Crusher studies the Acamarian medical records and discovers a similar murder. Fifty three years earlier, the Lornack eradicated another clan, and their leader died of cardiac arrest while awaiting trial. Visual records show a surprising link between the two cases: Yuta. Apparently, she hadn't aged a day in over fifty years. Another link is also discovered: Chorgan is also a member of the Lornak clan.

Riker is determined to stop any further assassinations and beams over to the Gatherer ship in time to stop Yuta's next killing. Riker confronts her, but Yuta tries to complete her task, for Chorgan is the last Lornack, and she was the one chosen from the five survivors of her clan to undergo genetic life extension and carry out their final revenge.

Riker fires a phaser at her twice, but she can resist maximum stun settings. After a final warning, he increases the setting to its most deadly, and when she makes a final attempt to kill Chorgan, he vaporizes her. The truce with the Gatherers is achieved, but Riker has to wonder at the price that was paid and the generations of hatred which had kept the feud alive.

EPISODE FIFTY-EIGHT: "THE DEFECTOR"

Written by Ronald D. Moore
Directed by Robert Scheerer
Guest Cast: James Sloyan, Andreas Katsulas, John Hancock, S.A. Templeman

A Romulan scout ship fleeing across the border of the Neutral Zone is detected by the Enterprise. The scout ship is being pursued by a deadly Romulan warbird. When the pilot of the scout ship requests asylum, he is rescued by the Enterprise which warns off the Romulan pursuit vessel.

The Romulan defector claims to be a minor logistics officer with important information: the Romulans are preparing for war, and have built a hidden base in the Neutral Zone, close Federation outposts.

Jean-Luc finds this information all too convenient. Analysis of the fight they witnessed indicates that the Romulan warship slowed down to let the scout ship escape. The Romulans have previously tricked opponents into appearing to be the aggressor by duping them into attacking somewhere in the Neutral Zone and thereby establishing the Romulans right to retaliate. A probe dispatched to the area of the supposedly secret Romulan outpost does report traces of low level subspace transmissions.

On the Enterprise, Data takes the Romulan defector to a holodeck simulation of a valley on Romulus. At the sight of a place on his homeworld which he'll never see again, the Romulan admits he's really an Admiral who had been censured for counseling against war.

He has defected to prevent his Empire from destroying itself, and has a wealth of information. Armed with this new information, Jean-Luc risks entering the Neutral Zone to investigate the base. But once there he finds nothing—except for two Romulan warships lying in wait. The Romulan Admiral had been fed misinformation to test his loyalty.

Picard confronts the threat of the Romulan ships with a bold front. Suddenly the captain of the Enterprise he reveals that he has his own surprise for the Romulans—two cloaked Klingon warships who were with him all along. Once the Klingon ships appear, the two The Romulan ships clear out and high tail it back to their homeworld.

The Enterprise returns to Federation space, only to find that the Romulan defector has poisoned himself. He leaves behind letters for his wife and daughter, letters which can never be delivered so long as the Romulans refuse to live in peaceful co-existence with the Federation. The Romulan Admiral believed that his cause was just and was willing to sacrifice himself to try to make life better for all Romulans.

EPISODE FIFTY-NINE: "THE HUNTED"

Written by Robin Bernheim
Directed by Cliff Bole
Guest Cast: Jeff McCarthy, James Cromwell

Roga Danar is an escaped Angosian prisoner who continually evades capture until Data second-guesses his next move. He is held on the Enterprise until the Angosians can pick him up. Angosia, which has achieved peace, is applying for Federation membership. Deanna Troi senses the prisoner's pain, and goes to him, to discover the truth of his violent nature.

In fact, he seems peaceful, only to have been physically altered to make him a perfect soldier. Investigation of his records is baffling: he has no criminal record, and his military record is exemplary. The Angosians, it seems, turned their volunteers into soldiers through biological and mental tampering. Once their war was won, they shunted their soldiers off to a lunar colony, where they were provided with a comfortable existence. This was not enough for Roga Danar.

Danar escapes during transfer. Modifications to his body enable him to fight the transporter beam, as well as making him invisible to the ship's sensors. He leaves traces intentionally, however, leading Data to conclude that he is misdirecting them.

Worf finds some of these traces of Danar in Cargo Bay Two. They discover that a pressure suit is missing. Attention shifts to the airlocks, but Danar is actually still hiding in the cargo bay. When Worf finds Danar, they fight, until the power goes out when an overloaded phaser, left by Danar, explodes in a Jeffrey's Tube. Danar knocks out Worf, powers the cargo bay transporter with a phaser, and beams onto the Angosian police shuttle, getting the drop on his would-be captors.

Down on Angosia, Danar leads a revolt, and confronts the agents of the government at the sides of his comrades. The soldiers are not programmed to fight unarmed opponents, but can defend themselves if attacked: will the government try to coerce them, or listen to their position?

When the Angosian Prime Minister requests help from the Federation, Picard invokes the Prime Directive, stating that the Angosians to work out their own problems since those problems are clearly of their own making.

EPISODE SIXTY: "THE HIGH GROUND"

Written by Melinda M. Snodgrass
Directed by Gabrielle Beaumont
Guest Cast: Kerrie Keene, Richard Cox, Marc Buckland, Fred. G. Smith, Christopher Pettiet

Beverly Crusher is kidnapped while helping victims of a terrorist bombing on Rutia IV. Ansata terrorists have been fighting the Rutian government for years, and have an undetectable mode of transport. They need a doctor because their DNA has been warped by constant use of the Inverter, which transports by means of a dimensional shift.

Their leader, Finn, hopes to draw the Federation into the conflict. Concerned that the Federation is providing medical supplies to his enemies, he becomes convinced, despite Crusher's protestations, that the Federation has chosen sides.

They study a device found on a captured terrorist, but Data cannot identify its function. Suddenly Wesley remembers reading about early experiments in dimensional shifting, long abandoned due to the hazardous price they exacted on the person using the device. Now Picard knows just how the Ansata are transporting, and why they need a doctor; the Ansata are slowly killing themselves every time they use the dimensional shifting to transport.

Wesley develops a program that will trace the power source, although the device must be used a sufficient number of times to get a fix on it.

On Rutia IV, Riker's presence as an observer at interrogations convinces Finn that the Federation is his enemy and that they have sided with the Rutian government. They launch an offensive against the Enterprise, but it fails. Never ones to give up, the Ansata strike again, this time capturing Captain Picard and taking him to their secret underground base.

The Ansata demand that the Federation impose an embargo on Rutia within twelve hours, or Picard will be executed. By now, Wesley has located the power source, and an Away Team beams down to rescue the Captain and Dr. Crusher. In the battle, Rutian police kill Finn. The Ansata have been crushed, for now, but their disputes with the ruling regime remain. Will they work out a peaceful settlement or will the Ansata rise again?

EPISODE SIXTY-ONE: "DEJA Q"

Written by Richard Danus
Directed by Les Landau

Guest Cast: John deLancie, Corbin Bernsen, Richard Cansino, Betty Muramoto

Attempts to keep a planet's moon from dropping out of orbit seem futile. When Q appears on the bridge, naked and claiming to have been stripped of his powers, Picard immediately suspects that he has a hand in the imminent disaster. Q is actually telling the truth.

Placed in the brig, Q tries to adapt to mortality, but is frightened by such unfamiliar sensations as sleep and hunger. When the Enterprise is probed by a mysterious force, it becomes obvious that Q's enemies are out to get him in his vulnerable state, and the ship is attacked by a diffuse energy being.

Q tries to advise Geordi on what to do about the tumbling moon, but without the powers of the Q, the only thing he can suggest is to change the gravitational constant of the universe. For Q, this would have once been a simple thing to do. While this is impossible for humans to duplicate, the idea does inspire Geordi to try to reduce the moon's gravity by enclosing it in a warp field.

This works, but is cut short when the alien uses the drop in shield power to attack Q again. Data is damaged trying to help Q. The Enterprise nearly enters the planet's atmosphere. While the descent of the moon has been delayed, its orbit remains dangerously unstable. It is only a matter of time before it falls to the planet below.

Although being human is unbearable to him, Q admits that Data is a better human than he is, and, bored with mortality, takes a shuttle to face the energy being and spare the Enterprise further attacks. When Picard tries to get the shuttle back, nothing works on it; unknown to the Enterprise crew, another Q has stepped in.

Amazingly to the Continuum, Q has actually shown something along the lines of genuine selflessness. Q's powers are restored, enabling him to get rid of the energy being. Q returns to the bridge of the Enterprise in triumph, and with a mariachi band to celebrate.

This is the same old Q and Jean-Luc is not amused. Before Q departs, he gives Data a gift in appreciation for helping him. Briefly, Q allows Data to experience laughter. Then Q sets the moon back in a perfect orbit, ending the crises threatening the planet below.

EPISODE SIXTY-TWO: "A MATTER OF PERSPECTIVE"

Written by Ed Zuckerman
Directed by Cliff Boles
Guest Cast: Craig Richard Nelson, Gina Hecht, Mark Margolis

When the Tanuga IV orbiting research station explodes just as Riker beams back to the Enterprise, Commander Riker is accused of the murder of Dr. Nel Apgar. Picard talks Tanuga's Investigator, Crag, into reviewing the case on the Enterprise holodeck. Dr. Apgar had been working on producing Kreeger waves. The Kreeger converter on the station was the focus for an energy generator on the planet's surface, but apparently was not ready.

First Will Riker relates events as he recalls them. He reveals that Apgar resented the Federation's intrusion; he seemed concerned that Riker would block his access to a certain element needed in his research. To further complicate matters, Mrs. Apgar tries to seduce Riker.

When Apgar intrudes on this, he hits his wife and she falls to the floor when Riker sidesteps a blow meant for him. The next day, after Mrs. Apgar and an assistant have beamed down to the planet, Riker returns to the Enterprise. As the hearing goes on, the Enterprise is subjected to periodic bursts of an unknown radiation.

Mrs. Apgar's testifies that Will Riker attempted to seduce her, then tried to force her to do his will. When Apgar intervened, Riker hit him, and warned that charges filed would result in a negative report to the Federation.

Apgar's assistant relates Apgar's version of events as he told it to her. According to Apgar, Riker and his wife seemed equally culpable in their infidelity, and the doctor beat up Riker in his righteous anger.

Since the Enterprise is in Tanugan space, extradition must take place, and evidence to prove Riker's innocence seems nonexistent. But Geordi, Data and Wesley come through with the evidence which breaks the case wide open. Radiation bursts have been occurring at regular intervals; except for a slight time variation. The deadly explosion also occurred at a multiple of this interval.

It turns out that Dr. Apgar succeeded in creating Kreeger waves after all, but he was stalling the Federation in the hopes of developing them into an offensive weapon he could sell to the highest bidder. Riker was a potential threat because he could cut off the supplies Apgar needed. Apgar tried to stage a transporter accident by striking the transport beam with Kreeger waves, but the wave was deflected from Riker's position, which accounted for the time lag, and blew up the reactor core instead.

The radiation plaguing the Enterprise was, in fact, Kreeger waves, converted from the planetary generator by the holodeck's recreation of Apgar's fully functional converter. The investigator from Tanuga remains skeptical until Geordi programs another holodeck program which is timed to coincide with the energy transmission. This program demonstrates precisely how Dr. Apgar accidentally engineered his own demise while attempting to kill Commander Riker. Riker's innocence is proven beyond the shadow of a doubt.

EPISODE SIXTY-THREE: "YESTERDAY'S ENTERPRISE"

Teleplay by Ira Steven Behr, Richard Manning, Hans Beimler and Ronald D. Moore.
From a story by Trent Christopher Ganing and Eric A. Stillwell
Directed by David Carson
Guest Cast: Denise Crosby, Christopher McDonald, Tricia O'Neil

As the story begins, a Federation ship emerges from a temporal rift; as it does so, the timelines shift, and the Enterprise becomes a war vessel. The Federation has been fighting the Klingon Empire for the past twenty-two years.

Tasha Yar is still head of security on the Enterprise as she encountered the creature Armus in "Skin of Evil." Due to the war with the Klingon empire, Worf does not exist in this Enterprise crew.

The other ship which has been discovered coming through the rift is the Enterprise-C, which vanished around the time of the failed peace talks with the Klingons. Guinan somehow knows that none of this is right and tries to convince Captain Picard that the Enterprise-C, damaged by the Romulans, must go back to its own time despite its almost certain destruction. Reluctantly, Picard eventually comes around to this view

The Enterprise-C seems to be a key factor in history, for it was defending a Klingon outpost from a Romulan sneak attack before its trip through time. Had it succeeded, the Klingons may have been impressed by the sacrifice. Picard confides to the other Enterprise's captain, Rachel Garrett, that the war is going badly for the Federation— a war which has already cost four billion lives.

Lieutenant Castillo and Tasha Yar become involved with one another as she works with him on making repairs aboard the Enterprise-C. Due to comments made by Guinan, Tasha becomes increasingly aware that something is wrong with her presence on the ship.

The two Enterprises are soon under attack from a greater Klingon force, as the Enterprise-C prepares to return through the destabilizing rift. But when Captain Garrett is killed, Tasha Yar volunteers to join Castillo on his doomed ship. Tasha is determined that this time her death will mean something.

As the Enterprise-C makes its way to the rift, the outgunned Enterprise-D provides cover for it. Just as the Enterprise-D sustains damage which will destroy the vessel in seconds, the Enterprise-C enters the rift.

Suddenly the timelines are restored. Everything is as it was before and this time Lieutenant Worf reports only a brief fluctuation in the sensor readings of the rift they see. Nothing emerges from it.

Aboard the Enterprise-D, only Guinan retains any knowledge of the alternative reality. In Ten Forward she joins Geordi for a drink and asks him to tell her about Tasha Yar.

EPISODE SIXTY-FOUR: "THE OFFSPRING"

Written by Rene Echeverria
Directed by Jonathan Frakes
Guest Cast: Hallie Todd, Nicolas Coster

Data becomes a father; he has built an android like himself. Lal, a humanoid without distinct features, calls Data 'father' and chooses the form of a young human woman for her permanent appearance.

Picard is concerned that Data made such a bold move without consulting him. Despite this, he takes Data's side when a Starfleet Admiral expresses his intent to remove Lal from Data's care and take her away for study, going so far as to contradict a direct order from the Admiral.

He feels that the Admiral is not recognizing or respecting the rights and liberties that the androids possess as sentient beings in the Federation. Ironies build up: Picard himself has never had children, but the Admiral, who is a father several times, seems, at least outwardly, to be quite heartless in this matter, and promises Picard that his stand may cost him dearly.

Lal is advancing and making great strides as she is gaining both from experience and from a series of neural transfers from Data's brain. There are even indications that she is surpassing her father in some ways. One is her self-developed ability to use contractions in her speech, something Data cannot do. The other change becomes evident when she realizes that the Admiral intends to separate her from her father and the Enterprise.

She runs to Deanna's quarters and reveals that she is actually feeling fear. She has achieved real emotion, but only as her systems begin to fail. Data and the Admiral strive to repair her, but her neural pathways shut down faster than Data can restore them.

Shaken by the experience, the Admiral realizes too late that there was more involved here than mere cybernetic devices. Lal was indeed a daughter to Data, and she had developed the emotions capable of enabling her to both love and feel anguish.

Data informs Lal that he must shut her down permanently; she thanks him for her life, and tells him that she loves him. Data cannot feel love, but certain love is evident in his actions even though he does not realize it. As Lal dies, Data transfers all her memories to his brain so that everything that Lal was will be preserved inside Data's positronic brain.

EPISODE SIXTY-FIVE: "SINS OF THE FATHER"

Teleplay by Ronald D. Moore and W. Reed Moran
From a story by Drew Deighan
Directed by Les Landau
Guest Cast: Charles Cooper, Tony Todd, Patrick Massett, Thelma Lee

A Klingon exchange officer reveals that he is Worf's brother Kurn. When Worf and his parents went to the outpost later destroyed by the Romulans, Kurn was left behind, presumed dead by the Empire but actually raised by another family. He found Worf after all these years because their father has been accused of helping the Romulan's notorious attack, and only the eldest son can challenge charges of treachery in the High Council. Otherwise, the stigma of a traitor will be borne by their family for seven generations. If Worf's challenge fails he will be executed.

When Jean-Luc has Data access all the records of the massacre, they determine that the charges against Worf's father were based on the records of a recently captured Romulan vessel. When Data compares these to the sensor records of the Federation ship Intrepid, which was nearby at the time, he finds a discrepancy in the time codes. The records have been deliberately altered.

On the Klingon homeworld, Worf goes to answer the charges, and is accompanied by Picard and Riker. When Worf's brother is ambushed, he barely escapes with his life. Picard steps in as Worf's "second." The Council sessions seem to offer little hope for Worf's cause until Data also learns that another Klingon, Worf's nurse, survived the massacre as well.

Picard ventures into the heart of the ancient Klingon capitol to find her, only to have her refuse to give any aid. On his way back he is attacked by assassins. He is saved only by the old woman's change of heart, for she stabs the assassin in the back when she catches up with Picard.

Her appearance at the Council throws things into an uproar. The head of the Council calls everyone into his private chambers. Finally the truth is revealed so that it cannot be denied: the father of Worf's accuser was the real traitor. When the Romulan records were seized, this information threatened the entire power structure of the Empire, for the traitor was a member of a very ancient and powerful family. Since Worf, apparently the sole survivor of his line, was away serving in Starfleet, a decision was made to cast the blame on his father. No one believed that he would ever challenge the charges.

The honor of the Klingon Empire outweighs that of any single family, a point that even Worf must agree upon. Worf agrees to undergo discommendation, in effect "de-Klingonizing" himself, for the good of the Empire in order to prevent disgrace from coming down on the High Council and threatening the stability of the Klingon government.

This demonstrates true Klingon honor because it proves Worf's loyalty to the Empire. But one day Worf will demand that his honor be returned to him. In the meantime he is willing to wait and live under the humiliation his family must endure.

EPISODE SIXTY-SIX: "ALLEGIANCE"

Written by Richard Manning and Hans Beimler

Directed by Winrich Kolbe

Guest Cast: Steven Markle, Reiner Schone, Joycelyn O'Brien, Jerry Rector, Jeff Rector

Picard finds himself held captive in a small space with two other humanoids, while an impostor helms the Enterprise.

When the impostor inquires about the nearest pulsar, he sets course for it, and forbids all communication. His irrational actions slowly begin to erode the confidence of the crew. The impostor continues to act in an uncharacteristic fashion by coming on to Beverly Crusher, joining the officers in their poker game, and ordering a round of drinks for everyone in Ten Forward. To make matters worse, he seems intent on taking the Enterprise dangerously close to the pulsar.

Meanwhile, the real Captain Picard is having problems to contend with. When a fourth captive materializes, it turns out to be a large, vicious feline creature from a wild, anarchic planet, and it rejects the food their captors provide. It prefers to kill and eat its own food, but explains that he can go three or four days before his hunger becomes dangerous.

The prisoners begin to question each others' identities: could one of them be an agent of their captors? When Picard's identity is questioned, the Starfleet cadet is quick to confirm it, citing a number of Picard's accomplishments. Picard restores an uneasy balance, and all four of them cooperate in a new escape attempt. This time, the door opens, only to reveal another barrier behind it.

On the Enterprise, Riker takes command when the false Picard endangers the ship by straying so near the pulsar that the shields begin to fail.

Elsewhere, the real Jean-Luc has determined that their captivity is all just an experiment. Picard turns to his fellow captive, a young Starfleet cadet, and suggests that he can confirm this for all of them. The young cadet is actually an alien. Picard pierced his disguise because when the cadet cited one of Jean-Luc's accomplishments, he was discussing a classified mission which could only have been appropriated by reading Picard's mind.

The alien assumes its true form, and is joined by an identical member of its species. Their kind, being identical, have no concept of leadership, authority or power, and have been experimenting by mixing up beings with different attitudes to authority.

With the experiment concluded, the captives are returned to the places they were originally kidnapped from. On the bridge of the Enterprise, Jean-Luc sees his double just before it assumes its true form. But before the aliens can depart, they find themselves imprisoned in a force field. Picard keeps them there just long enough for them to appreciate how unpleasant it is to be held against ones will, and then he releases them so that they can depart and consider what they have just experienced.

EPISODE SIXTY-SEVEN: "CAPTAIN'S HOLIDAY"

Written by Ira Steven Behr
Directed by Chip Chalmers
Guest Cast: Jennifer Hetrick, Karen Landry, Michael Champion, Max Grodenchik

Picard takes a shore leave that is anything but relaxing. A greedy Ferengi, mysterious Vorgons and the beautiful archaeologist/treasure hunter Vash all manage to interrupt his reading of James Joyce's ULYSSES. Picard gets involved in their intrigues, especially when the Vorgons appear and tell him that he is destined to find the Tax Uthat, a powerful device stolen from their future and hidden on Risa. Picard joins Vash on her expedition to the site described on the disc, despite constant problems with the annoying Ferengi. Along the way, romance develops, even though he doesn't really trust Vash.

Upon reaching the archaeological site, the Vorgons appear to watch. The Ferengi treasure hunter pulls a gun and makes Vash and Picard do the digging. When it finally becomes evident that the Uthat is not there, the Vorgons vanish. Unwilling to believe that he's failed, the Ferengi, picks up a shovel and begins to dig for himself, determined not to give up.

Picard finds Vash at the resort preparing to leave. Jean-Luc confronts Vash with his belief that the expedition was all a ruse. He thinks that Vash has had the Tax Uthat all along and just wanted to throw the Ferengi off the track. Knowing she's been outsmarted, Vash shows it to Picard.

Just then the two Vorgons reappear and at gun point demand that they hand the Tax Uthat over to them. Picard questions them, since they, too, might be thieves, perhaps the ones that stole it from the future in the first place. The Vorgons insist that Picard give them the device.

After Jean-Luc puts it on the ground he signals Riker to implement "Transporter Code Fourteen." The device is destroyed before all their eyes. This is just what the Vorgons had hoped to avoid as future history texts record that Jean-Luc Picard was the destroyer of the Tax Uthat. All along their plan had been to prevent Picard from destroying the device, but they failed. They fade away and Picard returns to his command, oddly relaxed by all this adventure.

EPISODE SIXTY-EIGHT: "TIN MAN"

Written by Dennis Putman Bailey and David Bischoff
Directed by Robert Scheerer
Guest Cast: Harry Groener, Michael Cavanaugh, Peter Vogt, Colm Meaney

The Enterprise pick up Betazoid Tam Elbrun, a specialist in first contact. A possibly sentient space ship, nicknamed Tin Man, is circling a near-nova star, and Tam is to try to contact it. Deanna studied Tam at University. Unlike most Betazoids, his mental powers did not develop at adolescence, but were functional at birth, leaving Tam a brilliant but tortured telepath.

He is best known for his involvement in a disastrous first contact where forty-seven Federation lives were lost. Uncomfortable around other humanoids, he seeks out exotic life forms. He becomes intrigued with Data, who he cannot read telepathically.

The Romulans have learned about Tin Man and have dispatched two ships to try and beat the Enterprise there. One of the Romulan ships actually manages to catch to the Enterprise and attacks, damaging the shields. The Enterprise stops for repairs while the Romulan proceeds.

Tam is outraged that the Romulans will succeed in making first contact. When he senses that the Romulans mean to destroy the entity, he warns it, and it destroys the warship in an amazing display of power. Tam is forced to reveal that he has been in contact with the being for quite some time; his powers are greater than ever suspected.

"Tin Man" is thousands of years old, the last of its kind; once it lived symbiotically with a crew of some unknown race, but that crew was destroyed long ago, leaving it alone. It is circling the doomed star in order to end its life.

Picard questions the motives behind Tam's need to beam aboard the entity. He relents when Data volunteers to go along. Once they aboard the Tin Man, Tam reveals that he intends to remain there. Far from any other entities, his mind will be at peace rather than filled with the babble he can otherwise never entirely shut out. Now the only voice he'll hear is Tin Man's.

When a second Romulan vessel attacks, Tin Man hurls both it and the

Enterprise 3.8 billion kilometers away just as the star goes nova. Data had been returned to the Enterprise just before Tin Man hurled it away from the exploding star, but no trace of Tam and Tin Man can be found. They were either destroyed or they escaped into deep space, never to be found again.

EPISODE SIXTY-NINE: "HOLLOW PURSUITS"

Written by Sally Caves
Directed by Cliff Boles
Guest Cast: Dwight Schultz, Charley Lang, Colm Meaney

Diagnostic Engineer Reginald Barclay's fantasies have gotten way out of hand. His holodeck fantasy, which involves berating his superior officers, ends when he is called to duty and he stands revealed as a reclusive, insecure man. He makes others nervous: Wesley has nicknamed him "Broccoli", while Riker wants him transferred.

Picard, however, insists that Geordi try to draw him out. When an anti-gravity unit carrying medical samples from a nearby planet malfunctions, Geordi assigns Barclay to investigate. This attention only serves to make Barclay more nervous.

Geordi gets annoyed when Reginald Barclay is late for his shift and tracks him down to the holodeck. Upon entering the holodeck, Geordi finds Barclay battling three musketeers who resemble Geordi, Data and Picard. Geordi realizes that Barclay has a problem. More engineering problems arise as transporters begin to malfunction. A food replicator reverses the molecular structure of another engineering officer's glass; there seems to be no explanation for these phenomena.

Later, Riker storms to the holodeck looking for Barclay and is furious when he encounters a foolish caricature of himself. Deanna tries to see it as harmless diversion until she meets Barclay's sexy version of her. Barclay is in more trouble, but a new crisis has arisen: the Enterprise has begun to increase its speed and cannot be stopped.

Barclay suggests that all the problems the Enterprise has been experiencing might well be linked. Geordi and Data investigate this and Barclay turns out to be right. When the antigravity unit dropped the medical supplies, two officers were contaminated with a rare substance used in medical containment units on the planet in question. They have been contaminating the Enterprise themselves. The problem is resolved, and Barclay finally has done something worthwhile outside of his fantasies.

EPISODE SEVENTY: "THE MOST TOYS"

Written by Shari Goodhartz
Directed by Timothy Bond
Guest Cast: Jane Daly, Nehemiah Persoff, Saul Rubinek

Space trader Kivas Fajo fakes Data's death, kidnaps him, and adds him to his collection of unique objects. Fajo insists that Data sit in a chair, on display, and that he get rid of his uniform. Data refuses. When Fajo brings a rival collector to see Data, the android assumes an inert position.

Fajo becomes furious, and later threatens to kill one of his own associates if Data does not sit in the chair. Data complies. The woman, who had accompanied Fajo for fourteen years, turns against him because of this, and helps Data escape.

Data has worked out a plan to escape, but they are ruined when Fajo catches them. To demonstrate his anger at Data's escape attempt, Fajo kills the woman who was helping him. The cold ruthlessness of the murder drives Data to turn a disrupter on Fajo. But Fajo is certain that the android will not harm him. Androids won't kill an intelligent being, or so Fajo believes.

Just then the Enterprise arrives, having pierced the scenario which was supposed to make them think Data had been destroyed, and they tracked him down to Fajo's complex. They abruptly beam up Data, but before they can reintegrate him they have to deactivate the disrupter the android was holding. It apparently discharged in transit, or had Data pulled the trigger the moment he was hit with the transporter beam, having intended to kill Fajo? Fajo will never know, and Data doesn't directly address the question himself.

EPISODE SEVENTY-ONE: "SAREK"

Television story and teleplay by Peter S. Beagle
From a story by Mark Cushman and Jake Jacobs
Directed by Les Landau
Guest Cast: Mark Lenard, Joanna Miles, William Denis, Rocco Sisto

When the Legarans finally agree to meet with the Federation, there's only one diplomat for the job: Sarek. Sarek is preceded by two assistants, one human, the other the Vulcan Sakkath, who insist that the Ambassador must rest. Sarek attends a Mozart recital but leaves suddenly when the music moves him to shed a tear.

The crew begins showing signs of tensions, first scattered and on a small scale, but finally culminating in a huge brawl in Ten Forward. Even Riker is punched during the melee. Deanna reports that during the recital she sensed that Ambassador Sarek had lost emotional control, something virtually unheard of for a Vulcan.

Dr. Crusher suspects that Ben Dai Syndrome, a disease affecting Vulcans of advanced age, could be the cause of Sarek's problem. If this is the case, then Sarek's Vulcan telepathy may be the cause of the strange disruptions among the crew. Sarek's human assistant will admit to nothing, but Sakkath tells Data that he has been using his telepathy to help Sarek maintain control.

When Sarek learns that Sakkath has been using his own telepathic abilities to secretly aid the ambassador, he dismisses him and agrees to be tested for Ben Dai syndrome. But Sarek refuses to delay the vital negotiations while they await the test results.

When Picard questions the wisdom of this, Sarek loses his temper, another uncharacteristic action for a Vulcan to indulge. Sarek calms down and sees that something must be done. Picard agrees to a mind meld. Sarek will take Picard's self-control, while Picard will hold the emotional side of the Vulcan's mind.

Sarek is his old self at the negotiations and concludes them successfully. But simultaneous, in his quarters, Picard experiences the awful pressures of Sarek's deep regrets and his long unvoiced love for his first wife Amanda and for his estranged son, Spock.

Finally Sarek returns to his quarters and relieves Picard of his emotional torments. Sarek leaves the Enterprise to return to Vulcan. This has been the ambassador's last hurrah as he now slips into retirement to deal quietly with the disease which is slowly destroying his mind.

EPISODE SEVENTY-TWO: "MÉNAGE À TROI"

Written by Fred Bronson and Susan Sackett
Directed by Robert Legato
Guest Cast: Majel Barrett, Frank Corsentino, Ethan Phillips, Peter Slutsker, Rudolph Willrich, Carel Struycken

Tog, the main Ferengi at a diplomatic reception, is taken with Lwaxana. He kidnaps her, Troi and Riker. Of course, Tog's lust is also fueled by the idea that Lwaxana's telepathy might be of some use in negotiations.

Tog attempts to woo Lwaxana, while Riker and Deanna try to find some way out of the Ferengi brig. Riker kibitzes a chess game two Ferengi are playing, and winds up playing a game, from a distance, with the constant loser. After a while, he gives up, since he can't really see the board. The Ferengi, desperate to win, lets Riker out to continue the match— only to be KO'd.

Lwaxana tries to plays up to the Ferengi captain to distract him while Riker works to access the ship's computer. But without Tog's security code he can't send a transmission. Deanna contacts her mother telepathically, and Lwaxana, who has Tog wrapped around her finger by this point, tries to get the code.

She almost succeeds, but the Ferengi ship's Doctor intrudes at the wrong moment. Tog, embarrassed, allows the Doctor to perform neural scans on Lwaxana's telepathic brain, a procedure which could kill her.

An Away Team investigating the abduction of the two Enterprise officers finds the ugly flowers, which do not grow on Betazed but thrive on the Ferengi homeworld. Picard and crew head off in search of Tog's ship.

Although Commander Riker is unsuccessful at breaking the Ferengi security code, he does comes up with an alternative plan. The Ferengi ship has a warp field phase adjuster, which controls the warp drive's tendency to interfere with subspace transmissions. Riker uses this to set up a repeating pattern in the Ferengi subspace channels.

The Enterprise tracks down the Ferengi ship before Lwaxana can be subjected to the deadly neural scans. As part of a bargain, Lwaxana offers to stay behind if Riker and Deanna are returned to the Enterprise. Tog agrees. When Lwaxana begins going on and on about Jean-Luc being one of her former lovers, Picard picks up on what she's trying to do and begins to play the part.

Tog hastily beams Lwaxana back to Picard. Although Jean-Luc was happy to be able to help Deanna's mother, he wishes that Lwaxana would not express her gratitude in such a grand and grandiose fashion. He's convinced that she loves seeing Captain Picard squirm.

EPISODE SEVENTY-THREE: "TRANSFIGURATIONS"

Written by Rene Echevarria
Directed by Tom Benko
Guest Cast: Mark Lamura, Charles Dennis, Julie Warner

The Enterprise encounters a severely damaged escape pod and rescues the humanoid being inside. Geordi assists in regulating the nervous system of the alien and doesn't notice when a strange light enters his head. Aboard the Enterprise, the alien regains consciousness but appears to be experiencing amnesia. The being heals from his injuries at an amazing rate, but seems to be undergoing additional mutations that are unrelated to his healing process.

Geordi begins acting differently. While before he was shy and almost terminally embarrassed around women, he suddenly begins to exhibit a new found confidence in dealing with the opposite sex. When Data investigates an unknown variety of information storage device found in the wreckage; it seems to use chemical configurations, but resists decoding.

Meanwhile, the amnesiac alien, dubbed John Doe, is beginning to exhibit periodic energy bursts, which cause him great pain and make his body glow. When O'Brien comes into sickbay with a dislocated shoulder, Doe instinctively heals him with a touch of his hand.

Doctor Crusher is very impressed with Doe, and is attracted to him, but his mystery continues until Geordi and Data discover that the information matrix uses memory RNA to store its data. This reveals a navigational chart which enables them to extrapolate Doe's point of origin.

Doe is alarmed at this, for despite his amnesia he knows he must not return to his home. A ship from that area is speeding at high warp to intercept the Enterprise. Doe senses that he is endangering his rescuers, and attempts to steal a shuttle. When Worf tries to stop him, he accidentally falls from a great height and breaks his neck, only to be brought back to life by Doe's healing touch.

When the other vessel intercepts the Enterprise, it is revealed to be crewed by Zalkonians. The Zalkonians claim that the mysterious amnesiac is from their world and is a danger who must be destroyed. Picard refuses to deliver a being who has not been proven to have committed a crime just on the Zalkonians' say so. To do so would be to participate in the alien's death.

It is clear that the Zalkonians fear this being greatly. Finally the facts are revealed. The Zalkonians are actually evolving to another level of existence, a higher life form, but when one of them begins to exhibit the signs of this metamorphosis, they destroy them.

Due to the delays engineered by Picard, the alien named Doe has reached the breakthrough point and undergoes the final metamorphosis into a bodiless being of pure energy. Freed from the confines of a physical body, he chooses to return to his homeworld of Zalkon to reveal the truth to his people. The Zalkons will continue on their metamorphosis in spite of the fear of those who have not yet been touched by the change.

EPISODE SEVENTY-FOUR: "THE BEST OF BOTH WORLDS" (PART ONE)
Written by Michael Piller
Directed by Cliff Bole

Guest Cast: Elizabeth Dennehy, George Murdock

The Enterprise finds a colony and its nine hundred inhabitants missing. A vast crater now exists where the settlement once stood. Admiral Hanson and a Commander Shelby join the Enterprise; they think the Borg are responsible. The Federation is not ready for the Borg.

Commander Shelby, an ambitious woman, is gunning for Riker's first officer chair. Will Riker has been offered his own command for the third time, but chooses to remain on the Enterprise, something that Shelby cannot understand. To her, even the Enterprise is a stepping stone to something greater. Riker and Shelby immediately mix like oil and water.

The Enterprise is contacted when it is confirmed that the Borg has destroyed a Federation vessel. The Enterprise intercepts the Borg ship and hail it. In return the Borg recognize Picard and address him by name. The Borg latches on to the Enterprise with a tractor beam and only just manage to break free. But breaking free and fighting the Borg are two different things. The Borg can adapt quickly to any change in phaser frequency or shield harmonics.

Picard steers the Enterprise into a nebula cloud to avoid the Borg's weapons, but the Borg manage to drive the great starship back out. Another attack ensues, during which several Borg appear on the bridge and kidnap Picard. Once they have him, they ignore the Enterprise and head towards the Earth.

Riker has no choice but to take over command of the Enterprise. He plans to attack the Borg ship with a concentrated phaser burst through the deflector shield. He sends an Away Team commanded by Shelby onto the Borg ship in an attempt to rescue Picard. They fail in this but manage to disrupt the ship's systems and force the Borg to drop out of warp, delaying its journey to Earth. Before they beam back to the Enterprise, they discover that Picard has been transformed into one of the Borg.

Picard now calls himself Locutus of Borg and has been chosen to speak for the Borg collective. Locutus orders the Enterprise to surrender. Instead, Riker prepares the Enterprise to fire on the Borg ship, and if possible to destroy it so that the deadly vessel will never threaten Earth. Worf is given the order to fire. Picard or no Picard, the Borg must be stopped, at any cost.

Talk about a real grand slam of an ending. It was one long, endless summer after this cliffhanger aired!

END OF SEASON THREE

Michael with Levar at the Bonaventure Hotel for Creation Con cast Q&A.

SEASON FOUR

SEASON FOUR

Season four began with the follow-up to the third season's cliffhanger, and set a standard that future two-parters would be hard pressed to live up to. To top that off, the aftermath of the Borg War would form the backdrop to a third episode, "Family," in which various characters used the lull after the storm to pick up the pieces and consider more personal matters.

"Brothers," the sequel to the obvious evil-twin machinations of first season's "Datalore," redeemed the idea of Lore and gave Brent Spiner a chance to really strut his stuff as both androids and their creator, Dr. Soongh.

The Worf family saga would take a tragic turn in "Reunion" and continue in "Redemption."

A real mind-bender was the episode "Future Imperfect." Riker would also play a key role in the classic format-breaker "First Contact." All in all this would be a great season, marred perhaps only by "Night Terrors," a real clunker damaged by cheesy flying effects.

EPISODE SEVENTY-FIVE: "THE BEST OF BOTH WORLDS" PART TWO

Written by Michael Piller
Directed by Cliff Bole
Guest Cast: Elizabeth Dennehy, George Murdock

The attack by the Enterprise on the Borg ship fails. The Borg, having absorbed Picard into their group mind, now possess all of his knowledge and experience, and resume their course to Earth. The Federation assembles an armada of forty of their own starships, in addition to the Klingons. They are even considering contacting the Romulans. Riker receives a field commission, and promises to join the Federation forces as soon as the Enterprise is functional again. Shelby becomes First Officer.

Admiral Hanson contacts the Enterprise, informing them that the Federation fleet has engaged the Borg, and the battle is not going well. His transmission is cut off abruptly. When the Enterprise reaches the battle site, they find a scene of complete devastation. Riker plans to separate the saucer section of the Enterprise for a diversion. While Picard knew of this plan, Riker has altered it considerably, hoping to outwit the memories of his former mentor.

The transporter beams from the Enterprise are being blocked by the Borg so Worf and Data take a shuttle over and use its escape transport to beam onto the Borg ship. Once there they successfully recapture Picard/Locutus. They return to the shuttle, clear the Borg field, and beam back to the Enterprise just before the shuttle is destroyed. The two ship sections reconnect.

The Borg mind is still in contact with Picard/Locutus via a subspace signal. Data creates a neural link via this subspace signal and eventually makes contact with the Borg command system. It is divided into various command subunits, but he cannot access any of the vital areas. The Borg halt their advance towards Earth and attack the Enterprise. Riker orders a last-ditch, warp-speed collision with the Borg ship.

Jean-Luc's personality begins to re-emerges. Semi-conscious, Picard repeats the word "sleep," which Dr. Crusher takes as an expression of fatigue. Data thinks otherwise and finally determines that the Captain is telling them how to stop the Borg. Since the regenerative system is of low priority, easily accessed, and Data uses it to convince the Borg that it is time for a regenerative cycle, effectively putting them all to sleep.

The Borg attack is halted as the Borg shut down. A power feedback caused by this induced malfunction causes the Borg ship to self-destruct. This finally frees Jean-Luc from the Borg sub-space link and allows them to safely remove the Borg machinery from him. The Enterprise returns to the nearest starbase for repairs and Shelby leaves to supervise the task force which will rebuild the fleet and prepare for the next incursion from the Borg.

EPISODE SEVENTY-SIX: "FAMILY"

Written by Ronald D. Moore
Directed by Les Landau
Guest Cast: Jeremy Kemp, Samantha Eggar, Theodore Bikel, Georgia Brown, Dennis Creaghan

Following his harrowing encounter with the Borg, a shaken Jean-Luc Picard returns home to France for the first time in many years. His older brother Robert, is a farmer keeping the family traditions alive. Robert prefers the old family ways and is openly resentful of Jean-Luc for abandoning them.

While Picard is physically recovered from his ordeal, he still has psychological scars to contend with and has chosen to wrestle with these problems by returning home and seeing his brother again. Robert has always regarded Jean-Luc as arrogant and ambitious. This comes out when Jean-Luc arrives at the family estate and meets his young nephew, Rene. The boy remarks that Jean-Luc doesn't look arrogant. When Jean-Luc meets his brother for the first time in nearly twenty years, Robert barely says hello and acts distant and preoccupied.

Over dinner, a small argument develops in which Robert complains that "Life is already too convenient" when the talk of getting a food synthesizer comes up. When Rene remarks that he won a ribbon for his paper on starships, Robert is clearly annoyed. The boy has already remarked to his uncle that some day he's going to be a starship captain, too.

Jean-Luc Picard's old friend Louis visits him; Louis is involved in a project to raise a section of the sea floor for a new sub-continent and believes that Picard would be the ideal man to direct the project. Louis remarks that Jean-Luc was always reaching for the future while Robert was reaching for the past.

The project directors are more than eager to have Jean-Luc lead them. Picard is tempted, but uncertain. On one hand, he is dedicated to Starfleet; on the other, his experience with the Borg has left him uncertain of his ability to go on in any leadership position.

Tensions mount between the Picard brothers when they're talking in Robert's vineyard. Robert had always resented the way Jean-Luc broke every one of their father's rules and got away with it. Jean-Luc had been an athletic hero in high school as well as the school valedictorian and Robert admits that he was jealous.

Robert had earlier asked what had happened to Jean-Luc out there, remarking that he understands that his brother must have been humiliated. "But then I always thought you needed a little humiliation, or a little humility."

They finally get to the bottom of their resentments as Jean-Luc tells Robert that he was a bully and challenges the older man to try and bully him now. Robert lashes out at his brother and a fight erupts. They roll around in the vineyard until they're covered in mud, at which point they break out laughing. Jean-Luc's laughter soon gives way to tears, for he has been unable until now to face the self-doubt raised by the Borg's use of him.

"They took everything I was. They used me to kill and to destroy and I couldn't stop them. I should have been able to stop them! I tried so hard, but I wasn't strong enough. I wasn't good enough. I should've been able to stop them!" Now that his emotions have broken through, he can begin to deal with

them. Robert points out that Jean-Luc will have to live with this for a very long time, whether below the sea with Louis or in space on the Enterprise. Jean-Luc makes his decision and decides to return to command the Enterprise.

As Jean-Luc prepares to return to the Enterprise, young Rene once more expresses his desire to be a starship captain. In Rene, Jean-Luc sees himself when he was a boy; a child whose eyes were always on the stars. Robert has realized this as well and has had to come to terms with the fact that his son will undoubtedly follow in his uncle's footsteps, not his father's. Even after Jean-Luc has left, Rene sits outside staring up at the stars. His mother remarks, "It's getting late." But Robert replies, "Let him dream." Both brothers have come to terms with what the future holds.

EPISODE SEVENTY-SEVEN: "BROTHERS"

Written by Rick Berman
Directed by Rob Bowman
Guest Cast: Cory Danzinger, Adam Ryen, James Lashly

Data seems to undergo a sudden malfunction as he abruptly takes over the Enterprise. He is obviously controlled by some outside force, but no one can stop him as he takes the ship to a distant planet. Once there, he beams down and is restored to normalcy by an old man who reveals himself to be Dr. Noonian Soong, the creator of Data.

Soong, presumed dead, had escaped the crystalline entity and taken refuge on a distant planet, where he has brought Data by means of a homing signal. Sensors on the Enterprise pick up a single life form on the planet below, as well as a space vehicle, with no life signs, approaching.

The shuttlecraft contains Lore, who had drifted in space for two years before being reassembled by traders. The homing beacon Dr. Soong sent out for Data, also brought Lore as Soong did not know that Lore had been reassembled. It turns out that much of what Lore once told Data about their past proves to be lies: Data was built without emotions because that was the one program which went awry with Lore.

Dr. Soong summoned his creation because the cyberneticist has perfected the component that will give Data genuine human emotions, without the side-effects which made Lore so dangerous. Lore, in a fit of jealousy, overpowers Data and dresses in his Starfleet uniform. Thus disguised, Dr. Soong is tricked into implanting the emotional chip into Lore. This causes the already unstable Lore to become completely unbalanced. Lore attacks Dr. Soong, hastening the scientist's demise, and then flees.

When Commander Riker arrives with an Away Team, he reactivates Data, who watches his creator and last chance to acquire genuine human feelings die.

EPISODE SEVENTY-EIGHT: "SUDDENLY HUMAN"

Teleplay by John Whelpley and Jeri Taylor
Story by Ralph Phillips
Directed by Gabrielle Beaumont
Guest Cast: Sherman Howard, Chad Allen, Barbara Townsend

The Enterprise rescues the crew of a disabled Tellerian training ship. This crew consists of five teenaged crew members, one of whom is apparently human. When a genetic scan is done of the boy, it is determined beyond question that he is Jonathan Rossa, whose parents were killed in a Tellerian border war.

Jonathan's grandmother is a Starfleet admiral. But this isn't as simple as it seems. The boy calls himself Jono and he has been fully assimilated into the Tellerian culture. He is scornful of women, and also refuses to remove his gloves to avoid contamination by aliens, such as the crew of the Enterprise.

Picard finds himself forced to assume the role of surrogate father since he is the only human Jono will respond to because he is the highest ranking male on board. Jean-Luc tries to reintroduce Jono to his former culture. This is complicated by the arrival of Jono's adoptive Tellerian father, Captain Endar.

Tricorder scans reveal traces of healed injuries which seem to suggest that Jono may have been abused by his father or other Tellerians. Picard refuses to release the boy to his father until this is explained. This action leads to the danger of renewed conflict with the Tellerian race. Memories of his real parent's death begin to haunt Jono.

He attempts to stab Picard, expecting to be killed for the transgression; death seems the only resolution for his growing dilemma. The wound is superficial and Jean-Luc is relatively unscathed, although it could easily have been as serious as the boy intended it to be.

It is determined that the old injuries were the result of harsh training and childhood accidents, not deliberate brutality. Realizing that Jono is, in essence, no longer a human but a real Tellerian, Picard returns him to his Tellerian father, Endar. Honestly

impressed by Captain Picard, Jono removes his gloves before he departs, and honors the Captain by shaking his hand, the sign of respect for an equal.

EPISODE SEVENTY-NINE: "REMEMBER ME"

Written by Lee Sheldon
Directed by Cliff Bole
Guest Cast: Eric Menyuk, Bill Erwin

Crusher greets Dr. Quaice, her old teacher, who has just come aboard the Enterprise. Then she visits Wesley, who is conducting an experiment with a static warp field. The warp field collapses, and a momentary flash of light appears. Crusher goes to Quaice's quarters to visit him, only to find no trace of him or his belongings.

He is not on the Enterprise, and there is no record of him having ever come aboard. Further investigation reveals no record of him anywhere in the Federation. Could the static warp field have had something to do with this?

Slowly, more and more members of the medical team vanish without a trace, until Crusher is the only medical staff member on board. This seems perfectly normal to the bridge crew, for one doctor should be sufficient for a crew of 230. Crusher protests that the crew should exceed one thousand. But by now her fellow crew members are starting to wonder about her. The crew keeps shrinking, but only she registers this change. A strange vortex threatens her in sick bay, but she resists it.

Worf, Wesley, and the rest of the Enterprise crew vanish, leaving her and Picard alone on the bridge. She is about to say something to him when Jean-Luc abruptly vanishes as well, just before the vortex returns. Resisting its powerful influence, Beverly fights its pull and the vortex disappears again.

Meanwhile, aboard the real Enterprise, Wesley and LaForge are trying to rescue Crusher from the warp field. The Traveler (first seen in the season one episode "Where No One Has Gone Before") appears to help them establish a stable gateway into the field. Dr. Crusher has created the reality within it with her own mind, and must realize her situation and choose to go through the portal in order to escape. The vortexes she fought were Wesley's attempts to rescue her. The Traveler and Wesley try to create another portal, but both of them begin to phase out in the process.

Inside the warp field, Beverly realizes that her universe actually consists of a sphere 705 meters in diameter, and it's collapsing. The truth finally dawns on her. Racing for engineering as her reality vanishes around her, she makes it

to the vortex and leaps into it just as the warp field collapses. Aboard the Enterprise once more, Beverly is reunited with Wesley and her friends, and this time they won't be disappearing on her.

EPISODE EIGHTY: "LEGACY"

Written by Joe Menosky
Directed by Robert Scheerer
Guest Cast: Beth Toussaint, Don Mirault

A Federation freighter sends out a distress signal while orbiting the planet where the late Tasha Yar was born. A world with a violent history, it promises death to any outsiders who land on its surface. The freighter explodes, but its two crew members manage make it to an escape pod, which crashes on the planet's surface.

The Enterprise responds to the distress call and an Away Team beams down but cannot locate the survivors. Instead, they encounter a group called the Coalition, which tells them that the crewmen are being held by their enemies, the Alliance. These two groups have divided the capital city since the government fell, the inhabitants having moved deeper and deeper underground during the lengthy civil conflict. A stalemate exists between the two groups, for all their members have implants which trigger the opposing side's proximity detectors. Conflict is limited to supply raids and minor skirmishes.

The Alliance holds the Federation crewmen as hostages and demand Federation assistance. When the Coalition learns that Tasha Yar had served on the Enterprise, they produce her sister, Ishara, along with an offer to help the Enterprise rescue the crewmen from their enemies.

Ishara feels that Tasha abandoned the struggle on their homeworld, but learns of her valor from the Enterprise crew, especially from Data, who establishes a tentative friendship with Ishara. Ishara even seems interested in following in her sister's footsteps, but her first, (and secret) obligation is to the Coalition.

Doctor Crusher removes Ishara's implant so that she can guide the Away Team to rescue the hostages. The rescue mission is a success, but Ishara then slips away on a private mission of her own. Ishara intends to destroy the Alliance's defense system, which would enable her side to attack without detection.

Data discovers her and discerns her plan. He knows he has to stop her, or the resulting deaths will be on the Federation's hands. Data tracks her down and following a brief standoff, he stuns her and halts the planned sabotage. Data discovers that the phaser Isahara had pointed at him was set to kill.

Picard realizes that they were all misled by their desire for Ishara to be just like their much-missed comrade, Tasha Yar. But now it is clear that Ishara will never have the opportunity to carry on where her valiant sister left off.

EPISODE EIGHTY-ONE: "REUNION"

Teleplay by Thomas Perry and Jo Perry
&
Ronald D. Moore and Brandon Braga
From a story by Drew Deighan and Thomas Perry and Jo Perry
Directed by Jonathan Frakes
Guest Cast: Suzie Plakson, Robert O'Reilly, Patrick Massett, Charles Cooper, Jon Steuer, Michael Rider, April Grace, Basil Wallace, Mirron Edward Willis

Worf has another encounter with K'Ehleyr, who has some news of great interest. The leader of the Klingon High Council is dying and wants Picard to discover which of the contenders for his position has been poisoning him. K'Ehleyr also has a surprise for Worf: their first encounter years before produced a son, Alexander. K'Ehleyr is now willing to make the marriage vows she earlier declined, but Worf resists because of his discommendation.

The arriving Klingon contenders for the throne discover that Picard has been chosen by their leader as the arbitrator, who determines the challenger's right to battle for the ascension. At the preliminary ritual, a bomb goes off, killing two Klingon aides. Picard delays further ceremonies by insisting on an archaic ritual which demands a long recitation of the challengers' accomplishments, a ritual which could take hours or days.

It turns out that the bomb used is a type which is of Romulan origin, and that it was implanted in the forearm of the aide of one of the challengers: Worf's old enemy, the Klingon responsible for Worf's family dishonor. It seems that he, like his father, is a traitor, doing business with the Romulans.

As this goes on, K'Ehleyr tries to discover the reasons for Worf's discommendation, which neither Worf nor Picard will reveal to her. She manages to put together the truth, but is discovered and killed by the traitor. Worf discovers her body and beams over to the Klingon's ship, claiming right of revenge.

His claim is questioned until he reveals that K'Ehleyr was his mate. Worf fights his enemy to the death, triumphing over him seconds before a security teams arrives to escort him back to the Enterprise. (Apparently, right of vengeance outweighs dishonor in Klingon ethics.)

Worf's action finds approval with the Klingon High Council since the Klingon he killed was revealed as a traitor. Picard is not so approving and will put his remarks as a reprimand on Worf's record but exact no other punishment. Although his enemy is dead, Worf still has to keep secret the truth behind his discommendation until the time comes when he can force the Klingon High Council to give him back his honor.

EPISODE EIGHTY-TWO: "FUTURE IMPERFECT"

Written by J. Larry Carroll and David Bennett Carren
Directed by Les Landau
Guest Cast: Andreas Katsulas, Chris Demetral, Carolyn McCormick, Patti Yasutake, Todd Merrill, April Grace, George O'Hanlon, Jr.

Riker regains consciousness in sick bay after a hazardous Away Team mission. Dr. Crusher addresses him as "Captain." It seems that he was infected by a virus when he beamed down, a virus that lay dormant for sixteen years and then wiped out all of his memories dating back to the time of the original infection. A bearded Admiral Picard boards the Enterprise, informing Riker that he is the key man in peace negotiations with the Romulans, and must proceed in that capacity despite his amnesia.

There are other surprising changes as well: Ferengi have joined the crew, LaForge has cloned eye implants instead of his VISOR, and Riker has a son named Jean-Luc! Riker is uneasy in these circumstances. The computer seems to be operating slowly, Riker still can't play "Misty" on his trombone and something always distracts him when he tries to find out who his wife was. When he finally manages to access visual records, Riker learns that his wife was Minuet, who was never a real person and who only existed as a hologram program.

Riker confronts Picard and the Romulan ambassador on the bridge. In the face of his realization, the Romulan reveals that it was all a holodeck-type simulation using neural scanners to read Riker's mind. The Romulans are surprised to learn the truth about Minuet, for Riker's emotions regarding her seemed quite real.

The Romulans put Riker into a cell with a captured Earth boy, Ethan, who they'd used as Riker's "son." Ethan helps Riker get away, but strange discrepancies begin to creep into this reality. Ethan refers to the Romulan commander as an ambassador. When Riker questions this slip, the Romulans recapture him, but he ignores them, having realized that the boy is the one responsible for the illusions he's experienced. The illusions all have one common factor—the boy.

The Romulans and all their trappings vanish, revealing a barren cavern. The boy is actually an alien whose mother concealed him there years before when their race was about to be destroyed. Neural scanners in the cavern walls have provided him with everything he needed, but he tricked Riker so that he could have some real company to ease his loneliness. Riker explains that he needn't hide in the cave from enemies any more and they both beam up to the Enterprise.

EPISODE EIGHTY-THREE: "FINAL MISSION"

Teleplay by Kacey Arnold-Ince and Jeri Taylor
Story by Kacey Arnold-Ince
Directed by Corey Allen
Guest Cast: Nick Tate, Kim Hamilton, Mary Kohnert

When Wesley is accepted to Starfleet Academy, Picard takes him along on one final mission when he goes to negotiate a dispute on a mining colony. Picard and Wesley board a mining shuttle owned by a colorful old pilot and head toward their destination. The ramshackle vessel loses a thruster and goes out of control, crash-landing on a moon of the mining planet.

Picard and Wesley are stranded with the shuttle pilot on the barren desert world with no food or water. Tricorder readings indicate magnetic field fluctuations in a nearby mountain range, so they head toward it, leaving an arrow on the ground to indicate their direction.

Meanwhile, the Enterprise discovers that Gamilon V's gravitational field has captured a 300-year-old space barge filled with radioactive wastes which threaten the population of the planet. LaForge uses remote construction modules to attach thrusters to the barge in order to steer it into the system's sun, but the barge begins to break up, and the Enterprise must tow it with a tractor beam, through an asteroid belt, while radiation levels on the ship approach lethal levels.

Following a journey through the desert, they reach the mountains, and the shelter of a cavern which has a fountain of water inside. Unfortunately, a force field prevents them from reaching the water. But the shuttle pilot is desperate for water and becomes irrational, firing on the force field with his phaser, which causes a cave-in which seriously injures Jean-Luc. Further attempts to pierce the force field unleash an electromagnetic "sentry" which kills the pilot.

Wesley eventually rewires his phaser, tricorder and communicator into a device which overrides the sentry mechanisms, enabling him to reach the life giving water. A short time later an Away Team arrives to rescue them as the Enterprise has returned from its emergency mission to Gamilon V.

EPISODE EIGHTY-FOUR: "THE LOSS"

Teleplay by Hilary J. Bader and Alan J. Adler and Vanessa Greene
Story by Hilary J. Bader
Directed by Chip Chalmers
Guest Cast: Kim Braden, Mary Kohnert

The Enterprise cannot change course, and is being pulled slowly along by an unknown force. Troi realizes that she has lost her empathic powers, which for a Betazoid is like going blind. Data attempts to analyze the strange malfunctions. He discovers that they are caught in a field of two-dimensional particles, which may be sentient, although there seems no way to determine this. An attempted overload jump to warp speed fails to free the Enterprise. They, and the particle cluster, are headed inexorably toward the gravitational field of a cosmic string fragment.

Troi resigns as ship's counselor when she realizes she can no longer adequately serve her patients. Without her ability she cannot really tell what they are feeling. She re-evaluates these feelings when a current patient turns out to have made an important breakthrough in her last session: Troi's intelligence and experience are just as vital and important as her empathic ability.

Deanna determines that if the mysterious cluster is sentient, it might be going toward the string fragment by choice, unaware that it is pulling the Enterprise along with it. Data arranges to have the ship's deflector dish set up a vibrational echo of the string fragment which is behind the Enterprise. This succeeds in confusing the cluster long enough for the Enterprise to break free. Once the Enterprise is free of the cluster, Troi's powers return as they were just being suppressed by the presence of the cluster.

EPISODE EIGHTY-FIVE: "DATA'S DAY"

Teleplay by Harold Apter and Ronald D. Moore
Story by Harold Apter
Directed by Robert Wiemer

Guest Cast: Rosalind Chao, Sierra Pecheur, Alan Scarfe

Data sends Commander Maddox a letter describing a typical day aboard the Enterprise in order to help him better understand what life for the android is like. On this particular day, Data is scheduled to stand in for the father of the bride in the wedding of Keiko to Chief O'Brien. When Keiko calls the wedding off, Data misgauges the effect that the news will have on O'Brien.

The android also has a long way to go in learning the use of friendly jibes and insults, although he does not offend LaForge when he calls him 'a lunkhead.' When LaForge assures him that Keiko will change her mind again, Data resumes his preparations for the wedding, and arranges for Doctor Crusher to give him dancing lessons, since her records indicate that she won a dance competition many years earlier. It is also revealed that Data keeps a pet cat, named Spot, in his quarters.

Meanwhile, Vulcan Ambassador T'Pel, who is on a mission of utmost secrecy, beams aboard the Enterprise to meet with Captain Picard. Her mission will take them into the Neutral Zone. The Ambassador questions Data about the Enterprise's security. Although she has the correct clearance codes, he tells her he must inform Picard. T'Pel abruptly withdraws the question, claiming that is was merely a test of his own security precautions.

When a Romulan warbird arrives at predetermined coordinates, T'Pel beams over to begin secret negotiations. But this is terminated when a mysterious transporter malfunction apparently results in T'Pel's death, leaving only minute organic traces on the transporter pad.

The Enterprise departs, but investigations reveal that the traces do not correspond with the records from when T'Pel beamed aboard. The Romulans somehow managed to alter their own transporters to fake T'Pel's death.

Picard chases down the Romulan ship and demands the return of the ambassador. But to his surprise Picard learns that T'Pel was not a Vulcan after all, but a Romulan spy. The Enterprise returns to Federation space.

The wedding of Keiko and Chief O'Brien goes on as planned in a traditional Japanese ceremony officiated by Captain Picard. Data has learned more about humans on this particular day, but he also now has more questions he'll need answered about human nature and its many strange and contradictory facets.

EPISODE EIGHTY-SIX: "THE WOUNDED"
Teleplay by Jeri Taylor

Story by Stuart Charno, Sara Charno and Cy Chernak
Directed by Chip Chalmers
Guest Cast: Bob Gunton, Rosalind Chao, Mark Alaimo, Marco Rodriguez, Time Winters, John Hancock

Picard is informed that the peace treaty with the Cardassians has been broken by the Federation ship Phoenix, commanded by Ben Maxwell. Maxwell has been out of communication for some time, and is apparently acting on his own initiative: the Phoenix destroyed a Cardassian science station without provocation. The Federation orders Picard to investigate, and to take a Cardassian team aboard as observers.

This brings up bitter memories for Chief O'Brien. O'Brien served with Maxwell during the Cardassian conflict and knows what the man went through. Maxwell lost his family in a border skirmish, which may account for his actions, while O'Brien recalls a battle in which he killed a Cardassian to save his own life. O'Brien finds it difficult to deal with Cardassians, not because he hates them, but because they remind him of his only act of aggression against another living being.

The Enterprise's sensors locate the Phoenix but not soon enough to prevent it from destroying another Cardassian warship and freighter. Pursuing the Phoenix at high speed, the

Jonathan alongside his captain, Patrick, at Paramount Studios for the Roddenberry dedication in honor of STAR TREK's 25th Anniversary.

Photo © 1994 Albert L. Ortega

Denise at
the Saturn
Awards
for
Science
Fiction.

Photo ©
1994
Albert L.
Ortega

Enterprise catches up and discovers that Maxwell believes the Cardassians to be re-arming. He agrees to return to Federation space, and Picard allows him to keep command of the Phoenix. Maxwell soon breaks away and heads toward another Cardassian freighter.

If Picard will not board the freighter and see that Maxwell is right, then Maxwell will fire upon it. Picard in turn threatens to use force against the Phoenix.

Picard agrees to allow Miles O'Brien to beam over and act as an intermediary between Picard and the rogue commander, assuming O'Brien can get through Maxwell's shields. O'Brien uses his expertise to beam over through a cyclic break in the Phoenix's shields, and talks to Captain Maxwell, reviewing their past together and showing him the error of his ways. Even if Maxwell is right about everything he says, he dealt with it in the wrong way. Sadly, Maxwell surrenders, ready to face Federation justice.

When the Cardassian captain thanks Picard, Jean-Luc states flatly that he believes Maxwell's claims, but acted as he did to preserve the peace. Picard warns the Cardassian that the Federation will be keeping an eye on them and that it would not be in their best interest to be preparing for another war.

EPISODE EIGHTY-SEVEN: "DEVIL'S DUE"

Teleplay by Philip Lazebenik
Story by Philip Lazebenik and William Douglas Lansford
Directed by Tom Benko
Guest Cast: Marta Dubois, Paul Lambert, Marcelo Tubert, William Glover, Thad Lamey, Tom Magee

The people of Ventax 2 believe that an impending apocalypse is about to occur. They are experiencing earthquakes and other signs, as predicted in the Legend of Ardra, a thousand-year-old document which seems to be a contract which promised a thousand years of peace in exchange for the ownership of the planet and its people.

Oddly enough, this world has enjoyed an idyllic millennium, which was preceded by a period of great strife. Ardra, their equivalent of the Devil, is a legendary figure credited with bringing this change about— but now the contract is up and the superstitious fears of many people are reacting to the current crisis.

Jean-Luc doesn't believe that a one thousand year old legend could really have returned to threaten the planet and intends to get to the bottom of this mystery. Picard beams down to negotiate the release of the science team, who are being held hostage, but the government is in hysterics.

When a beautiful woman appears in a burst of energy and claims to be Ardra, Picard is not impressed, but she does demonstrate remarkable powers. She can alter her shape at will, becoming various creatures, including a Klingon demon and Earth's Devil. The Away Team beams up, leaving Data behind to study the ancient contract.

Jean-Luc wonders if Ardra could be another renegade Q from the Continuum. Suddenly Ardra appears in the Enterprise bridge. She cannot be removed, even by transporter beam, and she keeps returning. Data informs the Captain that the contract is in complete accordance with the Ventaxian law, and cedes to Ardra everything on land, sea, air— or in orbit. Ardra claims the Enterprise is hers under the contract, and vanishes.

Picard is convinced that Ardra is nothing more than a cosmic con artist, and he intends to outsmart her. He arranges for arbitration, and Ardra, confident, agrees, with Data as the arbitrator. If Picard cannot disprove Ardra's claim, she wins him. The case seems to go against Picard, as Ardra demonstrates her various powers. Picard cannot explain them, particularly when she apparently causes the Enterprise to vanish.

Picard argues that the social changes on Ventax Two took place gradually, which is proven by the historical record. After the contract was signed, the legendary Ardra left, and did not oversee any of the reforms that took generations to heal Ventax's ecological and social problems. Even this pressing argument seems to fail, until Picard learns that LaForge has located a ship, cloaked with a copy of a Romulan device; the Enterprise was merely concealed by a shield extension, and is right where it should be.

Jean-Luc disputes Ardra's claim by "stealing" her powers. He seemingly creates minor earth tremors on command, changes shape, and causes Ardra to vanish. Picard proves that this so-called thousand year old legend is, as he suspected, a con artist. An Away Team has taken over her ship, is in control of her device and is able to give Picard her "powers," which involve the use of transporters, tractor beams and other existing technologies to trick the Ventaxians. "Ardra" tries to make a deal, but she has nothing to deal with as she's arrested and taken away.

EPISODE EIGHTY-EIGHT: "CLUES"

Teleplay by Bruce D. Arthurs and Joe Menosky
Story by Bruce D. Arthurs
Directed by Les Landau

Guest Cast: Pamela Winslow, Rhonda Aldrich, Patti Yasutake, Thomas Knickerbocker

The Enterprise detects a Class-M planet with a wormhole-like energy fluctuation nearby. Just as the ship enters the wormhole, everyone on board but Data falls to the floor unconscious.

The crew regains consciousness and find that the wormhole has apparently taken them one day's distance from their previous location in a matter of seconds. Still, peculiar things have happened. Moss cultures begun by Crusher have undergone 24 hours worth of growth. Could the wormhole have had some strange effect on them? Picard sends a probe back to the planet, but it is no longer a Class-M world. It is now completely inhospitable.

Picard wonders if 24 hours have elapsed. If so, then Data is lying— but why? Did they go through the wormhole? Bio-scans, compared with Transporter traces, reveal that the crew's cellular functions do not correspond with a lapse of a thirty seconds, but make perfect sense if 24 hours have passed. On the other hand, no one has any beard growth.

The computer chronometer seems to have been tampered with. Only LaForge and Data could have changed it, and only Data was functional during the lost time. Examinations reveal noth-

ing wrong with the android officer, but Picard is suspicious of him. Perhaps Data even rigged the probe to send back a false image. Troi feels dizzy for a moment, and is disoriented by her own mirror reflection. She seemed to sense an alien presence in it.

Worf turns out to have broken his arm and to have had it reset, all in the past 24 hours, but he has no memory of it. LaForge discovers that the probe was programmed to send back a library image of another world. When confronted, Data says he can neither confirm or deny anything.

He cannot say what happened, but does not deny that he did anything. A new probe confirms the original sighting of a Class-M planet, and no evidence of a wormhole. Data will not reveal anything, so Picard heads back to the planet, armed and ready.

When they reach their original destination, a green energy field enters the Enterprise and possesses Troi. In a powerful alien voice, Troi tells Data that the plan failed. Data tells Picard that they must leave immediately, but the captain refuses. He demands that Data reveal who ordered him to cover up the events of the missing day. Data reveals that the order was given by Picard himself.

It seems that the planet is occupied by a reclusive, xenophobic race that wishes to keep its existence secret. The "wormhole" was a trap which induces a biochemical stasis and diverts any ships from discovering the secretive beings.

Data, not being biological, instituted emergency automatic defense procedures and revived the crew. The alien presence occupied Troi, and broke Worf's arm when he tried to intervene. Crusher reset the injury. When the alien explained its wishes, Picard suggested that it suppress their memories, and ordered Data to reset the chronometer, and to never reveal the truth to anyone.

The aliens now feel that they must destroy the Enterprise to preserve their secrecy. Jean-Luc states that their curiosity was aroused by the various clues left behind, and suggests that the aliens remove all traces and reminders of their passing. The aliens agree, and the entire process is repeated. Once again the Enterprise crew awaken on the other side of a small wormhole, but this time no one but Data knows that the Enterprise faced death twice, and escaped it.

EPISODE EIGHTY-NINE: "FIRST CONTACT"

Teleplay by Dennis Russell Bailey, David Bischoff, Joe Menosky, Ronald D. Moore and Michael Piller
From a story by Marc Scott Zicree

Directed by Cliff Bole
Guest Cast: George Coe, Carolyn Seymour, George Hearn, Michael Ensign, Steven Anderson, Sachi Parker, Bebe Neuwirth

Riker has been surgically altered to resemble a Malkorian and sent down to the planet to secretly study them. The Federation is interested in Malkorian society as it is on the verge of achieving interstellar flight. But when Riker is injured in a freak accident, he's taken to a hospital where he physicians discover that he's an alien. Although this is kept a secret from the public, it sends shockwaves through the government which had been unaware that there is life on other worlds.

Riker tries to explain away his anatomical differences by stating that they're hereditary defects, and that his phaser is a toy for a neighbor's child. But his story doesn't fly and Riker is kept in a security ward while the Malkorian government investigates the matter.

Picard decides to confront the problem head on and beams down with Troi to introduce himself to the Malkorian Science Minister, Mirasta. She is a forward-looking woman who is largely responsible for her world's great leaps towards warp technology. Mirasta is indeed open minded, and willingly visits the Enterprise. She explains that many are not like her as the Malkorian culture tends to be very conservative and ethnocentric, believing themselves to be the center of the universe. The planetary Chancellor is fair-minded if cautious, but the Security Minister, Krola, is a fanatic about his traditional way of life.

When Mirasta and Picard beam down to the Chancellor's office, he is skeptical of the Federation's aims, although Picard does win his grudging respect. On Mirasta's advice, however, he does not mention the covert survey teams. The Chancellor is beamed up to the Enterprise, where he and Picard share a toast with the wine given Picard by his brother on his last visit to Earth. Still, the Chancellor is uncertain what to do. Later, when he learns about Riker and the covert operation, he is very disturbed by its implications and the specter of invasion it raises.

Lanel, who is fascinated by the concept of aliens, offers to help Riker escape—if he will make love to her—making love with an alien has long been her fantasy! Afterwards, when Riker tries to slip out of the hospital, he is detected, and attacked by a frightened crowd. He suffers kidney damage and internal bleeding, and is taken into intensive care, where the doctor struggles to help him.

The Security Minister, Krola, arranges to be alone with Riker when he awakens. Krola has figured out how to operate the phaser, and places it in Riker's weakened hand, intending to kill himself while making it look like murder. Krola's death will put an end to any notion of contact with aliens. Riker struggles to keep the phaser from firing, but Krola succeeds in triggering it, and is blasted across the room.

The discharge of the phaser allows the Enterprise a get a fix on Riker's position. Dr. Crusher beams down to the hospital in time to save both Riker and Krola, who did not realize that the phaser was only set on stun. Krola awakens in the Enterprise's sick bay.

Krola's plan is deduced by the Chancellor who chides him for such a foolish undertaking. And yet this proves to him that his people are not yet ready to make contact with other worlds. The Chancellor regretfully asks Picard to leave his world and not to return. The entire incident will be covered up, and funds will be diverted from technology to education in order to help eradicate ancient prejudices.

Mirasta, who has long dreamed of space travel, asks to be taken with Picard aboard the Enterprise. He and the Chancellor agree, since she would now be subject to too many restrictions on her home world, both because of what she knows, and because funding for her technological research into space flight will be cut off. On the Enterprise, Mirasta prepares to be the first of her people to explore space—a dream she never expected to come true this soon, or in this way.

EPISODE NINETY: "GALAXY'S CHILD"

Teleplay by Maurice Hurley
Story by Thomas Kartozian
Directed by Winrich Kolbe
Guest Cast: Susan Gibney, Lanei Chapman, Jana Marie Hupp, April Grace

LaForge is happy to learn that they are taking on an important passenger: Dr. Leah Brahms, who LaForge "met" as a holographic projection in "Booby Trap." His expectations are dashed by the real article, however, for Brahms is angry about LaForge's altered specifications. They don't get along too well, and LaForge finds himself on the defensive as Brahms examines his work.

She is alarmed to find some design changes already planned for the next class of starship, not realizing that LaForge had devised them by collaborating with "her." LaForge tries to start over by inviting her to dinner. She relaxes somewhat, but is put off by LaForge's

attentiveness. He is surprised to learn that she is married.

Meanwhile, the Enterprise finds a creature that lives in the vacuum of space. When the Enterprise probes it, it responds with a probe of its own, and then attacks the starship. A low-level phaser blast, intended in self-defense, kills the creature. Soon, however, new energy readings are detected in the body: apparently, it was about to give birth, and the baby is still alive. With Dr. Crusher's guidance, the Enterprise uses a phaser beam to help the creature get out of its parent's body.

When the Enterprise leaves, the baby follows, having imprinted on the ship. It thinks that the Enterprise is its mother and what's more, the creature feeds on energy, attaches itself to the hull and begins to drain power. Data extrapolates the parent creature's course, which leads them to an asteroid belt inhabited by more of the creatures, but the attempt to dislodge the baby from the Enterprise fails.

Leah Brahms becomes intrigued by Geordi's work and examines his records— including the holodeck program. When LaForge realizes she is doing this, he rushes to the holodeck, but he's too late. A furious Dr. Brahms is standing face to face with her own holographic image. She feels as if her privacy has been violated, and, despite

LaForge's protestations, wonders just how far he went with her simulation. Following much debate and discussion they arrive at an understanding as Geordi explains himself.

Leah and LaForge come up with a means of "weaning" the space infant. They alter the vibrations of the ship's power, in essence "souring the milk." Finally the creature detaches and joins the adults of its species, which were on the verge of attacking the Enterprise. As a result Geordi has become friends with the real Leah Brahms whose hologram once helped him save the Enterprise.

EPISODE NINETY-ONE: "NIGHT TERRORS"

Teleplay by Pamela Douglas and Jeri Taylor
Story by Shari Goodhartz
Directed by Les Landau
Guest Cast: Rosalind Chao, John Vickery, Duke Moosekian, Craig Hurley, Brian Tochi, Lanei Chapman, Deborah Taylor

Troi has strange dreams in which she drifts in a dark cloudy vortex. The lights shine in the distance, and the phrase "eyes in the dark" is repeated. The rest of the crew also begins to have odd experiences. Chief O'Brien becomes convinced that Keiko is cheating on him, for no good reason.

Picard hears his door signal chime repeatedly, only to find no one at the waiting to enter. Crusher and Troi visit him, but must knock on his door before he realizes that they're there. Crusher fears that the Enterprise is starting to experience the same problems that recently beset the Brittain. Picard orders the ship to clear the area, only to find that they cannot. They are adrift.

Finally they determine that the Enterprise is trapped in a rift in space which is draining the ship's energy. No one on board has had any dreams for the past ten days, except for Troi, who is afflicted by the same nightmares over and over. Data, who does not sleep, is the only one unaffected. Hallucinations begin to crop up: Picard is assaulted by a renegade turbolift, Riker finds snakes in his bed, and Crusher is menaced by the corpses of the Brittain's crew in the autopsy room.

The lack of REM sleep is causing a chemical imbalance which threatens to drive everyone insane. Worf, unable to cope with an invisible enemy he cannot attack, attempts Klingon ritual suicide, but is stopped by Troi. Data finally takes command of the ship when Jean-Luc makes the decision that neither he nor any of the crew can can be trusted to adequately do the job any longer.

Troi realizes that the dream she's having is in reality a telepathic message, perhaps from a ship on the other side of the space rift. The transmission is what is blocking everyone else's ability to dream. She can pick it up because her Betazoid brain works on a different frequency.

"Eyes in the dark" seems to indicate the nearby binary star. Data realizes that the binary star resembles a model of the hydrogen atom. Hydrogen can trigger a violent explosion with a rare element, but does the other ship have hydrogen, or do they need it? And, can Troi signal them back at the right time? The crew is going crazy, and a brawl in Ten Forward is averted only when Guinan pulls a vicious looking weapon from behind the bar and fires a warning shot.

Finally Troi enters electrically induced REM sleep and signals "now" to the other craft, as the Enterprise releases hydrogen gas into the rift. The explosion caused by jettisoning the gas sets free both the Enterprise and the unknown ship on the other side of the rift.

EPISODE NINETY-TWO: "IDENTITY CRISIS"

Teleplay by Brannon Braga
Story by Timothy De Haas
Directed by Winrich Kolbe

Guest Cast: Maryann Plunkett, Patti Yasutake, Amick Byram, Dennis Madalone, Mona Grudt

Geordi investigates the disappearance of a science team. Tattered Starfleet uniforms and strange alien footprints are the only clues to be found. Worf senses that they are being watched, but their instruments cannot sense any life forms on the planet. LaForge stops Susannah from wandering off; she is acting strangely, and insists that their former companions are alive, and nearby. Back in sick bay, tests reveal that her blood chemistry has gone completely haywire, and she seems obsessed with returning to the planet.

Tests reveal alien skin cells on the torn up uniforms, but the footprints match no known species. LaForge and Susannah review the Victory tapes, but the light from the view screen hurts her eyes, and she collapses. Her hands seem to be fusing, and her skin develops blue veins: the changes match the alien cells. She is taken to sick bay, and it seems that she is changing into another species. The cause of this metamorphosis baffles Dr. Crusher.

LaForge has the computer recreate the Away Team visual records on the holodeck, and isolates a shadow that doesn't belong to anyone from the Victory team. Extrapolating its source, he discovers that some sort of humanoid was nearby all along.

Susannah's changes continue. Her skin can simulate light, and her body seems to generate a disruptive field which interferes with instrument readings. Crusher finally locates a parasite in Susannah's thymus gland, a parasite which uses the immune system to spread genetic instructions. The parasite is removed surgically, but it is up to Susannah's own system to heal itself.

Meanwhile, LaForge has undergone the same mysterious transformation and transports down to the planet. Data rigs an emergency beacon to the Ultra-violet range, which might be able to "see" the aliens. An Away Team beams down to LaForge's Transporter coordinates, taking the recovering Susannah along at her own insistence.

The UV light reveals the humanoid forms as glowing blue outlines. The others are too far gone for help, but LaForge is still partially human, but afraid to come back. Susannah manages to coax Geordi into trusting her, perhaps because the change in him is not so far gone. Geordi is saved and returned to normal after the alien parasite is removed from him in an operation.

EPISODE NINETY-THREE: "THE NTH DEGREE"

Written by Joe Menosky
Directed by Robert Legato

Guest Cast: Dwight Schultz, Jim Norton, Kay E. Kuter, Saxon Trainor, Page Leong, David Coburn

LaForge takes Barclay along in a shuttlecraft to investigate a mysterious probe. The alien probe is resistant to all scans until they try a positron beam, which triggers a blast of light from the device. The shuttle computers are disabled, and Barclay is knocked out, while LaForge's VISOR protects him from the blast. LaForge returns to the ship, and the probe begins to follow. Although Reginald Barclay seems to be all right, he begins to suggest new medical techniques to Crusher which are clearly out of his field.

The probe is following on a collision course with the Enterprise, and is emitting an unknown but threatening field. It also matches the ship's speed, resists phasers, and remains too close to the ship to make a photon attack feasible. Barclay suddenly takes charge in engineering without consulting with anyone. The Enterprise drops to impulse power when he uses the warp field generator to boost shield power 300 per cent, which makes it safe to hit the probe with photon torpedoes despite its close range. The probe is destroyed and the Enterprise is saved.

The reason for Barclay's new and amazing abilities is that his brain has increased its production of neurotransmitters by 500 per cent, and the two hemispheres of his brain seem to be acting as a single unit. With an IQ between 1200 and 1450, he may be the smartest human who ever lived. This bothers the Captain, but Barclay has done nothing wrong, so all Picard can do is keep an eye on him.

In saving the Enterprise from the explosion, Barclay links his mind with the computer, and stays linked with it after the crisis has passed. Most of his higher brain functions and memories have expanded into the computer core. Any attempt to return these functions to his physical brain would be fatal.

Barclay begins to see the universe as a single, simple equation, and sees how the ship's speed can go far beyond warp. His intentions are completely in line with the Enterprise's mission, but Picard doesn't like the idea much.

Barclay begins to create a subspace distortion which pulls the ship into it. The distortion is intense, but eventually ends, and the Enterprise winds up in the center of the galaxy, some thirty-thousand light years from where it started. Suddenly, the computer returns to normal, and the huge image of an old man's head appears on the bridge, looking over the crew with a quizzical expression.

Reginald Barclay, no longer part of the computer, returns to the bridge and

explains. The Cytherians have the same basic mission as the Enterprise, except that they stay at home and bring other entities to them for an exchange of information. Their probes were meant to instruct other beings how to reach them, and Barclay wound up as their instrument, and was returned to normal once he'd brought the ship to them.

After remaining in Cytherian space for a time for the purpose of data exchange, the Enterprise returns to familiar space. Barclay muses on the experience he had. To his surprise, Troi takes Reginald up on an earlier offer he made of a walk through the trees, an offer he nervously accepts. Everything is back to normal.

EPISODE NINETY-FOUR: "QPID"

Teleplay by Ira Steven Behr
Story by Randee Russell and Ira Steven Behr
Directed by Cliff Bole
Guest Cast: Jennifer Hetrick, Clive Revill, John deLancie, Joi Staton

In orbit around Tagus 3, the Enterprise is the site of an archeology symposium. Jean-Luc is nervous about his keynote speech, but Troi assures him that it'll be fine. Upon returning to his quarters, Jean-Luc is amazed to find Vash waiting for him. The last time he saw her was on Rysa, and happily he picks up their affair where they left off.

When Beverly Crusher drops in for tea the next morning, she encounters Vash there with Picard. While Jean-Luc told Vash all about his crew, he didn't tell his crew about her. Dr. Crusher takes Vash on a tour of the Enterprise. She recognizes Riker from Picard's impression of him, when the First Officer tries his charm on her, but once again learns that Picard has not talked about her to his friends. By the time of the official reception, she is very annoyed, and accuses Picard of being embarrassed by her. (Worf notes that she has nice legs— "for a human.")

When Jean-Luc goes to his office, he finds Q at his desk. This is not a pleasant surprise. Q is keen on helping Picard in some way, since he owes him a favor from their last encounter and wants to free himself of the obligation as soon as he can. Picard tells him to forget it, but the mischievous Q won't take no for an answer, and vanishes.

When Jean-Luc starts to deliver his speech to the archeology symposium, Q interrupts by changing the costumes of the executive staff, culminating in Picard's refurbishment in a Robin Hood outfit complete with mustache and goatee. Then everyone disappears only to reappear in an Earth-like forest. Clearly, they are meant to be Robin and

his band, even though Worf is adamant that he is "not a merry man!" Riker is Little John, Data is Friar Tuck, and LaForge is the minstrel Alan A-Dale.

Worf is injured with an arrow when they are attacked by Sir Guy of Gisbourne. Q appears on horseback, having taken the role of the Sheriff of Nottingham, and explains that he has set in motion a scenario that will last until the next afternoon, at which point the Enterprise crew will be returned to their proper places. Q is merely an observer until then.

Picard is content to sit and wait until the time is up, until Q points out that Maid Marian is being held by Sir Guy, who will kill her if she doesn't marry him. Picard is not impressed until he realizes that Maid Marian is Vash, and orders his crew to stay behind while he rescues her. Q, meanwhile, is astounded to learn that Vash has agreed to marry Sir Guy.

When Picard tries to save Vash, she grabs his sword and turns him over to Sir Guy. Q is more and more impressed by Vash's shiftiness, but catches her trying to send Riker a message, and reveals her trickery to Sir Guy. The next day, their execution is interrupted when the Enterprise bridge crew, disguised as monks, come to rescue the Captain. An old-fashioned swashbuckling melee ensues, and Picard vanquishes Sir Guy.

Q is disappointed that everyone survived, but keeps his word and restores everything to normal. Q is so impressed with Vash that he offers to take her anywhere she wants to go in the universe, and she accepts, much to Jean-Luc's surprise and disappointment. Vash takes off with Q on an interstellar treasure hunt. Jean-Luc is left behind on the Enterprise, dismayed by what this has revealed about the opportunistic Vash.

EPISODE NINETY-FIVE: "THE DRUMHEAD"

Written by Jeri Taylor
Directed by Jonathan Frakes
Guest Cast: Jean Simmons, Bruce French, Spence Garrett, Henry Woronicz, Earl Billings, Anne Shea

J'Dan, a Klingon exchange officer, is caught accessing security codes. When the Romulans obtain secret information concerning the dilithium chambers, J'Dan is believed to be the spy who gave the Romulans the information. When one of the chambers explodes, it raises the possibility of sabotage, but J'Dan denies all charges. Troi senses that he is lying.

Starfleet calls retired Admiral Satie in to investigate the situation.

The daughter of an important Federation lawmaker, she brings along two aides, including a full Betazoid, Sabin. The damaged area can't be examined until radiation levels drop, so they can only interrogate J'Dan again.

The Klingon allegedly needed injections for a certain disease, but Worf discovers that his hypo has been converted so that it can read isolinear chips. Converting the information into amino acid sequences, the device can be used to inject the information into someone's blood. Faced with this, J'Dan admits his spying, but denies having sabotaged the dilithium chambers. Sabin believes this to be true. But how did the information leave the ship? Satie suspects a conspiracy.

Satie concentrates her investigation on Simon Tarses, a medical crewman who helped J'Dan with his injections. Born on the Mars colony, Tarses is mostly human but says that his paternal grandfather was a Vulcan, a claim which would explain his elongated ears. Sabin senses that Tarses is lying about something, and suspicion begins to build.

A hearing convenes, with Riker as defense, and Tarses is hammered with questions. Satie demands the names of anyone J'Dan talked to in Ten Forward. Sabin falsely suggests that the explosion was caused by a corrosive chemical. Tarses is completely off guard when he is accused of lying about his grandfather, who was a Romulan. On Riker's advice, Tarses refuses to answer under the Seventh Guarantee, the Federation equivalent of the Fifth Amendment.

Picard warns Worf, who is an enthusiastic supporter of Satie, that things may be getting out of hand. He tells him about the drumhead trials of the 19th Century, when military officers in the field would sit on an inverted drumhead and dispense summary justice, with no right of appeal. The Captain then talks to Tarses, who admits that he lied about his ancestry for fear of prejudice. Now his career seems to be completely ruined.

Picard confronts Satie, who defends the lie about the explosion as a useful tactic. She reveals herself as a self-important chauvinist for the Federation, and accuses Picard of blocking her investigation. She has already gone over Picard's head, and called more hearings. Admiral Henry of Starfleet Security will be taking part as well. Picard vows to fight her all the way. Later, Picard receives a command from Satie to report for questioning at the next hearing.

Picard requests to make an opening statement at the hearing, which Satie refuses to grant. But Jean-Luc invokes the specific regulation that guarantees this and questions the entire proceeding, asking that it end before it hurts anyone else. Satie accuses Picard of violating the Prime Directive nine times while commanding the Enterprise. She also brings up his capture and use by the Borg, and all but accuses him of being responsible for the loss of 39 ships in that conflict.

Jean-Luc maintains his self-control and quotes from writings about freedom, which regard as evil the very practices Satie is using. Satie tries to silence him, but not before he reveals that these words were written by her father. Satie rises to her feet and demands that Picard not sully her father's name and loses control, threatening to destroy Captain Picard, accusing him of being in on her imagined conspiracy.

Admiral Henry rises without a word and walks out of the room. Sabin calls a recess. Everyone exits the chamber, including Sabin, leaving Admiral Satie standing alone. The hearings are terminated, and Satie leaves the ship in disgrace, having ultimately ruined her own Federation career in her blind determination to find a conspiracy where none existed.

EPISODE NINETY-SIX: "HALF A LIFE"
Teleplay by Peter Allen Fields

Story by Ted Roberts and Peter Allen Fields
Directed by Les Landau
Guest Cast: David Ogden Stiers, Majel Barrett, Michelle Forbes, Terrence M. McNally, Carel Struycken

Lwaxana Troi tags along when Picard goes to greet Dr. Timicin, a scientist from Kaelon-2. This is the first Federation involvement with Kaelon-2, an insular world with a dying sun. Timicin's life work is in solar helium fusion enhancement, which will use modified photon torpedoes to revitalize his sun. The Enterprise is taking him to test his technique on a star identical to his own. Lwaxana keeps barging in on Timicin and the engineering crew, but Timicin, a widower, finds her attractive.

The experiment almost works but then fails and the Enterprise flees the resulting nova, and Timicin is despondent that his life's work is over. Lwaxana comforts him, saying he can always try again. But Timicin reveals that, on his planet, 60 is the age of The Resolution, a ceremony celebrating the life of a person— and culminating in his or her ritual suicide.

Lwaxana is outraged at such a barbaric practice. Timicin admits that he has his own doubts about this because there is so much more that he could contribute to his people, if only he were allowed to have the time.

Timicin's involvement with Lwaxana deepens, and he decides to continue his work, and asks Picard for asylum. Picard grants it.

But by turning against his society's traditions, the planetary government refuses to communicate with him or receive any of his findings. He's threatening the status quo. Even his daughter begs him to reconsider, which outrages Lwaxana. She cannot understand why someone would be expected to kill themselves just because they are getting old.

Two ships from the surface prepare to attack the Enterprise for agreeing to harbor Timicin. Finally, he realizes that he cannot go against the beliefs he has always upheld, and agrees to undergo the Resolution after all. Lwaxana is deeply hurt by this, and refuses to speak to him, but finally decides to take part in the ceremony as a final gesture of her love for Timicin. She doesn't agree with this practice, nor understand it, but ultimately she respects his decision and hopes that one day the people of Kaelon-2 will abandon this horrible tradition.

EPISODE NINETY-SEVEN: "THE HOST"

Written by Michel Horvat
Directed by Marvin V. Rush

Guest Cast: Franc Luz as Odan, Barbara Tarbuck, Nicole Orth-Pallavicini, William Newman, Patti Yasutake, Robert Harper

Odan is an emissary on his way to negotiate a dispute between two moon colonies. Odan's father brought peace to two moons a generation before, and the Governor of the parent world has called Odan in to avert another bitter conflict there. Beverly Crusher has become involved with Odan during his brief sojourn on the Enterprise. When Odan refuses to use a transporter, Commander Riker agrees to pilot him to the surface in a shuttle. Suddenly a ship from the Beta moon attacks the shuttle and Odan is injured.

Dr. Crusher works desperately to save Odan and is amazed to discover some sort of parasitic growth in his abdomen. Actually, Odan is the parasite, and the humanoid body is merely a host for it. Odan is a Trill. While the host body can die, the parasite can live on in a new host body. While Beverly can keep Odan alive in stasis for a few hours, she needs a temporary host until a replacement arrives in forty hours.

Will Riker agrees to the risky operation, which succeeds with only one complication. Riker's personality is submerged beneath that of Odan, who proclaims his continued love for Crusher. This places her in an unusual position.

Everything she loved about Odan still exists, but in Riker's body, and Riker has been like a brother to her. She cannot bring herself to face Odan again. Riker's body threatens to reject Odan, who persists in pursuing Crusher. Finally, she gives in to her confused passions.

The negotiations proceed without much progress, but Odan insists that he be removed from Riker in 24 hours, no matter what happens, as he cannot risk Riker's life for his own. The host body is delayed. Picard comforts Crusher, who is completely confused by her emotional dilemma. Odan emerges from the successful talks, but then Riker's body collapses. The Enterprise intercepts the ship with the host body, while Odan is removed from Riker and put in stasis.

To Crusher's surprise, the new host body turns out to be female. This proves to be too much for Beverly. When she fell in love with Odan she didn't know that he was a Trill or that he could conceivably switch to new bodies. She tells Odan that it just won't work as all these changes are too much for her to deal with.

EPISODE NINETY-EIGHT: "THE MIND'S EYE"
Teleplay by Rene Echevarria
Story by Ken Schafer and Rene Echevarria

Directed by David Livingston
Guest Cast: Larry Dobkin, John Fleck, Edward Wiley, Denise Crosby (Majel Barrett receives screen credit as the voice of the computer for the first time in the history of the series.)

The Enterprise takes a Klingon ambassador to K'Reos, a Klingon colony where a fight for independence is under way. The ambassador and Picard are headed there to investigate the planetary governor's claim that the Federation is supplying the rebels with armaments.

Geordi LaForge returns to the Enterprise from a conference just as it arrives at K'Reos. He seems happy and relaxed, recounting details of his vacation. Troi detects nothing wrong. In fact she is pleased that he seems so happy. Data's instruments detect a blip on the E-band wavelength but cannot determine the cause.

Picard and the ambassador beam down to see the governor of K'Reos. The governor reveals that Federation medical supplies have been found in rebel camps, but Picard counters by saying that the Federation does not restrict access to such supplies. Governor Vagh counters this argument by producing a Federation phaser rifle.

He insults Picard with a choice Klingon epithet and is surprised when Picard leans forward and curses Vagh in fluent Klingon. The governor is so impressed by this that he compliments Picard, stating that he must have some Klingon blood in him.

When Data and Geordi LaForge examine the phaser rifle, they determine that it is a Romulan replication, perfect in every way except that it was charged with a Romulan power source. It is evident that the Romulans are trying to crack the Klingon/Federation alliance. Data also detects more E-band emissions. Shortly afterwards, when he is alone, LaForge overrides the computer and routes a cargo bay transporter's power to the auxiliary replicator system and beams weapons down to the planet, then erases all memory of the event from the computers.

Governor Vagh intercepts the shipment of arms and accuses Picard of complicity. Suddenly the Enterprise finds itself surrounded by Klingon ships. Ambassador Kell convinces the governor not to act until he contacts the Klingon High Command. Meanwhile, Data detects yet another E-band transmission and believes that it may have Romulan origins.

Shortly thereafter, LaForge goes to the quarters of Ambassador Kell, who is revealed to be a spy as he knows that LaForge is under Romulan control. Kell intends to have Governor Vagh beam up to supervise the investigation on board the Enterprise, whereupon LaForge will kill Vagh in front of witnesses and claim that he was acting on order from the Federation.

Data compares the E-band blips he's detected with all known phenomena and determines that the E-band could be used to affect human brainwaves if processed through a system set up to process the electro-magnetic spectrum. Data goes to investigate LaForge's shuttle where he finds traces of tractor beam stress on the shuttlecraft. Closer examination of the memory chips in the shuttle's computer reveal that they have been replicated using Romulan technology.

When LaForge will not respond to Data's communication, Data contacts Worf and orders him to arrest Geordi. Geordi enters the cargo bay where he is seen by Worf. But the other Klingons are between Worf and LaForge and refuse to allow the dishonored Klingon to pass. Worf's shout alerts Picard, who deflects LaForge's aim upwards just as he fires a phaser. Worf then removes LaForge from the area.

Data arrives and explains his deductions and discoveries. Data has determined that the only two people with LaForge at the time the E-band transmissions were detected were Picard and Ambassador Kell. Picard suggests that they both be searched, but Kell refuses, declaring his diplomatic immunity.

When Governor Vagh says that Kell will be searched by Klingons instead, Kell realizes his danger and demands Picard grant him asylum. Picard agrees to grant asylum, after Kell has been searched by the other Klingons. Kell is arrested and beamed down to K'Reos.

In sick bay LaForge and Councilor Troi begin the slow process of restoring LaForge's genuine memories, which will not be easy. Geordi feels a great deal of guilt over what happened even though he understands that he was not at fault.

EPISODE NINETY-NINE: "IN THEORY"

Written by Joe Menosky and Ronald D. Moore
Directed by Patrick Stewart
Guest Cast: Michele Scarabelli, Rosalind Chao, Pamela Winslow

Data's study of human behavior leads him to a romance with another officer, Jenna. Jenna, who is on the rebound, tells Data about her childhood. His various logical comments make her laugh, and she wonders aloud why she's never met a man as supportive as he is.

She becomes embarrassed and turns to go, but returns to kiss Data on the cheek. Jenna tell's him that he is very handsome and gives him an even more passionate kiss, and then leaves. Data begins to seek advice about his new relationship. Guinan just tells him that the next move belongs to him, and that he'll have to figure things out for himself.

When Data returns to his quarters, LaForge joins him and returns his cat Spot, whom LaForge had found outside. Data wonders how the doors opened for the cat to escape, since the doors are keyed only to humanoids. The computer tells him that there have been no intruders. LaForge advises Data to ask someone else for romantic advice.

Data takes flowers to Jenna and tries to woo her. He is successful, even though he tells her that he has developed a "romance" program to help him out. Meanwhile, Picard discovers everything knocked off the desk in his ready room, but there is no apparent explanation.

Jenna visits Data to give him a gift, but must point out the appropriate responses to her android suitor.

The Class-M planet seems not to be at the proper coordinates, but soon reappears. Then the computer reports depressurization in the main observation lounge. But when this is investigated, everything is presently all right, except that the room is a shambles.

Data tries to act natural with Jenna but his routine is a matter of derived

behaviors: when he arrives, he calls out "Honey, I'm home!" He is very solicitous and romantic, but he is drawing on a database rather than real feelings, and Jenna is bothered by his behavior.

Thinking that a lover's quarrel might improve matters, Data acts angry, but this only adds to the confusion. When he explains that he is drawing on extensive cultural and literary sources, Jenna tells him to stop, and just to kiss her. When she asks him what his thoughts are during the kiss he tells her: he was working on a warp drive problem, reviewing the works of Dickens, calculating the safest pressure for the kiss, and other matters. Jenna is distressed by this, but at least she was in his thoughts somewhere.

As the Enterprise moves through the nebula cloud, certain systems malfunction, and explosive decompression occurs between two decks. When LaForge and an engineering team go to investigate for structural damage, one of them dies, caught between two levels in a grisly accident.

Data determines that the preponderance of dark matter in this region of space is causing gaps in normal space. When the ship encounters one of these, parts of the ship phase out, hence the decompression and the strange death of the crew person.

These "holes" are moving through space, but can be detected. A shuttle some distance ahead of the ship could detect them early and, with navigational linkage, guide the Enterprise through the nebula to safety. Picard insists on piloting the shuttle and he guides the ship most of the way through, but the gaps in space become more numerous, and the shuttle is damaged and goes out of control. Jean-Luc is beamed out just as the shuttle explodes. The Enterprise then manages to get through the rest of the nebula and escapes the danger zone, setting course for the nearest Starbase.

Jenna explains to Data that their relationship won't work because even though the android is attentive and concerned, he lacks real emotions and therefore cannot adequately provide everything a relationship requires. Data agrees and Jeena leaves him alone in his quarters with Spot, his cat.

ONE HUNDRED: "REDEMPTION I"

Written by Ronald D. Moore
Directed by Cliff Bole
Guest Cast: Robert O'Reilly, Tony Todd, Barbara March, Gwynyth Walsh, Ben Slack, Nicholas Kepros, J.D. Cullum, Denise Crosby

Gowron's ship appears and the Klingon confers with Picard: he needs help to avert a Klingon civil war. The family of Duras, who Worf killed awhile ago, is still very powerful, as two sisters survive Duras. While the female members of a clan cannot take part in the Klingon High Council, it is believed that they have concocted some sort of subterfuge as they have at least three fleet commanders on their side.

Picard agrees to act out his final obligations as the arbiter of succession, but cannot promise Federation aid in any civil conflict. Meanwhile, Worf asks Gowron for his help in restoring his honor, but Gowron refuses since that would alienate the Council by revealing Duras treachery.

Worf asks Picard for a leave of absence, which is granted. Then Worf meets with his brother, Kurn, who feels that the Klingon leadership has betrayed the Empire and must be swept away. He is certain that Gowron will be killed by Duras' family, but promises to do it himself if he is not slain by them.

Kurn has four squadron commanders sworn to help him. Worf, being the elder brother, chooses to change these plans. They will support Gowron, but not until he is backed into a corner by his many enemies and agrees to restore Worf's honor. Kurn agrees and talks all but one of his allies into going along with this new plan.

Picard appears before the Klingon High Council and asks if there are any challengers to Gowron's claim. At this point, Lursa, Duras' sister, appears with her other sister accompanied by a Klingon youth whom they claim is the son of Duras. Under Klingon law, Picard must consider this claim as well. But later we see that Lursa is actually acting in a secret conspiracy with the Romulans to gain control of the Klingon High Council.

Picard rejects the boy's claim because he has no experience, and back's Gowron. As predicted, the boy accuses Picard of serving Federation interests. The rest of the council backs the Duras family, leaving Gowron alone.

Later, Worf visits Gowron's ship and offers him aid in return for restoring his family's honor. Gowron scoffs, but when their ship is attacked by two other Klingon vessels, Worf takes command of the weapons station and destroys one of the attackers after tricking it into lowering its shields.

Gowron's ship is at the mercy of the other attacker until Kurn's ship appears and drives them off. The Enterprise, meanwhile, has withdrawn from the battle area as Picard realizes that he cannot get involved any more deeply than he already is. Back in the nearly empty Council hall, Gowron is sworn in as Council leader. His first act is the restoration of Worf's family honor. Worf grasps the naked blade of a Klingon dagger in the ceremony but does not flinch.

They travel to the Enterprise where Gowron again asks for Picard's help. Worf also asks, but Picard states that he cannot risk drawing the Federation into a civil war. He orders Worf to return to duty. Worf refuses and resigns his commission in Starfleet in order to join with Gowron to fight in the Klingon civil war.

Worf prepares to leave the Enterprise and so Picard goes to his quarters to see him off. The entire crew lines the hallway leading to the transporter room and they all stand at attention as he passes. It is obviously a moving experience for the Klingon as he leaves the ship and the friends he has there.

Down on the planet, the Duras family and their Romulan cohorts receive the news with some happiness. Only the boy is angry, since he wants to kill Picard for passing him over. The Romulan commander, with whom the Duras family is secretly aligned, counsels patience.

She's certain that Picard will be back soon enough. The Romulan commander steps into the light, revealing her face. She is a Romulan and yet she is also the seeming twin of Tasha Yar, the Enterprise bridge officer who died valiantly to bring peace to the Federation.

END OF SEASON FOUR

Patrick at Paramount Studios for the Rodden-berry building dedication.

Photo © 1994 Albert L. Ortega

Brent at the Director's Guild for a tribute to Whoopi.

Photo ©
1994
Albert L.
Ortega

SEASON FIVE

SEASON FIVE

A bit uneven after the third and fourth seasons, season five of THE NEXT GENERATION looks better in retrospect than it did at the time. The problem with the previous season's cliffhanger "Redemption" ending is that the conclusion proved a bit disappointing. But then, season five's cliffhanger would prove to be a real disaster. In between, however, the episodes ranged from mostly good to a few great ones.

The big news, of course, was the appearance of Spock in the two parter "Unification." But this, too, would prove rather disappointing, more like an advertisement for the theatrical release of STAR TREK VI—THE UNDISCOVERED COUNTRY later that year. (There was also an exceptionally long holiday hiatus for the series, which, oddly enough, coincided with the first two months of the movie's release.)

Good episodes include "Darmok," and the introduction of a new character, "Ensign Ro" (Michelle Forbes.) But the real season highlight would be the Picard episode "The Inner Light," another format-breaking story that payed great dramatic dividends.

EPISODE ONE HUNDRED ONE:
"REDEMPTION II"

Written by Ronald D. Moore
Directed by David Carson
Guest Cast: Denise Crosby, Tony Todd, Barbara March, Gwynth Walsh, J.D. Cullum, Robert O'Reilly, Michael G. Hagerty, Fran Bennett, Nicholas Kepros, Colm Meaney, Timothy Carhart

As the Klingon crisis continues, Worf and Kurn narrowly escape their enemies, and Picard argues that the Federation must cut the supply line between the Romulans and the Klingons. Twenty Federation ships assemble a tachyon grid to detect any cloaked ships. Picard assigns Riker and Geordi to command one of the ships. Data is assigned to command the Sutherland.

The Federation ships deploy the tachyon web and wait. Sela, the Romulan who is conspiring with the Duras family, arrives in a ship and decloaks near the Enterprise. She contacts Picard. He cannot believe his eyes. She taunts Picard, revealing that Tasha Yar was her mother. Then she orders the Federation to leave within twenty hours. Picard doubts her claim, but Guinan states that Tasha Yar was on the Enterprise-C twenty-three years before, and that Picard was the one who sent her there.

Worf is kidnapped by the Duras sisters. B'Etor tries to seduce him to her side. He refuses.

Sela agrees to meet with Picard and reveals the truth about Tasha Yar. A Romulan general took Tasha as a consort in exchange for sparing the lives of the other prisoners. Tasha was executed when she attempted to escape with her four year old daughter. Sela cried out, not wanting to leave, resulting in Tasha's capture.

Picard tells Gowron that an attack on the Duras side would pressure the Romulans to run the blockade. The Romulans flood the area near the Sutherland with tachyon radiation to cancel the net. Data determines that this action will also leave a trail. He detects the radiation signature and attacks, exposing the position of the Romulans, who retreat.

The tide turns against the Duras. A Romulan tries to kill Worf, but is defeated. The illegitimate son of Duras is captured when the Duras sisters flee, leaving him behind. As a result of his efforts, Worf's discommendation is lifted as the Duras family has been disgraced by their attempts to involve the Romulans, who are the traditional enemies of the Klingon Empire. Worf requests permission to return to the Enterprise and Picard agrees.

EPISODE ONE HUNDRED TWO: "DARMOK"

Teleplay by Joe Menosky

Story by Philip Lazebnik and Joe Menosky

Guest Cast: Paul Winfield, Richard Allen, Colm Meaney, Ashley Judd

The Enterprise has been assigned the delicate task of negotiating with a race with whom successful negotiations have never been made. While the Federation has encountered the Children of Tama before, they could never manage to communicate with them. Though they were able to translate the language into English, it made no sense to them.

Without warning, the Tamarians beam Picard and their own commander, Dathon, down to the surface of the planet they are orbiting. When Picard comes face to face with Dathon, he's uncertain what to expect. Is this a contest between the two captains? The Tamarian tells Picard, "Darmok and Jalad at Tanagra, when the walls fell."

When Picard fails to grasp the significance of this, Dathon is disappointed. When darkness falls, they each make separate camps within sight of each other. Dathon builds a fire for warmth, but when he notes that Picard fails in making a fire, he tosses a flaming branch to him, stating, "Temba—

his arms wide." Picard denotes this as a signal of friendship.

On board the Enterprise, Data and Troi try to determine the meaning of "Darmok at Tanagra." Through cross-referencing they determine that Darmok was a warrior leader and Tanagra an island.

Down on the planet, Dathon comes running out of the forest, pursued by an alien beast. The creature can appear and disappear at will. Picard moves to retreat, but the Tamarian refuses, saying, "Shaka, when the walls fell." Picard and Dathon attack the beast, with some success. But suddenly Picard is caught by a transporter beam, which removes him from the fight.

Picard doesn't want to leave Dathon alone and the transporter beam cannot quite get Picard off the planet, but it prevents Jean-Luc from coming to the immediate assistance of Dathon. When Picard is able to help Dathon, it is too late for the alien commander has been gravely wounded. Picard continues to strive to understand the Tamarian language. The Tamarians speak in metaphors. "Darmok at Tanagra" was a situation similar to what Picard and Dathon are going through. Sadly, the Tamarian succumbs to his wounds.

Riker attacks the Tamarian ship, disrupting the jamming field. Picard is beamed up. The Tamarians strike back at the Enterprise. Picard goes to the bridge and speaks to the Tamarian first officer on ship-to-ship linkup. "Temarc! The river Temarc in winter!"

The Tamarians are amazed. They understand what Picard means. Dathon risked, and sacrificed, his life so that two peoples could finally communicate with each other at last. Dathon's sacrifice was not in vain.

EPISODE ONE HUNDRED THREE:
"ENSIGN RO"

Teleplay by Michael Piller
Story by Rick Berman & Michael Piller
Directed by Les Landeau
Guest Cast: Michelle Forbes, Scott Marlowe, Frank Collison, Jeffrey Hayenga, Harley Venton, Ken Thorley, Cliff Potts

Admiral Kennelly wants Picard to find Orta, a Bajoran terrorist leader, and get him to halt his attacks. Up until now, Orta has only attacked Cardassian targets but recently a Federation colony was assaulted.

Kennelly has Ensign Ro Laren, a Bajoran, transferred to the Enterprise. She is a Starfleet officer who was court marshaled and sent to prison for an incident on Garon Two. Picard is angry at the transfer as it was made without consulting him. Riker dislikes the idea

as well. They mistrust Laren, but Kennelly states that because she's Bajoran, her experience will help them locate Orta. When Ensign Ro reports for duty she makes it clear that she doesn't like the assignment either, but it's better than prison.

The Enterprise sends down an Away Team to meet with Jas Holza at a Bajoran refugee camp on Valo Three. They hope to find a lead to the terrorist, Orta. Ro complains that they're wasting their time with Holza because he's just a figurehead trotted out to deal with the Federation. Ro Laren recommends Keeve Falor, but he won't help the Federation because they have used the Prime Directive as an excuse to allow the Cardassians to repress the Bajorans. Picard is troubled by the conditions he sees in the camps and orders blankets and medical supplies for the people there. Then Keeve agrees to help Picard.

Guinan approaches Ensign Ro in Ten Forward, but she rejects Guinan's friendly overtures and just wants to be left alone. Guinan inquires about what really happened on Garon Two, but Ro doesn't care to discuss it. Ro leaves when she is notified that a subspace message has come in for her. It's from Admiral Kelley. It seems that she's on a private mission for the Admiral which Picard knows nothing about.

The Enterprise has been directed to a spot on the third moon of Valo, and when they arrive there, Ro beams down six hours ahead of schedule, without informing anyone on the Enterprise that she has left. The rest of the Away Team beams down to search for her and Orta when they're suddenly surrounded by Bajorans and taken prisoner.

Orta meets with Picard but mistrusts the Federation. He denies involvement in the attack on the Federation colony. Could someone else be trying to draw the Federation into the conflict?

Picard is furious with Ro for leaving the ship without orders and restricts her to quarters. Guinan visits Ro and convinces her to talk to Picard. Ro confesses that Admiral Kennelly assigned her to secretly offer arms to the Bajorans. Picard accepts Ro's admissions and asks her to convince Orta to go along with a plan which could expose the conspiracy. The Enterprise contacts Kennelly and tells him that they will escort Orta's ship to a Bajoran camp on Valo Three.

Two Cardassian warships are detected which demand that the Bajoran terrorists be turned over to them. They give the Enterprise one hour. Kennelly recommends giving up the terrorists. Picard accuses the Cardassians of plotting to involve the Federation in the war, but watches as the Bajoran ship is destroyed.

But this was a decoy ship. Picard has evidence that the Cardassians staged the attack on the Federation colony on Solarian Four, then tricked Kennelly into supporting their plan to capture the Bajoran terrorists. For engaging in tactics against Federation policy, Kennelly faces court martial. Ro Laren is offered the chance to remain on the Enterprise.

EPISODE ONE HUNDRED FOUR: "SILICON AVATAR"

Teleplay by Jeri Taylor
Story by Lawrence V. Conley
Directed by Cliff Bole
Guest Cast: Ellen Geer, Susan Dion

The Crystalline Entity, last seen in "Datalore," suddenly threatens a Federation colony. After it destroys the outpost, as well as two colonist, the Enterprise is sent to track it down. Dr. Kila Marr, an expert on the entity, has been studying the scenes of its attacks for years. Riker and his Away Team are the only survivors of any of the entity's attacks.

Dr. Marr wonders why there were survivors this time, although Riker points out that two colonists did die. When Picard assigns Data to work with her, Dr. Marr resists because Data's brother, Lore, once assisted the entity. Dr. Marr mistrusts Data. She wonders if Data collaborated with the monster to save those hiding with him. Dr. Marr reveals that her son Renny was killed by the entity when it ravaged the world Data originated on. She vows that if she discovers that Data helped it in any way, she'll see to it that he's destroyed.

The Enterprise traces the path of the entity, but Picard reveals that he will only destroy it as a last resort. He wants to try to communicate with it. Dr. Marr is shocked that he doesn't want to destroy it outright. Riker thinks the entity should be destroyed on sight as well. He's afraid that by trying to communicate with it they could lose their chance to destroy it.

The Enterprise pursues the entity and uses graviton emissions to lure it. The entity approaches; the Enterprise raises shields. The entity seems to respond to their signal. It's trying to communicate. But Dr. Marr changes the signal and locks it into a beam which destroys the crystalline entity. "I did it for you, Renny," she says.

Dr. Marr is escorted to her quarters by Data. Her career is over. She misused her position and went against Picard's orders. She asks Data to tell her that Renny would have approved, but Data replies that he doesn't think the boy would have approved of her taking an action which destroyed her career.

EPISODE ONE HUNDRED FIVE: "DISASTER"

Teleplay by Ronald D. Moore
Story by Ron Jarvis & Philip A. Scorza
Directed by Gabrielle Beaumont
Guest Cast: Rosalind Chao, Colm Meaney, Michelle Forbes, Erika Flores, John Christian Graas, Max Supera, Cameron Arnett, Dana Hupp

The Enterprise has hit a quantum filament. When a second one hits the vessel as well, Monroe is killed on the bridge at her computer console when it explodes. Troi and O'Brien remain on the bridge but cannot raise Picard on the communicator. The various decks on the ship are cut off from each other as emergency procedures went into effect, including the automatic sealing off of the various decks from one another.

Picard and three children are trapped when a turbolift comes to an emergency stop. The children are frightened and Picard has suffered a broken ankle.

O'Brien transmits a distress call but can't be sure it's going out. Ensign Ro makes it to the bridge by climbing up the turbolift shaft but they're trapped there as emergency bulkheads have closed cutting off areas of the ship. With Monroe dead, Troi is the senior officer on the bridge.

Riker, Data and Worf are stuck in Ten Forward. Riker and Data try to reach engineering. In the crawl space, they encounter an electrical arc from a malfunctioning panel.

Ro and O'Brien discover that the containment field is weakening. If it drops to 15% the ship will explode.

In the crawl space, Data uses his body to block the energy arc, but this damages him, and Riker must remove his head to continue to engineering.

In Ten Forward, Keiko goes into labor with only Worf to help her.

On the bridge, Ro Laren suggests a saucer separation to get away from the drive section. Troi refuses to abandon their comrades who may still be alive and instead instructs them to divert power to engineering to enable anyone there to see the danger and prevent the containment breach. Picard and the children climb up the turbolift shaft in search of a door they can access a corridor through.

Keiko is in labor with Worf overseeing. He took a computer simulated course in delivering a baby and was quite good at it.

On the bridge, Ro is pressing to have a saucer separation or risk having

everyone die. Only if someone in engineering notices the readings and acts in time can the ship be saved.

In Engineering, Data's head is attached to the computer. Riker notices the containment field readings and, following Data's instructions, stabilizes the containment field in the matter-anti-matter chamber. The bridge crew sees this and realizes that someone is in engineering. The ship is saved.

Picard and the children find a door and enter a corridor through it. Picard congratulates the children for what they all accomplished.

Keiko finally gives birth and Worf cuts the umbilical cord.

Things get back to normal on the Enterprise as it heads to Starbase 67 for repairs.

EPISODE ONE HUNDRED SIX:
"THE GAME"

Teleplay by Brannon Braga
Story by Susan Sackett & Fred Bronson and Brannon Braga
Directed by Corey Allen
Guest Cast: Ashley Judd, Katherine Moffat, Colm Meaney, Patti Yasutake, Wil Wheaton

Riker is on shore leave on the planet Risa with an alien female named Etana. He is obviously enjoying her company when she shows him a device which fits easily over his head and periodically projects beams into the eyes, rewarding him with pleasure each time he completes a level.

Riker returns from Rysa. The Enterprise is on its way to an uncharted area called the Phoenix Cluster. Wesley will be joining them during a break from Starfleet Academy.

Riker brings the Game back with him. He shows Troi the Game, which he says is even better than chocolate.

Wesley beams over to the Enterprise. Troi tells Dr. Crusher about the Game. In Engineering, Wesley meets Robin Lefler.

Crusher calls Data to sick bay and disconnects him while Troi and Riker assist. They work on Data's brain and leave the android shut down. Riker shows Geordi the Game.

Wil spends time with Robin, who demonstrates that she knows a lot about him. She invites Wil to dinner.

Picard is still mystified by Data's condition.

Wes finds his mother playing the Game. She tries to get him to try it but he's in a hurry to meet Robin. Beverly keeps pushing Wes to try the Game. He finds her persistence curious. Wes and Robin investigate the Game with the medical computers. It reveals that the Game is addictive. Wes reports his find-

ings to Captain Picard, who promises to investigate, but when Wes leaves, Picard puts on his own headset. Nearly everyone aboard is addicted to the Game. Wes and Robin discover that Data has been deliberately damaged.

The Enterprise meets a ship piloted by Etana, who tells them where to distribute the Game. The Ktarians are behind this conspiracy.

When Wes meets with Robin again, he realizes that she's been taken over, too. He uses a preprogrammed escape plan involving intership beaming, but he is finally tracked down and captured. Riker and the others finally force Wesley to wear the Game.

Data steps onto the bridge and the lights dim. He flashes a hand-held whose pulses cancel out the hypnotic effects of the Game. He has programmed lights in computer consoles throughout the ship to do the same and free the rest of the Enterprise crew. Picard captures the Ktarian ship in a tractor beam and takes Etana prisoner to be delivered to Starbase 82.

Later, Wesley prepares to leave to be returned to Starfleet Academy. He kisses Robin goodbye, knowing that they have been through a lot together and will remain friends forever because of their ordeal.

EPISODE ONE HUNDRED SEVEN: "UNIFICATION I"

Teleplay by Jeri Taylor
Story by Rick Berman & Michael Piller
Directed by Les Landeau
Guest Cast: Joanna Miles, Stephen Root, Graham Jarvis, Malachi Throne, Norman Large, Daniel Roebuck, Erick Avari, Karen Hensel, Mark Lenard, Leonard Nimoy

Picard journeys to Vulcan to learn why Spock has gone to Romulus without authorization. Meanwhile the Enterprise investigates a crashed Ferengi ship with traces of Vulcan metal in it.

When Picard arrives at Sarek's residence, he learns that Sarek is dying. Shocked to hear that Spock is on Romulus, Sarek reveals that Spock knows Pardek, a Romulan senator. Spock called for maintaining an open dialogue with the Romulans, but he would never defect.

The Enterprise goes to Gowron, the Klingon leader, to obtain a cloaked ship. Data and Picard begin to be prepared with Romulan disguises.

Geordi determines that the metal parts from the crashed Ferengi ship are from the T'Pau. The T'Pau is supposed to be in storage at the Qualor Two.

Data and Picard board the cloaked Klingon ship. The Klingon captain dis-

likes the secrecy of the mission. The Enterprise travels to Qualor Two to investigate how an old Vulcan ship wound up in Ferengi hands. They contact Dokachin, who manages the junkyard, and he reluctantly assists them. Dokachin is furious to discover that the T'Pau is indeed missing. Aboard the Klingon ship, Picard receives a message that Sarek is dead.

Data and Picard, disguised as Romulans, beam down to Romulus from their cloaked orbit around the planet. Someone is watching them. Data and Picard see Pardek and follow him, but are stopped at gun point and taken to a secret cave where Pardek waits for them. When Picard explains that he seeks Spock, Spock steps out from behind a wall.

EPISODE ONE HUNDRED EIGHT: "UNIFICATION II"

Teleplay by Michael Piller
Story by Rick Berman and Michael Piller
Directed by Cliff Bole
Guest Cast (Additional): Denise Crosby, Vidal Peterson, Harriet Leider

Spock tells Picard that his mission is no concern of Starfleet. He's on a personal peace mission. Romulans are there in the cave to learn more about Vulcan philosophy and discuss a reunification of Vulcan and Romulus. Spock explains that many centuries before, the Vulcans and the Romulans were a single people.

Spock states that he took this avenue of diplomacy because he did not want to risk anyone else getting involved because of what happened when he urged James Kirk to become involved in the original peace overture with the Klingons many years before.

Data beams up to the Klingon ship and tries to pierce the Romulan communications net.

Spock and Picard discuss reunification and the possibility of a Vulcan peace initiative. Pardek tells Spock that the Proconsul has agreed to meet with him.

Riker traces the T'Pau to the wife of a dead smuggler. Riker questions Amarie, the four-armed widow of the smuggler. She's not bothered that her husband is dead and is amused that Riker was on the ship which killed him. Her husband dealt with Omag, a fat Ferengi.

Pardek takes Spock to see the Proconsul Neral, who tells the Vulcan that he supports unification. Neral explains that he'll support talks between Vulcan and Romulus. When Neral is alone, Sela enters and smiles.

Picard questions the logic of the Proconsul's support. Spock is also suspicious, but he'll still meet with Neral as planned. Picard questions the wisdom of this. Spock explains that he must discover if the Romulans have an ulterior motive.

Spock beams up to the Klingon ship and helps Data pierce the communications net.

In the alien cantina, the Omag enters. Riker beams down and questions him. The Ferengi is obnoxious so Riker threatens him and he talks, revealing that he delivered the T'Pau near the Neutral Zone. Riker reports this information to Picard and they plan a rendezvous.

Picard and Data are meeting with Spock when the Romulan treachery is revealed. Romulans led by Sela capture them in the cave. Spock deduces that Pardek is the traitor.

The Romulans plan to use the unification movement as a cover to conquer Vulcan and achieve unification their own way. Sela has written a speech for Spock stating that a peace envoy is heading to Vulcan, which will allow the Romulans to seize control before anyone can stop them. Spock refuses to cooperate. He knows that logically she will kill them anyway. Sela presents a hologram of Spock which she will use instead.

The Enterprise detects three Vulcan ships en route towards Vulcan from the Neutral Zone. Suspicious, they move to intercept them.

Sela returns to her office and finds her prisoners missing. She is fooled by holograms which Data programmed by breaking into the Romulan computer system, and Sela is captured. A fake distress call almost lures the Enterprise away from the mysterious ships. Then a message from Spock reveals that the Vulcan ships contain a Romulan invasion force.

Data uses a Vulcan neck pinch to render Sela unconscious. Their plans exposed, a cloaked Romulan ship suddenly appears beside the Vulcan transports and destroys them, along with the 2,000 Romulan troops who were aboard them.

On Romulus, Spock explains that he has decided to remain on Romulus to continue to work with the genuine Romulan underground. But before Jean-Luc leaves, Spock mind melds with him in order to access Sarek's final message for him. During all the years they lived, Spock and his father had never mind melded. Spock melds with Picard and is visibly moved by the final message he receives from Sarek.

EPISODE ONE HUNDRED NINE:
"A MATTER OF TIME"
Written by Rick Berman
Directed by Paul Lynch

Guest Cast: Matt Frewer, Stefan Gierasch, Sheila Franklin, Ghay Garner

When a type C asteroid strikes Pentara Four, the Enterprise goes there to assist the planet. Worf reports a space-time distortion and a small object is detected. A man beams over and identifies himself as Berlinghoff Rasmussen. He explains that he's a 26th century historian whose focus of study is the 22nd through the 24th century.

Why he has appeared that day will become evident, but the dangers of time travel prevent him from revealing anything from the future. Riker wonders whether Rasmussen could be an impostor? Scans indicate that the small vessel he came in, now in the cargo hold, is unlike anything on record.

Pentara Four is growing colder. Three underground pockets of carbon dioxide could be released with drilling phasers which would cause the atmosphere to grow warmer. The drilling phasers successfully release the carbon dioxide, causing temperature increases that will give the planet time to mend its system.

Rasmussen keeps annoying everyone with questions. A series of earthquakes strike Pentara Four. They originate beneath the drill sites. Planetary conditions are worsening beyond what they could have expected from the asteroid strike.

While Rasmussen is speaking to Data, the scientist slips a tri-corder into his pocket.

Data and Geordi come up with a plan to ionize the particles in the atmosphere and move them off into space. But any errors could burn off the planet's atmosphere.

Picard discusses his dilemma with Rasmussen, who refuses to tell him the outcome. But to Picard, Rasmussen's past is his future and it hasn't been written yet. He decides to proceed with the plan after the planetary government approves it. They fire phasers and use shield inverters to clear the atmosphere. It works.

Rasmussen gets ready to leave in his time machine, but Picard insists on looking inside the vessel. Objects have been reported missing. Rasmussen allows only Data to enter. The objects are all there. Rasmussen points a phaser at Data, revealing that he'd stolen the pod from a 26th century time traveler. The auto timer is set to return the pod to the 22nd century, where Rasmussen plans to "invent" the stolen items himself.

Rasmussen tries to stun Data with the phaser, but it has been deactivated. Rasmussen is led away to a holding cell, the time pod having vanished according to the previous settings. The thief and killer is now marooned in another age and will experience all the worst that the future has to offer him.

EPISODE ONE HUNDRED TEN: "NEW GROUND"

Teleplay by Grant Rosenberg
Story by Sara Charno & Stuart Charno
Directed by Robert Scheerer
Guest Cast: Brian Bonsall

The Enterprise arrives at Lemma Two and Dr. Ja'Dar briefs them on the Soliton Wave discovery. The wave will be generated on the planet's surface and then propel an unmanned test ship waiting in its path. The wave will then take the ship to Lemma Two, three light years away. On Lemma Two a scattering field will be generated to dissipate the Soliton Wave. The Enterprise will be following the ship to monitor the progress of the experiment.

An embarrassing incident occurs when Alexander is caught stealing in the lab after he'd denied taking anything. Worf is incensed as it is dishonorable for Klingons to lie. Worf lectures Alexander on Klingon honor, explaining that one does not just dishonor oneself with a lie, but one's family as well. Thus a lie told by Alexander also dishonors his father. The boy understands and says that it won't happen again.

The test begins and the test ship enters warp. The Soliton Wave fluctuates, affecting the Enterprise; Picard orders an immediate shutdown. The wave shifts again and the test ship is torn apart.

The Enterprise warp drive is off line for two hours.

Worf is told that Alexander is still lying and being disruptive. He tracks down his son and finds him in the holodeck, using Worf's Klingon workout program, set on its lowest level. Worf observes Alexander battle a foe with Worf's sword and defeat him. Worf is proud, but when he confronts the boy about his problems, Alexander is defiant. Worf announces that he will send the boy to a Klingon school, an idea the boy hates.

The Enterprise restores its sensors and is still working on the warp engines on line when they discover that the Soliton Wave, still bound for Lemma Two, has increased to warp 4.1. By the time it reaches Lemma Two its energy will have increased by a factor of 200, which will destroy the colony and much of the planet as well.

Worf discusses his problem with Troi, who points out that Alexander may have felt that his father abandoned him by sending him to Earth. Troi also wonders if Worf might still be angry with K'Ehleyr for having kept

Alexander's existence a secret. Worf goes to Alexander to explain his feelings, but the boy is packing and is too angry to talk with his father.

Geordi reports that the Soliton Wave will reach Lemma Two in two hours. To stop it the Enterprise has to get in front of it and use photon torpedoes to disrupt the wave. In order to get in front of the wave, the Enterprise will have to fly through it.

Confined to his quarters, Alexander leaves and returns to the biolabs to see the Gilvos lizard, which he considers his only friend. The Enterprise enters the Soliton Wave and he's knocked to the floor by the impact. Ion contamination will occur in certain sections of the ship when the photon torpedoes are exploded; Picard orders those areas evacuated.

A scan reveals that there are still life forms in the biolab, including Alexander. The transporters are down and warp drive will fail in four minutes, so they cannot delay firing the photon torpedoes for very long.

Worf and Riker race to the biolab and force open the doors, encountering a fire. They find Alexander trapped under debris. Worf lifts the debris himself to save the boy. But Alexander wants the Gilvos saved, so Riker reluctantly rescues the lizards. They all escape the lab as the photo torpedoes are fired and detonated.

The Soliton wave dissipates. Worf decides to let Alexander stay with him, feeling that it would be an even greater challenge for the boy than a Klingon school.

EPISODE ONE HUNDRED ELEVEN: "HERO WORSHIP"

Teleplay by Joe Menosky
Story by Hilary J. Bader
Directed by Patrick Stewart
Guest Cast: Joshua Harris, Harley Venton

When an Away Team beams over to the Vico, a disabled exploratory vessel, they find everyone dead except a young boy, and beam him back with them after Data frees him from debris. Timothy reveals that the Vico was attacked by a ship and aliens beamed in and killed everyone. Both of Tim's parents were killed aboard the Vico.

Data and Geordi analyze the Vico's computer logs. Data asks Geordi if he ever had a traumatic experience. Tim is entered in the school but he's always distracted and can't seem to relate to what the class is doing.

Picard tries to figure out what happened to the Vico. He has doubts about Tim's story, but why would the boy lie? Troi is also worried about Tim's behavior, so Picard assigns Data to spend time with the boy. Data helps Tim assemble a building model. He explains to the boy that androids have no emotions. The Enterprise goes deeper into the black cluster, piercing the graviton wave fronts to approach the core of the cluster.

Troi goes to see Tim, who is seriously imitating Data now. Troi goes along with the routine. She later explains to Picard that this is one stage of Tim's healing process. Data spends more time with Tim, hoping to get to the underlying truth of what happened to the Vico.

The Enterprise penetrates deeper into the black cluster and experiences gravity feedback to the shields.

Data talks to Tim about the advantages of human behavior. Because he has no emotions, while he can never experience sadness, neither can he ever experience happiness.

The Enterprise tries to fire its phasers, but they are ineffective. This casts further doubt on Tim's alien attack story. Data breaks down Tim's story until finally Tim blurts that he was responsible for the destruction of the Vico. He fell against a computer panel when the ship rocked and a moment later the ship was wrecked. Data explains that this was a coincidence and Picard confirms this as the computer has safety procedures to prevent such accidents from affecting the ship.

The gravity wave front buffeting the Enterprise increases in intensity. Data asks Tim to tell him everything he remembers happening before the accident. Tim says the same thing happened on the Vico, with people shouting "more shields." When they decide to route the warp engine power into the shields, Tim says they did that on the Vico, too.

Data tells Picard that they must drop all shields. Picard resists at first, but when he agrees and the shields are dropped, the graviton waves disperse. They had been experiencing wave front feedback all along. The more power they put into the shields, the more it was reflected back at them. Tim's information saved the Enterprise.

In school, Troi and Data observe Tim, who seems to be recovering now and acting like a boy again. Tim admits that he misses his parents, because now he's all alone. But Data states that he would be proud to accept Tim as a friend.

EPISODE ONE HUNDRED TWELVE: "VIOLATIONS"

Teleplay by Pamela Gray and Jeri Taylor
Story by Shari Goodhartz & T. Michael and Pamela Gray
Directed by Robert Wiemer
Guest Cast: David Sage, Eve Brenner, Rosalind Chao, Ben Lemon, Rick Fitts, Doug Wert, Craig Benton

A delegation of Ullians— telepathic humanoids— is being transported by the Enterprise. Tarmin's son Jev is in the delegation, as is an older woman named Inad.

Tarmin demonstrates his telepathic ability in harmless ways. He asks Crusher if she'd like to remember her first kiss. Not all Ullians can read memories, but Tarmin is quite skillful at it. His son is angered by these displays and leaves dinner in a huff.

Troi follows Jev to try to calm him down. He's just annoyed at his overbearing father. Troi says she understands. Later, in her quarters, Troi is haunted the memory of her last romantic encounter with Riker, which turns into a memory of a vicious rape. Riker's face turns into Jev's just before Troi screams and passes out.

Troi is found in a coma. Crusher doesn't know how to awaken her. Riker questions Jev, who was the last person to see her. Riker says he wants to test the Ullians for any diseases. Jev is angry and resentful over the request.

When Riker returns to his quarters, he also experiences a mental episode involving the death of a crewman. He lapses into a coma. Troi and Riker share an abnormal brainwave pattern which seems to indicate Iresine Syndrome, a rare neurological disorder. But it seems unlikely that two people would both fall prey to it so close together.

Worf wants to quarantine the Ullians, but Picard doesn't want to anger the delegation without proof of their involvement. When Picard explains the situation to them, Tarmin becomes angry while Jev tries to soothe tempers. Crusher suggest that she monitor the group while they perform memory probes.

Crusher examines Keiko, who experienced a memory probe from Tarmin, but she speaks positively of the experience. After Keiko leaves, Crusher is haunted by a memory of her husband's death and lapses into a coma. She is found like this by Data and Geordi.

With events getting so out of hand, Picard has Data investigate the planets the Ullians previously visited in search of any similar occurrences.

When Troi finally awakens, she cannot remember anything.

Picard confines the Ullians to their quarters until the matter is resolved. Jev offers to solve the mystery by helping Troi to retrieve her lost memory. Although reluctant, he knows that Keiko suffered no ill effects from her memory probe.

Data and Geordi begin to discover similar incidents on planets visited by the Ullians. Those comas had also been explained as Iresine Syndrome.

Jev helps Troi recall the memory, which she does, but now when she's attacked it's not Jev she sees in her mind but Tarmin. Tarmin is taken into custody.

Data and Geordi continue their record searches. In two cases, Tarmin was not present, but Jev was. Jev goes to Troi's quarters to apologize for his father, but he reveals his attraction for Troi and invades her mind again. Troi realizes that Jev was behind the incidents all along.

Worf, Data and a security team enter the room. Worf punches Jev to subdue him. Riker and Crusher awaken and Tarmin promises help in their healing. They experienced a form of mental rape which no one on their world has been guilty of for centuries.

EPISODE ONE HUNDRED THIRTEEN: "MASTERPIECE SOCIETY"

Teleplay by Adam Belanoff and Michael Piller

Story by James Kahn and Adam Belanoff
Directed by Rick Kolbe
Guest Cast: Ron Canada, Dey Young, John Synder, Sheila Franklin

A previously unknown colony is a sealed off, balanced and all-too-perfect society. Their main problem now, is that a stellar core fragment is headed toward their home world of Moab four. When Picard sends a message to their colony, they increase their defensive shields. The leader of the Genome colony, Aaron Conor, responds and indicates that they do not interact with outsiders. Conor explains that their biosphere can withstand quakes measuring 8.7 magnitude. Data replies that the stresses caused by the core fragment will create disturbances beyond that level.

Picard recommends that they evacuate the colony, but Conor insists that there must be another way. Conor reluctantly agrees to allow a small Away Team to beam down. He's clearly amazed by the concept of matter transmission. Riker, Troi and Geordi beam down. They are met by Conor, as well as by Martin Benbeck. Benbeck doesn't like the intrusion into their biosphere by outsiders.

Conor explains their reluctance to leave is because their genetically engineered society has spent two centuries building to their current level. Each person has a rigid place in their society and it is more than just a colony. It is a grand experiment in creating a perfect society. Seeing Geordi, Benbeck points out that no one in their society would be permitted to be blind.

Conor apologizes for Benbeck, insisting that they need outside help if their society is to survive the approaching crisis. Geordi meets with Hannah Bates, a scientist, and they begin working together to solve the impending problems.

Troi is shown around by Conor, who has been friendly from the start and is clearly interested in her. Hannah suggests that perhaps the Enterprise can move the stellar fragment to keep it from wrecking havoc on the planet. The Genome colony had detected the approach of the stellar fragment but lacks the kind of power generating facilities required to move it. Hannah seeks permission to leave the colony to work with Geordi on the Enterprise in solving this problem. Conor permits it but Benbeck dislikes the idea.

Troi reports to Picard, explaining that she feels that Conor is a noble leader who must be convinced that whatever they do will be for the good of the colony.

Tremors begin to shake the planet as the stellar fragment approaches.

The more Conor and Troi work together, the closer their relationship becomes.

Geordi and Hannah succeed in creating the type of multi-phase tractor beam needed to try to divert the stellar fragment. Meanwhile the biosphere is undergoing a massive refortification. Fifty enterprise crewmen are needed to install new shield generators, which Conor reluctantly allows.

When Troi beams up, she breaks off her affair with Conor, explaining that it would never work. He is devoted to his colony and she to her starship counselor duties. Conor pleads with Troi to remain but she says that she cannot.

The Enterprise follows a course parallel with the stellar fragment. The tractor beam requires all available power and they barely succeed in diverting it in time as they were nearing a power overload. When Conor congratulates Hannah, she informs him that she's thinking of leaving the colony and remaining on the Enterprise. Conor is shocked.

The biosphere sustains only minor damage when the stellar fragment passes. At first Hannah reports a breach in the wall, but Geordi doublechecks this and discovers that she's wrong. He knows that she deliberately falsified the information. Hannah wants to leave the colony. She was bred to be a scientist and the Enterprise technology is far beyond anything they've developed in the biosphere. Troi now believes that the so-called "perfect society" is a lot less perfect than she would have believed before.

When Captain Picard and Counselor Troi beam down, they find Conor, Hannah and Benbeck arguing. Conor and Picard meet alone where the colony leader pleads with Picard not to let anyone from the colony leave lest it completely disrupt what they've worked to create. Jean-Luc states that he'll advise them not to make any rash decisions, but he cannot in good conscience refuse passage to anyone who wants to leave.

Connor pleads with his people to wait six months, whereupon the Enterprise will return. Hannah points out that all this will mean is Connor and others pressuring them to change their minds for six additional months. She insists on leaving now. Conor states that when she chooses to come home, she will be welcome. Finally 23 colonists choose to join the Enterprise.

Picard isn't certain whether they really did the colony a favor by showing up in that by allowing members of the carefully balanced colony to leave, they have disrupted it as much as the threat from the stellar fragment did.

EPISODE ONE HUNDRED FOURTEEN: "CONUNDRUM"

Teleplay by Barry Schkolnick
Story by Paul Schiffer
Directed by Les Landau
Guest Cast: Erich Anderson, Michelle Forbes, Liz Vassey, Erick Weiss

The Enterprise is investigating subspace signals and encounters a small vessel which begins scanning them. The computers go down and a wave of light sweeps through the inside of the ship. When it passes, no one can remember who they are or what they're doing there.

Commander Keiran MacDuff, a new bridge crewman, states that he has suffered a memory loss as well. They discover that while they still possess their skills, they've lost their identities. Worf decides that he must be the captain since he's the only Klingon aboard the ship.

Drifting debris nearby leads them to believe that they may have been attacked. When they attempt to interface the computer, they can't access anything other than the directory. Worf asks the crew throughout the ship to report on their status. They determine that the Enterprise has one thousand people on board, all without memories of who they are. Because of the weapon-ry the ship carries, they believe that they must be on a battleship.

Riker and Ro are very friendly as they check out the ship together, even though they don't know who they are and had been bickering before they lost their memories. In Ten Forward they find Data working as a bartender.

When they finally access identity records, Worf discovers that he's the security chief and feels chagrined. The computer records indicate that the Federation is at war with the Lysians and that their mission is to attack Lysian Central Command.

Troi questions whether the information they have is valid since they have no way of double-checking it. But Picard points out that their orders insist that they maintain radio silence. Troi says that nothing feels right, but she seems attracted to Riker.

When Riker returns to his quarters after getting off duty he finds Ro Laren there and likes the idea. She comes on to him and he responds.

The Enterprise enters Lysian space where they encounter a Lysian destroyer. Picard resists attacking, but MacDuff insists that they should. When the Enterprise refuses to reply to its hailing, it attacks. Picard fights back, destroying it.

Crusher comes up with an idea for regaining memory, but access to the medical files in the computer is still blocked. Data wonders about his identity, if perhaps he's from a planet of androids.

Troi tells Riker that she doesn't feel right about the war. Geordi is suspicious because anything in the files relating to personal knowledge is missing.

Crusher tries a memory stimulus on Commander MacDuff but he has a bad reaction to it. When Crusher isn't looking, he smiles.

Picard remains suspicious of the situation, as though he's being set up. MacDuff agrees but says they could prolong the war by not following orders.

MacDuff goes to Worf and plays on his Klingon pride, explaining that at the moment of truth everything may depend on him.

The Enterprise nears the Lysian Central Command. They find little armament or firepower as they destroy unmanned sentry pods. When they reach the Central Command, their sensors reveal fifteen thousand people on the station.

Riker wonders how their enemy could be one hundred years behind them in weapons technology. MacDuff insists that they attack. When Riker still refuses to attack without further deliberation, MacDuff tries to take command and when Worf resists this, he attacks the Klingon. Worf and Riker

fire hand phasers, which reveal the stunned MacDuff to be a non-human.

The impostor is a Satarran, a race long at war with the Lysians. The Satarrans needed the Enterprise technology to fight the Lysians.

His memory restored, Riker encounters Ro and Troi in Ten Forward. The two women are amused by what happened and take great joy at seeing Riker squirm with embarrassment. Clearly the dynamics of their relationship have changed.

EPISODE ONE HUNDRED FIFTEEN: "POWER PLAY"

Teleplay by Rene Balcer and Herbert J. Wright & Brannon Braga
Story by Paul Ruben and Maurice Hurley
Directed by David Livingston
Guest Cast: Rosalind Chal, Colm Meaney, Michelle Forbes, Ryan Reid

Troi, Data and O'Brien are taken over by hostile alien entities after they beam down to a planet while investigating a distress signal. At first, the aliens try to pose as these crew members. Troi tries to get Picard to investigate the southern polar region of the planet they're orbiting. Then Data tries to convince Riker to begin their search for the Essex, missing for years, in the same area, but Riker prefers to begin at another point.

Data becomes furious and attacks Riker, with O'Brien's help. They flee the bridge with Troi, who angrily tells them that if they'd waited she would have convinced the captain to go to the southern pole. Security halts the turbolift, but Data overrides it.

The three enter Ten Forward and commandeer it, taking everyone there hostage. When Worf and a security team arrive, they shoot it out with Troi, Data and O'Brien. Worf and the team are stunned while Troi, Data and O'Brien seem immune to phasers.

Riker dispatches security teams to cover the entrances to Ten Forward while O'Brien takes the transporters off line. Picard contacts Ten Forward to discuss terms. Data threatens Worf who refuses to show fear. Amid those in Ten Forward who are among the cowering hostages is Keiko, O'Brien's wife, with their baby daughter.

Troi orders Picard to place the Enterprise in a polar orbit.

Picard trades himself for the wounded hostages. After Picard enters Ten Forward, he meets with Troi, who seems to be the trio's leader. She claims to be Bryce Shumar of the starship Essex and that the other two are her officers from the crashed vessel. She explains that all she wants is to get her crew's remains from the planet where their consciousness have been trapped for two hundred years.

Geordi and Ro set up a microscopic drill above Ten Forward. They plan to shock the entities out of Troi, Data and Ro and then trap them in a containment field.

The Enterprise approaches the southern pole— the supposed crash site of the Essex. Troi insists that they beam up the remains of the Essex crew to take to Earth for proper burial, but Jean-Luc refuses to do anything unless all of the hostages are released.

When the plasma field is activated in Ten Forward it only snares Troi and O'Brien. Data goes wild, grabbing Picard by the throat and stating that he'll kill everyone if they others are not released. Picard orders the attack to stop and the entities return to the bodies of Troi and O'Brien.

The Enterprise is given coordinates of what to beam up but Riker explains that the transporters aren't working properly. They must go to a cargo bay and Picard promises safe passage. Transporter control is transferred to Ten Forward where they lock it out except to a special access code O'Brien programs in.

The three each take a hostage and go to the cargo bay. Once there Picard challenges Troi/Shumar to reveal who they really are as he can't believe that Federation officers would act so dangerously.

On the bridge, Riker explains that Picard directed them to that cargo hold because it's possible to blow the outer door which would send everyone in the hold out into space. He tells Ro that he'll blow the hold when he thinks there's no other choice.

The other entities are beamed up from the planet, whereupon Troi reveals that they are actually all condemned prisoners sentenced to that moon five hundred years before. But when a containment field is thrown around the new entities, Troi threatens to kill everyone. Picard replies that they're all willing to die to save the ship from them. He offers to return them all to the surface if Troi and the others will release the bodies they have taken over. Troi reluctantly agrees. Before she is beamed down, Shumar warns Picard not to pass this way again.

The entities free the bodies of Troi, Data and O'Brien and the prisoners are transported back down to the surface of the cold and lonely moon.

EPISODE ONE HUNDRED SIXTEEN: "ETHICS"

Teleplay by Ronald D. Moore

Story by Sara Charno & Stuart Charno
Directed by Chip Chalmers
Guest Cast: Caroline Kava, Brian Bonsall, Patti Yasutake

When Worf's spine is crushed, questions arise. Dr. Crusher wants to use existing technology to help him regain most of his motor functions. Dr. Toby Russell, a neuro-geneticist, wants to try an experimental new technique of cloning a new spine and transplanting it.

Because of his injuries, Worf sees himself as useless and wants to do things the Klingon way by committing ritual suicide. Riker refuses to help him. Riker tells Picard what Worf wants. The captain states that they should respect Worf's beliefs if it finally comes to that.

Alexander wants to see Worf, but Worf would feel shame to have his son see him in such a helpless condition. Troi explains to Alexander why Worf doesn't want to be seen. Troi goes to Worf and pleads for Alexander.

Crusher explains a technique of implants which could give Worf a sixty to seventy percent recovery of his mobility. Worf dismisses the idea. He will not live as an object of pity, hobbling around the corridors.

Dr. Russell uses this opportunity to reveal her process of genetic replication and the possibilities it holds for Worf's complete recovery. Crusher takes

Dr. Russell into the next room and registers her objection to having told Worf about this dangerous experimental technique. Crusher believes that Russell is just using Worf's desperation to try her procedure since Starfleet has turned down her requests for humanoid experimentation three times.

Alexander goes to see Worf and finds him standing. But when Worf falls, he demands that his son leave.

The survivors from the starship Denver are beamed on board and a triage system is set up in sick bay. In triage, Dr. Russell tries a new remedy on a severely injured patient and the man dies. Crusher relieves Russell of all medical duties on the ship.

Picard meets with Crusher about Dr. Russell. He wants Dr. Russell to use the genetronic operation on Worf. Crusher insists that Worf should learn to accept his condition just like anyone else would, but Picard states that it just won't happen. Klingons have a different value system. Crusher just doesn't believe that the operation will work, but Jean-Luc states that it really is Worf's only choice.

Riker visits Worf who still wants to perform the suicide ritual. Will refuses and thinks that Worf is being selfish. But he's also looked into it and learned that the ritual is supposed to be performed by a family member, preferably the oldest son. Worf refuses to consider the idea, but Riker leaves Worf to think about it.

Worf tells his son that he has decided not to kill himself but will undergo a dangerous operation.

Crusher reluctantly grants Worf's request for the operation. The operation is begun by Crusher and Dr. Russell and Worf's back is opened. Picard and Riker are elsewhere, together, waiting.

Worf's spine is removed and genetic replacement of the damaged parts of the spine is begun. The spine is replaced and tissue growth proceeds properly. Worf is fully reconnected to his spine but they encounter trouble. Worf goes into cardiac arrest. They use a cortical stimulator but it doesn't seem to work. Worf is declared dead.

Crusher comes out to tell Alexander that his father has died. The boy demands to see him. He stands next to the body, but Crusher detects something and reactivates the bio-monitor. Worf is alive. A back-up synaptic system in his body saved him.

Dr. Russell comes to say good-bye to Crusher. Crusher is very pleased that Worf will live but she still believes that Russell takes too many shortcuts.

EPISODE ONE HUNDRED SEVENTEEN: "THE OUTCAST"

Written by Jeri Taylor
Directed by Robert Scheerer
Guest Cast: Melinda Culea, Callan White, Megan Cole

The Enterprise has been contacted by the J'Naii, an androgynous race. The J'Naii need assistance in locating a missing shuttle. Some of the J'Naii have beamed over and are on board helping in the search. In the process they discover an area of null space in the region which had never previous need detected.

Riker has been working with the aliens in the investigation, and his partner is a J'Naii named Soren. The J'Naii are a species without gender, but Riker likes the androgen he's working with. Not everyone on the Enterprise likes the J'Naii, though. Worf in particular is made uncomfortable by being around the androgynous people. Soren is coy but curious. She asks Riker what gender is like, something he finds difficult to explain.

When Riker and Soren take the shuttle out to chart the pocket of null space, Soren inquires about human mating practices. Soren asks the commander about his sexual organs, which startles him at first as he admits that it's not a normal subject for casual conversation.

Suddenly the shuttle encounters trouble and loses an engine. The turbulence throws Soren to the floor where she's knocked unconscious. Soren is beamed to sick bay but the J'Naii only has a minor concussion. Initially when Soren is examined by Dr. Crusher the J'Naii appears nervous, but this soon passes. Soren asks Dr. Crusher what it's like to be female and she tries to explain but basically says that it is the way she has always been.

Dr. Crusher states that long ago the female used to be considered inferior to the male, but that is no longer true. When Riker comes to see Soren in sick bay, her unspoken response to him makes it evident to Dr. Crusher that Soren is attracted to Will Riker.

Alone with Riker, Soren confesses affection for him. Soren explains that she was "born different" and is a throwback to the time when her people were born with gender and had a tendency to be male or female. But now the J'Naii consider gender to be offensive. The J'Naii feel that by evolving away from gender they have moved onto a higher form of life.

Soren explains that on her world such a thing as a strong inclination to one gender or the other is forbidden. Those who are revealed to possess such feelings are ridiculed and given psycho treatments. Soren has lived with the secret of her having female gender emotions for a long time, living a life of pretense and lies.

Riker and Soren take the shuttle out again and penetrate the area of null space. They find the J'Naii shuttle and rescue its two unconscious inhabitants and then are beamed back to the Enterprise when their own shuttle starts experiencing trouble.

Noor, the J'Naii leader, holds a banquet in honor of the Enterprise for rescuing the shuttle crew. Riker and Soren go off alone in the woods and kiss. Back on board the Enterprise, Riker goes to Troi and confesses his relationship with Soren. But Deanna had already noticed and isn't surprised. When Riker goes to Soren's temporary quarters on the ship he finds that Soren is gone and instead Krite is there in her place. Krite reveals that they know about Soren and that Soren has been taken into custody.

Riker beams down and bursts into the hearing where Soren is being tried for her social crime. To his credit, Riker stands up for Soren and takes the blame himself for what happened. But Soren decides to stop hiding and says that Riker is just trying to help. Soren confesses that she is female.

"I am tired of lies," she admits. "I have had these feelings, these longings, all of my life. It is not unnatural. I am not sick because I feel this way. I do not need to be helped. I do not need to be cured. What I need, and what all of those who are like me need, is your understanding and your compassion."

The judge isn't impressed by the speech and in fact Noor has no doubt heard similar things before. The judge replies, "Your decision to admit your perversion makes it much more likely that we can help you."

While Soren is being led away, Riker steps up to the judge and objects, offering to take Soren back to the Enterprise never to return to trouble the J'Naii society. But Noor, the judge, explains that on this world everyone wants to be normal, and the J'Naii take their responsibilities to their people very seriously. For the Federation to interfere would violate the Prime Directive.

Back on the Enterprise Riker meets with Picard to discuss the situation. Will Riker feels guilty about all this and blames himself, and well he should, for while Soren initiated the romance, Riker was the one who was reckless enough to kiss Soren on the surface of her own world. Picard counsels Riker against doing anything rash but he won't stand in Will's way.

Riker plans an escape attempt and Worf offers to help. The Klingon has come to terms with his discomfort. While he had initially disliked the J'Naii he respects the idea of individuality. Plus he is loyal to Riker and states, "A warrior does not let a friend face danger alone."

They beam down but when they rescue Soren, it's too late. She's already been brainwashed and claims to be happy. When Riker tells Soren that maybe Dr. Crusher can reverse the treatment, Soren is surprised at the suggestion and rejects it. Why would she want to go back to the way she was? Soren's personality has largely altered and with it any feelings she had for Riker have been neutralized. Regretfully, Riker agrees to Soren's wishes and he returns to the Enterprise without her.

EPISODE ONE HUNDRED EIGHTEEN: "CAUSE AND EFFECT"

Written by Brannon Braga
Directed by Jonathan Frakes
Guest Cast: Michelle Forbes, Patti Yasutake, Kelsey Grammer

The story begins on Stardate 45652.1, as the Enterprise enters the uncharted Typhon Expanse.

A poker game is in progress between Data, Riker, Worf and Crusher are also playing. They bet. Data and Worf fold. Crusher winds because Riker was bluffing.

Crusher is summoned to sick bay to see Geordi, who is suffering from dizziness. Crusher experiences déjà vu as she's certain that Geordi has come to her before for this same problem.

In her quarters, Crusher lies down to sleep, then wakes up upon hearing a babble of voices. But by the time she stands up and turns on the light the voices are gone. At a staff meeting, Beverly reports hearing the voices, and that ten other people heard them as well at the same time.

Worf reports unusual readings 20,000 kilometers off the starboard bow. It's a highly localized distortion of the space-time continuum. Picard has the Enterprise back off slowly, but power levels on the ship begin to drop. Suddenly another ship appears in front of them from out of the time disturbance. Shields aren't working and the other ship is on a collision course. They use a tractor beam to divert the other ship, but it hits one of the nacelles on the Enterprise. The Enterprise spins out of control and explodes. . . again.

It's stardate 45652.1 again. The same poker game is being played. Crusher seems distracted. Riker folds stating that he had a feeling she was going to call his bluff. Crusher is called to sick bay to see Geordi. When she examines Geordi, both of them experience déjà vu over this. In her room, Beverly has an odd feeling. She suddenly hears a strange babble of voices, but then it fades. She goes to report this to Picard. Both of them are experiencing déjà vu.

At the next staff meeting for the command personnel, they discuss the anomalies and then Worf reports the distortion in the space-time continuum. The accident happens again. The Enterprise is destroyed once again. . .

It's stardate 45652.1 again. The poker game is being played, but now Worf and Beverly have déjà vu. Crusher knows what cards are to be dealt, as does Worf and Riker. Data says that this is highly improbable. Crusher says that she knows that Geordi is about to enter sick bay.

Beverly reports to Picard about the feelings of repetition. Geordi's visor is seeing distortions which read like afterimages in time. That night Beverly knows what's about to happen and uses her tricorder to record the voices. She takes it to Geordi and Data who try to determine what the sound is. Data has the computer filter it and then do continuous playback. Data listens and determines that it's one thousand voices—the Enterprise crew.

At the staff meeting, Geordi reports that they're in a time loop. Data has analyzed the recording and isolated Picard ordering them to abandon ship. Can they escape the time loop? Picard decides to stay on course. Geordi suggests trying to send a message into the next loop. They think that Data can pick up the message subconsciously by adjusting his brain.

The Enterprise is approaching the time distortion. The accident sequence begins again. Riker suggests decompressing the shuttle bay to move the Enterprise out of the path of collision. Data suggests a tractor beam which they try instead. The Enterprise is hit and just before it explodes Data sends his message into the time continuum.

It's stardate 45652.1 again.

In the poker game, they think they know the cards that Data is going to deal but instead he deals all 3's. Then he deals everyone three-of-a-kind. Beverly goes to sick bay to treat Geordi again. Beverly and Geordi talk to Picard. Data keeps encountering the numeral three an inordinate number of times.

They get the voice recording again. They know about the accident and the time loop, but where does the number three enter into it? Maybe Data is receiving a message. They get the unusual time-continuum readings again. The other ship appears. The Enterprise begins to lose power again. Impact with the other ship in 36 seconds.

Data realizes that his tractor beam suggestion won't work and he decompresses the shuttle bay. The Enterprise is pushed out of the path of the other starship. No collision occurs. The number three referred to the number of insignia on Riker's uniform, indicating that his suggestion was the correct one to save the ship.

They discover that they have been in a the time loop for seventeen days. The other vessel is the USS Bozeman, a Federation ship, Soyuz Class, a type not used for eighty years. Captain Picard communicates with Captain Bateson on the other vessel. Bateson thinks it's still 2278—the 23rd century rather than the 24th century. Jean-Luc suggests that Bateson to beam over to the Enterprise so that he can have a talk with him.

EPISODE ONE HUNDRED NINETEEN:
"THE FIRST DUTY"

Written by Ronald D. Moore & Naren Shankar
Directed by Paul Lynch
Guest Cast: Ray Walston, Robert Duncan McNeill, Ed Lauter, Richard Fancy, Jacqueline Brookes, Wil Wheaton

Starfleet Academy contacts Picard to tell him that there's been an accident. Wes was hurt, but not seriously. Another cadet was killed. Admiral Brand states that they're investigating and taking depositions from Nova Squadron.

At Starfleet Academy, Wes meets with his mother and Picard. He is also visited by Nicholas, his squadron leader. After Picard and Crusher leave, Nicholas tells Wes that they have to stick together. Wes reluctantly agrees.

Picard wanders the grounds of Starfleet and encounters the groundskeeper, Boothby, who was there when Picard was a cadet. Their discussion reveals that he once did Picard a favor.

Nova Squadron is ready for the inquiry and are standing together. They describe what happened, saying they were in a diamond formation when their ships collided. They claim that they didn't deviate from their flight plan but then admit that they did, slightly. No one claims to have seen the collision because they were flying on sensor readings only.

Nicholas blames the accident on Josh Albert, the one who died. He says that Josh panicked. The panel recesses to reconvene the next day. Back on the Enterprise, Picard asks Geordi and Data to reconstruct the accident with the computer.

Wes and Nicholas get into an argument because they had agreed not to lie and Wes feels that they're blaming everything on their dead friend when it wasn't really his fault. More happened than they're willing to admit. To admit too much would destroy their careers. The next day information from the flight recorder in Wes's ship is to be played, although the information is incomplete. Before the hearing, Josh's father talks to Wes and thanks him for all the help he gave to Josh. He tells Wes that he's sorry that Josh let him down.

When Wes Crusher testifies, he's hammered with new information consisting of a satellite photo of the ships flying wing-to-wing, contrary to their sworn testimony. Wes has no explanation for the photo, but Picard thinks that he does.

Jean-Luc believes that the Nova Squadron was practicing a forbidden maneuver when the accident happened. The maneuver, outlawed for one hundred years, involves all five ships igniting their plasma trails while flying in close formation. Picard confronts Wes, but the boy won't answer. Picard tells Wes that the first duty is to the truth! Either Wes tells the truth to the board of inquiry or he will.

When Wes tells Nicholas that Picard knows, he wants Wes to deny it. But Wes won't be put into the position of calling Picard a liar. Wes wants to tell the truth and says that they should all come forward. But Nicholas explains that it would be a pointless sacrifice for them to make. Josh is dead and nothing they can do will bring him back.

Admiral Brand expresses suspicion over the testimony they have heard, but suspicion is not proof. The Admiral is about to close the case and exonerate the Nova Squadron when Wes stands up and reveals what really happened. If Josh did panic it was because he was pushed into performing a dangerous and illegal maneuver he wasn't ready to do.

Punishment is handed out to all concerned. Wes Crusher has to repeat his final year of classes at Starfleet Academy. Nicholas is expelled because he decided to step forward and accept full blame for both the incident and the cover-up. Jean-Luc tells Wes that while he has difficult days ahead, he did the right thing as the first duty is always to the truth.

EPISODE ONE HUNDRED TWENTY: "COST OF LIVING"
Written by Peter Allan Fields

Directed by Winrich Kolbe

Guest Cast: Majel Barrett, Brian Bonsall, Tony Jay, Carel Struycken, David Oliver, Albie Selznick, Patrick Cronin, Tracy D'Arcy, George Ede, Christopher Halsted

Worf and Alexander's relationship continues to show some strains. They argue in Troi's office, and she suggests that they draw up an agreement. Troi is then told that her mother has come aboard. Lwaxana tells Troi that she's getting married again and that she wants the ceremony performed in Ten Forward.

Troi is surprised and wants to know who the groom is. He's Compio from Constelaine, but Lwaxana has never met him in person. Worf and Alexander are having difficulty drawing up their contract and they enter Troi's quarters to speak to her. Lwaxana takes a shine to Alexander and doesn't like the idea of the contract. Riker tells Picard that he's to give away the bride. As they speak they don't notice that some kind of energy entity has penetrated the hull of the Enterprise.

When Alexander is on his way to his meeting with Troi, the boy encounters Lwaxana, who takes him in hand. Alexander reveals that he hates his father because he's expected to do everything right all the time and he doesn't know how. Lwaxana takes Alexander to the holodeck to experience a mud bath. Deanna comes to Worf's quarters looking for Alexander and when they check the computer they learn that the boy is with Troi's mother in the holodeck.

Worf and Troi are not pleased that Mrs. Troi took Alexander without permission. Troi thinks that her mother is giving Alexander mixed messages. Lwaxana states that she gave Troi mixed messages at that age and she still turned out deadly dull. Lwaxana reveals that she won't be having a Betazoid wedding but will wear a dress. Troi is shocked that her mother won't appear naked at her own wedding.

Alexander visits Lwaxana. He's sorry if he got her in trouble. She admits that she's lonely and that's why she's getting married. Malfunctions plague the Enterprise. Nitrium was absorbed from the replicator and the stabilizer. Something is eating the nitrium.

Lwaxana's future husband, Minister Compio, beams on board with his Protocol Minister. Compio and Lwaxana are talking when Alexander enters. Compio wants to discuss the wedding and other subjects. Troi and Worf enter and want Alexander to go home. An argument erupts over who should do what first and finally Lwaxana walks out on all of them.

Lwaxana and Alexander go to the holodeck again where Lwaxana notices that a wall of the holodeck is breaking down.

Picard and his staff determine that a certain asteroid field would be the best place to lose the parasites from the ship, but it will take five hours to reach that site. In the meantime the parasites are busy. Life support starts shutting down on some decks. Oxygen levels are dropping and Picard orders Data to carry out the plan if everyone else on the bridge passes out. As the Enterprise reaches the asteroid field, Data uses an emitter beam to lure the parasites off the ship. With the parasites gone, repairs begin and Data transfers power from the warp engines to the life support systems.

Lwaxana's arrives in Ten Forward for her wedding, naked, in the Betazoid tradition. Compio is stunned and says nothing, but his Protocol Minster dubs the incident "Infamous!" and leads Compio out of Ten Forward. The wedding, it seems, if off, but Lwaxana doesn't mind a bit. For her it's back to the holodeck mud baths, only this time she's determined that Worf will learn how to enjoy them as well.

EPISODE ONE HUNDRED TWENTY-ONE: "THE PERFECT MATE"

Teleplay by Gary Perconte and Michael Piller
Story by Rene Echevarria and Gary Perconte
Directed by Cliff Bole
Guest Cast: Famke Janssen, Tim O'Connor, Max Grodenchik, Mickey Cottrell
Michael Snyder, David Paul Needles, Roger Rignack, Charles Gunning, April Grace

Two warring planets have agreed to a ceremony of reconciliation to end their decades long conflict. An item in the cargo bay is vital to this peace ceremony.

One planet's ambassador is shown the holodeck set-up arranged for his ceremony which recreates an ancient temple from his world.

A Ferengi bent on stealing the object for one of his own clients sneaks into the cargo bay. There he sees a glowing translucent object floating above the floor. Security detects him. When they surprise him the Ferengi accidentally disturbs the object, which opens. They witness the emergence of a beautiful woman who walks up to Picard and says that she is for him. She is an empath—a gift to the planetary leader they are going to meet.

Picard is disturbed by this as he considers using a human being like this to be slavery and a violation of Federation rules. She is an empathic metamorph who can sense what a mate wants and needs. Female metamorphs are rare. She states that she does this of her own accord.

Her name is K'Malla and she's in her final stage of sexual development when she will imprint on one man. K'Malls comes on to Riker when he leads her to her quarters, but he resists her undeniable charms, stating that he never opens another man's gift.

Crusher argues with Picard about allowing the woman to be delivered into a life of prostitution. Picard points out that it would violate the Prime Directive to interfere. Picard visits K'Malla and is impressed by her intelligence. The Enterprise reaches the coordinates of the conference.

Picard assigns Data as K'Malla's chaperone so that she can leave her quarters safely. She and Data enter Ten Forward where men start coming on to her and she clearly appreciates it. Things get a bit rowdy until Worf steps in. She even knows how to excite Worf, much against his will as he's surprised at himself after she leaves Ten Forward.

K'Malla agrees to stay in her quarters—if Jean-Luc will visit with her. She then tries to get Picard aroused.

The Ferengi try to bribe the ambassador. They offer him a great deal of money to sell them the metamorph. When the ambassador states that he's going to report this to the captain, they attempt to stop him and the ambassador is knocked down, injuring himself. Although the ambassador is unconscious in sick bay, the conference must go on.

When they suggest that Picard take over, K'Malla agrees to help him prepare and learn the ceremonies and rituals. K'Malla explains to Jean-Luc that she's been prepared for her role since she was four years old. But she finds herself attracted to Picard. She likes to talk to him and likes the sound of his voice. But he doesn't want to use her as other men do. She is scheduled to be presented to her future husband the next morning.

Picard visits K'Malla's future mate and finds him only mildly interested in her. When Jean-Luc visits the metamorph one last time, K'Malla admits that she will never really love her mate because she has already bonded with Picard. But she has her duty to perform and her mate will never know the difference. The presentation ceremony is performed while Picard watches silently.

EPISODE ONE HUNDRED TWENTY-TWO: "IMAGINARY FRIEND"

Teleplay by Edithe Swensen and Brannon Braga
Story by Jean Louise Matthias & Ronald Wilkerson and Richard Fligel
Directed by Gabrielle Beaumont
Guest Cast: Noley Thornton, Shay Astar, Jeff Allin, Brian Bonsall, Patti Yasutake, Sheila Franklin

Troi talks to Clara Sutter, a little girl who's telling her about Isabella, her imaginary friend. Troi tells Clara's father that his daughter's imaginary friend is just Clara's response to her frequent relocations. Troi feels that Clara will fit in once she's made new friends on the Enterprise.

The Enterprise arrives at a nebula which has formed around a neutron star. A glowing entity enters the vessel and explores the ship. It enters the botanical gardens, passes unnoticed through Clara's head and then assumes the form of a little girl with blond hair. Isabella, Clara's imaginary friend, has become real.

The Enterprise shudders as and its speed diminishes slightly. Shields indicate they hit something but sensors say they didn't. Their speed is still dropping. Clara enters engineering during this situation and her father sees her and tells her to leave. Isabella makes sure that she is invisible when grownups are around since they don't believe in her anyway.

Isabella wants to go where there's lots of people. They run down the corridor playing and run into Worf. He says that this isn't an area for children, but after he leaves they slip past and continue on their path.

Sutter talks to Geordi about what it was like growing up with parents in Starfleet and if it was difficult on him. Geordi says he may have missed out on some things but that it was really just one long adventure to him.

Clara enters Ten Forward and Guinan talks to her. Guinan had an imaginary friend as a child, but it was a razorbeast that purred her to sleep at night. Troi encounters Clara and invites her for a walk. Troi explains that Ten Forward is for grownups, but Clara says that Isabella insisted on going there. In the turbolift Troi pretends to talk to Isabella. Clara says that Isabella says to leave them alone. Later Isabella apologizes to Clara for getting her in trouble. Isabella has decided she doesn't like grownups and wants to go to engineering.

Troi enters to talk to Clara and invites her to ceramics class, but she can't bring Isabella, who is angry at being left out.

The speed of the Enterprise drops again by 1.1%, but they don't know the origin of the drag coefficient. They discover that they've been encountering strands of energy and they want to discover how many there are. The Enterprise manages to make the strands visible and discovers that there are 47 million of them. They decide to turn around and leave the nebula.

At the children's ceramics class, Clara is teamed with Alexander. In Troi's quarters her cup of hot chocolate mysteriously falls over by itself. Back in the ceramics class, Isabella knocks over Alexander's model but Clara can't convince him of the truth.

As she turns and runs out, Isabella hits Alexander from behind with a piece of clay, which really confuses him. Clara runs down to the botanical gardens where she cries because of what happened. Isabella appears and says that Clara is going to die along with everyone else when the others come. The Enterprise is 12 minutes from clearing the nebula but its speed is dropping further.

Sutter calls Troi to his quarters where Clara is afraid to enter her room because of Isabella. She tells Troi what Isabella threatened. Isabella appears and attacks Troi. In sick bay, Troi tells everyone what happened. Picard contacts Worf and describes Isabella, whom Worf reports having seen earlier. They order a security alert.

As the Enterprise's speed drops by another 22%, they detect life forms approaching which begin to drain the shields. When Picard, Clara and a security team go to the botanical gardens to search for the mysterious Isabella, the child appears to them, stating that she is there to determine if they are a threat. Isabella states that she believes that the crew are cruel, unfair and restrictive.

Jean-Luc explains that the rules are to keep children from harm. Finally Isabella comes to understand and appreciate what he is saying and smiles. The threatening entities depart and Captain Picard has an energy beam directed into the nebula for the entities to feed on.

Clara sees Isabella one last time. The entity has come back to apologize for the trouble she caused and hope they can meet again one day. Then Clara's imaginary friend is gone.

EPISODE ONE HUNDRED TWENTY-THREE: "I, BORG"

Written by Rene Echevarria
Directed by Robert Lederman
Guest Cast: Jonathan Del Arco

When a young Borg is found alive at a crash site in, Picard is stunned by the news. Picard orders the Away Team back to the ship but Crusher argues against leaving the young Borg to die. Riker points out that the transmission is undoubtedly a homing signal. Worf wants to kill the Borg and make it look like it died in the crash.

Picard allows the injured Borg beamed aboard for treatment, but insists that it be confined in a detention cell. He has Geordi neutralize the Borg's internal homing signal.

Troi's concerned that Picard might be having a bad reaction to having a Borg aboard the ship, but he insists that he's fine.

In the cell, Picard observes Borg. Some of its implants are damaged and will have to be replaced. Picard suggests introducing an invasive programming sequence through its biochip system which would infect the entire Borg collective. He wants something which would cause total systems failure and destroy the Borg race within months.

Crusher questions whether they have the right to kill an entire race. Picard points out that the Borg are the ones who have carried out acts of war against the Federation and that there are no innocent civilians in the Borg collective.

The Borg prisoner awakens and doesn't know what to do since it is cut off from the collective. Crusher says that he looks scared.

Picard fences with Guinan. They take a break and she asks about the Borg prisoner. She doesn't understand why they are helping it. They fence again and Guinan demonstrates through a trick how feeling sorry for an opponent can be a mistake.

The Borg wants to return to the collective. It calls itself, "Third of Five" in reference to the Borg which were in the five man craft which crashed. Crusher explains to the Borg how she saved its life. Geordi asks it questions and it responds. It asks if it has a name and repeats the word "you" which sounds like "Hugh," and Geordi thinks that name would be perfect.

Crusher gives the Borg perception tests and it allows Geordi to examine its eyepiece. Hugh describes what it is like living on a Borg ship with the thoughts of thousands of others in its head.

Geordi tells Guinan that the Borg seems like a lost child, a description which she bristles at. She points out that the other Borg will come for him and destroy them all if they can. Geordi says that she should see the Borg for herself.

The Enterprise picks up a small Borg ship on its long range scanners. It will arrive in the system in thirty-one hours.

Guinan visits Hugh and tells it how the Borg destroyed her people and scattered them throughout the galaxy. It recognizes that she is lonely, just like it is. Guinan is taken aback by this sensitive observation from what she regards as a creature.

Geordi explains to Hugh why he and his friends don't want to be assimilated. Later Geordi completes the device, a paradox designed to create an endless and unsolvable puzzle, which will infect the Borg collective. But now Geordi has concerns about using the Borg in this way as he feels that he has genuinely gotten to know it.

Guinan tells Picard about the Borg, which he hasn't observed since it has awakened. Picard states that he doesn't care that some of the crew seem to have turned it into some sort of pet. She wonders why Picard hasn't looked it in the eye if he's going to use it to destroy its race. Guinan just isn't certain that it's really a Borg any more.

Jean-Luc decides to visit the Borg alone. When he enters it recognizes him as Locutus. Picard questions it to see what it really thinks. It likes Geordi and doesn't want him to die. Hugh calls Geordi a friend and refuses to assist Locutus when he suggests that they should assimilate Geordi. The Borg has a real human personality and refers to itself as "I" when speaking to Picard.

Picard decides not to use the destructive program in Hugh but they know that they still must erase his memories of them on the ship. But even so he may retain the knowledge of self and singularity, which could have dramatic implications in the Borg collective. He gives Hugh a choice, and Hugh decides to return. They drop him off at the crash site, where he is reunited with the Borg.

EPISODE ONE HUNDRED TWENTY-FOUR: "THE NEXT PHASE"

Written by Ronald D. Moore
Directed by David Carson
Guest Cast: Michelle Forbes, Thomas Kopache, Susanna Thompson, Shelby Leverington, Brian Cousins, Kenneth Meseroll

Geordi and Ro are declared dead after an apparent transporter accident. This occurred during an attempt to save a damaged Romulan ship. The Romulan ship is still in danger of exploding, and its engine core has to be ejected from the Romulan ship and the Enterprise extends their shields to protect the other ship when the core explodes in space.

Picard walks right by Ro without seeing her. She's lying on a corridor floor and wakes up. She enters sick bay but no one pays any attention to her. Ro overhears Picard and Crusher talking about her but no one can see or hear her. Picard walks right through her as though she's an invisible ghost. Ro attempts to communicate with Crusher, but to no avail.

On the Romulan ship, power is transferred from the Enterprise so that the other ship can make it back to Romulus.

On the Enterprise, Data asks Picard if he can conduct Geordi's memorial service. He considered Geordi his best friend.

Geordi finds Ro Laren again and reveals that he's discovered the same things that she has. While they are solid to each other, Ro nevertheless believes that they're spirits or souls. Geordi refuses to accept this as even being a possibility.

Meanwhile, Data is investigating the accident and detects Kromiton particles from the Romulan ship's cloaking device and decides to investigate matters further aboard the Romulan ship.

Geordi finds Ro and insists that they accompany Data on the shuttle to the Romulan ship. Ro reluctantly agrees to accompany him. She still thinks that they're both dead. Once they're on board the Romulan ship, Geordi and Ro look around while Data investigates. Geordi finds a strange phase invertor

which could have been combined with a cloaking device. He's convinced now that an accident made them phase and that now they have to find a way to reverse the process.

Geordi and Ro overhear the Romulans planning to sabotage the Enterprise in order to keep their interphase generator from being discovered. Now more than ever they have to find a way back in order to warn the others. But unknown to them there is a Romulan present who has also been phased and he follows them.

The Romulan follows when Geordi and Ro return to the Enterprise on the shuttle. Meanwhile, Data detects more Kroniton fields on the Enterprise. Geordi realizes that he and Ro are leaving the Kroniton fields whenever they touch something.

It's only a matter of time before Ensign Ro encounters the Romulan. He points his disruptor at her and wants to know how to be de-phased. The Romulan thinks that Geordi and Ro may have the answer. Elsewhere on the Enterprise, Geordi tries to alert Data to his presence and guesses a way he might be brought back.

The Romulan leads Ro at gun point but suddenly she attacks him and flees. He follows, firing his disruptor as he chases her. Data tracks the new Kroniton fields this unleashes.

When the Romulan catches up to Ro they get into a hand-to-hand fight. Just then Geordi encounters them, takes in what is happening and rams into the Romulan, knocking him through the bulkhead into space. The Romulan drifts helplessly away. Aboard the Romulan ship the Enterprise technicians have helped the Romulans install a new engine core. With that completed, they beam back to the Enterprise and begin preparations to leave.

Geordi and Ro want to get to where the Kroniton decontamination is and see if it will make them briefly visible. They go to Ten Forward where where they find a party going on as people share their memories of Geordi and Ro. Ensign Ro sets her disruptor to overload and its explosion dramatically increases the Kroniton fields. The decontamination field is increased as well, causing Geordi and Ro to partially materialize. Picard and Data witness this and the android figures out what to do.

Data figures out how to bring them back and Geordi and Ro reappear. They tell Picard about the Romulan's plot to sabotage to the Enterprise, and they barely manage to avert it.

Data welcomes Geordi back.

Ro and Geordi, alone, have their first meal in two days. Geordi is digging in but Ro seems distracted. She admits that for awhile she thought she was dead and had begun to believe in what the Bajorans had taught about the afterlife, but now she doesn't know what to believe.

EPISODE ONE HUNDRED TWENTY-FIVE: "THE INNER LIGHT"

Teleplay by Morgan Gendel and Peter Allan Fields
Story by Morgan Gendel
Directed by Peter Lauritson
Guest Cast: Margot Rose, Richard Riehle, Scott Jaeck, Jennifer Nash, Patti Yasutake, Daniel Stewart

An ancient alien probe renders Picard unconscious. As his body lies on the bridge, attended by Crusher, he finds himself in a strange place, tended by a strange woman, Helene, who calls him Kamen and says that he's had a fever for three days. He leaves the house and finds a community of people.

The township is fighting a drought which has been plaguing them for some time. Picard meets Batai, a friend of Kamen's and a council leader. Picard feigns amnesia and learns that he's on the planet Katan. Picard goes for a walk to investigate this place. He returns "home" to Helene after dark, where he finds his wife very worried about him.

Picard angrily insists that this is not his life. He asks about their communications system and learns that Katan has no interplanetary capabilities. He finds that Kamen is an iron weaver and plays the flute. Helene, his wife, wants him to come to bed. Picard is reluctant. He notices her necklace looks just like the probe that the Enterprise encountered.

Living as Kamen, Picard settles into his life on Katan and has been there five years already. He tells Helene that his life on the Enterprise was real and he can't just give it up. He meets with an administrator and says that they should build water condensers, but it's clear that the administrator thinks that this is premature.

Picard has learned to play the flute during those five years. Picard/Kamen tells Helene that he wants to start a family. They embrace and kiss.

On the Enterprise they think they can trace the probe to its origin point.

On Katan, Kamen/Picard has a five year old daughter and a newborn son. He names the boy Batai for his friend who died a year before the child's birth. Suddenly Kamen collapses. On the Enterprise they're disrupting the beam and Picard is starting to die without it, so they restore beam contact. Picard stabilizes, but he's still unconscious. On

Katan, Kamen's daughter is a young woman now. Picard has been on Katan for twenty-five years by this time.

The Enterprise has traces the probe to the world of Katan where all life was destroyed one thousand years ago when that systems star went nova.

Kamen working on his telescope, which he built thirty years before. His son, Batai, is grown now and wants to be a musician rather than a scientist like his father. Kamen is going to present evidence he has proving that Katan is doomed. He discovers that the council already knows, but they do have a plan to try something to preserve something of their race. Kamen is summoned home by Batai—Helene is dying. He goes to her side and watches as she passes away quietly.

Kamen is playing with his grandson when Batai comes in and tells his father that they're going to see a missile launched. Kamen is reluctant to go. He's angry, knowing Katan is dying and that his grandson will never live to have a full life.

When Kamen goes outside to see the launching he discovers that it's a satellite. Suddenly Batai—Kamen's long dead friend—appears and explains that this probe is being sent to find someone in the future who can be a teacher and tell about the people of Katan. Picard realizes that he is that someone that the probe is going to seek. Helene appears to

Kamen and says that the rest of them have been gone a thousand years. "Tell them of us, my darling."

Suddenly Jean-Luc awakens on the Enterprise bridge. Picard has been unconscious for twenty-five minutes. With the beam having deactivated by itself, the probe is brought into the cargo bay. Later, in his quarters, Picard is looking at things which he hasn't seen in 30 years. The probe has been opened and inside was a package containing the flute, a flute identical to the one Jean-Luc learned to play on Katan. Picard clutches to him and then begins to play, just as he did when he was Kamen living on the lost world of Katan.

EPISODE ONE HUNDRED TWENTY-SIX: "TIME'S ARROW" PART ONE

Teleplay by Joe Menosky and Michael Piller
Story by Joe Menosky
Directed by Les Landau
Guest Cast: Jerry Hardin, Michael Aron, Barry Kivel, Ken Thorley, Sheldon Peters Wolfchild, Jack M. dock, Marc Alaimo, Milt Tarver, Michael Hungerford

Excavations beneath San Francisco reveal evidence of alien visitors on Earth in the late 19th Century— along with Data's severed head!

On the Enterprise, Data's head is studied. Data casually observes that he's destined to die on Earth in the 1800's. They trace an object in the cave to another world investigate. Geordi and Data discuss the fact that Data knows that he's destined to die. Geordi tells Guinan about it, but it doesn't seem to bother her. She remarks to herself that it's a full circle.

Riker and Troi discuss the Data situation and how it's like discovering that someone you love has a terminal illness. Data encounters them and notes that they, like others lately, stop talking when they see him. They admit this is true and discuss their feelings. Arriving at their planetary destination, sensors note a cave containing triolic waves beneath the surface. An Away Team is sent. Data wants to go but Picard won't let him. "One cannot cheat fate," Data observes, but Picard wants to try.

In the cave, Troi senses hundreds of terrified humans. Could they be trapped in time? They seem to be temporarily out of phase with the people in the cave. But to get in phase, Data must join the Away Team. Data establishes a communications link with the Away Team and then makes himself in phase with the temporal distortion. He reports what he sees—blind entities unaware of him. Data encounters further temporal distortion. They lose contact with him, his tricorder device the only thing left to indicate that he was there.

Data finds himself on a San Francisco city street. in the 19th century. He goes to a hotel where he gets into a poker game, passing himself off as a Frenchman. Using his poker skills and positronic brain, Data wins a lot of money and checks into a hotel room. Data gives the bellhop an extensive list of supplies to get for him.

Not far from the hotel, two strangers walk up to an old miner and shoot him with a strange ray which emerges from a handbag. The old man dies and the two people walk away.

On the Enterprise they decide that they must investigate the time disturbance and whether it's a threat to 19th century Earth. They plan to look for Data as well. Worf points out that it may be their fate to die with Data as their remains in that cave would have turned to dust long ago.

In San Francisco, Data has constructed an electronic device in his hotel room. He looks at a copy of the latest edition of the newspaper which the bellhop has brought up to him and sees a photo of Guinan, who has reportedly just arrived in town. At the reception for Guinan, Samuel Clemens speculates on man's place in the universe.

Data arrives at the reception and sees Guinan. He believes that she some-how followed him from the future, but when he manages to talk to her, she doesn't recognize him. But when Data mentions the word starship she quickly ushers him off to one side where they can talk privately. Data realizes that Guinan is older than he thought and that she is visiting Earth, perhaps like an alien tourist. Data explains that he's from the future where he serves with her on the Enterprise.

Just then Samuel Clemens reveals that he's been eavesdropping on them.

In the future, Picard, Riker, Troi, Geordi, Worf, and Crusher beam down to the alien cave on Devidian Two. There they set up a device to duplicate the phase shift Data experienced. Picard had not planned to go, but Guinan explains that he must, but she cannot explain why he must. Worf beams back up to the Enterprise as there is no way that he could be adequately disguised on Earth of the 19th century.

Geordi activates the field device on Devidian Two and they see strange a glowing portal which the Away Team enters. The portal closes after them. The question remains. . . how will this bizarre sequence of events turn out?

END OF SEASON FIVE

James at Paramount Studios for the Rodden- berry building dedication.

Photo © 1994 Albert L. Ortega

Levar with wife Stephanie Cozart at the Santa Monika Pier for a lunch with underpriviledged children from Venice, California.

Photo ©
1994
Albert L.
Ortega

SEASON SIX

SEASON SIX

Year six is a mixed bag with a wide range of stories and story-telling styles from human dimension ("Tapestry" and "Second Chances") to hard SF ("Timescape"). Unfortunately the disappointing conclusion to "Time's Arrow" did not initially bode well for the season. The meandering storyline in part two completely undercut all of the excitement established in the first part as it lurched from one scene to another, dragging Samuel Clemens along for the unnecessary ride.

"Realm of Fear" features the return of Barclay, the crewman first seen in "Hollow Pursuits." It's nice to see a recurring character who is actually portrayed as having personality problems. Too many of the characters we meet on TNG don't have much of a personality at all.

Surprisingly, Scotty's crossover appearance on THE NEXT GENERATION in "Relics" is better written than Spock's was in "Reunification." James Doohan is actually given some acting to do for a change, particularly in the portrayal of him as a man out of time—an old man who just doesn't fit into the new world he's been brought into.

"Rascals," on the other hand is one of those "I don't believe what I'm seeing" episodes. When Picard, Ensign Ro, Guinan and Keiko are turned into children by the transporter, it happens just in time for them to outsmart some Ferengi who

attempt to steal the Enterprise. What an unfortunate final appearance for Ensign Ro.

Michelle Forbes was unceremoniously written out of TNG after she angered Rick Berman by turning down the offer to be a regular on DEEP SPACE 9 after Berman went to the trouble of establishing the character of Ro on TNG. Rather than recast the part he created a new character and Michelle Forbes was made persona non grata on the Paramount lot. We haven't seen much of the actress in the last year have we?

"The Quality of Life" is a strange episode in which Data determines that a new type of droid has achieved the definition of true life as the robots are aware of their own existence and unwilling to risk their "lives" because of that self-awareness. Although its heart is in the right place it never quite convinces, particularly in light of the fact that Data never got this concerned when the holodeck characters started exhibiting a sense of self and a desire for self-preservation. The logic is the same.

This was the season which decided to show that Captain Kirk wasn't the only Enterprise commander who was a man of action. "Starship Mine," in which Picard finds himself trapped aboard the Enterprise between two deadly points of opposition, is clearly DIE HARD on a starship.

Some fans have expressed disappointment with season six, but episode by episode, it clearly emerges as being at least as good as season five.

In the Trek Classic blooper reel there's a scene from 1966 where a 10 year old boy wearing pointed ears walks onto the bridge and says to Mr. Spock, "Hi, daddy." That child was Leonard Nimoy's son, Adam. Twenty-seven years later, Adam Nimoy, an entertainment attorney turned director, is at the helm of "Timescape," one of the more challenging episodes of the sixth season.

The directing by Adam Nimoy is quite good, particularly in light of the complicated requirements of the story. This episode is both suspenseful and imaginative and keeps you guessing right up to the climax. It's quite an accomplishment. Nimoy also directed "Rascals," which didn't give him quite so much to work with. Maybe Adam is the one who should have directed season five's "Unification."

Since the end of season three, THE NEXT GENERATION has been striving to craft cliffhangers which would keep the viewing audience on the edge of their seats throughout the summer as they awaited the fall premiere. This has never been better accomplished than with "Descent," the sixth season climax.

While setting us up for the return of "Hugh" the Borg from the fifth season, we instead encounter Lore, Data's "evil twin" last seen in the fourth season episode "Brothers." Just when we'd practically forgotten the miscreant, he returns, and in the worst way possible—leading a contingent of the Borg. Sadly, like "Time's Arrow," the conclusion to "Descent" would prove to be decidedly lackluster.

THE NEXT GENERATION has accomplished a great deal and this was well exemplified in season six. Although Roddenberry had frozen the show into an unrealistic idealism where the crew of the Enterprise existed in perfect and absolute harmony, "Chain of Command" aptly demonstrated just how that harmony could be ruptured and even showed Picard acting like an actual torture victim who was being used and degraded.

That one episode showed many of the unrealized potentials that still exist in the characters on the series. "Realm of Fear" also demonstrates this with Barclay, who, while a little overcooked at times, comes far closer to acting like a genuine, complex human being than anyone else on TNG normally does.

Out of all the regulars, Riker has been allowed to show the most range of character, acting lustful ("The Game") as well as grumpy and even a bit of a tightass at times. Riker shows signs of stress in small as well as large ways and is more human for that. The series has clearly grown in its six going on seven years.

EPISODE ONE HUNDRED TWENTY-SEVEN: "TIME'S ARROW" PART 2

Written by Jeri Taylor
From a story by Joe Menosky
Directed by Les Landeau
Guest Cast: Jerry Hardin, Michael Aron, Barry Kivel, Ken Thorley, Sheldon Peters Wolfchild, Jack Murdock, Marc Alaimo, Milt Tarver, Michael Hungerford

In San Francisco in the 19th century, Samuel Clemens has decided that he must do something to expose the aliens he has discovered in the city. Those aliens, of course are Data and Guinan.

Meanwhile, Capt. Picard, Lt. Riker, Dr. Crusher and Geordi have arrived in San Francisco after passing through the Devidian time portal. They masquerade in contemporary 19th century garb and begin looking for traces of the aliens from Devidia Two. They find indications of them among the victims in the cholera morgue. Dr. Crusher uses her tricorder to determine that electro-chemical energy has been drained from some of the bodies.

Clemens bribes a bellboy to let him into Data's hotel room where he discovers the time-shift detection instrument. Upon removing a transceiver from it, the device shuts down. Hearing talking from outside, Clemens hurriedly hides in the closet.

Data and Guinan enter the room, discussing that she knows where the cavern is which Data has been looking for. When Data discovers that his mechanism has been tampered with he easily figures out that Clemens is in the closet.

But instead of being fearful, Clemens accuses the pair of being from the future intent on disrupting the past and he vows to stop them for the sake of humanity. Clemens leaves the room, after Data gets his missing transceiver back from him.

Picard and the others are working at the infirmary, searching for clues to the aliens. They learn about a doctor and nurse who have been appearing at the clinic and the tricorder indicates that these may well be the aliens. When the aliens return to the clinic, the Away Team confronts them, but the Devidians vanish using their time/space shifting device, but not before Geordi grabs their snake-head.

The time-shifting by the aliens activates Data's device and he rushes to the location of the disruption. When Data arrives in a horse-drawn carriage, he aids the escape of the Away Team.

When Picard meets Guinan he's quite pleased although she has never met him before. Picard explains that some day she'll know him quite well.

At Data's room, they determine that the cavern where Data's head was found in the future must be the focal point for the time shifting and determine to go there. Guinan acquires a pass to the cavern as it is located beneath the Presidio, a military outpost in San Francisco.

Upon arriving at the cavern they discover that they were correct as it has been altered by the Devidians. They determine to destroy this portal. Just then Samuel Clemens appears, threatening them with a .45. But before they can deal with this threat the Devidians reappear, grab the snake-headed cane and activate it. Data tries to grab it but the resulting discharge blows the head from his body as the rest of Data goes through the portal back to Devidia Two.

As the alien male escapes through the portal, the others follow, including Clemens, and Picard is left behind. But Guinan, who is badly wounded, is left behind as well. Picard tends to her injuries as they discuss the future, where they will not meet for another 500 years. When she asks if they become friends, Picard replies, "Oh, it goes far beyond friendship."

On Devidia Two in the 24th century, Data's body, the rest of the Away Team and Samuel Clemens are beamed aboard the Enterprise. Riker turns Clemens over to Troi while Geordi turns

to trying to repair Data by reattaching his head. Only this is the head discovered in the cavern beneath San Francisco 500 years after Data lost it.

They know they must destroy the portal on Devidian Two but they also must retrieve Picard. Riker reluctantly decides that the menace to the past must take priority. Even if Picard cannot be rescued soon, the portal must be destroyed.

Geordi manages to successfully reattach Data's head whereupon the android discovers a message placed there by Picard when the detached head lay in the cavern 500 years before. If the Enterprise fires on the cavern on Devidia Two, there will also be a resulting explosion in San Francisco in the past in the cavern where Picard is, which will trigger an explosion which will threaten the Earth.

When their weapons are altered to prevent this, Dr. Crusher determines that the snake-cane can take one person back through the portal and bring one back from the past. Clemens volunteers to go and give the cane to Picard, even though he is fascinated by what he has found in the future.

Clemens goes through the portal and Picard returns to be beamed off the planet just before it is hit by photon torpedoes.

In the past Clemens helps Guinan from the cavern which can never again be used by the Devidians to feed on human beings.

EPISODE ONE-HUNDRED TWENTY-EIGHT: "REALM OF FEAR"

Written by Brannon Braga
Directed by Cliff Bole
Guest Cast: Dwight Schultz

When the U.S.S. Yosemite is reported lost, the Enterprise is dispatched to the Igo sector to search for it. The Yosemite may be lost in a plasma streamer it was sent to observe. When they cannot contact the ship, they link the transporter systems on the two ships so that an Away Team can be safely beamed aboard it.

Reginald Barclay is assigned to the Away Team, a duty he accepts with some reluctance. In the Enterprise transporter room Chief O'Brien explains that he'll have to beam them over one at a time and that it'll be a rough ride. Just as he's about to step aboard the transporter pad, Barclay changes his mind and bolts from the room, insisting that he cannot go through with it.

Barclay explains to Troi that he has transporter anxiety and has had it since he was a child. Miraculously he has never had to use a transporter dur-ing his Starfleet career and has therefore managed to keep this fear hidden. Troi shows him a Betazoid technique for easing his anxiety and Barclay decides that he'll try the transporter after all, but now, not later.

In the transporter room, Barclay confesses his fear to O'Brien, who admits in return that he was once afraid of spiders and was put in a situation where he was forced to overcome that anxiety in order to complete a job.

Aboard the Yosemite they find the body of one crewman but four are missing. When Barclay transports over, he does so without incident. But when he beams back he actually sees something coming towards him in the transport stream. It touches his arm just as he rematerializes.

Later Barclay reveals what he experienced to Geordi, who offers to run a diagnostic on the transporter to allay his fears. But neither Geordi nor O'Brien can find anything wrong. On top of this, Barlay's arm starts to intermittently ache and glow, leading Barclay to believe that he has transporter psychosis, for which there is no cure.

In sickbay Dr. Crusher is performing an autopsy on the dead Yosemite crewman and witnesses parts of dead the body function briefly and then cease. She believes that this was caused by high energy plasma exposure aboard the Yosemite.

Barclay wants to be beamed aboard the Yosemite again as he needs to know if there's something in the transporter stream. When Barclay transports, he sees it again and upon beaming back to the Enterprise he insists that the senior staff be assembled. Dr. Crusher confirms that Barclay's arm is contaminated with the same ionization found in the body of the dead crewman.

When Geordi, Barclay and Data reconstruct an experiment they believe took place aboard the Yosemite (except that a containment field is added for safety) a container containing a plasma sample explodes. The explosion is contained but Barclay faints, half of his body now glowing from plasma infection.

They determine that complex energy microbes are living in the plasma and were forced out by a frequency scan. Some of these microbes have infected Barclay. They determine that if they transport Barclay they can use a bioscan to separate the microbes from him, but he'll need to be suspended in transport for up to 40 seconds. But if he's suspended too long his pattern will degrade and won't be able to be re-integrated.

While Barclay is suspended in transport he sees the amorphous shapes approaching him once again. But this time he grabs one just as he is reintegrated. To everyone's shock, Barclay reappears holding one of the missing Yosemite crewmen. A security team is transported and returns with the other three missing crewmen. The plasma stream kept their patterns from degrading.

Later in Ten Forward, Barclay is met by O'Brien, who opens a box to reveal his pet spider—a tarantula. While O'Brien goes to get their drinks, the spider creeps across the table towards Barclay, who never got around to mentioning that he's afraid of spiders, too.

EPISODE ONE-HUNDRED TWENTY-NINE: "MAN OF THE PEOPLE"

Written by Frank Abatemarco
Directed by Winrich Kolbe
Guest Cast: Chip Lucia, Stephanie Erb

The Enterprise responds to a ship in distress which is being attacked near the planet Rekag-Seronia. Rekag ships break off their attack and withdraw when the Enterprise arrives on the scene.

The captain of the transport requests that the Enterprise carry his passengers to their destination at Seronia. Rekag-Seronia is a planet divided by political conflicts which are expanding and threaten Federation trading routes. One of the passengers, Ves Alkar, is a Lumerian ambassador and he is there to try to find a way to end the conflict.

When Ves Alkar and his mother, Maylor, beam aboard the Enterprise, Maylor abruptly confronts Troi who is there to greet them, proclaiming that her son couldn't possibly be attracted to her. Alkar tries to explain that his mother hasn't been well, but Troi remains confused.

Later, Troi is at a martial arts class conducted by Worf when they are joined by Alkar. Troi detects how serene the ambassador is and compliments him on it. Alkar replies that he could accomplish more as an ambassador if he were empathic like Troi because his people are only empathic within the same species. Troi agrees to assist him in his negotiations.

As Troi walks with Alkar back to his quarters, Maylor confronts Troi again, demanding to know if they've mated yet. Alkar takes his mother into their quarters while Troi is once more left confused and upset.

Later Troi discusses the incident with Riker when they are suddenly summoned to Alkar's quarters. His mother has suddenly died. Deanna agrees to perform a funeral meditation with him.

In Troi's quarters, Alkar removes some small stones from an ornate box. As part of the ceremony he touches a stone Troi is holding with another one of the stones. The stones glow and afterwards Troi feels uncomfortable.

Dr. Crusher wants to perform an autopsy on Maylor but Alkar states that his Lumerian beliefs forbid it.

During a workout, Troi suddenly feels sensual and goes to Alkar's quarters where she tries to seduce him, but he rebuffs her advances while not seeming very surprised by them. But on her way back to her quarters, Troi catches the eye of a young ensign and lures him back to her quarters.

Later, Riker arrives at Troi's quarters and finds her garbed only in a robe while the ensign is apparently just finishing getting dressed. Embarrassed, the ensign departs but Troi gets nasty with Riker, who decides to leave as well.

When the Enterprise arrives at Seronia, Alkar and the rest of his delegation, which includes Liva and Jarth. Seronia is on the verge of open war with Rakar.

Meanwhile, Troi is becoming more irrational and enters Ten Forward looking as though she has aged decades in a matter of hours. Troi walks up to Liva and confronts her the same way that Maylor confronted her when she came aboard the Enterprise.

Troi continues to age and act more irrational, attempting to attack the Lumerians as they're about to beam down. Picard is cut during the attack and Troi is restrained by security.

Crusher performs an autopsy on Maylor under Picard's orders and discovers that she wasn't Alkar's mother at all but a 30 year old woman. Picard and Worf beam down to confront Alkar with these facts and demand answers.

Alkar admits that he empathically channels his darkest thoughts into others and that his consorts usually live for years. Maylor was supposed to live through the negotiations, but when she abruptly died he turned to Troi. Alkar refuses to release Troi and armed security prevent Worf and Picard from forcibly returning him to the Enterprise.

Aboard the Enterprise, Dr. Crusher explains that if they allow Troi to die, Alkar will break the link and then they can resuscitate her so long as it is within 30 minutes.

As the negotiations end, Alkar acts stricken and returns to the Enterprise with his delegation. He is now consumed by dark emotions but insists that the Federation guarantee him safe passage back to his world in spite of Picard's desire to see Alkar answer for his crimes.

Later, Alkar begins the ceremony with Liva, which is interrupted at a cru-

cial point when Liva is beamed out of the ambassador's quarters. Alkar dies as Worf and the security team look on and Dr. Crusher neutralizes the neuro-transmitters in Troi's brain, reversing the aging process and returning her to normal.

Later, Troi thanks Will for sticking with her and he replies that he always will, even when she's old and gray.

EPISODE ONE HUNDRED THIRTY: "RELICS"
Written by Ronald D. Moore
Directed by Alexander Singer
Guest Cast: James Doohan

The Enterprise-D discovers something long theorized but never before encountered: a Dyson sphere. This is a construct built around a star. It's an immense sphere at an appropriate distance from the star, such as Earth's orbit, so that civilizations can live on the inside of the sphere, taking advantage of natural solar energy in an area vastly larger than the surface of a single planet. This discovery occurs because the Enterprise has detected an old Federation distress signal. Upon arrival at the impossibly huge artifact, they discover a small spacecraft, the Jenolan, that appears to have been wrecked on the outer surface of the Dyson sphere some seventy-five years earlier.

Geordi and an Away Team investigate and find no one alive on board—and no corpses. But Geordi is intrigued to discover that the transporters on the Jenolan are still functioning, although at a low power level. He discovers that someone had apparently set up a closed loop in the transporter pattern buffer. Two signals are locked in. One has deteriorated too much to be retrieved, but the other is almost at one-hundred per cent. An amazed LaForge brings back Montgomery Scott, who has been cycling through a transporter field for three quarters of a century!

Scotty is pleased to learn that he has been rescued by the Enterprise and expects to see Jim Kirk. Geordi knows that he must explain exactly how much time has passed. When Scotty sees Worf and realizes that there is a Klingon lieutenant in Starfleet, he starts to understand what has happened on his own.

In the Enterprise sickbay, Scotty explains that he was a passenger in the Jenolan on the way to a retirement colony on Norpin Five. Scotty loves talking about the old days. When he takes a tour of the Enterprise engineering room he keeps poking his nose into things he's 75 years out of date on until Geordi finally explodes in anger and

tells Scotty to stop interfering with his job.

In Ten Forward, Scotty orders a scotch and is unpleasantly surprised by the synthahol substitute Data gives him. Trying to be helpful, the android finds a bottle of genuine brew behind the bar and offers it to Scotty, who gratefully accepts it.

Slightly tipsy, Scotty visits the holodeck he's been told about and conjures up the bridge of the original starship Enterprise, drinking a toast to old companions. Captain Picard joins him and they drink a toast to their old commands.

Later, Picard orders Geordi to return to the Jenolan with Scotty to download the computers as he wants Captain Scott to feel useful. Geordi reluctantly complies.

While Geordi and Scotty are aboard the grounded Jenolan, the Enterprise inspects the surface of the Dyson sphere and inadvertently triggers the entrance doors and tractor beams which pull the Enterprise inside as the massive doors close behind it.

When Geordi cannot communicate the Enterprise, they try to get the Jenolan functioning again and between Scotty's old know-how and some devices Geordi brought along, they get it up and running.

Inside the Dyson sphere Data determines that the instability of the star is why the sphere was abandoned, and unless they get out soon the solar flares will begin to imperil the Enterprise.

The Jenolan takes off and begins tracking the impulse ion trail of the Enterprise, which leads them to the two huge doors. They figure out what must have happened and determine that if they get the doors to open again they might be able to jam them open long enough for the Enterprise to escape. The plan works but Scotty and Geordi are beamed off the small ship only just in the nick of time before the Jenolan is destroyed.

As a reward for his service to them and to Starfleet, Picard grants Scotty the permanent loan of a shuttle, which Captain Scott gratefully accepts. He's decided not to retire after all. "Maybe some day I'll end up there, but not yet," he states as the command crew of the Enterprise-D bid Scotty a fond farewell.

ONE-HUNDRED THIRTY-ONE: "SCHISMS"

Written by Brannon Braga
From a story by Ronald Wilkerson & Jean Matthias
Directed by Robert Wiemer

The Enterprise has arrived at the globular cluster known as the Amargosa Diaspora. Their purpose is to map that star region.

Riker awakens, anything but refreshed, and he looks it when he arrives at the morning briefing. Later, during a reading of bad poetry by Data, Riker falls asleep. Riker is embarrassed but explains that he hasn't been sleeping well recently. Dr. Crusher examines him for any biological reasons for the fatigue but is unable to find anything.

Geordi has recently amplified the ship's sensor array and it detects an explosion in Cargo Bay Four which further investigation reveals never occurred. The sensor glitch causes Geordi some concern.

But Riker isn't the only one experiencing strange unexplainable problems. When Worf visits the annoying Mr. Mot to get a haircut, the Klingon reacts badly to the sight of the barber's glistening metal scissors being held so close to him. He practically attacks Mot in reaction to his involuntary feelings, and then leaves the barber station with both of them very confused.

Other crew members are also experiencing fatigue and its explained away by the need for shore leave, although that doesn't explain a strange malfunction which Geordi experiences in his VISOR. Nor does it explain how

Data's chronometer is off by 90.17 minutes, as though the android is suffering from missing time. Since Data's missing time and other problems all took place in Cargo Bay Four, they begin their investigation there.

This investigation by Data and Geordi leads them to discover an emission point in Cargo Bay Four for tetryon particles, an indication of an opening between subspace and normal space.

Troi reports that other crew members are reporting disturbing involuntary reactions to certain seemingly commonplace objects, as though they have all experienced the same dream—an impossibility.

Taking the various crew members to the holodeck, their bits of memories are used to construct what finally appears to be an alien examination room which all of them recognize.

Further investigation reveals that Data was not on board the Enterprise during his missing 90 minutes. A more detailed bioscan on Riker reveals that the lower portion of one of his arms had been amputated and then reattached using microsurgery which was almost undetectable.

Things worsen as the formerly invisible subspace portal begins to grow to the point that it could soon threaten the integrity of the Enterprise hull. Geordi has a way of sealing the breach but only at its source. Since Riker has been taken several nights in a row, he volunteers to take the device with him.

Riker is given a stimulant to counteract the alien sedative as well as a homing device and tricorder. Riker is suddenly taken through the portal and opens his eyes in the alien examination room. A missing crewmember is on a table next to him. Aliens dressed in long robes move about the room.

Geordi locates the source of the tetryon emissions but Riker and the other crewmember must escape before the subspace breach can be permanently sealed. Geordi proceeds to start weakening the breach and as the aliens react to that, Riker uses the distraction to plant the device, rescue the unconscious crewmember and leap through the portal.

Just after they appear in Cargo Bay Four, the portal is sealed but not before a tiny, glowing alien probe escapes from the closing rupture and disappears out into space through the Enterprise hull. None of them can be certain that the probe was a harmless exploratory device. This is because one of the Enterprise crewmen who disappeared had been returned earlier. His blood was replaced by a liquid polymer as though part of some hideous experiment.

ONE HUNDRED THIRTY-TWO:
"TRUE Q"

Written by Rene Echevarria
Directed by Robert Scherrer
Guest Cast: Olivia D'Abo, John de Lancie

A new crewmember, 18 year old Amanda Rogers, joins the Enterprise crew while the vessel is en route to the Argolis Cluster. She is the winner of a student competition whose prize is the opportunity to intern aboard the Enterprise.

Riker escorts her to her quarters and after he leaves she remarks that she could have brought her menagerie of dogs with her, whereupon a dozen puppies appear which she makes disappear again by remarking aloud, "Oh no—I didn't mean it!"

The Enterprise arrives at Tagra Four, a planet which suffers from ecological devastation. Everything the Enterprise wants to send down to the surface must go via shuttle due to the intense ionization in the atmosphere created by the barystatic filters in place on the planet.

In the cargo bay, Amada notices a heavy crate falling towards Riker which she diverts with a wave of her hand. Riker considers it a close call as he doesn't realize that Amanda used some sort of power to knock it out of the way.

Later in engineering, the warp core begins to fail and moments before an impending explosion Amanda raises her arms, forces the breach back into the core and repairs all damage in a matter of moments.

Not only are her actions miraculous, but so was the accident. As Geordi explains, it wasn't natural as everything was normal and then suddenly all the laws of physics failed.

To answer that, Q miraculously appears. He caused the accident to force Amanda to reveal her powers. Amanda's parents, who died when she was an infant, were Q who had taken human form and chosen to live on Earth. The Q continuum suspected that their daughter would have the powers of the Q as well.

Q, as an expert on human affairs, has been sent to properly school Amanda in her powers and return with her to the Q continuum. Picard agrees to allow this only so long as Amanda can make this decision for herself.

Amanda meets with Dr. Crusher and explains that her powers began to manifest themselves just six months before. Q thinks she has potential and wants to return with her to the Q continuum right away, but Amanda doesn't like Q and rebuffs his strange attempts at befriending her. In fact she wants to remain with Starfleet and have a human family. Q doesn't think much of this idea.

Q tries to make amends and explains that the Q are omnipotent—that she can have anything she wants. She summons up an image of her parents but turns to find that Q has vanished.

Meanwhile, Data has been exploring Amanda's records and discovered the curious fact that her parents were killed by a tornado in a region which operated under weather control which should have prevented it. Picard's suspicions are aroused.

Q convinces Amanda to play hide and seek with him, which enables her to realize that her powers are even more fantastic than she could have ever imagined as she finds that she can actually walk on the outside of the Enterprise hull itself.

Later, when Amanda's advances are gently rebuffed by Riker, she uses her powers to make him like her, but it is unsatisfying because she knows Riker is just acting like a puppet at her command, so she releases him.

Picard confronts Q who admits that Amanda's parents were killed for defying the Q continuum. He also suggests that the Q might respond to Amanda similarly if she refuses to join the continuum. After all, the cintinuum feels a responsibility not to let omnipo-

tent beings roam free and unchecked in the universe. It has a disturbing logic to it which Picard still argues with.

Picard confronts Q in front of Amanda regarding the truth of the situation. Q states that they had decided not to harm her but to offer Amanda a choice—join the Q or remain among humans but never use her power. He points out that her parents made that choice but couldn't resist using their powers.

Below on Tagra Four, an unstable reactor is threatening to overload which will kill thousands. Making a decision, Amanda uses her power to repair the reactor and clear the pollution from the planet's atmosphere. Amanda understands that she, too, would eventually be tempted to use her powers again. She agrees to join the Q continuum, after revealing the truth to her adoptive parents back on Earth.

Amanda says that she hopes to visit the Enterprise again some day, to which Dr. Crusher points out that as a Q she can do anything she wants.

ONE HUNDRED THIRTY-THREE: "RASCALS"

Teleplay by Allison Hock
From a story by Ward Botsford, Diana Dru Botsford & Michael Piller

Directed by Adam Nimoy

Guest Cast: David Tristan Birkin, Brian Bonsall, Michael Snyder

Captain Picard, Guinan, Ensign Ro and Keiko O'Brien are returning to the Enterprise from shore leave aboard one of the shuttles. Picard has some specimens with him from an archaeological dig and Keiko is holding a tray of plants. But before they can reach the Enterprise the shuttle passes through a strange stellar cloud which badly rattles both the craft and its passengers.

Chief O'Brien locks onto the four and beams them out of the shuttle just before the craft explodes. But when they materialize on the transporter pads they all appear to be adolescent children rather than the mature adults they really are.

The four are examined by Dr. Crusher who determines that mentally the four are the same. Only by studying the cloud they passed through can she determine whether the effect can be reversed.

Before Crusher can accomplish this the Enterprise is summoned to Ligos Seven to aid a science team which has sent out a distress call. When Picard walks onto the bridge and tries to start ordering everyone to their stations, they just stare at him with shock and disbelief. Dr. Crusher advises Jean-Luc that for the time being it would be better if he allowed Will Riker to assume temporary command. Picard very reluctantly agrees.

Guinan is enjoying the change while Ro Laren dislikes it because this reminds her of her own adolescence lived in a refugee camp. Chief O'Brien is having a particularly difficult time relating to his wife now that she appears to be only 12 years old.

Dr. Crusher's examinations determine that the four crew members have lost some specific viroxic sequences in their RVN, the portion of cell chemistry which changes with adolescence. The missing chemical sequences enable the body to mature to adulthood. Apparently a molecular reversion field masked these viroxic sequences when the four were transported. While the four will continue to age normally, it will take decades for them to return to their original age. Dr. Crusher believes that by using the transporter buffer she can return them to normal.

The Enterprise arrives at Ligos Seven but before they can find the missing science team they are fired on by two Klingon warships. Surprisingly, the Enterprise is disabled and invaded by a Ferengi boarding party. With seconds to spare, Riker gives the computer a coded command to block all command functions so that the Ferengi will be unable to operate the vessel.

The Ferengi, led by one Damon Lurin, declares the Enterprise his under the Ferengi salvage code. If the crew refuses to cooperate, the Ferengi threaten to execute them. Most of the crew are beamed off the ship down to the planet's surface where they will be forced into slave labor. The Ferengi already have a buyer for the Enterprise—the Romulans.

Guinan, Picard, Ro and Keiko are detained in the ship's school area where they have access to the school computer. Picard takes command and sends Ro and Guinan through the Jeffries tube to engineering. Picard sees a toy which Alexander is playing with and gets an idea.

The toy is used to lure a Ferengi crewman out of the transporter room so that Keiko and Picard are able to pilfer some phasers. In sickbay, Alexander steals several medical hypos.

The Ferengi believe that Picard is Riker's son and threatens to kill him unless Riker releases the computer control to the Ferengi. Riker agrees and begins explaining the computer control with a bewildering array of doubletalk which none of the Ferengi can follow. Under cover of this he releases command control to the school computer.

Picard takes advantage of this while the others manage to sneak up on other Ferengi and slap combadges on them. Then Picard transports those Ferengi into detainment fields. Keiko uses a medical hypo to knock out one of the Ferengi, which accounts for the small crew left guarding the vessel.

Picard arrives on the bridge and places Damon Lurin under arrest. The Ferengi alliance disavow any knowledge of the actions of the supposedly renegade Ferengi.

Dr. Crusher successfully returns Keiko, Guinan and Picard to normal. But when Guinan goes looking for Ro Laren, she finds that Ro is enjoying being a child and wants to wait just a little while before being changed back.

EPISODE ONE HUNDRED THIRTY-FOUR: "A FISTFUL OF DATAS"

Written by Robert Hewitt Wolfe and Brannon Braga
From a story by Robert Hewitt Wolfe.
Directed by Patrick Stewart
Guest Cast: Brian Bonsall

The Enterprise is having a two-day layover at a Starbase and so the crew are relaxing with their own private pastimes. Geordi and Data get permission from Picard to conduct an experiment involving using Data as an emergency back-up system in case of a catastrophic systems failure.

Worf prefers to be on duty, but when Picard has nothing for him to do, Worf agrees to go with his son, Alexander, to the holodeck for a 19th century western program in Deadwood, South Dakota. There they become Sheriff Worf and Deputy Alexander. Worf and Alexander easily deal with a criminal who is shooting up the saloon, but Alexander wants it to be more difficult. It's too easy. Worf increases the program difficulty to level four.

Worf once again confronts the criminal in the saloon and only captures him after a barroom brawl. Worf is starting to like this game. But the criminal, Eli Hollander, pulls his gun on Worf and is defeated only when Deanna Troi shows up and shoots the criminal's hat off.

Meanwhile, Geordi has linked Data to the computer net, but when Data experiences a sudden power surge, Geordi abruptly ends the experiment. As they leave the room, Data picks up his tricorder and twirls it like a gunslinger.

On the holodeck, Eli has been locked up by Worf but threatens that his father will come to rescue him.

Elsewhere on the Enterprise, crew members begin to experience minor computer problems.

In Deadwood, Alexander is kidnapped by Eli's cronies, something which is not in the programming they had entered for the holodeck routine. When Alexander tries to have the computer freeze the program, the computer ignores him. Now Alexander is frightened.

When Worf goes looking for Alexander, he encounters Eli's father, Frank, who looks like Data. It doesn't take long for Worf to realize that this isn't really Data at all. Frank knocks Worf around and even shoots him, with a real bullet. Now Worf really knows he's in trouble.

Back at the jail, Troi is still there and Worf tells her what is happening, but even with their combined efforts they cannot override the holodeck program. What's just as bad, they cannot contact anyone on the Enterprise outside of the holodeck. But Troi believes that if they can get the program to run its course that it will then end naturally.

Geordi and Data have determined that the earlier power surge caused some of Data's programming to replace certain ship's programming. While they talk, Data slips in an out of a Texan accent, much to both of their surprise.

When Frank comes to the jail, Worf agrees to trade Eli (who now also looks like Data) for Alexander. Frank agrees to make the exchange in two hours. But after he leaves, Troi points out that in westerns the bad guy always lies and will undoubtedly try to double-cross Sheriff Worf and kill him.

The time comes to make the exchange, and after the trade is made, Frank's hidden henchmen appear and start shooting at Worf. With Troi's help they defeat the gunmen. The program should end, but it doesn't.

Suddenly the saloon keeper, Miss Annie Meyers, rushes out to thank Worf and give him a kiss—but she looks just like Data, too. Reluctantly Worf accepts the kiss and the program ends.

Later, Alexander is sad, believing that his father will never want to go back to the Deadwood holodeck program, but Worf assures Alexander that whenever Deadwood faces danger again, the sheriff and deputy will be there to face it together. Alexander happily goes to sleep as the repaired Enterprise moves off through space.

ONE HUNDRED THIRTY-FIVE:
"THE QUALITY OF LIFE"
Written by Naren Shankar
Directed by Jonathan Frakes
Guest Cast: Ellen Bry

The Enterprise has been assigned to visit a space station to monitor work on a massive project on Tyrus 7-A, which the space platform is orbiting. The Tyan particle fountain is a new type of mining technology being supervised by one Dr. Farallon. Because of all of the delays and setbacks the particle fountain has encountered, Geordi is there representing the Federation to evaluate the project as to whether it should continue or be terminated.

Dr. Farallon defends her project and has even developed a type of small maintenance robot which she believes will facilitate the project immensely. She is able to demonstrate this when a power grid malfunction threatens the containment field, and the entire project, not to mention the safety of those on the space station orbiting Tyrus 7-A.

The small robots, called exocomps, are dispatched to repair the containment field and succeed miraculously. Even Geordi is impressed and moments before he had been expressing misgivings over the project's viability.

Geordi has Dr. Farallon bring one of the exocomps to the Enterprise for further study. There she meets Data, whom she is particularly fascinated by. On the other hand Data is particularly interested in the exocomps. The exocomps contain the ability to learn. Farallon ask Picard if he'll wait just 48 hours before passing his final evaluation on the project. Until then she will be able to use the Enterprise engineering staff, and her exocomps, to finish the project and increase the efficiency of the Tyran particle fountain to acceptable levels. Picard grants her the 48 hour reprieve.

Data assists Dr. Farallon but is intrigued when an exocomp returns from an access tunnel before its task is complete—just before the tunnel explodes. Data determines that the exocomp detected danger in the tunnel and fled in an act of self-preservation, clearly not the routine of a robot created to act as a mere tool.

When Dr. Farallon next prepares to use the exocomps, Data forbids her, stating that he believes that the robots exhibit the characteristics of a living, rather than merely mechanical, entity. Farallon opposes him but Picard agrees to investigate the situation more completely. If they are alive, Data contends that exploiting them as laborers is to treat them as slaves. Dr. Farallon argues that they are merely well programmed tools which she created.

On the space station, Picard and Geordi are inspecting the project when explosions shake the station. The project is seconds away from failing and flooding the station with radiation. While others are safely beamed out, Picard and Geordi are trapped aboard the station with only a force field protecting them from the increasing levels of radiation. But this will only protect them for 30 minutes.

Dr. Farallon suggests using the exocomps which can be programmed to explode in the particle stream and shut it down. Data objects but Riker states that the lives of Geordi and the captain must supersede Data's objections. But Data over-rides the transporter controls, stating that he does not believe in sacrificing one life form for another, and he is ready to face the consequences. Data offers to go in their place as he will thus be making the decision to sacrifice himself, a choice the exocomps do not have.

Riker suggests a similar compromise but it involves reconnecting the command pathways of the exocomps so that they can choose whether to self-destruct and complete the mission themselves. Data agrees. The exocomps alter their programming and Data believes they have come up with an alternate solution themselves.

The exocomps appear near the fountain core and siphon off enough power to open a window in the ionization field to allow Picard and Geordi to be beamed out. They are also able to retrieve two of the three exocomps but one had remained to keep draining the core and therefore sacrificed itself to save its fellow exocomps. The particle fountain shuts down safely and Dr. Farallon now understands the points Data was trying to make.

Data meets with Picard and explains that when the Federation challenged whether Data was truly alive, Jean-Luc stood up for him, for which Data will be forever grateful. But since the exocomps had no such advocate, Data chose to represent them rather than see them blindly sacrificed. Picard replies that it is the most human decision the android has ever made.

ONE-HUNDRED THIRTY-SIX: "CHAIN OF COMMAND" PART ONE

Written by Ronald D. Moore
From a story by Frank Abatemarco
Directed by Robert Scheerer
Guest Cast: Ronny Cox, David Warner

Vice-Admiral Nechayev of the starship Cairo rendezvous with the Enterprise in order to meet with Picard. She needs Picard to resign his command in order to undertake a secret mission. The mission involves the Cardassians, who recently withdrew from Bajor. The Federation believes that the Cardassians are preparing to invade another disputed system, but which one? Dr. Crusher and Worf will accompany Picard, but no one else aboard the Enterprise will know the purpose of their absence.

Captain Jellico is assigned command of the Enterprise in Picard's absence and will proceed to the border to negotiate with the Cardassians. Jellico previously helped to negotiate the Federation's original armistice with that alien race.

Worf and Beverly Crusher practice commando tactics on the holodeck but even they don't know the purpose of their mission yet.

Lt. Riker and Jellico do not hit it off too well and his abrupt changes of ship's routine grate on everyone's nerves. When Troi approaches Jellico about the morale problems being created, Jellico puts her in charge of the situation and tells her to remedy it. Jellico also orders Troi to begin wearing a standard uniform.

Picard, Crusher and Worf leave the Enterprise aboard a shuttle, whereupon Jean-Luc explains their mission. The Federation believes that the Cardassians are employing metagenic weapons, something which Picard is an expert in. The Federation believes that a secret lab exists on Celtris Three. Picard arranges a secret passage to the planet with the aid of a Ferengi mercenary pilot.

Meanwhile, the Enterprise rendezvous with a Cardassian ship, the Reklar. Captain Jellico chooses to keep the Cardassian negotiator, Gul Lemec, waiting to create a strategic advantage. When they do finally meet, Troi is with him.

At Celtris Three, Picard, Worf and Beverly Crusher arrive and enter the subterranean caverns. There they encounter steep cliffs and are menaced by giant bat-like creatures, but they continue towards the bio-research site hidden in the caverns.

Aboard the Enterprise, Gul Lemec reveals that he knows about a security team sent into Cardassian territory, which catches Jellico off-guard.

Thus when Picard, Crusher and Worf reach their destination they discover that the installation is nothing like they were told. They have been decoyed into a trap. The Cardassians attack. While Worf and Beverly escape, Jean-Luc is captured.

At the same time the theta-band waves being broadcast from Celtris Three cease, seemingly indicating that Picard was successful. But upon contacting Admiral Nechayev, Captain Jellico is told that the Federation has heard nothing from the raiding party.

Picard is imprisoned in an interrogation room where he meets the Cardassian, Gul Madred, who reveals that Picard was indeed set up and trapped. When Picard asks why, he is sternly told, "In this room you do not ask questions. I ask them. You answer. If I am not satisfied with your answers, you will die."

END OF PART ONE

EPISODE ONE HUNDRED THIRTY-SEVEN: "CHAIN OF COMMAND" PART TWO

Written by Frank Abatemarco
Directed by Les Landeau
Guest Cast: David Warner, Ronny Cox

A prisoner of the Cardassians, Picard is drugged and tortured to get information on his mission, which the Cardassians know all about anyway as they tricked the Federation into sending Picard on it to begin with.

On the Enterprise Captain Jellico is negotiating with the Cardassians and each wants the other to withdraw their forces from the disputed border zone. The Cardassians accuse the Federation of attacking Celtris Three with an assault force led by Jean-Luc Picard, whom they reveal they have captured.

Jellico reveals the mission to Riker and dispatches him in a shuttle to the rendezvous point which Worf and Troi would have headed to if they escaped. Jellico and Riker are not getting along and the captain considers Riker to be a poor First Officer, but he recognizes that Riker's skills are needed for the shuttle mission.

On Celtris Three, Gul Madred tries to charm Picard, and when that fails he makes it clear that the best Jean-Luc can hope for is a trial and punishment. When the Cardassian demands the Federation defense plans for Minos Kova, Picard refuses to reveal them. Gul Madred has Picard hung by his wrists from a bar and begins to torture him.

The following day Picard awakens to find that a device has been implanted in his chest which can inflict excruciating pain at Madred's command. Madred enjoys this method of torture and wants Picard to do whatever he says. When he points to a row of four lights, he tells Picard to state that there are five. When he refuses, Madred activates the pain implant.

Riker returns to the Enterprise with Troi and Worf but Captain Jellico refuses to authorize a rescue mission since the Cardassians would clearly be expecting it. Besides, the Federation has disavowed Picard's mission, which leaves the captain open to being treated as a terrorist, a position not protected by the provisions governing the treatment of prisoners of war. When Riker challenges this negotiating strategy as being life-threatening to Picard, Jellico relieves Riker of command.

Picard manages to get under his torturer's skin when he sees the man's daughter and questions what kind of person she will become being exposed to such things.

When the Cardassians break off negotiations with Captain Jellico, the Federation surmises that the colony on Minos Kova will be the point where the Cardassians will launch their attack. There is a nebula nearby where a Cardassian fleet could safely hide for three days without experiencing any problems.

Madred offers to let Picard go, stating that he had captured Worf and Crusher. With Worf dead, the Cardassian will torture the information he needs out of Crusher. Picard has no way of knowing that this is a lie and so chooses to remain with the Cardassian. Madred is pleased.

Captain Jellico plans to set a trap for the Cardassians but he needs to send an experienced shuttle pilot into the nebula to lay mines which will attach themselves to the Cardassian ships. Reluctantly, Jellico knows that Riker is the best man for the job and asks him to undertake the mission. Riker angrily accepts.

Riker and Geordi use the shuttle to successfully distribute a pattern of anti-matter mines. Captain Jellico contacts the Cardassian ship the Reklar where he confronts Gul Lemec. The Cardassians are shown the difficulty of their position and they reluctantly agree to surrender. The terms include the release of Jean-Luc Picard.

Gul Madred tells Picard that the Enterprise has been destroyed and that he'll live forever under the control of the Cardassians. But his lot will be improved if he chooses to do what Madred commands—just say there are 5 lights even though there are four. Picard refuses. Then the Cardassians release him, much to his surprise.

When Picard returns to the Enterprise and resumes command, Captain Jellico tells his senior staff that it was an honor to serve with them, but none reply in kind.

Picard later admits to Troi that at the end he actually could see five lights, but told Madred that there were four anyway just to be contrary.

EPISODE ONE HUNDRED THIRTY-EIGHT: "SHIP IN A BOTTLE"

Written by Rene Echevarria
Directed by Alexander Singer
Guest Cast: Daniel Davis, Dwight Schultz, Stephanie Beacham

On the holodeck, Data is acting as Sherlock Holmes in the 221B Baker Street simulation. Data announces his deduction, which "Watson" (Geordi) points out is flawed. Data freezes the program and notifies Barclay that the holodeck is malfunctioning.

Barclay runs a diagnostic on the holodeck and encounters a protected memory file. Activating it he sees Prof.

Moriarty appear in the same form he took during a holodeck session Data had run years before. Moriarty tells Barclay that he wants Captain Picard to come and explain why he has been locked away for so long as Jean-Luc had made certain promises to him. Barclay shuts Moriarty off, but the image reappears by itself a few seconds later.

Picard is informed of the encounter on the holodeck and the strange request that a hologram made of him. Picard and Data accompany Barclay to the holodeck where they encounter James Moriarty. Prof. Moriarty insists that he be allowed to leave the holodeck, although Picard patiently tries to explain why that won't work.

Moriarty believes the contrary and proves it by stepping through the holodeck door into the ship's corridor, where he remains unaffected. Moriarty claims that it is simply mind over matter.

In sick bay Dr. Crusher examines Moriarty and pronounces him human. He wants to explore the Enterprise. Picard is suspicious but Moriarty explains that his criminal nature was a creation of Arthur Conan Doyle and he's quite different from the fictional portrait.

Moriarty also wants to bring the Countess Regina Bartholomew with him as she had been created by Data to be Moriarty's lover. Picard says that he'll take it under consideration.

But before Picard can spend much time thinking about it, Moriarty locks out the command controls of the Enterprise. Moriarty repeats his demand and Picard orders Data to get on the problem. In engineering Geordi and Data work on using transporter technology to move the countess from the holodeck to the rest of the ship which could retain her physical integrity.

Barclay sets up pattern enhancers in the holodeck to experiment on a chair, but it doesn't work. What's really odd, though, is that the computer has no record of them ever using the transporter for these tests. After further experimentation, Data tells Picard that they've never left the holodeck, which is how Moriarty seemingly entered the corridor. It was all a holodeck simulation.

When Picard gives his command code to the computer, it doesn't recognize him. But Data realizes that Picard has just given Mariarty the information he needs to gain control of the real Enterprise.

On the real bridge, Moriarty appears on the view screen, having now gained control of the real Enterprise. He tells Riker that he'll release the Enterprise back to him in exchange for being freed from the holodeck. Moriarty explains the experiment Barclay tried on the holodeck using pattern enhancers with the transporter. Geordi and Riker agree to make the attempt.

Moriarty has placed a force field around the holodeck so that no one can get in and override his programs. Picard tells the Countess that uncoupling the Heisenberg Compensators could enable an object to be beamed out of the holodeck and maintain its integrity. She passes the information along to James Moriarty who tells Riker to try it, particularly since the Enterprise is starting to tumble towards a gas giant and will collide with the star in 25 minutes unless the command functions are released by Moriarty.

Moriarty sets up pattern enhancers around himself and the countess and they are activated. The duo appear in the transporter room, very much intact. But before Moriarty will relinquish the Enterprise he demands a shuttle which will allow him to leave. Riker reluctantly agrees.

After leaving in the shuttle Moriarty releases the lockout command. Picard tells the computer to store program Picard delta one in active memory and to end the simulation. The shuttle bay disappears and they are on the empty holodeck.

Exiting the holodeck they find that Riker has regained control of the Enterprise and they are safely pulling away from the gas giant. Picard had managed to program the holodeck from inside and thereby trick Moriarty into thinking he had left the holodeck the same way that Moriarty had tricked them into thinking that they had left the holodeck earlier.

A cube on the table contains a miniature holodeck on which Moriarty and the countess are inside a shuttle-craft exploring strange new worlds. The enhancement module contains enough active memory to provide Moriarty and his lady love with a lifetime of experiences, and they need never know the truth.

EPISODE ONE HUNDRED THIRTY-NINE: "AQUIEL"

Written by Brannon Braga & Ronald D. Moore
From a story by Jeri Taylor
Directed by Cliff Bole
Guest Cast: Renee Jones

When the Enterprise makes a routine stop at a space station near the border with the Klingon empire, the station is found to be deserted. Two officers who were stationed aboard the station seem to have disappeared. What they do find is a live dog, and a glob of cellular residue which Dr. Crusher reports to be the remains of one of the missing Lieutenants. Blood at the scene matches that of Lt. Aquiel Uhnari but no other trace of her can be found, although the station's one shuttlecraft is missing.

Geordi hopes to find out what happened by accessing the computer logs. The main computer control has been tampered with, as though someone were attempting to bypass security locks. Going to Lt. Aquiel's quarters, Geordi has better luck there and accesses the lieutenant's personal logs, which reveal concern about working with her arrogant comrade, Lt. Rocha.

The other evidence indicates that a Klingon vessel may have stopped at the station and boarded it, but Picard doesn't want to risk a diplomatic incident without more compelling proof.

As Geordi reads more of Aquiel's logs, he finds himself attracted to her image, but is just as intrigued by references to a Klingon, Morag, who had been trying to intimidate station personnel. When Worf finds traces of Klingon DNA at the relay station, that gives them the evidence they need to file a report with the Klingon governor of that region.

Governor Torak arrives and presents Picard and company with the missing Lt. Aquiel. They had picked up her shuttle. Aquiel explains that Rocha had abruptly attacked her one morning for no reason and she had managed to flee the station in the shuttle. She doesn't know what happened after that. She also cannot adequately explain why she fled instead of reporting the incident to someone in Starfleet.

Geordi takes charge of Aquiel, hoping to learn more. After all, he knows a lot about her after having gone through her records. She seems friendly enough and is particularly happy to see that her dog, Maura, is safe with them.

Starfleet records show that Rocha was an exemplary officer whereas Aquiel was often cited for being argumentative and difficult to work with. Also, further exploration of the space station reveals that a phaser is missing. Geordi doesn't want to believe that Aquiel committed any crimes and admits that he is growing to care for her a great deal.

But the missing phaser is found on the shuttle and Dr. Crusher's analysis of the cellular residue left on the space station indicates that the person was killed by a 60 second level 10 phaser blast, or else a Klingon disruptor. Accessing Rocha's logs can't help as someone has erased them.

Meanwhile Morag, a Klingon commander, arrives and is confronted with the evidence. He admits to stealing the computer access codes but not to killing anyone. He claims the station was abandoned when he got there.

Geordi confronts Aquiel who admits to deleting Rocha's files because he was about to dispatch a negative evaluation of her to Starfleet. It looks bad for her although she insists she didn't kill Rocha.

Dr. Crusher discovers that the cellular residue she found is part of an organism which needs to absorb other life forms to survive, and it duplicates whatever it absorbs, even down to the cellular level. Rocha may have been such an organism which attacked Aquiel when it needed to absorb a new body. If this is the case then either Aquiel or Morag could be this coalescent. Aquiel is taken into custody, much to Geordi's dismay.

Geordi is alone in his quarters with Maura, Aquiel's dog, for company when it alters form and attacks him. The dog is the coalescent! Geordi manages to dodge the creature, pull out a phaser from his desk and destroy it.

Aquiel now understands that the coalescent had attacked her and drained some of her memories, but then she got the phaser, defended herself and escaped, which is when the coalescent turned on the dog. Aquiel is going to Starbase 212 for reassignment and perhaps one day she'll be good enough to be assigned to the Enterprise.

EPISODE ONE-HUNDRED FORTY: "FACE OF THE ENEMY"

Written by Naren Shankar
From a story by Rene Eschevarria
Directed by Gabrielle Beaumont
Guest Cast: Carolyn Seymour, Scott MacDonald

Counselor Troi awakens and when she instructs the computer to turn on the lights, nothing happens. She gropes her way to a wall, finds a light switch, and when it is activated she is shocked to see her reflection—a reflection of a Romulan woman in full uniform.

She is soon visited by a Romulan, Subcommander N'Vek, who reveals that she is on a Romulan warship, the Khazara. Troi had been drugged and kidnapped while she was on Bokara Six at a neuro-psychology seminar. She was surgically altered and given the identity of Major Rakal of the Tal Shiar of Imperial Romulan Intelligence. The Tal Shiar are a type of secret police who have authority even over the commanders of Romulan warbirds.

Troi is to order the ship's commander, Toreth, to take the warbird to the Kaleb sector. If she doesn't, her imposture will be exposed and she'll be executed. Then everything will be explained to her. Her empathic abilities tells her that N'Vek is being truthful, but for what final purpose?

Troi quickly adapts to her role of Major Rakal and gains the upper hand with commander Toreth regarding the mysterious cargo which was beamed aboard. The Khazara is on a secret mission and it's not healthy to challenge the Tal Shiar over the details of such things.

Meanwhile, the Enterprise picks up one Stefan DeSeve at Research Station 75. He is an ex-Federation ensign who defected to the Romulans years before and has seen the error of his ways. DeSeve is placed under arrest but wants to speak to Picard. DeSeve gives Picard a message from Spock regarding what the Vulcan described as "further cowboy diplomacy."

Picard recognizes that it is indeed from Ambassador Spock. The Enterprise is supposed to meet a Corvallen freighter in the Kaleb Sector within 12 hours to pick up its cargo and return it to Federation space. Picard accepts the message as genuine and has the Enterprise set course for the Kaleb sector.

Aboard the Romulan warbird, N'Vek reveals the nature of their mission. The secret cargo consists of members of the Romulan underground who have been placed in stasis. These include Vice Proconsul M'ret of the Imperial Romulan Senate and his two top aides. This mission is meant to open an escape route for other Romulan dissidents who wish to defect. In the Kaleb sector they are to transfer their cargo to a Corvallen freighter.

When they rendezvous with the freighter, Troi's empathic abilities reveal that the Corvallen's intend to betray them and when she informs N'Vek, he fires the warbird's weapons and destroys the freighter. Troi orders the cloaked Romulan ship to maintain its position, in spite of angry demands from Commander Toreth who wants to know what's going on.

Soon the Enterprise arrives, which further inflames Toreth's anger and suspicions. She orders the cloaked warbird to slowly leave the area.

Troi talks to one of the dissident crewmen who manipulates the engines so that the Enterprise can just barely detect the presence of the cloaked warbird.

When Commander Toreth realizes that the Enterprise can detect them, she orders that the warbird fire on it, but Troi countermands the order and relieves Toreth of command. Troi contacts the Enterprise and Picard is silently surprised to see Troi in Romulan attire addressing him from the view screen. She offers to come to the Enterprise to discuss the situation over the destroyed freighter. Picard figures out that she's asking to be rescued.

When the Enterprise drops its shields so that Troi can beam over, she instead orders the ship to fire on the Enterprise. The disrupter fire is very weak and is actually a cover for beaming over the secret cargo onto the Enterprise.

Toreth sees through the subterfuge and confronts Troi and N'Vek. When N'Vek pulls his sidearm, he's killed by one of Toreth's aides. When Toreth orders the ship to drop its shields so that they can cloak and go to warp, the Enterprise beams Troi off the vessel.

On the Enterprise Picard states that the mission has been a success as now further dissidents will be able to escape. N'Vek's sacrifice was not in vain.

EPISODE ONE HUNDRED FORTY-ONE: "TAPESTRY"

Written by Ronald D. Moore
Directed by Les Landeau
Guest Cast: John de Lancie, Ned Vaughn

Captain Picard is brought unconscious into sick bay following a sneak attack on the Away Team he was leading to a peace conference. Picard has a blackened wound on his chest from the blast of a Lenarian compressed teryon beam. Dr. Crusher is working to save him desperately but it appears that fate is working against her.

Picard, still unconscious, finds himself in a place filled with a bright light from which a figure slowly emerges wearing long white robes. When Picard reaches out and takes the figure's hand, it turns out to be Q. "Welcome to the afterlife, Jean-Luc. You're dead."

Jean-Luc refuses to believe that Q runs the afterlife, although when Q introduces Picard to his deceased father, it gives him food for thought. Q blames Picard's death on his artificial heart which was fused by the blast. When Picard explains that he lost his real heart as a result of a rash act in his youth, Q is intrigued.

Picard admits to starting the fight with the three nasty Nausicaans because he was a cocky young ensign. He admits that if he had to do it all over again he'd avoid the fight and therefore still have his real heart 30 years later. Q wonders if that's true.

Suddenly Picard finds himself 30 years in his own past on the verge of reliving the events which led up to the brawl with the Nausicaans. Q tells Picard that what happens from then on is entirely his own decision.

Picard encounters his friends Corey Zweller and Marta Batanides. They are gambling and approached by a Nausicaan who wants to challenge him at Dom-Jot. Picard knows that the Nausicaan will cheat and this will eventually lead to the altercation. After the loss, Picard tries to talk Corey out of seeking revenge, but he just gets mad at Jean-Luc and storms off.

Marta is impressed. This is a different side of the brash, reckless Jean-Luc. Marta and Jean-Luc return to his quarters that night and make love, something which never happened before. The following morning Marta is upset, believing that this has altered their friendship and Picard now realizes this is true. He made a mistake, one he didn't make previously.

Corey is back trying to beat the Nausicaan again, much to Jean-Luc's dismay. When he is called a coward by the Nausicaan, Picard prevents a fight, thereby seemingly betraying his friendship. Both Corey and Marta turn their backs on him, apparently forever. The fight was averted, but at what cost?

Back in real time, 30 years later, Picard is on the Enterprise but as a Lieutenant, junior grade. Captain Thomas Halloway is in command of the Enterprise. Picard played it safe his whole life, never took risks, and therefore never rose to his fullest potential. Picard doesn't like it.

Suddenly back in limbo, Q chides Picard for complaining about the second chance he's been given. But Jean-Luc doesn't consider living out his life in a tedious second-rate position on the Enterprise to be much of a life. Without facing death, he never had a revelation of mortality which focused his life and made him seize the moment time after time.

Picard wants another chance to become the man he was. He'd rather die as that man than live as that pitiful Lieutenant, j.g.

Back at the Bonestall Facility, when the Nausicaan calls Corey a coward, it is Jean-Luc who throws the first punch. When he is stabbed in the back, as he knew would happen, he goes down laughing.

Picard wakes up in Sick Bay, still laughing. Dr. Crusher has stabilized his injuries and he'll live.

Later Jean-Luc tells Riker about his experience and can't decide whether it was a dream or not. While there were things he did in his youth that he regretted, he discovered that by pulling on one of those threads he unraveled the entire tapestry of his life.

EPISODE ONE HUNDRED FORTY-TWO: "BIRTHRIGHT" PART ONE

Written by Brannon Braga
Directed by Winrich Kolbe
Guest Cast: Siddig El Fadil, James Cromwell

Shortly after the Federation takes charge of space station Deep Space Nine orbiting Bajor, the Enterprise arrives to assist the Bajorans on the surface who are in need of technical assistance following the destructive evacuation of the Cardassians.

Worf beams aboard the station where he is approached by an Yridian named Jaglom Shrek. Shrek knows who Worf is and offers to sell the Klingon information on where he can find his long lost father. Worf is outraged at the attempted deception, stating that he knows his father died at the hands of Romulans on the planet Khitomer. But Shrek insists that Worf's father was a prisoner of war taken to a secret Romulan prison planet.

Turning his back on the Yridian, Worf returns to the Enterprise, but not even a vigorous workout can take the edge off his anger. Finally he reveals what happened to Counselor Troi and explains that a Klingon would prefer death to the indignity of being taken prisoner. Were his father discovered to be alive, his entire family would be dishonored by the fact.

Dr. Bashir beams aboard the Enterprise to use its advanced equipment to analyze a strange alien device he has found. Data and Geordi assist him, and during an experimental activation of the device, an energy bolt shoots into the android's tricorder and knocks him to the floor.

But instead of being harmed, Data experiences an hallucination. In the vision he is walking down a corridor of the Enterprise where he finds a 19th century blacksmith pounding on an anvil with a hammer. The man looks at Data who sees that it is a young version of Dr. Noonian Soong, his creator.

When Data revives he learns that he was in shut down for a full 30 seconds, although his memory clearly records the vision. Data is perplexed but Dr. Bashir suggests that Data had a dream, which would be an entirely novel experience for the android.

Worf talks to Data about a vision he once experienced of Kahless, the legendary Klingon warrior. Worf states that if Data had a vision of his father then he should try to understand all that he can about it as such visions are considered important to Klingons.

All this talk has convinced Worf that he must get to the bottom of what Shrek suggested and looks him up on Deep Space Nine. Worf intimidates Shrek into taking him to the Romulan prison camp, stating that he will not be paid unless he is telling the truth. If Shrek is lying then Worf will kill him.

Shrek takes Worf to the planetoid and gives him a homing device, promising to return in 50 hours as it would not be safe for the shuttle to just wait there. Worf explores the jungle choked area for awhile before suddenly coming upon a small pond where Ba'el, a young Klingon woman, is washing herself. Worf tells her that he is there to take her home, which confuses her as this world is her home. When Worf detects a Romulan guard approaching, he hides.

Meanwhile, Data is exploring the nature of his vision through painting. He has done 23 paintings of the images he has seen in order to make more sense of them. The paintings have images Data does not recall from the dream and asks Geordi to help him recreate the vision. Geordi is uncertain and believes that it's dangerous to try. But by including certain safeguards, Geordi and Dr. Bashir recreate the incident under controlled conditions.

Data re-experiences the vision, but now a large black bird is in the dream as well and it flies along the corridor, causing the dream to change again. Dr. Soong is there, explaining that Data doesn't need to understand his dreams. The fact that he has them is proof that he has advanced, just as Dr. Soong had planned. "Data, you are the bird," and Data understands as he sees what the bird sees, including when it flies through the hull of the Enterprise and out into space.

Data awakens and tells Dr. Bashir that the dreams are the result of a dormant program which was activated by the plasma surge, a program Data intends to explore each day.

On the Romulan prison planet, Worf finds the prison camp and encounters another Klingon, named L'Kor, who is amazed to see Worf. Worf asks about his father, Mogh, and is told that Mogh did indeed die on Khitomer, but survivors of Khitomer still live in the prison camp. Worf wants to rescue the other Klingons, but they do not wish to leave, and by summoning their Romulan guards they intend to prevent Worf from leaving as well.

EPISODE ONE HUNDRED FORTY-THREE: "BIRTHRIGHT" PART TWO

Written by Rene Echevarria
Directed by Dan Curry
Guest Cast: Alan Scarfe, Richard Herd, Christine Rose, Sterling Macer, Jr., Jennifer Gatti

The Klingons in the Romulan prison camp do not want to be rescued because they believe they "died" at Khitomer and to return to the homeworld now would be to return in disgrace. Originally the Romulans had intended trading the prisoners for Klingon concessions, but the Klingons refused to accept the concept of the Romulans even having Klingon prisoners.

The Klingons were raised in captivity and came to accept their fate rather than go home and dishonor their families by having failed to die in battle rather than be imprisoned. A Romulan commander took pity on them and allowed them to live out their lives on the planetoid in peace for 20 years.

Worf said if he had located his father he would not have found it in his heart to feel shame. But L'Kor says that if his son found him, he hoped that he would be Klingon enough to slay his father.

Worf sees a Klingon youth, Toq, working in a garden with a Klingon ceremonial spear as though it is just a tool. Worf is shocked that Toq knows nothing of his heritage. Toq says that there is no war as his parents came to that world to escape it.

When the young Klingon woman Worf met earlier approaches him, he talks to her comes to realize that the

Klingon children have no idea their parents were prisoners of war who abandoned their heritage out of shame.

Worf gets the transponder beep from Shrek telling him that the shuttle is waiting for him.

The Romulan commander, Tokath, explains to Worf that the Romulan command gave him the choice of executing the Klingon prisoners or overseeing them from then on. Tokath has since married a Klingon woman and will not allow Worf to disrupt their lives.

Worf manages to escape, but before he can reach the shuttle he is tackled by Toq and recaptured by the Romulans.

Once Worf is 12 hours overdue, Picard determines to search for him by tracking the Yridian shuttle.

Back in the prison colony, Worf is determined to maintain his Klingon individuality by working out, which attracts the attention of some of the Klingon youths. Worf tells the youths tales of Klingon warriors, such as the legendary Kahless.

Ba'el is particularly interested by Worf and when he responds to her advances he is shocked to discover that she has pointed ears. She is half Romulan, half Klingon, a concept that repulses Worf. Later Worf apologizes for his reaction, explaining that ordinarily Romulans and Klingons are hereditary enemies.

Worf starts getting to know the other Klingon youths better and teaches them about the real purpose of the various weapons they have been using as tools.

Tokath doesn't like what Worf is doing and orders him to live with them in peace or be killed. Worf prefers death to living in dishonor. He'll show the others how a Klingon dies. Ba'el urges Worf to escape, but he refuses. It's not the Klingon way. As Tokath prepares to execute Worf, Toq enters in full Klingon regalia and vows to die with Worf. Others of the Klingon youth join him. The Klingons plead for their children and the Romulans relent. Worf tells the children that if they leave then this place must be kept a secret, for their parent's sake.

When the Enterprise receives a signal from Worf, he is picked up along with Toq and some of the other Klingon youths, whom Worf states are "crash survivors." The secret of the prison planet will be kept, and Ba'el chooses to remain behind knowing that her Romulan heritage would never be acceptable on the Klingon homeworld.

EPISODE ONE HUNDRED FORTY-FOUR: "STARSHIP MINE"

Written by Morgan Gendel
Directed by Cliff Bole

Guest Cast: David Spielberg

The Enterprise docks at the Remmler Array where it is scheduled to be cleared of baryon particles. In order to do this the Enterprise must be cleared of all personnel, who are evacuated to the Arkaria Base.

The command personnel are invited to a reception given by Commander Hutchinson, reportedly the most boring man in Starfleet. Picard excuses himself by stating that he's going horseback riding below and he returns to the Enterprise to retrieve his saddle from his quarters.

At the reception, Data is intrigued by Command Hutchinson's pointless babbling and decides to imitate it, all too successfully for Will Riker and Dr. Crusher's taste. When Data starts talking to Hutchinson himself, the Commander is fascinated by Data's pointless observations.

After Picard retrieves his saddle, he sees one of the technicians, Devor, near an open junction box and carrying a laser welder. When Picard questions the technician, the man threatens the captain, who hits him with the saddle. When Picard tries to get to the transporter room before the automatic systems shutdown begins, he almost runs into two more of the technicians.

Picard retrieves the unconscious Devor and hides him in sick bay, then hears the others talking over the man's communicator. The group is led by a woman named Kelsey who is working on a secret project in engineering. When Picard tries to investigate what is going on, he is captured by Kiros, who takes him to engineering.

Back at the reception, Geordi detects some strange radiation at the hors d'oeuvre table. Seeing that they may be discovered, Orton and a waiter grab their guns from beneath the table, fire their weapons, killing Hutchinson and wounding Geordi. Then they take everyone else at the reception prisoner.

Aboard the Enterprise, Picard is marched at gun point into engineering where Kelsey and the others are draining trilithium resin from the warp core into a portable container. Picard claims he's the ship's barber, Mott, who came back to get something before the baryon sweep started.

In the Arkaria Base, Data has Dr. Crusher give medical aid to Geordi while Data uses this as a cover to reset Geordi's VISOR. If he can get it to emit a hypersonic pulse, it will knock out everyone else in the room, except for Data.

In the corner where he's being guarded, Picard pulls out the laser torch he'd hidden in his belt and uses it to set off a sensor which causes gas to flood the compartment, allowing Picard to escape, although one of the technicians soon follows him. By doing this Picard has also sabotaged the diverter field which the saboteurs were using to protect them from the baryon sweep.

Picard escapes into a Jeffries Tube, and the guard who follows him is tricked into getting caught in the baryon sweep and killed.

Kelsey and her aide, Neil, have no protection from the baryon sweep and have to move forward in the ship until they can be picked up by their confederates. Neil wants to leave the trilithium behind, but Kelsey refuses because that's what all of this has been for. Neil protests that it is unstable and dangerous to just carry around, but Kelsey insists.

Picard goes to Worf's quarters to find weapons which wouldn't have been deactivated by the baryon sweep. He decides to take a crossbow and some arrows. In sick bay he also prepares some chemicals for his special use. When he encounters one of Kelsey's men he shoots him with a drugged arrow, but is then cornered by Kiros who takes him to Kelsey.

Kelsey is tired of Neil's whining. She shoots him and takes the trilithium herself.

On the Arkaria Base, as a ship is detected approaching, they put their plan into effect. Geordi's VISOR gives off the hypersonic burst and when it momentarily disables everyone, Data acts.

Picard tries to get Kelsey to leave the trilithium since he knows she plans to sell it to someone for the purpose of making terrorist weapons. Picard struggles with Kelsey but she manages to break away from him and is beamed off the ship with the trilithium.

Picard contacts the Arkaria Base and hears Data respond. Data is able to halt the baryon sweep just inches from where Picard sits crouching against a bulkhead.

Through a port in Ten Forward, Picard sees Kelsey's ship explode. He had managed to pull the safety catch from the trilithium container, making it even more dangerous to handle.

EPISODE ONE HUNDRED FORTY-FIVE: "LESSONS"

Written by Ronald Wilkerson & Jean Louise Matthias
Directed by Robert Weimer
Guest Cast: Wendy Hughes

While on night watch, Picard encounters Lt. Commander Nella Daren, the new chief of the Stellar Sciences department. Picard keeps encountering her and finding her more interesting at each meeting. When he attends a concert and discovers that she is also a marvelous pianist, he is even more intrigued. When she learns that he has an interest in music he explains that he's just an amateur.

She arrives at his quarters soon after while Picard is playing his Ressikan flute. Nella has brought a portable keyboard and she coaxes Picard into accompanying her on his flute. Later Nella takes Picard to the fourth intersect of Jeffries Tube 25 because it is ostensibly the most acoustically perfect place in the ship. Picard plays a lullaby on his flute which deeply touches Nella. His music stops when they embrace.

The Enterprise is dispatched to Bersalis Three to study the fire storm cycle of that world.

Picard discusses the situation with Counselor Troi as to whether it is wise to become involved with a co-worker. But Troi explains that it is unwise for him to cut himself off from his feelings.

During an intimate dinner with Nella, Picard is interrupted by an urgent summons from the bridge. The firestorms on Bersallis Three are endangering the Federation outpost which will need to be evacuated. While the outpost was constructed to withstand ordinary firestorms, this raging inferno is double the size of anything previously recorded.

The Enterprise at its best speed will still arrive only one hour before the storm hits, so Nella Daren suggests that by erecting thermal deflectors they can buy themselves some time. It will take 24 crewmen to operate the 12 deflectors and Lt. Daren intends to be one of them. This will put them at risk because they will be the last personnel on the ground to be evacuated.

Nella is put in charge of the task, which troubles Picard because of the risk factor. But Nella points out that they had agreed that their relationship should not affect their work. Nella and her team beam down to the planet to erect the deflectors while the evacuation is in progress.

The storm will hit in four minutes but they need ten minutes to complete evacuation, which means that the ground crew will have to remain with the deflectors. Theoretically this should protect them, although the deflectors have been giving them some problems. Picard is clearly concerned over Nella's safety but won't single her out for premature evacuation.

Four of the teams are rescued when the storm hits but interference prevented beaming out the other two, which included Nella Daren. Picard is overwhelmed as chances are slight that Nella could have survived.

But soon Worf reports that survivors have been beamed up. Nella is not in the first group and Picard accepts the truth, but then the transporter activates again and Nella appears.

She and Picard meet in her quarters later after she has been examined in sick bay and cleaned up from her ordeal. They discuss what has happened and how she feels about the fact that Picard would have blamed himself if she had died.

"I've lost people under my command; people who were very dear to me. But never someone I've been in love with. And when I believed that you were dead, I just began to shut down. I didn't want to think. I didn't want to feel. I was here, in my quarters, and the only thing I could focus on was my music, and how it would never give me any joy."

Nella decides that she must transfer because of the pressures being on the same ship puts on both of them. They hope to see each other again but it might be a long time. She asks Picard to promise not to give up his music.

EPISODE ONE HUNDRED FORTY-SIX: "THE CHASE"
Written by Joe Menosky

From a story by Ronald Moore & Joe Menosky
Directed by Jonathan Frakes
Guest Cast: Norman Lloyd, Linda Thorson, John Cothran Jr., Maurice Roeves, Salome Jens

Picard's old archeology teacher, Professor Galen, pays a visit to the Enterprise. By way of introduction Galen brings the captain an unusual relic, a small statue called a naiskos from the Third Kurlan dynasty. What makes the carved figure so rare is that it is intact. Picard is extremely impressed.

Galen is there to offer to share his latest discoveries with him, so long as Picard agrees to accompany the professor on his newest exploration. He is scheduled to rendezvous with a Vulcan shuttle in two days. Galen has been doing a study of fossil records on a microscopic level. He wants Picard to accompany him on what could prove to be the most fantastic discovery of his or anyone else's career—but he won't reveal the nature of that discovery. Picard is flattered by the offer but feels that he has a responsibility to Starfleet to live up to.

Galen is angry, feeling that Picard is rejecting his offer so that he can continue to live life as a grandiose security guard. Prof. Galen compares Starfleet with the centurions of the Roman Empire and clearly doesn't feel that what Picard is doing there is very important. It turns out that he is still resentful that Jean-Luc, his prize student, chose a career in Starfleet over one in exoarcheology.

A few days later the Enterprise receives a distress call from Prof. Galen. His shuttle is under attack from an Yridian destroyer. The Enterprise arrives on the scene quickly and when it is forced to fire on the Yridian ship, the destroyer explodes. But they are too late to save Galen. As he lies dying, he tells Jean-Luc, "I was too harsh." In spite of Galen's forgiveness, Picard feels a measure of blame for Galen's fate.

The Yridians were apparently trying to steal information from the shuttle's computer files. Although Data and Geordi have retrieved the information from Prof. Galen's files, they don't know what the link between the bits of information is.

They backtrack to Galen's last stop, the planet Ruah Four which has no signs of civilization, and therefore no archaeological significance. Galen's next stop was to be Indri Eight, where they head next. But at Indri Eight, someone has been there before them as the planet has been blasted with a plasma weapon, destroying all life signs, primitive as the life on that uninhabited planet had been.

This makes them wonder whether the information from Prof. Galen's computer has something to do with organic matter, such as DNA strands. It turns out that the information consists of DNA codes from 19 different worlds, some of which interlock as though into a prearranged pattern.

The design is an algorithm coded at the molecular level into a pre-arranged program. This could not be accidental. The linking fragments have been a part of the DNA strands on far flung worlds since life on them began eons ago. But how could a code have been created in such a way unless all of those life forms have a common source?

Prof. Galen was searching for the strands which would complete the program, but it's impossible to know what the completed program would signify. The Enterprise next travels to Loren Three where they are greeted by two Cardassian warships which try to warn the Enterprise off, although they won't explain what disturbance the Enterprise is causing. The Cardassian commander, Gul Ocett, makes veiled threats until a Klingon ship suddenly decloaks and joins the conversation. Captain Nu'Daq wants to know what the other two are doing there.

Picard suggests that the two rival captains join him aboard the Enterprise to resolve the situation. Jean-Luc makes it clear that he knows what the others are doing there and points out that only by joining forces can they solve the mystery now that Indri Eight has been blasted of all life signs. Gul Ocett is outraged over the news and begins arguing with the Klingon since it is evident he was responsible for what happened to Indri Eight.

Gul Ocett and Nu'Daq reluctantly agree to join forces with Picard, although neither of them have any additional clues as to what the program signifies. The Klingon thinks it's a weapon and the Cardassians believe it the secret to a source of limitless power. Picard explains that even with the information the Cardassians and the Klingon have, that a piece is still missing. The Enterprise computers will determine where the missing strand can be found.

When Data announces that the fragment can be found in the Rahm-Izad system, Gul Ocett suddenly beams to her ship, fires at the Enterprise and the Klingon ship, and then speeds off. But Geordi had earlier detected tampering which had been done to the defensive systems of the Enterprise and prepared for this. The blasts from the Cardassian ship didn't harm the Enterprise at all, and Data deliberately gave Gul Ocett the wrong information.

But the Klingons, although prepared, did not defend their ship as well and it suffered some minor damage. Rather than delay, Nu'Dag agrees to accompany Picard and company on the Enterprise to the true destination in the Vilmoran system.

Upon arriving they find only one planet capable of supporting life, and even this primitive life is all but gone. A landing party consisting of Picard, Worf, Nu'Daq and Dr. Crusher beam down. No sooner do they do so than they are greeted by four Romulans, who had been silently tracking them. Then Gul Ocett appears, having discovered that she was tricked and back tracked the Enterprise. She threatens to destroy the only sample they found there rather than let the Romulans get it.

While they argue, Dr. Crusher finds another sample, enters it into her tricorder and a hologram appears. It is of an ancient humanoid alien from a long dead race. Their scientists seeded other worlds with life, all of which was in their basic humanoid form, however different they may look on the outside.

"It was our hope that you would have to come together in fellowship and companionship to hear this message. And if you can see and hear me, our hope has been fulfilled. You are a monument—not to our greatness but to our existence. That was our wish, that you, too, would know life and keep alive our memory. There is something of us in each of you, and so, something of you in each other. Remember us."

The hologram ends and the Klingons and Cardassians are all disappointed that the message did not offer some more tangible reward. Gul Ocett in particular is annoyed at the thought that Cardassians and Klingons could have anything in common. They beam out and the Away Team returns to the Enterprise.

Before leaving orbit, Picard receives a hopeful message from the Romulans, who apparently appreciated the basic message of the hologram and its significance far more than the Klingons and Cardassians did. The Romulan commander suggests that perhaps one day their people will indeed come together in fellowship, just as their creators intended.

EPISODE ONE HUNDRED FORTY-SEVEN: "FRAME OF MIND"

Written by Brannon Braga
Directed by Jim Conway
Guest Cast: Andrew Prine, Gary Werntz, David Selburg, Susanna Thompson

Riker is in an asylum for the insane, patiently trying to explain to his doctor that he's all better now. Then Riker becomes more and more angry and we see that he's on stage in the theatrical auditorium aboard the Enterprise. He's rehearsing the play "Frame of Mind" which Beverly Crusher is directing.

On the way back to his quarters Riker almost bumps into an alien in the corridor who stares at Riker without speaking.

Picard tells Riker about their scheduled mission to rescue a research team which was kidnapped by terrorists on Tilonus Four where the government has collapsed and anarchy has resulted.

Riker will go in alone to avoid attracting attention and is brief by Worf who is acting strangely and accidentally cuts Riker on the temple with a knife he's demonstrating. Dr. Crusher tends to the wound but Riker still feels pain afterwards, which isn't normal.

When the play is performed, it is well received and the audience gives Riker a standing ovation, except for one alien who sits and says nothing. Suddenly the audience is gone and Riker is alone in a real cell, not a mock-up on a stage. The alien doctor who sees him looks just like the lieutenant he saw in the auditorium.

The alien, Dr. Syrus, tells Riker that the memories of being on a starship are a delusion. He is in Ward 47 of the Tilonius Institute for Mental Disorders. When Riker is taken to the common area to eat he meets another inmate who also claims to be from a Federation starship, but she is clearly insane.

When Riker is told that the crime he was arrested for was stabbing a man nine times and mutilating him, Riker rejects the claim and attacks the attendant. Riker is subdued with a hypo.

He wakes up in his bunk aboard the Enterprise, before he has done the play. It was all a dream, or so he thinks. Riker performs the play and once again it turns into the real asylum.

Riker finally accepts that the visions and memories of the Enterprise are delusions. When Dr. Crusher sneaks in and tells him that he was captured and they are there to get him out, he rejects her as an hallucination. When Geordi and Worf beam in and rescue Riker, he struggles to resist them even after they return him to the Enterprise.

In sick bay, Dr. Crusher heals Riker's head wound, which starts bleeding again. He rejects this all as a delusion, grabs a phaser, points the weapon at himself and fires. Sick bay vanishes like a shattered mirror and Riker is once again in the asylum with Mavek, Dr. Syrus and Mr. Suna.

Riker rejects this image as well as he still has the phaser. He puts it on the highest setting and fires again, destroying this image as well. Now Riker is on

the stage on the Enterprise along with Mr. Suna. Riker's head wound starts bleeding again and he attacks the walls of the set, which also shatter.

Will Riker awakens as everything up until now had been a dream or memories of true events. He's on an examination table and a probe is attached to his temple in the spot he feels pain. Riker attacks the attendants, grabs the disguised communicator he had with him and is rescued via emergency transport.

On board the real Enterprise now, Dr. Crusher works at rebuilding Riker's memory. He had been on the solo mission, exposed, attacked and taken for interrogation to the asylum where the aliens attempted to perform a neurochemical drain on him. Riker had used the play as a defense mechanism to keep himself sane.

Finally Riker has one last act to perform. In the Enterprise auditorium he knocks down the sets to "Frame of Mind," destroying the last vestige of the nightmare he lived through.

EPISODE ONE HUNDRED FORTY-EIGHT: "SUSPICIONS"

Written by Joe Menosky and Naren Shankar
Directed by Cliff Bole

Meeting of the Treks.

Michael along with original Trekkers James Doohan and George Takei and DS9's Terry Farrell in Las Vegas for the '93 VSDA (Video Software Dealers Association).

Photo © 1994 Albert L. Ortega

Will with Brent, Patrick and Levar at the L.A. County Museum for a night of STAR TREK with Q&A by the Academy of Television Arts & Sciences.

Guest Cast: Peter Slutsker, James Horan, Joan Stuart Morris, Tricia O'Neil

When Guinan comes to see Dr. Crusher about treating her tennis elbow, Beverly reveals that she cannot help her as she has been relieved of duty. Beverly is packing to return to Earth for a formal hearing on the charges of violating medical ethics, disobeying a direct order and causing an interstellar incident. She finally agrees to treat Guinan's tennis elbow and explains how she got into this mess.

It began after meeting the Ferengi scientist, Dr. Reyga, when she decided to convene several observers from the scientific community aboard the Enterprise so that Reyga could demonstrate his discovery. His metaphasic field could be an important breakthrough.

It is a shield so durable that it can even protect a craft from the radiation in the corona of a star while using a power source small enough to fit aboard a shuttlecraft. Because he is a Ferengi, Dr. Deyga's theories have not received serious consideration and Beverly intends to set that right.

The scientists who arrive to observe the experimental metaphasic field are a Klingon—Kurak, a Takaran—Jo'Bril, T'Pan of the Vulcan Science Academy and her human husband. The scientists are openly skeptical but agree to give Dr. Reyga's theory a chance.

One of the shuttles of the Enterprise is outfitted and Jo'Bril agrees to be the pilot during the experimental flight. Jo'Bril guides the shuttle into the corona of the star Vaytan. Suddenly Baryon particles flood the compartment and when the shuttle is yanked back by the tractor beam of the Enterprise, Jo'Bril is dead. But when Dr. Crusher examines Jo'Bril he doesn't appear to have died from radiation poisoning but from something else entirely.

Dr. Reyga wants to pilot the shuttle himself next time to prove that his equipment did not fail, but Dr. Crusher doesn't want to risk any more lives. A short time later Dr. Reyga is found dead with a plasma infuser in his hand as though he shot himself with it.

Beverly refuses to accept this possibility. She believes that someone murdered the Ferengi scientist to cover up the fact that his device is a success. But who? Who would gain from stealing the technology for themselves?

Dr. Crusher needs to perform an autopsy to prove that it wasn't suicide, but Ferengi death rituals prevent such post mortems. Captain Picard states that he will not allow an autopsy unless Beverly can provide other evidence that a murder was committed.

Beverly questions the other scientists, and Kurak reacts violently when Dr. Crusher accuses her of lying. Reyga did accuse Kurak of sabotaging the experiment, but she didn't kill him because of that.

Beverly decides she has only one course of action—to perform the autopsy against orders. She does so and finds nothing. Picard is furious and Starfleet relieves her of duty after the Ferengi file a formal protest.

This is the story Beverly relates to Guinan, who seems somewhat unconcerned. When Beverly gets angry, Guinan tells her that she should put that anger to good use and keep investigating. She does.

When Beverly questions Data about whether the shuttle could have been sabotaged, he explains that this would have had to happen when it was in operation, and only J'Bril could have sabotaged it, which seems unlikely since the sabotage would have resulted in his own death.

Beverly does some more checking and then makes an unauthorized departure in the shuttlecraft to test her theories about Dr. Reyga's metaphasic field. Her mission into the corona is successful, but just as she reports this to the Enterprise, her transmission abruptly ends.

Aboard the shuttle Jo'bril has stepped from hiding, leveling a phaser on Dr. Crusher. Takarans can simulate death, which he did in order to sabotage the experiment and steal the technology for himself.

Beverly struggles with him and gets the phaser. She shoots a hole in him which doesn't slow him down at all. Finally she disintegrates Jo'Bril with the higher phaser setting.

Dr. Crusher is reinstated and Dr. Reyga's discovery is vindicated. When Beverly tries to thank Guinan by presenting her with a tennis racquet, Guinan explains that she doesn't play tennis, and never has. She was just there to listen to Dr. Crusher at a crucial moment and guide her in the right direction.

EPISODE ONE HUNDRED FORTY-NINE: "RIGHTFUL HEIR"

Written by Ronald D. Moore
From a story by James E. Brooks
Directed by Winrich Kolbe
Guest Cast: Kevin Conway, Robert O'Reilly

Worf has been acting strangely, and when he is reported overdue for his shift, Riker becomes concerned. When Worf doesn't respond at his door he has a security team break in. Inside, Worf is in a trance which he awakens from. Around him are small ceremonial fires which have filled the compartment with smoke. Worf seems strangely disoriented.

He confesses to Captain Picard that he has been undergoing a crisis of Klingon faith. Following the rescue of the Klingons from the Romulan prison camp, he has questioned his own beliefs. While he instilled the strength of their heritage in the Klingon youth he rescued, he didn't feel that his own passion was truly as strong as theirs.

Picard grants Worf a leave of absence so that he can visit the planet Boreth where a temple has been built to honor the legendary Klingon warrior Kahless, who lived hundreds of years before. Kahless had long ago united the Klingon people and promised to one day return and lead them again. At Boreth, the followers of Kahless have been waiting for that promised return for centuries.

At Boreth, Worf undergoes ceremony and ritual, watching as other Klingons speak of visions they have had, although Worf has had no visions of his own. If anything this makes him even more dispirited. When Worf expresses his concern to Koroth, the leader of the acolytes, he is chided since all Klingons have been waiting for Kahless to return for 1500 years.

During a fire ritual, Kahless appears, and not just to Worf but to all the Klingons who are present. This is no mere vision but is Kahless in the flesh. After 15 centuries he has returned at last to lead his people.

When Kahless is challenged by Boreth to prove his identity, he reveals the story of the forging of the bat'leth sword, a secret known only to the high clerics on Boreth. The acolytes declare that this is indeed the real Kahless.

Kahless is to be taken to the Klingon homeworld aboard the Enterprise. Once on the homeworld, Kahless will meet with Gowron. But Koroth and the others fear that Gowron will oppose being replaced by Kahless, which could divide the empire in a bitter conflict.

Worf meets with the command crew who question him about Kahless. When Data presses for evidence, Worf admits that his opinion is largely based on faith as Kahless has become a religious figure over the centuries.

Gowron chooses to intercept the Enterprise before it arrives in Klingon space so that the question of Kahless' identity can be settled before he reaches the homeworld. Gowron brings with him the sacred knife of Kirom which is stained with the blood of the real Kahless. A genetic analysis proves that the man calling himself Kahless is a perfect match for the blood on the 1500 year old knife. Worf at last feels that they have the hard evidence for proving the identity of Kahless beyond question.

In the holodeck, Gowron is formally presented to Kahless and challenges him with a knife. Gowron easily defeats Kahless and then openly questions the Klingon's identity. How can this be the greatest Klingon warrior of them all? Even Worf is now uncertain.

Worf demands that Koroth reveal the truth or he will slay him on the spot. Koroth admits that Kahless is a clone grown from the blood on the knife of Kirom. Even the new Kahless did not know this. When he appeared on Boroth, that was the first conscious moment for the new Kahless, who until that moment on the Enterprise even believed himself to be the original Klingon legend.

Koroth defends their actions as they need Kahless to hold the empire together in the face of the corruption which is tearing it apart under Gowron. Worf goes to Gowron and tells him the truth, but states that the truth doesn't matter. Many Klingons will still stand with Kahless against Gowron because they need something to believe in that will give their life meaning. If Gowron openly opposes Kahless, civil war will tear the empire apart.

Worf suggests making Kahless Emperor, a post long unused in the Klingon empire. Gowron will still lead the high council and have the real power whereas Kahless will provide moral leadership for the Klingon people.

Addressing Kahless, Worf explains that he will have the power to hold the people together and turn them towards honorable things. Gowron and Kahless accept the compromise.

Although Worf is still uncertain about his own beliefs, Kahless tells him that the legacy the real Kahless left behind is still vital and important and those teachings should be followed as the truths they are. Worf considers this as he bids Kahless farewell.

EPISODE ONE HUNDRED FIFTY: "SECOND CHANCES"

Written by Rene Echevarria
From a story by Michael A. Medlock
Directed by LeVar Burton
Guest Cast: Mae Jemison

The Enterprise approaches Nervala-Four, a planet surrounded by a distortion field which makes transporting to and from the surface difficult. Only when the planet's orbit takes it close enough to its sun does it become possible to find low enough levels of distortion to transport through.

This happens every eight years. Eight years earlier, an Away Team from the Potemkin had rescued the inhabitants of a science station on the planet. The leader of that team, Lieutenant William Riker, had been the last to beam up, and had almost failed to make it back.

On the bridge, Data and Riker discuss the situation. Their mission is to retrieve the scientific information left behind in the computer database on Nervala-Four eight years earlier. Improvements in transporters in the past few years make the job a bit easier, but even so there will only be three transporter "windows" over the next several days. If the database is not retrieved in this time, it will have to wait another eight years.

The first transporter window arrives and Riker beams down to the science station with Data and Worf. Data detects an approaching humanoid life form with his tricorder. Drawing their phasers as a precaution, they watch as the figure steps from the shadows. It is Will Riker, dressed in a tattered yellow lieutenant's uniform!

The two Rikers stare at each other, dumbfounded. They begin to quiz each other. Each believes that they are the true Will Riker, and rejects the other one's claim. Data steps in and asks Lieutenant Riker how he got there.

Lieutenant Riker recounts the story of how he led the Away Team from the Potemkin eight years earlier. His version differs in one important detail: the distortion field kept him from being able to beam up, and he has long assumed that he was left for dead.

Lieutenant Riker agrees to a medical examination, and beams up to sickbay with Worf. Dr. Crusher finds him in good health, although she detects that one of his arms had been broken and healed; he admits that he had to set it himself. Picard arrives to meet the new arrival and questions Crusher about him. Could he be a clone?

Crusher doubts it, as there is no genetic drift detected in her exam. Not only is Lieutenant Riker genetically identical to Commander Riker, his brain patterns are also the same, with slight differences easily accounted for by eight years of different experiences. Lieutenant Riker is the same person as the Commander, although he exists separately— but how?

Geordi LaForge checks out the transporter logs from the Potemkin and believes he has found the answer to that question. When the Potemkin was beaming Riker back up, its transporter chief had trouble getting a lock on Riker's signal, so he boosted the transport beam with a second containment field, apparently intending to reintegrate the fields at the beam-in point.

Riker beamed up in the first beam, and the second one was shut down— but it, too, had picked up Riker, and somehow the second beam reflected off the distortion field surrounding the planet, beaming Riker back down to the science station at the same time that he was also beaming back up to the Potemkin! There's no getting around it. Both Rikers are real.

Another Away Team is planned to go after the database. Picard suggests that they take Lieutenant Riker along, since he did a lot of reconfiguration on the station computer, removing components and using them to keep the station's radiation shields operational. Deanna volunteers to go to Lieutenant Riker's quarters and ask him if he's willing to join the mission.

When Deanna enters Will's quarters, she hardly has time to ask him anything, as he takes her in his arms and kisses her passionately. Deanna draws back and tries to explain how her feelings for Commander Riker have changed. Lieutenant Riker remembers their last meeting as lovers, at the Generan falls on Beta-Zed.

There they promised to meet on Rysa in six weeks. The meeting never took place. For Lieutenant Riker, this has one meaning. But Deanna tells him that Commander Riker never made it, either, as his career on the Potemkin moved so fast after the Nervala-Four rescue that he never had a chance to reunite with Deanna until they both joined the crew of the Enterprise, by which time their passions had cooled, resulting in their present friendship.

Lieutenant Riker points out that, while his counterpart may have given up his passion for Deanna, he has not. In fact, it was the thought of seeing her again that kept him going throughout all his years as a castaway.

Deanna changes the subject and asks Lieutenant Riker if he will join the Away Team. He says that he will. But as she goes to leave, he reminds her that his feelings have not changed since they last met on Beta-Zed.

Lieutenant Riker is late for the beam down, and Commander Riker is angry. Apparently Lt. Riker hasn't adjusted to living on someone else's schedule again. Down on the planet, the Lieutenant explains that he had rerouted most of the computer lines. They cannot retrieve anything from the consoles; Lieutenant Riker had shunted the database to the central computer core beneath the station.

He crawls under a console to see if he can access the core database. As he works, Commander Riker wonders if they should tell their father that he now has two sons. Lieutenant Riker doesn't really think it's necessary— he has no desire to see his father again. But he's curious about how Commander Riker got in touch with Kyle Riker.

Commander Riker explains about the time he was offered the command of the Ares. Lieutenant Riker cannot believe that Commander Riker turned down that captaincy. Obviously, the two Rikers can find little to agree upon.

Lieutenant Riker discovers that the primary computer coupling is fused. There can be no link-up with the core, and it seems that the servo-link with the subterranean computer core has probably been damaged by the frequent seismic activity on Nervala-Four. There's no time to go down and fix it, however, as the transporter window is about to end. Lieutenant Riker wants to stay and work on it; he'll be done by the time of the third window. But Commander Riker vetoes this idea; the caverns are too unstable. Lieutenant Riker tries to stay anyway, but Commander Riker pulls rank on him, and they all beam up to the Enterprise.

Deanna receives a note from Lieutenant Riker, which gives her a clue that leads her to a transporter room. There she finds a flower and another note. A series of notes and clues leads her to various locations ending with Ten Forward, where she encounters Lieutenant Riker waiting for her.

He gives her a gift: a piece of metal on which he has etched, with a phaser beam, a depiction of the Genaran Falls. They talk about "their" past and more recent events, and something in him reawakens Deanna's interest. She confesses how disappointed she was when Commander Riker never made their rendezvous on Rysa.

Later, Beverly Crusher and Deanna are in the gym, practicing the Klingon exercises taught them by Worf. Crusher is quizzing Deanna on Lieutenant Riker's attentions to her. Lieutenant Riker appears, and Crusher leaves the two alone. Lieutenant Riker notes the similarity between the Klingon exercises and Tai Chi Ch'uan. They begin to compare techniques. Deanna throws Lieutenant Riker to the floor and kisses him passionately.

Lieutenant Riker receives word that, with Picard's help, he has been assigned to a post on the Gandhi, and will transfer in one week. He will be allowed to take family on board after six months— will Deanna marry him? Deanna can't commit to that, as her work on the Enterprise is important to her. She understands that Lieutenant Riker cannot stay on the same ship as Commander Riker, but she can't go with him, either. But when Lieutenant

Riker asks her if their relationship is over, she tells him that it is not.

The next transporter window arrives and both Rikers beam down to the computer core to repair it. Lieutenant Riker observes that there has been considerably more seismic damage since their last visit.

Lieutenant Riker and Commander Riker reach a catwalk that leads to the computer core. But as they are crossing it, it collapses, and Lieutenant Riker falls, only to be grabbed by Commander Riker. Both are in danger of tumbling into a vast chasm beneath them, and Commander Riker cannot pull Lieutenant Riker up unless Lieutenant Riker climbs.

Lieutenant Riker tells Commander Riker to let him fall, but Commander Riker refuses. They manage to get back to safety and repair the link to the computer core. Data and Worf retrieve the information, and the Away Team is beamed back up with no further mishaps.

Deanna and Lieutenant Riker say their farewells. It will be a long time before they see each other again, but matters are not yet closed between them. Lieutenant Riker has waited for her eight years— he can wait a little longer. Commander Riker gives Lieutenant Riker a trombone as a gesture of conciliation, and the Lieutenant

leaves Deanna with Commander Riker, asking his alter-ego to take good care of her.

EPISODE ONE HUNDRED FIFTY-ONE: "TIMESCAPE"

Written by Brannon Braga
Directed by Adam Nimoy

Riker is called to the bridge when the Enterprise receives a distress call from a Romulan ship.

Meanwhile, Captain Picard, Geordi, Data and Troi are in an shuttle returning from a conference. They are sitting and talking when to Troi's amazement Geordi and Picard momentarily freeze, and then begin talking again as though nothing happened. She describes what she saw and suddenly finds Picard and Geordi standing next to her as she also just experienced a time lapse. They also experience seeing a bowl of fruit rot and one of the shuttles engines burn itself out from running continuously for 2 days, all in a matter of seconds.

A sensor probe indicates that there are time-space pockets nearby, which if they are careful they can avoid. When the shuttle reaches the rendezvous point where they are supposed to meet the Enterprise, it isn't there. Some scanning reveals where the

Enterprise is and they see it and a Romulan warbird frozen in time, apparently in the middle of a battle.

They need to beam over to the Enterprise, but since it is in a time pocket, they would be affected as soon as they materialized. Geordi configures a device they can wear in an armband which will create a force field to shield them from the time/space effects.

Geordi, Data and Troi are beamed to the bridge of the Enterprise where they see two Romulans on the bridge. The frozen consoles indicate trouble in different parts of the ship so they split up to investigate.

In sick bay Troi sees the frozen tableau of a Romulan firing a disrupter at Dr. Crusher. When Troi leaves to report what she's seen, a Romulan woman in sick bay is watching her—apparently immune to the time distortion effect.

In the transporter room, wounded Romulans are apparently being brought aboard. But isn't the Enterprise battling the Romulan ship? Something is not what it appears to be.

The biggest shock is in engineering where the Enterprise is experiencing a warp core breach which will destroy the vessel as soon as time resumes its natural course. And what's worse, Data has determined that time is not really frozen on the ship at all, just moving extremely slow as they can actually see minuscule movements in the frozen warp core explosion.

Picard starts having a bizarre reaction to things and they determine that its a malfunction in his armband. They beam Jean-Luc back to the shuttle where he recovers and Geordi replaces him on the Away Team.

When they beam over to the Romulan ship they see that it is being evacuated and is not in battle at all. Also there is some sort of power transfer going on between the Enterprise and the Romulan ship.

In the Romulan engine core chamber they find an aperture in the time space continuum which may well be the source of all the trouble. Data scans it with his tricorder, seeing dark spots which register as life forms. Data's scanning causes a response and time momentarily resumes its natural flow. On the shuttle, Picard sees the Enterprise explode and then watches as time moves backwards to its previous halted position.

Data determines that his tricorder scans activated the temporal rift. When Geordi points to a Romulan who wasn't there before, he is attacked and the contact between the Romulan and Geordi's force field knocks both of them unconscious. Geordi goes into shock and is near death when Troi pulls off his armband, freezing him in time and saving his life.

They take the Romulan back to the shuttle and when he awakens they learn that he is a life form from the time continuum disguised as a Romulan. The young of their species are trapped in the Romulan gravity well, which they took for a natural well and were trapped in it when they entered it.

This causes the problem the Romulan ship sent a distress call about. When the Enterprise did a power transfer, the aliens in the continuum thought they were being attacked and tried to destroy the Enterprise in response. Then the false Romulan fades away.

Knowing that the tricorder can affect the time rift, they decide to reverse it and prevent the Enterprise from doing the power transfer which started the major problems.

Data beams into engineering and when time reverses, he prepares to halt the power transfer but is attacked by another false Romulan. He is stunned and delayed from stopping the power transfer.

When time resumes its flow, Riker is startled to see Picard standing next to him, ordering the Romulan evacuation to be accelerated and that Geordi must be beamed out of the Romulan ship immediately.

In sick bay, Troi pushes Dr. Crusher out of the way of the disrupter, which the Romulan had actually fired at a false Romulan who had tried to attack him.

Picard is told by Data what has happened and via remote control they use the shuttlecraft to disrupt the transfer beams and thereby shut them down when the shuttle explodes. Then the evacuated Romulan ship breaks up and vanishes, along with the remaining false Romulan who had attacked Data.

Time has returned to normal with no danger of it rupturing there again. Picard directs the Enterprise to the Neutral Zone to return the Romulans to their home base. Riker is thoroughly confused and Jean-Luc says that this will take some time to explain.

EPISODE ONE HUNDRED FIFTY-TWO: "DESCENT"

Written by Ronald D. Moore
From a story by Jeer Taylor
Guest Cast: John, Jim Norton, Stephen Hawking

Data is on the holodeck experimenting with representations of Albert Einstein, Isaac Newton and Stephen Hawking to see how they would interact during a game of poker. But this delightful exercise is terminated when the Enterprise responds to a red alert. The Federation outpost on Ohniaka Three is being attacked.

When the Enterprise reaches that world, they see an orbiting spacecraft which does not fit the configuration of anything they've encountered before, but it doesn't attack them. Beaming down, the Away Team finds that all 274 members of the outpost have been murdered—and the killers are still there. A pitched battle results when members of the Borg ambush them.

During the fight, Data sees an Enterprise crewman slain and in an undeniable fit of anger the android brutally attacks one of the Borg and kills him. The Borg flee back to their vessel which fires on the Enterprise as it leaves orbit and vanishes into space.

Picard is told that the Borg did not react like members of the collective as they referred to one another by name and reacted to individual deaths. They wonder if this could be connected with the Borg they named Hugh who learned about individuality while a captive on the Enterprise two years before?

Data is concerned about his exhibit of anger as he is not capable of emotions, or hasn't been until now. Geordi does a diagnostic and finds nothing wrong with the android. Data is also unable to recreate this reaction. He's troubled by the fact that his first genuine expression of emotion was violent and negative.

Picard informs Starfleet of this latest incursion by the Borg. Admiral Nechayev prepares to assemble a fleet and criticizes Jean-Luc for not proceeding with his plan to destroy the Borg when he had the chance with Hugh. Picard suspects that Hugh may well be connected with this group of Borg individualists.

The Enterprise is summoned when the Borg attack the MS-1 colony. The Borg ship turns to flee as the Enterprise arrives but the Federation starship is close enough to the Borg to be swept along with them into the transwarp conduit which the Borg use to transport their vessel from one area of space to another.

Upon emerging into normal space, the Borg fire on the Enterprise and disable it so that the aliens can escape without being followed. The Enterprise have taken a captured Borg, Crosis, into custody and while Data is examining it the Borg activates something on its body which causes a response in Data, who begins exhibiting negative emotions.

Data and Crosis flee the Enterprise in a shuttlecraft and disappear into a transwarp conduit. The Enterprise duplicates the effect and follows the shuttle, emerging 65 light years away near planets which have been decimated by Borg conquests.

Electromagnetic activity on the planet where the shuttle landed renders the sensors useless, so Away Teams are beamed down to search for Data. A team comprised of Picard, Geordi and Troi find a structure not far from where the stolen shuttlecraft landed. Upon entering the structure they are surrounded and captured by a large contingent of the Borg. Then they see someone they first take to be Data, but soon realize that it is Lore. Data soon joins him, wearing an expression just as malevolent as his brother's.

"The sons of Soong have joined together," Lore proclaims, and vows that together with the Borg they will destroy the Federation.

END OF SEASON SIX

PROBABLE FUTURES

If there was any doubt that Paramount would launch a fourth version of A STAR TREK, those doubts were removed in October 1993 when they announced STAR TREK-VOYAGER. While little information has been released at this point beyond the title, it is clearly intended to be the direct sequel to STAR TREK-THE NEXT GENERATION

How about a rumor? As I write this, various parties are fighting to buy Paramount Pictures. With STAR TREK-THE NEXT GENERATION still at the top of the ratings there is speculation that the new owners of Paramount may not want to pull the plug on a successful syndicated series this soon. After all, Paramount kept CHEERS going for eleven years. It will be interesting to see if NEXT GENERATION will return in a slightly reworked form in the fall of 1994 while the regular crew continues on in a series of motion pictures.

Christmas of 1994 will, of course, see the first NEXT GENERATION theatrical motion picture, which will reportedly include a crossover with some, but apparently not all, of the original STAR TREK actors.

What else? DEEP SPACE NINE continues to be a success and that success fuels the marketplace with growing numbers of STAR TREK novels (of all three versions) as well as books about STAR TREK, encyclopedias, comic books

and more. It's interesting to note that just ten years ago it looked as though STAR WARS was surpassing STAR TREK in popularity, but once George Lucas stopped producing new STAR WARS films, the phenomenon faded. It is only now slowly becoming re-established after all but disappearing by the late '80s.

STAR TREK continues to thrive, clearly revitalized by the addition to the mythos of THE NEXT GENERATION in 1987. STAR TREK is bigger now than it ever was and continues to soar into new frontiers.